Timekeeper:

A Steampunk Time-Travel Adventure

Book 2 of the Keeping Time Trilogy

by Heather Albano

Stillpoint/Prometheus

Stillpoint/Prometheus
Stillpoint Digital Press
Mill Valley California USA

FIRST PAPERBACK EDITION
First ebook edition published in 2011

Foreword copyright © 2016 by Kenneth Schneyer

Special Hardcover ISBN XXXXXXXXXX
Paperback ISBN 978-1-938808-41-8
Ebook ISBN XXXXXXXXXX
version 1.

The dingbat font used throughout is Nymphette, designed by Lauren Thompson, and the decorative fonts are Steampunk, designed by Marta von Eck, and Octant by Catharsis Fonts. All are used with permission.

∽

BY HEATHER ALBANO
Fiction:
Timepiece
Timekeeper
Timebound (Winter, 2018)

Games (Choice of Games):
A Study in Steampunk
Choice of Broadsides (with Adam Strong-Morse and Dan Fabulich)
Choice of Zombies (with Richard Jackson)
Affairs of the Court trilogy (with Adam Strong-Morse and Dan Fabulich)

∽

INTERESTED IN SPECULATIVE FICTION?
SIGN UP FOR NEWS, GIVEAWAYS, AND MORE AT
stillpointdigital.com/prometheus/news

For Mom, Dad, Molly, and Richard
and with thanks to Anise,
who let me have McLevy's pocket watch in the first place

ADVANCE REVIEW COPY

Timekeeper

Prologue

Waterloo, Belgium, June 18, 1815

John Freemantle felt every jolt of the cart like an explosion within his skull.

At least, he thought it was a cart. He had reason to think so; he had been carried semi-conscious in a cart once before, and it was not an experience one forgot. The sickening arrhythmic lurches, each one as bone-rattling as it was nauseating, had nothing in common with the plunging deck of a ship or the joggle of a properly sprung carriage. Moreover, each jolt seemed to give rise to a fresh bout of moaning in a variety of registers, from sources surrounding him at close range. Then there was the smell—sweat and blood, vomit and urine. He was becoming more certain every instant that his initial impression had been correct. He was in a cart.

What he could not determine was why. Freemantle cast his mind back, trying to recall some sequence of events that would logically end with his person residing in such a conveyance. The battle had been going badly, he remembered that. The British and their Belgian allies had been under heavy fire from the more numerous French. Between injuries, deaths, and desertion, Wellington's line was stretched almost to breaking, and when the news came that the farm La Haye Sainte had fallen, Wellington had no fresh troops he might move to plug the gap. The promised Prussian reinforcements had still not arrived, and so there was nothing for the Duke to do but—

Freemantle remembered with a jolt worse than anything the cart could throw at him, and jerked upright. Or tried to; he only got halfway before pain spiked through his temples and he sagged back down. The Duke had summoned the special battalion. The Duke had sent him, John Freemantle, to summon the special battalion. But something had ambushed him in the woods. And he could dimly remember, as though recalling a dream, a girl with a minx's face and an impossible pocket watch—

"Battalion," he croaked.

"Easy, John."

Freemantle turned his head toward the voice. The movement seemed to take a long time, and a green blur swooped across his field of vision as he did so. He wasn't sure if he had opened his eyes, or if the sickening haze was present only behind his lids.

He squeezed his eyes hard shut, then forced them open. This time they focused enough to recognize James Warren. Warren was propped upright against the side of the cart, chest and right shoulder bound with blood-soaked bandages, face paperwhite except for the dark shadows under his eyes.

"Battalion," Freemantle said again. "Burnley. I was—" The cart jerked underneath him, drowning the faint flicker of memory in a flood of queasiness. Freemantle drew a deep breath, holding it until the worst of the sickness past. "What—happened?"

"You were thrown from your horse," Warren said. He spoke almost without inflection. The gray eyes that regarded Freemantle seemed unnaturally wide, unnaturally steady.

Freemantle made one more effort to sit up, and this time managed it despite the spike of pain through his skull. "The message—"

"Hit your head," Warren added, as though that were the question he had asked. "They took you to the village to recover."

"The message, James. The battalion—"

"Didn't come," Warren said.

"Oh, God." The blur of green crashed over his head like an ocean wave. There had been a girl and a pocket watch and an impossible story, and he had— chosen not to bring the message? But no, that was impossible, that was a fever dream. Surely he could never have chosen to betray Wellington. Surely he was guilty of nothing but failure. "Oh, dear God."

"I wasn't there," Warren said, as though he were talking in his sleep. "Leeches wouldn't let me leave. But I heard. Heard the others talking. They said His Grace was waiting on the battalion. They said it looked like the Prussians might reach us—they were even in sight. But then the infantry broke under the last French charge. The Prussians thought the day lost, and made tracks. It didn't take long after that..."

"But the Duke," Freemantle said, struggling to comprehend it. The girl had said they could win without the special battalion. And because of that, Freemantle had chosen to— He shied away from the memory. "Never beaten— all those times on the Peninsula—conjuring possibilities from thin air—how could the Duke—" He stopped at the look on Warren's face. "Dear God. No."

"He was trying to rally them," Warren said hoarsely. "He was—being conspicuous, the way he always—Lord Uxbridge rode at him, shouting, 'For God's sake, don't expose yourself so!'—and then—A lucky shot, they said. Uxbridge was so close that the Duke's blood—the Duke's blood splattered—" Warren choked. He coughed, and the crimson stain on his bandages darkened and spread.

"Under Uxbridge," Freemantle said. It was the only part of the paragraph he could absorb. The other intelligence was too momentous, as though the universe had been pulled up by the roots, or broken and reformed into something entirely new. He could not comprehend it. He pushed it instead to the back of his throbbing brain. The girl had said that, to save the future, he must not bring the message. And he had *believed* her, as mad as that seemed now, he had chosen— "We're under Uxbridge. What are we about?" He looked around himself. Bleeding and hastily bandaged comrades-in-arms lay wedged and piled around him, groaning with each fresh lurch of the wheels. Past them, the green haze would not come into focus.

"Retreating," Warren said, still expressionless, eyes still staring. "Bonaparte sent in the Garde. Immortals. Undefeated."

"Retreating," Freemantle repeated. She had said they would win. "Where to? Brussels?"

"In Brussels," Warren said, "they are preparing feasts to welcome home their Emperor."

Of course they were. The Belgians had always been more French than Dutch, had never been likely to stand with Napoleon's enemies in the event of the Emperor's victory. Some had fled the battlefield, and some— Freemantle had an instant's memory of Belgians in the Forest of Soignes, but it fled when he tried to grasp it. The effort struck through his head, a blinding spear of pain. The girl had a handkerchief, and a pocket watch, and a glib tongue, and he had believed her, and he was worse than a traitor, worse than a fool. She must have been a French spy. If she were real at all. Perhaps she wasn't real. He wanted her to not be real.

If she wasn't real, this was not his fault.

"Bonaparte's done it," Warren said. "Separated us from the Prussians. They retreat across the Rhine, we back to the North Sea while the route home is still open to us. The French pursue, but Uxbridge left a small band of monsters to cover our retreat. He thinks they will be enough. He takes the rest home to garrison our shores. It's too late to use them any other way."

"Too late," Freemantle repeated. The words tasted awful on his tongue, slimy and nauseous.

"Not your fault," Warren said suddenly. But it was. "Even Wotten said so, when he came to fetch me from Mont St. Jean. You hit your head. The Duke oughtn't to have waited. He delayed too long in sending a second courier. He delayed too long in sending for the monsters in the first place."

Freemantle's guts twisted inside him. "No," he said, as the sky throbbed in time with the throbbing in his temples. "It wasn't his fault. Never his fault. It was mine—mine—I failed—I caused—" She had said, *The message must not get through,* and he had said, *I have a plan.* His hand had thrown the lamp, struck the guard, misdirected the message, lost the war. "I caused this. Oh, God."

He was no longer wearing his pistols. But a polished-smooth handle still rode on the belt at Warren's hip. Freemantle reached out, and Warren was too drunk on his own injuries and grief to stop him seizing hold of it.

Chapter I

London, August 28, 1885

The silence in the little sitting room was so profound that Elizabeth could hear the rain pattering on the cobblestones outside. Her soaked shirt and trousers had been hung to dry in the scullery, and she was now clad once more in a gown—her own, one of the two she had brought from 1815 in William's rucksack—with a worn gray blanket about her shoulders to ward off chill. Not that chill was a terribly probable consequence of her night's adventures; the air inside the warehouse-hideaway was so hot and still that she was more likely to melt than freeze. But Brenda Trevelyan had offered the blanket as an expression of kindness, and moreover playing with its frayed edge gave Elizabeth something to do with her hands, so she hugged it close and kept her attention on the loose threads under her fingernails. She did not want to meet anyone's eyes—especially not Katarina's, familiar and unfamiliar and unfriendly, or Maxwell's, bloodshot and anguished.

Finally she heard the expected step on the boards outside, and William came sidling through the door, a blanket wrapped around his own upper half and the young Prussian Emil Schwieger a watchful pace behind him. Schwieger had to hold the door open, as William's left hand was occupied in keeping the blanket clasped and his dangling right arm, injured back on the Peninsula, was no longer capable of opening doors or doing anything else.

Schwieger might have made the gesture look friendly, but he did not. He looked still like the guard he was, shoulders straight and mouth uncompromising. In response, William had arranged his own face into a look of resolute calm, but Elizabeth wasn't fooled.

"All right," Frederick Kent said then—not loudly, but in a tone that did not brook refusal. The tawny-haired man rose to his feet, drawing all eyes to himself. "Sit down. All three of you." Elizabeth was already seated at the dining table. Kent waited until Maxwell and William had drawn back chairs and joined her, then strode around the table to take the seat opposite. Katarina Rasmirovna sat in the chair on his right and Emil Schwieger moved to stand at his left—a decidedly unfriendly arrangement, Elizabeth thought. It reminded her of newspaper descriptions of a tribunal, or of being summoned to answer for naughtiness to her mother, father, and aunt all at once. Kent looked over as though to inquire whether Gavin Trevelyan wished to join the panel, but Trevelyan was seated on the arm of his wife's wing chair and did not look inclined to move. He was, Elizabeth thought, more witness than judge in any case.

Kent turned his attention back to her, and she had a sudden sympathy for the way a mouse must feel under the gaze of a hawk. Kent's intense blue eyes moved from her face to William's, then to Maxwell's. "Now," Kent said. "Start over from the beginning."

Maxwell ran a hand through his disheveled white hair, pressed his palms flat against the tabletop to stop their shaking, and started over from the beginning.

It sounded like a madman's story, Elizabeth had to admit that. The words sounded mad to her, and she had lived it. She could only imagine what they sounded like to the three on the other side of the table. Kent's posture pretended relaxation, but his hands rested only lightly on the arms of his chair, and he watched Maxwell almost without blinking.

"I am a time traveler," Maxwell began as he had the first time. "My young friends and I have most recently been in a version of 1885 very different from this."

"When and where were you born?" Kent interrupted him.

Maxwell hesitated a bare instant. "The year eighteen hundred and eighteen, in the north of England. But...I believe it was an 1818 very different from the one in your history books. It will have changed since last I was there."

"Because you changed it," Frederick Kent said.

"God help me," Maxwell said, "yes. I changed it while trying to change 1885."

There was another pause. The rain drummed the street outside, and Maxwell did not meet anyone's eyes. Elizabeth found herself stealing surreptitious glances from under her lashes to the others seated around the table. Kent's sternly handsome face was as expressionless as he could make it; he was deliberately reserving judgment, which was both somewhat reassuring and a fit with all Elizabeth had heard about him. But Emil Schwieger's face displayed open hostility, and—what was more painful—so did Katarina's. Elizabeth could understand why this Katarina would not immediately accept an unknown traveler with an incredible story, but they had become friends in the other 1885, and the seething mistrust in Katarina's luminous dark eyes now made Elizabeth feel as though she were in a boat cut free of its moorings.

Brenda Trevelyan's wing chair was positioned in a sheltered corner, where the shadows fell so Elizabeth could not see her expression. Not that it would have helped much if she could; there had so far been no hint as to what the sweet-faced woman thought of them all. From her shoulder, her husband watched the scene with perfectly readable sardonic eyes, and Elizabeth felt a flash of anger toward him. This Trevelyan knew Maxwell—not as well as had his counterpart from the other London, but at least a little. It was on Trevelyan's word that Maxwell and his friends had been permitted entry into this hiding place. Trevelyan really ought to be helping Maxwell tell his impossible-sounding story now. But he said nothing as Maxwell described the other timeline—the Battle of Waterloo, the special battalion, the monsters that roamed Britain in the years thereafter.

"Tell me about 'the other 1885,'" Kent said.

Maxwell took a breath. "To do so, I must tell you about the other 1815. In the world in which I was born—and in which Miss Barton and Mr. Carrington were born—the Duke of Wellington was not killed on the field of Waterloo. Indeed, he won the day and broke Bonaparte's power."

Kent leaned forward, interested as though despite himself. "How?"

"When the British feared Napoleon's invasion in 1805," Maxwell said, "they set to work on a weapon to defend their shores. Some fifteen years earlier, a young Genevese had built a secret laboratory on an island off the Orkneys, and in 1800 the, er, results of his experiments drew attention to themselves and were captured by British soldiers. By studying their captives and the Genevese's notes, the British bred an army of monsters—creatures created from dead flesh, from corpses cut apart and stitched back together, then re-imbued with the spark of life—taller and stronger than any man alive. When Bonaparte escaped from Elba in 1814, the British sent this 'special battalion' with Wellington and his ragtag army. The monsters were with Wellington at Waterloo."

"Yes," Katarina muttered. "We know. This is history. The Duke held them in reserve in the Forest of Soignes, not wishing to use them unless the need were absolute. In the end he did send for them to reinforce his line, but the message reached them too late, and the British were overwhelmed by the French."

Because of me, drummed in Elizabeth's head, in time with the rain outside. *Because of us. Because we waylaid the courier. All this, because of me.*

"In the world in which I was born," Maxwell said, "the message reached Burnley and his battalion in time. He brought the monsters to reinforce Wellington, and through them, Wellington won the day. The monsters slaughtered the French, the British captured the French Eagles, a messenger brought them home to lay at the Prince Regent's feet like the final act of an opera...and 'Wellington's monsters' became the nation's darlings. They were used, with similar success, in other military operations, and then to mine coal and work ranches in the colonies. And then they rebelled. They were never as stupid as we liked to think them, and they were everywhere, ideally placed to turn on their masters and destroy Britain from within. The revolt happened in stages, but by 1872, all of England was burning.

"We needed a weapon against them." Maxwell did not look at Gavin Trevelyan. "A student at the University of London—a brilliant young Welshman—created a mechanical monster to overcome the one we had made of flesh. His constructs, as they came to be called, were metal men twenty feet high, with rifles embedded in their arms and—"

Katarina jumped to her feet, her chair slamming into the wall behind her, Kent's hand raised too slowly to stop her. Trevelyan leaned forward, throwing a lean and rangy shadow across the light. Maxwell broke off, and for a moment the only sound in the room seemed to be Katarina's quickened breath. As far as Elizabeth could tell, Maxwell was not breathing at all.

After a moment, Katarina turned to Kent. "I told you," she said, "we could not trust them."

"No," Trevelyan said. "Wait. Tell me how they worked, these constructs."
Maxwell hesitated.

"Tell him," Kent said. He did not look at Katarina, but his hand reached out, took her arm, and guided her back down to her chair.

"Clockwork and steam," Maxwell said. "The first prototypes dragged their fuel behind them in wagons. Later, a more efficient boiler system was developed. Three men rode inside them, one to stoke the boiler, one to move the feet, one to fire the artillery. One arm was a cannon-mouth, the other a—a new type of rifle, called a Gatling. They were...very effective." Maxwell ran out of air and took a ragged breath before continuing. "By 1885," he said, "by the 1885 I knew, they had restored order and retaken the English countryside, and the Wellington monsters had long since ceased to be a threat. What few specimens remained were caged in zoos or laboratories. Perhaps two or three ran free on an isolated moor here and there. But the Prime Minister did not stand down the constructs. Instead he used them to enforce order in the colonies, in the countryside, finally even on London's streets. We lived in fear, by 1885. It was a terrible world.

"I knew you there." Maxwell took another breath. "You were freedom fighters. All three of you." He turned in his chair to face Trevelyan. "You had switched sides by then. You were trying to destroy the constructs you had created. When I knew you, you were creating a rifle that worked on the same principle as railway-cars, to power a javelin sufficiently to pierce a construct's hide, even the reinforced piece above the boiler." Not so much a reaction as a careful absence of one crossed Trevelyan's face. "You gave your life trying," Maxwell said. From Brenda Trevelyan came a startled little gasp. "All three of you gave your lives. Lord Sew—Frederick Kent was arrested on a treason charge, and two nights later, Katarina Rasmirovna and Gavin Trevelyan were shot dead by constructs in an alleyway, their rail-gun captured. And I—we—" He gestured to Elizabeth and William. "We went to Waterloo to stop it from happening. Wellington maintained until the end of his life that he could have won the battle without monstrous aid, and so we...took him at his word. We delayed his courier."

"This is absurd," Katarina said flatly. She turned angry eyes from Kent to Trevelyan. "You cannot seriously—either of you!—consider this outrageous story at all believable! It is far more likely that—"

"It is believable," Trevelyan cut her off. "For one thing, there's the matter of Mr. Maxwell having saved my life in Vienna and telling me we would meet again under precisely these circumstances. For another—do you still have the watch, Maxwell?"

"I still have the watch." Maxwell drew it from his pocket, popped it open, and laid it on the table before Kent.

Katarina stopped talking.

It was the fourth face that had silenced her, Elizabeth thought. The fourth face had a tendency to do that. The first three faces allowed one to set the date, time, latitude, and longitude to which one wished to travel—but it was not obvious at first glance that they did so fantastic a thing. One might conceivably mistake the pocket-watch-with-too-many-dials as the tool of a ship's captain or perhaps a physician. But the fourth face—the fourth face corrected any such misapprehension. The fourth face displayed images that moved, tiny simulacra as realistic as anything in the real world. Now Elizabeth watched their familiar forms flicker by, upside down.

Sunlight danced on a brook surrounded by waving green grass, fluffy clouds reflected in its depths. Then the brook faded out of existence, to be replaced by a ship struggling to remain upright in a gale, its sails strained to bursting and gray waves crashing against its side. Then the ship was gone, and knights in armor rode horses down a forested mountain path. Then a newspaper blew across a tired-looking London street, coming to rest in a pile of soot and rubbish. Elizabeth would have thought that last scene familiar, except no construct stomped its earth-shaking feet along the cobblestones or lit the sky blue with its lightning-weapons. There were no constructs ravaging London any longer. Because of her. *At least there's that. That's to the good, surely?*

The images continued to flicker past. The ship. The mountainside. The brook. The deserted street. The—battlefield?

She had not seen that one before. She leaned closer to peer at it. It looked for a moment like a painting one might encounter in a gallery—a huge landscape, storm-cloud sky and brown earth overwhelming the viewer's attention, tiny figures of men and horses frozen in an instant of victory or bloodshed.

Except these figures moved. Men. Horses. Cannon—she could see tiny sparks of light, miniscule pinpoint explosions. And Wellington monsters. Some wore red and some wore blue, and they were tearing each other to pieces, weapons flung aside, torn-off limbs hurled bloody to the ground.

Elizabeth swallowed against a wave of sickness and looked away.

"Impressive," Kent said at last. He lifted his head from his examination of the watch, and the flickering candlelight caught the silver strands among the tawny gold of his hair. "I must confess it is hard to disbelieve a story of time travel, with this sort of proof offered."

"It could be a trick," Katarina said between her teeth.

Kent shook his head—not in negation, Elizabeth thought, but in wonder. Light had kindled far down in his blue eyes. "And then there is the matter of Gavin having met Mr. Maxwell in Vienna."

"Briefly," Trevelyan said, "but memorably. He saved my life—on the second of April, 1882, by the way," he added in Maxwell's direction, "in the *meithaus* district, from a gas-main explosion. You said I was to tell you when I encountered you and your two young friends in London. I thought him mad," Trevelyan concluded, speaking once more to Kent, "but here we are."

"Here we are," Kent agreed. "That's the second point. And the third—" He met Maxwell's eyes. "—is that you continually begin to address me by a name not my own. That was the fifth time, just there. You catch yourself after a breath, but there is a name that rises to your lips every time you see me. I should judge, then...that, even if your tale is not true, something near to it is. I remind you of someone. Someone who looks like me, whose surname begins with an 'S'." The blue eyes watched Maxwell's face.

"I knew you as Lord Seward," Maxwell said simply, and Kent let out his breath.

"Indeed. That is...that was a title held by an ancestor of mine. Before." He nodded toward the window and the world beyond it. The fingertips of his left hand began to beat a restless rhythm on his chair arm. "It would be my title, in a world where the French had not overrun us."

"A fact someone sufficiently motivated could have discovered!" Katarina said. "Good Lord, you would think no one in this warehouse had ever engaged in a masquerade to obtain information!"

Trevelyan ignored her. "Kent's name, Maxwell's watch, my time in Vienna," he said, ticking the points off on his fingers. "And finally—" He looked to Kent, and Kent nodded.

William, silent until now, addressed his first question to the air midway between them. "'Finally,' sir?"

"Finally," Trevelyan said. He got up. "Come with me."

"You are mad," Katarina gritted.

"It may be I am," Trevelyan said, "but not for believing their story. They couldn't be crafting it from reading a treatise or peeking through a window-pane. Come with me," he repeated, and Elizabeth pushed back her chair and followed him to the door, William and Maxwell behind her, the others trailing after.

Trevelyan led them down the bare whitewashed corridor to the door of what had been his laboratory in the other 1885. He produced a key, inserted it into the lock, and the door swung open into blackness. "Come in," Trevelyan said, disappearing inside without a hesitation. "Stand just there." There was a hissing sound, and then the lights came up—not all at once like a matchstick touched to a lamp wick, but slowly, a yellow glow burning away the shadows.

The room lightened from velvet black to gray studded with darker gray, revealing itself to be laid out more or less as Trevelyan's laboratory had been in the other London. Elizabeth's straining eyes discerned the outlines of worktables running down the length of the two long walls—the spiny curve of the enormous spinning-wheel-thing in the back—the bellows of the cold blacksmith's forge. As well as something large and looming, standing still just in front of her.

It came clear as the shadows fell away from it, as the growing light shone off its burnished hide. This one was only eight feet tall, and constructed of a mismatched patchwork-quilt of metal scraps, but otherwise the details were sickeningly familiar. Elizabeth stared in horror at the mouthless mask-like face, the bolts driven into the chest, the cannon gaping at the end of the left arm, the slender cylinders of the Gatling gun grouped at the end of the right. A wagon of coal scraps was attached to one leg. Unseeing blue-tinted eyes stared forward, seeming to calmly meet her own.

Oh, no. She couldn't find the breath to say it out loud. Behind her, she felt William freeze and heard Maxwell's hiss of comprehension. *No.*

"A prototype," Trevelyan explained, heedless of their shock. "Only to prove that it does what it should. I mean to make them stand twenty feet high, and yes, each one will need a team of three inside it. I've a plan for improving the boiler design, but I've not captured it even in my own notebook as yet. So no spy could've discovered it," he added in Katarina's direction. "Either our guests come from where they say they do, or they've the power to read thoughts."

"No," Elizabeth breathed at last. Trevelyan's eyes dropped back down to her, interested but unconcerned.

There was no sense in trying to make him understand. She turned, pushing half-blind past Maxwell and William, to confront Kent.

His piercing gaze met hers—interested, she thought, as Trevelyan's had been, measuring her reaction, evaluating whether it also seemed to prove the truth of Maxwell's story—but also holding compassion for her distress. "You can't do this," she said, "you cannot do this—sir, you can't, you can't. You've done it before—in the other London—it led to horrible things, and you mustn't take a step down that road—"

"It's a bit late for that, Miss Barton," Kent said mildly, but he reached out to take her arm as though he feared she might turn faint. "The first step has already been taken, as you see, and several more besides."

"But you don't understand!" Elizabeth heard her own voice rise. "You have done this very thing before. In the other timeline, you did it in 1876. Nine years later, those who controlled the constructs had risen to power and held all of Britain with a boot to its throat."

"That won't happen this time," Trevelyan said. "With the booted feet of the French so fresh in everyone's mind, we'd hardly be making that mistake ourselves."

"What will stop you? I'm sure your counterparts said just the same—You can't do this, Mr. Trevelyan. We unmade a universe to undo this mistake. You can't make it again!"

"I must agree with the young lady," Herr Schwieger said unexpectedly from behind her. "She provides yet another argument to my cause. I do believe this is the wrong avenue for us to pursue. Again, I must say I would rather see us seek out the secret of the Genevese monsters, and restore Britain's defenders to their—"

Kent, still holding Elizabeth's arm, used his other hand to wave the young Prussian silent. "Enough, Emil."

But William had gone rigid. "I beg your pardon, sir, what?"

Schwieger glanced once at Kent before replying. Kent rolled irritated eyes, then gave permission with a nod. "The British special battalion retreated back to England with its masters, after the disaster at Waterloo," the young Prussian said. "For a time they enabled Britain to hold the line against the Empire, but the Empire had learned men under its own employ. French soldiers managed to take captive a badly injured monster, and French scientists discovered the secret of its creation. They made a battalion to serve France. They brought it across the Channel. The Battle of Dover was..." Schwieger trailed off, as though at a loss for words. "I believe your watch showed an image of it," he offered at last.

William nodded woodenly.

"The only thing that has ever been able to stop a monster is another monster," Schwieger said. "Or—" He inclined his head to Trevelyan in studied politeness. "—perhaps a construct. Someday. But perhaps not; or perhaps as we now hear, the risk would prove to outweigh the benefit. We know, however, that monsters can run over anything in their path—even the Imperial Garde. By the time Wellington's special battalion reached Waterloo, there was nothing left for it to save, but that was not the monsters' fault, and they guarded Britain quite well in the years before France found a way to match them. Now Britain needs them once again."

Elizabeth's throat felt too choked to speak. William had gone paper white, but he pushed onward. "But you said the French had a similar force—"

"Had," Schwieger agreed. "The monsters destroyed each other at Dover. There are none living now. The notes made by the original creator—notes that might guide us in creating more—were stolen from the Empire by a pair of Englishmen some decades ago. No one knows for certain where these notes might be, but I have an idea or two, and if they could be found, why then, we could breed again a force sufficient to send the Empire packing home."

"No," Elizabeth choked out. She looked desperately at Maxwell, hoping he would find himself capable of a more eloquent argument, but he said nothing. He was staring at the construct as though the sight had drained the last bit of hope from his body. He looked suddenly old, the lines on his face and the pallor of his skin a match for his white hair. Elizabeth wrenched her eyes back to Schwieger. "No. That would be just as bad—"

"No," Trevelyan said, in the tone of one engaged in an argument so familiar as to be boring. "We haven't time to breed and train a monster army. British children are being born into French slavery right now. That needs to be stopped right now. We need to bring it all down."

"And replace it with what?" William demanded. "What will fill the hole once you blow up Parliament—or trample it underfoot, or whatever it is you intend to do? Surely to goodness it would be better to work from within, grains of sand grinding rock smooth, a slowly diverted stream—"

"I haven't seventy years to play with," Trevelyan said sharply. "Even seven years is too long to wait. The constructs are the only solution I can see that has a hope of doing Britain any good in the next seven months. I'll keep my hand to the plow I've chosen."

"You'd—you'd keep your hand there still, when we've brought you something better?" Elizabeth said to Kent.

Her heart was hammering so hard and fast she could hardly breathe. But she tried to lift her chin confidently, tried to smile at Kent as though she were sure of her words. She had to stop them doing this, had to. If Maxwell wouldn't speak, she must. And Kent was the one to convince—there was no point in trying to sway Trevelyan and she did not know Schwieger and Katarina might as well have been a stranger—but it had been Kent's conspiracy in the other 1885, and it still was here and now. The others would follow where he led. If she could give him a third option, surely he would turn away from the two paths fated to end in disaster—and the third option was ready to hand, nothing less than obvious. By the look in his eyes, he was thinking the same thing she was.

"Mr. Kent," Elizabeth said, "haven't you ever wished for a way to warn those who fought at Dover?"

"I've prayed for such a thing," Frederick Kent told her. His smile made her think of the sun coming up. They might have been the only people in the room. "Are you an angel come in answer, then? Or a genie granting wishes?"

"I've certainly never been called an angel," Elizabeth said.

"A genie, then. I somehow wasn't expecting they'd look so prosaic." Kent started to pace. "A warning. You could take a warning back in time. Dear God. You could tell me what I wish I'd known during the mine revolts—or what Carter wished he'd known during the '41 Rising—or if you go back further, you could even stop Dover as you say. You could take dossiers, maps—I could get my hands on memoirs—"

"Because your jinn made such good use of maps and memoirs at Waterloo?" Katarina's voice cut like glass.

Kent paused mid-step.

"Katarina's right," Trevelyan said. He folded his arms and leaned back against the empty-eyed metal giant. "I might be owing sanctuary to Mr. Maxwell and his companions—I agreed to that in Vienna—but I can't say I think much of letting them mine the ground I'm standing on. Whatever world they create next might well be a mess I can't fix."

"You can't fix this one," Elizabeth shot back. "Not with constructs. Set constructs loose on British soil and you'll create a world worse than this. That's exactly what happened last time."

"Under entirely different circumstances."

"Under exactly the same circumstances! A threat that made it worth the risk, constructs that first seemed like protective angels, and then later—later it didn't matter about intentions. The—the crank turned itself, that's what Katarina told me." Elizabeth turned back to Kent. "Mr. Trevelyan wants you to use metal monsters, and Herr Schwieger wants you to use Wellington monsters, and I can offer you something better. Send us back with your warnings, and—"

"—and I won't have to stand here choosing between devils. Yes, I'd already grasped that's what you offer me." Kent looked off into the shadows. "It would be a risk," he said. "But if I could send you with good reconnaissance—And I think I can. As it happens, I know someone who fought at Dover. A very old man now, but alert enough of mind for all that. While I can't answer for the accuracy of his memories, his cottage is stuffed full of memoirs from the old days; he has all the maps and battle plans and firsthand accounts you could want. If I can get you up north to see him—"

Katarina made a hissing sound of dismay. "Have you lost your mind?"

"Oh, come, Kat," Kent said to her, genially enough. "Are you not always wishing us to act more boldly?"

"Always," Katarina said. "And you always tell me why we can't, and you're changing your strategy now, like this? Even if the watch proves their tale, nothing speaks to their motives, and you'd deliver Mr. Carter into their hands? What can possibly make you believe you can trust them?"

"The same way I trust everyone else who turns up on my doorstep and wants to aid my cause," Kent said, his voice dropping into a lower, more dangerous register. "On the word of someone already in my service—Gavin in this case—coupled with my own observation. When you command your own company, Katarina, you may of course employ different criteria, but I see no need to change the one that has served me well so far."

"Most of the people who turn up on your doorstep don't admit to having *betrayed the British at Waterloo*!" Katarina flung back.

Chapter 2

London, August 28, 1885

"Dover?" Maxwell snapped the instant they were left alone.

Elizabeth reeled from the fury in his voice—or maybe it was only the close air of the garret that caused her near-stumble. The rooms up here were even smaller than they had been the last time—of course they were; this garret was divided into four bedchambers instead of two—and the still, hot air pressed heavy and damp on every inch of her skin, choking her throat and making a deep breath impossible. Her head swam.

They really ought be resting while they had the chance, their growing fatigue being why Kent had sent them up here in the first place—or at least, that was the motive he claimed, though it was obvious that he also very much desired to remove the time travelers from eavesdropping range while he and his people continued their argument below—but instead of trying for sleep, the three of them had crowded into one of the tiny bedchambers to pursue a counterpoint dispute of their own. It was Katarina's chamber, given to Elizabeth for the few hours remaining until dawn—much to Elizabeth's discomfort and much against Katarina's will. Despite Elizabeth's pledge to touch nothing, the gypsy woman had snapped closed the lock of her trunk with ostentatious anger before storming back down the stairs. There was only one trunk standing against the wall this time, of course, and no men's boots to trip over. Gavin Trevelyan slept with his wife in the adjoining chamber.

"Dover?" Maxwell repeated, and all at once an answering flush of fury cleared Elizabeth's vision and stiffened her knees.

"Someone had to say something!" she retorted, facing him. "I didn't see you taking charge of the conversation!"

"After the carnage we caused at Waterloo, after the disaster we wrought, you want to meddle with another battle? We don't have enough blood dripping from our hands?"

"We succeeded at Waterloo!" Elizabeth retorted. "We changed something."

"Oh, so you like this world, do you?"

"No, *no*, of course not, but don't you see? You've never managed to change anything before, you said that. But the three of us together could, we *did*, so we can do it again."

"You think we can fix this by meddling with the Battle of Dover?" Maxwell repeated.

"Or something else! Perhaps not Dover. Perhaps there's some other opportunity—I hope there's one much earlier—but we can't know what chances exist until we learn something about their history, and we won't be able to get to history books and memoirs and old soldiers unless we have an ally willing to help us. Dover was the only battle they had mentioned by name, and I had to say something to catch Kent's imagination. Otherwise he'd yield to Trevelyan and unleash constructs or to Schwieger and unleash monsters—I had to say something to make him see there was another option. I didn't," she added, switching her glare from Maxwell to William, who had been quiet all this time, "notice either of you helping me."

"I find the strategy perfectly sound," William said, in a calm and reasonable tone that made Elizabeth want to scream. "But I saw no point in rushing to execute it. Trevelyan isn't able to unleash an army of constructs tonight, and Schwieger does not even know where those notes on the Wellington monsters might be. Offering a third option might as well wait a day or two or even longer, until we learn enough about our new allies to know what arguments will move them and they learn enough about us to know we may be trusted. This universe is seventy years old. If we succeed in unmaking it, it will never have been—so does it matter if we succeed when it is seventy years and three months of age instead of seventy years and two months? Don't we have time to move carefully?"

Elizabeth sagged a little. "It just feels as though...if we give it time to—to settle—then it becomes real. If we don't move immediately to unmake it, it will be harder to dislodge. I keep thinking of wheels sinking into mud." Which was foolish. The tiny clockwork wheels of the pocket watch were not threatened by mud or anything else. "I don't want it to be real."

"No. Of course you don't," Maxwell said.

She took his meaning plainly. Before her eyes rose an image of her hand seizing his sleeve. She had forced him to take her to Waterloo, she had forced the issue, she had forced the world to change. Into this. Into *this*. "Yes," she said to Maxwell. "It's my fault. I admit it. I did not appreciate how severe the consequences of my actions might be. But I *did something*. We changed something, which you've never been able to do alone. If you didn't want me to take action, you should never have sent me the watch!"

Maxwell stared. "What are you talking about?"

Elizabeth threw up her hands in exasperation. "I recognized your handwriting! In the barn outside Waterloo!" The injustice of it made her want to cry again. It made this whole horrible situation worse to know that she need never have meddled in the first place. She had considered herself under something of an obligation to do so—a grand and glorious obligation, to be sure—for when the pocket watch had arrived without explanation, she had assumed without really thinking about it that it had been sent by someone who knew what he was about, who knew what she would do with it, who entrusted her personally with the power to change history. But there was no larger plan and there was no one knowledgeable behind the scenes—just Maxwell, and her, and William. And two pocket watches, one broken because of her impetuousness. And the tricolor flag flying from the Tower of London. She barely managed to keep her voice steady as she added, "It's unworthy of you to maintain this pretense."

"No pretense," Maxwell said. "I've never in my life sent a pocket watch to you or anyone. So the question you are asking is, 'Why will I?' And the answer is, 'Damned if I know.' I can't imagine what would prompt me to send you such a dangerous tool after knowing the mess you'd make with it."

"That's enough." William did not speak loudly. "Sir," he added after a deliberate moment. "There were three people trying to change history at Waterloo. All three of us have blood on our hands. All three of us have the obligation to make amends for it. And we will." He took a breath. "We have lost an engagement. It happens. It is a misfortune that has been known to befall even the Duke of Wellington. One retreats in good order, one chooses better ground, and one counter-attacks. The Peninsula wasn't a single battle, and neither is this. It will be all right. We will fix it."

"Or we'll make it worse," Maxwell said. His brown eyes burned in his pale face. "Genies are bottled because of their power, because of the havoc they wreak when they—"

"I am not going to sit with my *hands folded* while the French rule Britain, just because I am afraid of what *might happen* if I act," Elizabeth flung at him. "You had chance after chance and changed *nothing*, and I at least managed something, even if it was the wrong something. Here I thought you knew what you were about, but now I think your caution is really cowardice—"

William turned on her. "That'll do, from you as well," he said, and though his voice was still quiet, danger outlined each word. She thought they must have taught him how to do that in the Army.

"What lovely symmetry." Maxwell turned for the curtained doorway. "Disillusionment appears to be the order of the day." Without offering further explanation for the comment, he stalked off to Kent's chamber.

*

Elizabeth lay down upon Katarina's bed, but she did not sleep. The air was too hot, and pressed too heavily against her skin and throat, and the rise and fall of voices downstairs jerked her awake whenever she did manage to drift off. What would those voices conclude? Whatever would she and the others do if Kent decided not to trust them?

Stay alive until tonight and then use the pocket watch to go somewhere else, she told herself, staring into the darkness above her head. *We'll learn history some other way, we'll decide where best to affect it, we'll proceed from there.* Assuming, of course, they could persuade any other local inhabitant to trust them where Kent had declined to, which upon reflection did not seem very likely. Without an ally, would they be able to discover trustworthy sources of history? There would be schoolbooks, Elizabeth supposed, but she did not think schoolbooks would answer. Maxwell had drawn his knowledge of Waterloo from Wellington's private writings; they would need something comparable for Dover and for all the opportunities that were not battles. The memoirs stored in the cottage of Kent's Yorkshire mentor—Mr. Carter, had Katarina said the name was?—seemed ideal. If only Kent decided to trust them. Elizabeth rolled over and buried her head in the pillow.

The blackness had only just begun to lighten into thick, gritty grayness when Elizabeth heard a step on the stair, and then Emil Schwieger's voice spoke her name from the other side of the curtain. "Herr Kent wishes to speak with you," he said. She could not tell from his tone of voice whether he was pleased or displeased at the intelligence he had been instructed to convey. He moved on to give the same message to William and Maxwell. A few short minutes later, Elizabeth followed him down the stair with a feeling halfway between vertigo and what the French called *déjà vu*—thinking of following Katarina up the same stairway a few days ago in a vanished universe, back when the whole matter was an adventure and a cause for giddy glee.

The sitting room seemed ominously quiet as she approached the doorway. She thought again of being called to face her aunt's wrath, then impatiently put aside the comparison. Surely her standards of "trouble" should have altered in the last few days.

And indeed, no trouble awaited her. When she entered the room, it was to discover that the silence proceeded from fatigue rather than anger on the part of its inhabitants. Mrs. Trevelyan appeared particularly exhausted, curled again in the wing chair, lashes cast down upon milk-pale cheeks. Her husband again perched on the chair's arm. He looked nearly as tired as she did, the bags beneath his eyes even more pronounced than they had been, and as the time travelers entered the room, he moved fractionally closer to his wife, looking over her head with the air of a protective bird of prey. Katarina had pushed one of the straight-backed chairs into the other corner and sat with her head leaning back against the wall, her face set and sullen.

Only Kent was still on his feet—hair rumpled, coat cast off and sleeves rolled up, but alight with energy still. Elizabeth suspected at once both that he had carried his point, and that he had done so by talking his opponents into exhaustion. He was standing at the dining table, bent over a pile of papers, but he looked up and straightened as soon as she cleared the threshold.

"Ah, there you are. Good." He paused to add, "Good morning. I hope you were able to sleep a little?" but did not wait for a reply before continuing. "I believe I have a method for getting you to Yorkshire without arousing French suspicion."

He had carried his point, then. He would trust them and they were going to see his mentor. Elizabeth felt instinctively it would be the wrong tactic to express delighted surprise, but she had to grope for a moment before she found another reaction to put in its place.

"Oh, have you?" It sounded inane to her own ears. "That's—ah—wonderful, thank you, sir. How shall it be accomplished?" She suddenly wished she had been able to take advantage of the brief respite to sleep. It might be easier to keep up with Frederick Kent if she were rested.

"It is difficult to travel from one part of England to another," Kent said. "Without papers, it is impossible, and even with them—But you are fortunate in your timing. I had in fact secured tickets on today's dirigible for certain members of my organization. We will put off their journey a week or so, and you will make use of the tickets instead."

Elizabeth opened her mouth to ask if a dirigible might be something like a locomotive-train, but William was already speaking. "It's very kind of you, sir. It will make matters easier to have you with us, to be sure."

Kent shook his head. "I never intended to make this particular journey, and in fact, I have responsibilities that must keep me in London. But Katarina was to go, in the person of one of her alter egos. She will be your guide."

Elizabeth cast a dismayed look at the woman rocking back the chair legs in the corner of the room. "I'm not pleased about it either," Katarina said without opening her eyes. "But as I have been reminded, I don't give the orders here."

"Emil Schwieger will go as well," Kent said, ignoring this, "though probably in a different guise than what we had planned. Those specifics still require a bit of thought. Emil, while I think, run off to see Matthews and the Johnstons and tell them their services will not be required today after all. Then I'll need you to rouse Gilbert out of his bed and get him to craft papers for our guests, ones that support the details of the cover story."

Schwieger nodded, brisk and martial and Prussian. "Yes sir. And those details—?"

"—will be finalized by the time you come back from your first errand." Kent grinned briefly. "Those specifics require a bit more thought as well. It will need to be a somewhat convoluted story, to explain the desired destination, our guests' unfamiliarity with England as it is now, and the accent of their spoken English, while still giving them the social class sufficient to ward off suspicion. But then, challenges are what make life worth living. Off you go, Emil. And Katarina, get to your greasepaints; we only have a few hours. Miss Barton." Kent turned to face her as Emil headed for the front door and Katarina without a word pushed herself off the chair and strode for the stairway. "Mrs. Trevelyan has offered the loan of her walking dress. If you would do me the kindness to go and don it now, so that we may be sure it fits while we still have time to correct problems, I would be greatly obliged. And then, Brenda—you should get yourself to bed." He spoke more gently to her than he had yet to anyone. Brenda Trevelyan seemed to call gentleness from her companions. "You look ready to drop, my dear."

Brenda smiled as she uncurled herself from the wing chair. "I'm well enough, nothing to worry over, and glad to help. *Yes*, Gavin, I mean to rest afterward!" She shook her head with affection, then turned her smile to Elizabeth. "Miss Barton, won't you come with me?"

"Mr. Carrington and Mr. Maxwell," Kent continued as Brenda took Elizabeth's arm and led her from the room. "I think we ought to be able to outfit you from the warehouse store of gentlemen's clothing—"

"Yes," Brenda murmured at Elizabeth's shoulder, and Elizabeth turned to see merriment dancing in the older woman's eyes. "What you were wondering—the answer is yes. Frederick Kent *is* always like that. He listens with all his soul until he is certain, and then he springs into motion, sweeping all up and driving all before him. Like being caught by the Wild Hunt, I always think." Elizabeth had to smile. They ascended the stairway while Kent's voice rose and fell below them, talking without apparent pause for breath.

So early in the morning, barely any light penetrated the Trevelyans' garret bedchamber, and so Brenda struck a match to the candle on the low table just inside the curtain. There were matchsticks in common use in this 1885 as well, it seemed. By the candle's light, the bedchamber was revealed to be as pleasant as such a cramped and airless apartment could be—the mattress bed crisply made, the clothing-chest gleaming with polish, the boards beneath bone-white with scrubbing. Brenda turned not for the chest, but for a curtain hung from the ceiling in such a way as to form an alcove.

Within, a dark blue gown seemed to stand under its own power. An illusion, Elizabeth realized almost at once, spotting the hook on the garret roof, but an understandable one. The stiff skirt brushed the floor; the bodice hung above was just as rigid. The last time Elizabeth had seen an outfit of this design, it had been worn by a woman falling to construct fire in the other London. She had thought then how hideously uncomfortable it must be. It looked even worse up close.

Yes, that was a wire cage serving as an underskirt. Yes, definitely whalebones reinforcing the sides of the wasp-waist bodice. The skirt pulled tight across the front and came into a puffed tail at the back. How on earth did one sit in it? Walk in it? From the chest, Brenda was taking a pair of black gloves, a black bonnet heavy with feathers and ribbon, and an assortment of underthings. The ensemble looked more like a suit of armor than anything made of cloth.

Elizabeth managed, "Is this…fashionable?"

Brenda looked up. "I fear it's a bit behind current fashion. I left Wales with the clothes on my back, and they serve me well enough for everyday—" She indicated her simple countrywoman's dress. "Especially in this part of the city. But sometimes it is necessary, for my own protection, to have the dress of… of that sort of woman who is not viewed with suspicion by the authorities, so Frederick acquired one for me. Well, he had Katherine do so, and this was the best she could manage with the funds he could spare." Her cheeks had turned pink. "I've no choice but to live on charity for now, but it won't always be so. And I can assure you it is close enough that you won't be drawing attention from those we must avoid."

"Oh, no, no, I didn't mean to—" Elizabeth floundered. What could she say that would unmake her misstep? "I am very grateful for your charity towards *me*. It's just—different." She indicated her own simple gown.

Brenda looked from Elizabeth's gown to the monstrous dress and back. "It must seem overwhelming," she agreed. "To be honest—" One cheek dimpled. "—it did to me when I first tried it on. Katherine had to show me how to get all the pieces fastened properly. But not to worry—I know how, now, and I'll have you ready for your journey in two shakes of a lamb's tail." She pressed something white and amorphously shaped into Elizabeth's hand. "I'll just step outside while you take off your own things and put on the combination, and then I'll be back to help with the corset." She slipped around the curtain before Elizabeth could protest.

Not that a protest would have been of any use. It *was* armor, apparently, this dress that made it possible for a woman to walk abroad and appear respectable enough, or possibly French enough, not be troubled by the French authorities. Brenda had not created the rules, so Elizabeth could not appeal to her for permission to ignore them.

She stripped off her gown and chemise, and stood in stockings and shoes to examine the undergarment. She thought at first it might be like the drawers Katarina had once loaned her, but it had too many leg holes. After a time she determined that the holes were for both legs and arms—oh, a *combination*. It wasn't too bad, once she had it turned the right way round—the bottom part fell loosely to her knees, and a waist similar to the top half of a chemise hung loosely from her shoulders. The fabric was muslin, light enough against her hot skin, decorated with frills and tucks. Perhaps this wouldn't be so uncomfortable after all.

Brenda peeped back through the curtain. "Oh, good. I thought we were near enough the same size. Now for the corset." She held it for Elizabeth to fit her arms into, then came around behind to lace it.

Elizabeth had worn stays before, of course, but she was not prepared for the way these clamping steel fingers forced the air from her lungs. Looking down the length of her body, she saw that she had a more womanly shape than she ever had before, but she did not consider this benefit a reasonable exchange for the ability to breathe. The little room seemed to swim around her. She forced her breath out and in again, to the fullest extent the cramping whalebone would allow.

The black dots before her eyes cleared, and she looked down again just as Brenda Trevelyan buckled the wire-cage underskirt around her waist. Elizabeth craned over her shoulder and caught a glimpse of the hard wire structure sticking straight out from the small of her back like a shelf. *You cannot possibly be serious.*

Brenda went again to the alcove and returned with a petticoat. "Lift up your arms," she said, and dropped the white garment over Elizabeth's head. She tugged it into place, then brought out the skirt. The heavy blue folds swished past Elizabeth's eyes. They hit the cage and stopped, and Brenda walked around, tugging and fastening them into place. The drag against Elizabeth's back was every bit as bad as she had thought it would be. And how did one *sit?*

"Here," Brenda said, reappearing with the bodice and holding it up. Elizabeth turned to slip her arms into it, and nearly stumbled as the tight front of the skirt trapped her legs.

That decided her. "I can't," Elizabeth said. "I can't possibly wear this."

Brenda paused, the bodice in her hands and a concerned line between her brows.

"I can't imagine how you do," Elizabeth said. "I won't know how to walk. I'll give us all away. Can't I wear my own gown? Or can't I go as a boy?"

"In that shirt and those trousers?" Brenda shook her head. "You'd look like—like no one who'd be allowed to board a dirigible. As for your frock—" She hesitated, obviously seeking a way to give Elizabeth what she wanted, but in the end shook her head again. "You could wear it indoors, perhaps, and pass it off as a tea gown, but never traveling with all those fine people. I cannot see how you can get to Mr. Carter's cottage without wearing proper walking dress. I fear you must either wear it or wait here with me. Not that I would object to your company, not at all, but—"

Elizabeth gritted her teeth. "Yes. All right. If it is what I must do to meet Mr. Carter, I shall do it. You must—you must teach me to walk in it."

Brenda nodded. "I shall. Here, the basque first." She helped Elizabeth coax her arms into the tight sleeves, and buttoned the tiny buttons from the waist all the way up to right under Elizabeth's chin. The heavy silk pressed tight against the cotton of the petticoat, which clung damply to the hard surface of the corset, which bit into her muslin-covered skin. The layers of draped skirts smothered her legs. Elizabeth drew in a gasping breath of the garret's scorching air.

"The skirt is pinned up like so," Brenda explained, suiting the action to the word, "and now it should be a little easier to walk." It wasn't, but Elizabeth persevered until she managed to cross the room and back with little mincing steps. Brenda nodded approval. "Sit right here, and I shall arrange your hair. How fortunate it curls naturally."

Elizabeth lowered herself with exquisite care onto the edge of the chest, feeling how the cage gave way in response to her weight. It would spring back into place as soon as she stood, she was certain, assuming she managed to stand. Brenda stepped behind her and continued the work of lady's maid, pulling a hairbrush painfully through her tangled curls, then sweeping her back hair into a heavy, hot mass on the top of her head and teasing the rest so it fell over her forehead in sticky ringlets. Atop this arrangement she pinned the hat—equally hot, equally heavy—and handed Elizabeth the gloves.

I will not faint. Elizabeth managed to lever herself upright. *Soldiers march in scarlet woolen coats, with packs and rifles; this cannot be worse; I will not faint.* She did not, not during the walk across the garret nor during the walk down the stairs.

"There," Brenda said, "you're doing beautifully. It's not so hard once you try, is it?"

Elizabeth turned her head enough to give the older woman a look, and Brenda winced. They descended the rest of the stairway and traversed the corridor to the sitting room, Elizabeth taking the short little steps that were all the front of the skirt would allow, feeling the back shift behind her with each one. Was it centaurs that had the bodies of horses and the heads of men? She wondered if she looked as much like one as she felt.

"Yes," Katarina's voice drifted from the direction of the sitting room, "but it won't explain why they know nothing of Prussia or the German language or current events."

"It has some drawbacks, to be sure," Kent's voice answered, "but it hits the salient points, and despite its slight omissions, this explanation has an elegant symmetry that pleases me. I think we'll do no better on such short notice."

At the other end of the shadowy corridor, the front door opened, and Schwieger came hurrying through. He stopped short at the sight of Elizabeth standing at the foot of the stairs, swallowing some obstruction in his throat. "My—my goodness, Miss Barton. You look lovely."

She barely bit back a snarl at him, and he looked startled and alarmed, as Brenda had. It was some small compensation for the way her back was already aching. Without another word, Schwieger bowed and hastened past her into the sitting room, ducking around Trevelyan, who stood leaning against the doorframe and drinking tea from a handleless cup like a farm laborer who knew no better table-manners—did the man *always* stand where he would block everyone else's path? Elizabeth regathered the folds of the skirt in her hand and made her way through the sitting room doorway.

William stood on Trevelyan's other side, now attired in a coat and waistcoat similar to the one Schwieger wore, with the odd pointy front that had been fashionable in the other 1885 as well as this one, and the baggy Cossack-style trousers. Both seemed a little loose on his slim frame, but not absurdly so. He was watching as Kent helped Maxwell adjust the collar of his coat—and it was Maxwell's own coat, Elizabeth saw, the one he had worn in the other 1885. "If we cannot find anything better, this will do," Kent was saying. "The tailoring is a little unusual, but that only means you will seem a little unfashionable. If we must choose, I think it will be better than loaning you one that does not really fit." Maxwell rolled his broad shoulders under the coat, and agreed.

An unknown young man lounged against the far wall, with one foot braced behind him, watching this show. He was dressed as smartly as William—more so, for his glossy-black coat, waistcoat, and trousers fit as perfectly as Kent's, much better than William's borrowed garb. In his own violation of good manners, he wore his top hat as well as his gloves indoors. Elizabeth thought for a moment he was a member of Kent's company she had not yet met—and then the luminous dark eyes came up, and she recognized the planes of the face and the gleaming black hair pinned up and slicked back under the top hat. "Good Lord, Madam Katherine!" she said. "What an astonishing transformation."

It was an understatement. Elizabeth's eyes darted between Katarina and William, and could discern no difference in their silhouettes. Katarina had bound and padded herself so that she appeared to be a tall, slim young man. Artfully applied grease-paint somehow suggested a heavier jaw, blunted the elegant cheekbones. Elizabeth regarded the casually propped foot with naked envy. *Why could I not also travel as a young man?*

Katarina did not show any pleasure at her admiration. "All part of my trade, Miss Barton." She pushed off the wall and sauntered to the other end of the room.

It felt like being slapped. Elizabeth stood still, burning, sweltering, unable to breathe. Then she turned and smiled at Brenda. "Mrs. Trevelyan, I do thank you for all your assistance. I am finding the skirt easier to manage now, and I am sure it is due to your tutelage. It was so very kind of you to loan your walking dress and help me prepare."

Brenda smiled back, surprised but pleased at the sudden friendliness. "I am glad to help, Miss Barton."

"It is so lovely to get to know you," Elizabeth added without thinking. "Truly, it is."

Brenda's soft brown eyes looked a question. "Did you not know me in your other London?"

Maxwell flashed her a warning look, too late. Elizabeth hesitated a breath, wondering how she might answer truthfully without revealing painful facts Brenda Trevelyan had no need to learn. "No," she said at last, "I did not have the pleasure."

Brenda accepted this without any concern, though her husband paused for one sharp look at Elizabeth before he came to take his wife's arm and urge her to bed. Then Kent was turning his incisive attention in Elizabeth's direction, and she forgot everything else. "Ah, Emil, you've returned, good. I've worked out a story for you to take to Gilbert. Miss Barton, you look very smart indeed. That will do nicely. One final touch—" He held his closed hand toward Elizabeth, and she reached back in unthinking response. He set something in her palm and drew his hand away with a conjurer's flourish, whereupon she found herself holding a small gold wedding band and almost dropped it. "Mr. *Kent*," she said.

His eyes sparkled. "High time I shared my plans with the rest of you, Miss Barton?" he interpreted. "Indeed it is. I said it was necessary to invent a story that would account for your accent, the limitations of your knowledge, and your desire to travel by dirigible to the middle of nowhere? I've decided on one." His looked from Elizabeth to Schwieger. "Emil, you'll be acquiring a wife for the duration," he began. Emil Schwieger's eyes widened, and beyond him, William Carrington's narrowed into slits.

Chapter 3

London, August 29, 1885

There were, William reminded himself, several matters more worrisome and more worthy of his attention than this business of Elizabeth Barton spending the day on Emil Schwieger's perfectly functional arm. Many matters. Of far greater importance. It was not even as though the pairing represented any stated preference on her part. It was a masquerade, no more.

William was still hard-pressed not to grind his teeth at the thought of it. He had yet to discuss with her the topic of their kiss in the village of Waterloo—they had shared very few moments alone since, and none had seemed quite the time to open the conversation—but right now, he wished he had opened it anyway, suitable opportunity or not. What were she and Schwieger talking about in the sitting room, anyhow? He could hear their voices, but not their words.

He stood in the scullery with Katarina Rasmirovna, once his friend, now a suspicious stranger, submitting with ill grace to her fingers tying his limp right arm up in a sling. A sling at least implied a recent injury; a war wound with no war save rebellions in the immediate past might well draw attention their party didn't need. He hated how every disguise must work to take the arm into account, and he hated how the sling forced him to wear Emil Schwieger's second best coat shrugged around his shoulders instead of properly fitted. Nor was he overly pleased at the idea of entrusting his safety and that of his two companions to the plainly hostile Katarina and the unknown Schwieger for the entirety of a journey to Yorkshire. He wanted to grind his teeth at that thought, too.

"—giving them kerosene and matches and setting them playing near a gas-main," Trevelyan's voice snapped from the corridor just outside. "What makes you think you'll prefer whatever universe they create next? What makes you think this one isn't preferable to the last?"

"We're through with this argument," Kent's voice responded. "You had your say last night. Now I've given my orders."

"Damn it, I have a family to protect—" Trevelyan said.

The voices passed on, and William looked up to see that Katarina's attention was fixed in the direction of the corridor, as his had been. It must be as uncommon here as in the other London for Trevelyan's colorless voice to so flush with warmth. Once William would have thought Trevelyan too cool of spirit to speak passionately of any subject at all; but since then he had seen the flash of relieved joy on the Welshman's face when the rail-gun worked, and the lightning-flare of hatred when he turned the rifle on a construct. There was not much Trevelyan cared about, William thought, but he cared intensely about those few things. Those few people.

The connection formed itself in William's mind with a suddenness that made his breath catch in his throat. *I have a family to protect.* Not a wife, a family. And, *The constructs are the only weapon that has a chance of making a difference in the next seven months.* William now thought he understood why seven months might be a meaningful measurement of time. And—God, and Brenda Trevelyan had been dead in the other 1885. Trevelyan couldn't know that, though, surely? Even if he did suspect—she had been killed by Wellington monsters in the other world; with no Wellington monsters, there was no reason to suppose her life in danger in some third universe. But William had the cold feeling that if Trevelyan once realized the risk, he would not be content to thus coolly reason out her chances for survival. Particularly not given her current condition. Men did...unreasonable things when children were at stake. William thought of Christopher Palmer struggling to walk on a mangled leg, struggling to live long enough get home to William's sister and their unborn child.

His thoughts were shattered by the sharp rapping on the front door, delivered in sets of three loud enough to shake the warehouse. "Emil?" Kent's voice called. "Your carriage is here."

The "carriage" was a pony-trap, such a conveyance apparently the one best suited to the roles the four of them were to play. Its driver, a young red-haired man named Johnston, silently lifted the brass-bound trunk containing their change of costuming, and Schwieger gave Elizabeth his hand to help her into the trap. William and Maxwell took their places, and the trap clattered away.

It was still early morning, but the air was already thick and heavy. *Dead,* William could not help thinking. The other London had been characterized by its noise—the constant undertone hum, the stomping of the constructs, the shrilling of the factory whistles. This London was profound in its silence. The very buildings seemed to sag into their foundations, enlivened by neither industry nor hope of any.

When they turned onto a street that fronted the Thames, William could see men dressed in rough laborers' clothes unloading cargo from a ship that flew the tricolor flag and was ornamented at every joint with ornately carved bees. The prow was a screaming eagle with outstretched talons. The crew unloading that ostentatious great ship seemed to be the only specimens of humanity at work that morning; whole long stretches of dock stretched silent and still under the rising sun, as though the turgid August air pressed too heavily to make movement worthwhile. Or perhaps it was the eagle's talons that restrained any who might otherwise have ventured out-of-doors. The effect of all the slow nothingness was mesmerizing—block after block of quiet street went by, until you stopped expecting to see anyone bustling about their affairs. William saw Elizabeth shift against the constraints of her gown, and he fought a similar urge to stretch against the trappings of his sling.

"There is not work enough at the docks for all who would seek it," Schwieger remarked like an answer to William's thoughts. "Since it has become nearly impossible for any to run a shop without French patronage, other options are few. Some say the city is dying, although that I suppose depends on your perspective." No one answered. After a time, Schwieger added, "Two or three French firms have factories farther down the Thames. Sometimes there is talk of others building here, but only talk so far."

"Why only talk?" William started to ask, but three men in blue coats stepped out from the cross-street just ahead, and the words dried up in his throat. The uniform had changed some in seventy years, but not nearly enough.

"Your business?" the guard greeted them.

Schwieger held out a sheaf of papers, all ornamented with colored ink and wax seals. "We have tickets for the dirigible to York."

The guard took his hand away from his pistol and plucked the bundle of passports and tickets from Schwieger's grip. His two comrades stayed alert, still fingering their weapons. "Prussia?" the dark-haired guard said, and looked up. "What do you do here, then?"

"My wife's father was born here," Schwieger said, nodding to Maxwell. "He emigrated to Prussia long ago. We have come to see the old country. My wife and her brother have never before visited."

The guard's eyes ran over Elizabeth, then turned to William. "What is wrong with your arm?"

William did not have to pretend the grimace. "Our carriage suffered an upset on the journey to take ship to England. I suppose I was fortunate to break only the arm."

The guard handed the papers back to Schwieger without further comment, and waved them on their way. William managed to hold his peace until he was sure they were out of earshot.

"I thought we would need the papers for the dirigible," he hissed to Schwieger then. "London is occupied still, seventy years later?"

Schwieger shrugged a little. "Under Napoleon I, it was the policy of the Empire to humiliate Britain as much as possible. The Emperor's own words. And policies have a way of outlasting their creators. Besides—" He chuckled a little. "—Britain has done all possible to make it known the yoke sits uncomfortably. Even seventy years later. Each time the Imperials turn their heads away, the British revolt in the mines, or explode a train, or some such. That is why the talk of factories is only talk."

The architecture had begun to change subtly around them. William had never been in Paris proper, and so it took him some time to identify the niggling familiarity as having come from sketches he had seen. These wide arcades and ironwork balconies were built in the French style—so this must be the respectable part of town. Here servants in livery scrubbed steps and otherwise prepared business for the day, and here other carriages clattered along the streets. Here, too, a great oval balloon blotted out the skyline.

They had nearly reached it when another set of soldiers stopped them. "Out early, aren't you?"

Schwieger produced again his papers and his explanations. This time the guard looked sharply at Maxwell. "When did you leave England? Why?"

"During the Troubles, in the spring of '45," Maxwell said. William wondered how many identities and life stories he had memorized at short notice, trying to fit into one time or another. "We were starving, as so many did in the north. The opportunities elsewhere in the Empire were better."

"You yourself were not part of the Rising?"

"Oh, no indeed," Maxwell assured him, and that, William thought, was at least true enough. The guard looked him over once more—paused long enough for cold sweat to start oozing down William's back—then returned the papers to Schwieger and waved them on.

The riverbank opened up into what was definitely a dockside. It would have made William think of Portsmouth, with its milling crowds waiting to board packet ships leaving for the Continent, except no ships nestled in the water. Instead, the huge dark balloon rose above the river, casting a silent shadow like a curved-beak hawk gliding over a meadowful of mice. The angle of the rising sun stretched the shadow, rendering it even more grotesque. The pointy nose of the prow bisected the street where the carriages rattled, while the mass of balloon and propeller stretched over the dockside itself. Like the cargo ship further downriver, it had Napoleonic bees worked in the basket suspended beneath the balloon, and a great screaming eagle painted upon the silken balloon itself. Upon the *envelope*, Kent had said it was called.

The expected guards were here, and Schwieger embarked upon the now-familiar ritual. "We are from Prussia; my wife and her brother were born there and have never seen their father's home village; we go now to visit it." This time a guard looked sharply at all the faces and their corresponding passports, making William hope with all his might that the forger Kent employed would live up to his patron's boast. The guard looked twice from Elizabeth's face to Maxwell's, but seemed to relax when he compared Maxwell's to William's. *You two look enough alike for the story to be believed,* Kent had commented. *Similar complexion, same color eyes. If you are challenged, say Madame Hoffman takes after her late mother.*

Madame Hoffman. It shouldn't irritate him so much to hear her called so, not with so many real dangers confronting them.

The guard returned their papers, and then there was nothing for it but to dismount from the trap and join the throng of gibuses and gleaming gold-topped canes, bustles and big hats heavy with flowers. The crowd spoke in well-modulated low tones, but the effect of so great a number could not help but be a roar—and they were all talking French. It was in its own way as frightening as Waterloo.

Maxwell twitched a little. "It sounds like Paris."

Schwieger smiled without humor. "I suppose much of southeast England might as well be. Frenchmen come for administrative posts, or French second sons for the opportunity, and then they stay. Their sons speak French in the home, go to French boarding schools, employ Englishmen who have learned to speak the *lingua franca* without accent. And so it goes. Some of these here speak English at home, but you will not find any in London who speak only English. For that you must go far outside the palisade, into the wild lands past York."

William watched the crowd, listening to the overlapping conversations. One group he took to be men of finance, some French and some Gallicized English. That priest there he thought to be English-born, though how odd to see an Englishman in Popish dress. Those two women—dressed in gowns that looked even more elaborate than Elizabeth's—were likely the English wives of the Frenchmen standing not far away. The women were discussing their sons, presently together at a Paris boarding school.

A whistle blew, and Elizabeth flinched from it. Schwieger patted her hand, and William gritted his teeth again. The crowd formed itself into an impressively orderly queue and commenced its slow promenade up the gangplank. It was in fact quite like boarding a packet ship, even to the way the deck seemed to shift slightly underfoot as William's boot touched it. Overhead, the edges of the elongated silken balloon, striped red and white and blue beneath the eagle, fluttered in a breath of air off the water.

Schwieger handled all necessary transactions for his "wife" and her "brother" and "father," shepherding his three charges under the curving bee-encrusted prow and safely to the observation deck. Here the shiny polished wood and gleaming brass reminded William even more strongly of a sailing ship. Poised as it was over the Thames, you could even look over the rail and through the enclosed glass window and fancy yourself about to set sail—if you took care to angle your view to hide the several-foot drop between the bottom of the basket and the water.

Elizabeth did not seem disconcerted by the drop, but she did seem to be having difficulty with the odor that wafted from the water. She sneezed once delicately, then again, and fished her handkerchief out of Brenda Trevelyan's borrowed reticule.

"How does the balloon fly?" she asked her "husband," leaning more closely to him than William thought was necessary, even for verisimilitude.

"The first ones had an open flame between the envelope and the basket," Schwieger answered. "The hot air rose as it does in a smokestack, and carried the balloon with it. But one could only float with the wind; it was not possible to steer. Elongating the envelope allowed them to add a rudder. See, you can see it, there."

"Where?" Elizabeth leaned forward eagerly, shoving her handkerchief back into her reticule with careless fingers. It was not the first time she had mistaken a fold of cloth for the opening of a reticule, William thought. The handkerchief fluttered free as a pocket watch once had, but Elizabeth did not notice. She was craning to look at the rudder.

"The elongated envelope proved to have its own problems," Schwieger continued. "Hot air will rise, but not spread. It was not until the use of helium was perfected that the dirigible would operate properly. The prototype was launched in 1818 or 1819. The fleet—" He spread his hands. "—well, as you know, set sail in 1820."

"Madame?"

All three of them turned at the voice, in time to see a sleek dark young man stoop and rescue Elizabeth's handkerchief from the other feet milling about the deck. He handed it to her with a bow, and she thanked him in English, then caught herself and repeated the thanks in French.

"My pleasure, Madame," Katarina Rasmirovna said—in English, and in a voice half an octave below her usual throaty tones. If William had not known who spoke to them—if he had not already seen the guise back at the warehouse—he never could have guessed. She moved with a swing of her hips and shoulders that was absolutely unlike any woman William had ever seen—even a woman wearing breeches. Even Katarina wearing breeches. The illusion was magnificent; William could not tell if he were more impressed or more disconcerted. "Colin Ramsey," Katarina added, touching her hat to Elizabeth. "At your service."

"Madame Emil Hoffman," Elizabeth murmured, indicating her "husband," and Katarina—Colin Ramsey—shifted to bow to him as well.

"Prussia? But your accent is so flawless, Madame. I would have taken you for an Englishwoman."

At this cue, Maxwell joined them, and it became the most natural thing in the world for he and young Mr. Ramsey to fall into conversation. "—to see the old homestead," Maxwell said for the fourth time that morning. "And you, sir, what brings you to York?" Above them, the boiler coughed, spluttered, then suddenly roared. Only for a moment; but Elizabeth's hand tightened reflexively on Schwieger's arm. *Damn him,* William thought. A pretty young woman standing near Katarina—near Colin Ramsey—shrieked and stumbled and clutched at the air for support. Katarina/Colin caught her, speaking cheerfully and soothingly until the young woman was reclaimed by her mother and father—both English, William thought, but aspiring to Frenchness—who scolded her in low icy tones and glared at Colin Ramsey until he retreated. Katarina looked up once they had gone, her sardonic eye catching William's for an instant.

After the first burst of noise, the dirigible rose—no, the water fell away—in utter spellbinding silence. William tried not to gawk. A man of his position must have certainly seen such a sight before, dirigibles being in use everywhere in the Empire. Another burst of noise, and the huge bee-encrusted prow swung about, and the balloon glided its silent way over London.

Behind him, Katarina and Maxwell resumed their conversation, exchanging bits of their pre-arranged and utterly false stories in English. Maxwell added an unrehearsed bit about his fictitious late wife. She was brave and outspoken, he said. To his great grief, she had died before her children were old enough to know her. William thought of the locket Maxwell kept hidden inside his shirt collar, and wondered if any of that story might be true. He did not know whose face might be within, as Maxwell took great care always that no one should see. If it held the face of some lost love, there was no way to tell the year of her birth—or the year of her death. William reflected, not for the first time, what an impossibly strange life this man must lead.

Above Maxwell's tale rose the conversation of the English mothers, still discussing their sons. The French businessmen were complaining about current economic conditions. Schwieger still kept Elizabeth on his arm, pointing out to her various items of interest. William looked down at the country below, slipping by all quiet and green.

The balloon's shadow moved as slowly as poured honey, drenching each swath of farmland in turn, passing smoothly on. The land below looked like a painting, captured on canvas, unchanging and unchangeable. Or trapped in amber, perhaps, frozen solid. *Unable to breathe,* William thought, looking up to find his eye caught by Elizabeth's tightly corseted waist. *Unable to breathe, let alone move, let alone grow. Is this what defeat looks like? Placid green farmland and the aspiration to speak accentless French?* It was obscene that this great sailing monster should move so silently and be so clean. It ought to be belching black smoke clouds into the sky, so the people below would hate it and remember to struggle.

"And then there is all that nonsense with those rebels in the northwest and the coal trains," one of the French businessmen said, and William caught the twitch of Katarina's smile. Schwieger had said that Britain had revolted against the Empire every time the Imperial attention was momentarily distracted. *Well, at least some people remember to struggle. And we'll fix it. We will. We'll go back with a message and mend our error and this will never happen.*

"Perhaps you would care to share a coach with us, young man?" Maxwell said to Katarina, easy and jovial, as the dirigible descended toward York some hours later.

"I'd be pleased to, sir," Katarina said, just as casually. Surely none of the finely dressed French speakers surrounding them could suspect collusion. "The countryside is a bit rough around here, but I know it well, and our paths lie together."

They engaged rooms at an inn for the night, as Mr. Colin Ramsey and as Herr Hoffman and his wife and her family. They discussed over supper in the common room their—diverging, naturally—travel plans for the morrow. And then before dawn they boarded the first coach of the day, one that had not been featured in the supper conversation, the costumes they had worn on the dirigible packed away in the trunk and all the grease-paint scrubbed off—except for Katarina's, as she still chose to pose as a young man. But now she wore comfortable country clothing, as did the men, and Elizabeth appeared in a state of bliss indeed after exchanging the hated walking dress for her own gown.

The complexities of this journey north made William's head spin. Now that he had time to think, he could not help but wonder whether all these machinations were truly needful, or whether any rather fed some unnecessary dramatic flair on the part of his hosts. He studied Katarina's and Schwieger's intent expressions, and came to the unwelcome conclusion that these layers of misdirection were indeed commonplace in the lives they led. "All along the city road, in and out the Eagle," Katarina murmured to herself as the coach rattled away. At William's inquiring look, she clarified, "A children's song. Sometimes heard in the music halls, suitably, er, modified. The Eagle is a tavern. In the children's song, at least."

"At least we needn't climb in one side of a train and out the other," Schwieger said.

"Only because there isn't one to hand." Katarina stretched her legs out as much as she could.

Elizabeth looked up at the word "train." "I wondered about that," she said. "Wouldn't it have been more discreet to travel by railway?"

"It would have been," Schwieger told her, "but Colin Ramsey, the secretary of M'sieur Levesque, travels on more distinguished conveyances."

"Yes, but why did Katarina Rasmirovna wish to travel on one?" Elizabeth looked hard at Schwieger. "Why did Mr. Kent have those tickets in the first place? What was it our arrival interrupted?"

"This time?" Schwieger said. "Nothing at all. Some other future dirigible journey might be less peaceful, but we first need to explore—"

"Emil," Katarina said.

Schwieger did not respond to her rebuke as quickly as he had responded to Kent's. "I am not telling her anything not public knowledge. All know the French use dirigibles for everything. If the service were to be disrupted, why, that could be most…disruptive to the gentlemen of the Empire."

"Could they not just use trains?" Elizabeth wanted to know.

"Oh, they could." Schwieger smiled. "But we've been very successful at disrupting those."

"Emil," Katarina said, and he subsided.

The coach deposited them at a cross-roads without a house to be seen in any direction. "This far outside the palisade, we may enjoy peace from Imperial attention," Katarina said. "Unfortunately, that means we may expect lack of decent transportation as well. I fear we have a trudge ahead of us. At least we can engage a hand-cart for the trunk in Danby." Until then, William inferred, they must carry the thing. He hefted one side with his left hand—because he could do that, damn it, and did not need to relinquish the duty to an older man or to a woman—and was pleased enough to see that the other end occupied enough of Schwieger's attention to preclude the possibility of the young man playing the gallant to Elizabeth. Freed of the corset and puffed-out skirts, she strode quite comfortably without needing to lean on anyone's arm, following Katarina briskly down a cow-path and then up an incline.

From the top of the rise, the village of Danby was visible—a ramshackle place boasting only a cluster of cottages and crumbling stone church—and they reached its outer edges perhaps half an hour later. There Katarina engaged a hand-cart from a man who called her "Mr. Ramsey" with matter-of-fact recognition, and the five of them continued on their way.

Their destination proved to be a cottage set some distance farther on from the village—the sort of place that wanted to be neat and pretty, William thought, and only succeeded in stretching halfway to the former. The white paint peeled from the lintel, and the upstairs windows had boards replacing their glass. What ought to have been the front garden was only a stretch of weeds and dirt, with a dilapidated-looking sundial on a brick base presiding drunkenly over all it surveyed.

A flock of chickens rose in a complaining cloud of feathers at the strangers' approach, and in response a middle-aged woman in a cap and apron came around the corner from the side yard. The anxious crease in her forehead smoothed as her eyes fell upon Katarina.

"Mercy me! Is it—" The woman seemed to choke on the words, and took a moment to swallow and choose different ones, shooting little glances at Katarina's companions. "—Mr. Ramsey, isn't it?"

"It's Miss Katherine," Katarina said, with the first smile William had seen from her. "At least, it is if Mr. Carter and Mr. West are home alone today. This lady and these gentlemen are—" She apparently could not bring herself to say the word "friends." Instead, she amended, "Mr. Kent sent me to bring them to Mr. Carter."

The woman smiled. "They're alone today, Miss Katherine."

Katarina pulled the cap off her head and started tugging pins from her hair. The heavy black coil slithered loose, for an effect that was most disconcerting indeed when combined with breeches and a coat, and Katarina gave a little sigh of relief and rubbed at her scalp. "How are you and your gentlemen, Janet?"

"Oh, well enough, Miss Katherine, can't complain." Janet resettled her own mobcap over her knot of fair hair. "Mr. West, he wanders in his mind, like, but Mr. Carter, he keeps his faculties wonderful well for a man so old. And ninety-five his next birthday and only needing a cane to support him! I've never seen the like before. But come right in, you and your friends, and I'll tell the gentlemen you've come to call." She bustled away ahead of them, under the cottage's crooked lintel.

The hall was likewise crooked and cramped and dark. Even the late summer sunshine could not brighten it. "Mr. West mostly sets in the front parlor these days," Janet said, pausing in front of the first door to the left. Over her shoulder, William could see a room barely large enough to contain a sofa, two sagging armchairs, a slender side table set against the wall, and a small glass curio case of books. The whitewashed walls were painfully bare, but the room still seemed so crowded he could not fathom how a party of their size could possibly fit into it. A second doorway led off to some darkened side room.

"He gets a bit of sun," Janet continued, "and besides, it's warmer for him here."

Was that really a concern, in August? The northern countryside did not share the oppressive humidity that characterized London, but William would hardly call it cool.

"I'll leave you with him, Miss Katherine, he'll be so glad to see you, and then I'll go and hunt up Mr. Carter." Janet raised her voice as she led them through the doorway. "Mr. West! Mr. West, look here who's come to call!"

The front parlor was indeed warmer than the summer afternoon outdoors—unpleasantly close, in point of fact—but the old man in the chair nearest to the empty hearth had wrapped himself in plaid shawls even so. He blinked confused eyes as Janet spoke to him, and extended a shriveled head on a leathery neck to peer at his guests. William could not help thinking of the tortoises he had seen in warmer climates, with their sand-blasted leathery skin drooping away from beaky noses and toothless mouths.

"Why, little Kat!" the old man rasped, and stirred enough to put out a clawlike hand. His smile chased some of the turtle-resemblance from his face. "What a surprise, to be sure. So nice of you to come by. And with more youngsters to liven my afternoon. How very nice indeed."

Janet beamed at the success of her introductions and bustled back out, now calling in cheerful tones for Mr. Carter. There was a pause, and then a creaky old voice answered, farther away but growing closer.

Mr. West did not react to it. Probably, William thought, Mr. West could not hear it. Instead, West peered past Katarina to the rest of them. He looked with interest from one face to another before his toothless mouth curved upward again in a smile of pleased recognition.

"My goodness me," he said. "Miss Barton, isn't it?"

Katarina's head snapped around to Elizabeth, and Maxwell's did as well. Elizabeth stood with her lips parted, eyes searching the old man's face with no apparent recognition. William wondered if meeting him was something she would do someday, and had not yet. If so, that was good, surely? For it meant she at least would live long enough to have some adventure after this one—

Mr. Carter entered from the side door at that moment. He was as lean and spare as Mr. West, and only slightly less reptilian in his facial features. His head still bore some white strands of hair, but it rose out of a shirt collar grown too big for him. He moved with slow, shuffling steps, balancing his feet carefully and bending over his cane, and nothing about his figure should have evoked a dashing young officer.

But William had seen him only two days before. He had been hunched over a staff for support then as well, pain lines carving his face exactly where the age lines carved it now, making his way step by agonized step to the infirmary while the Battle of Waterloo howled around him. William put his left hand out for something to steady himself, and knocked a small book from the side table to the floor.

"God in heaven," he said. *"Chris."*

A slow smile parted Christopher Palmer's lips. "William Carrington," he replied—not in shock, but rather in the satisfied tone of a man who has been handed the key to a puzzle.

Interlude

Provence, France, July 10, 1841

Shoveling horseshit was, no question, the worst part of the job. Not that Jack Sheffield particularly relished any of the other parts—he'd grown up on the streets of the city that gave him his name, and after that he had marched with the infantry, and thus he'd had little to do with horses before embarking upon his third career. He'd been gobsmacked when he first realized Hull actually *liked* the smelly beasts and didn't mind all that was involved in caring for them. But then, Hull was country-born, and moreover a sergeant who'd risen through the ranks, and so it made a sort of sense that he'd be comfortable both with horses and with being sworn at.

The Captain was the real surprise. You wouldn't expect a man like him to be accustomed either to stables or to taking guff from the men who ran the stables, but the Captain had slipped into the role as easy as—

No. Not the Captain. *Palmer* had slipped into the role as easy as you please. Sheffield had to stop thinking of Palmer as "Captain." Keep saying that inside his head, and it was only a matter of time before he slipped and said it out loud in front of the frogs, and that would draw down a deal of trouble they didn't need.

He usually didn't need to worry about what he called Palmer, because he and Palmer didn't usually work this part together. Usually it was Hull and Sheffield who played at being grooms, after Palmer had picked the house and provided information as to what they'd find inside and maybe written up some references if the household was particular about such things. Mostly the households weren't; English laborers were to be found throughout the French countryside, competing desperately for the sort of menial jobs that didn't require trust. Like shoveling horseshit.

Then once Hull and Sheffield had gotten hired on and settled in, the Sergeant would court a maidservant or the like and get her to leave a kitchen door unlatched overnight—maybe telling her he wanted to sneak some pie, maybe hinting he meant to come to the servants' attic and sneak sweeter things. Then he and Sheffield would follow Palmer's map to the room where the gentry hid their baubles and the Sergeant would stand watch while Sheffield broke into the strongboxes or cracked the safes. Later, Palmer would fence the jewels or the silver or whatnot, and then there was that much less for the frogs and that much more to fund the Rising back home. Easy as you please. They worked each job the same way, because it always worked smooth as Lyons silk.

But this time Hull was out readying their escape route and Palmer was working alongside Sheffield, because this time they were after something big. The Count kept a book in his safe upstairs, so Palmer had explained, and that book was worth more to the Rising than even the dirty great emerald they'd pinched last month. There were bound to be many other books in the safe, and only Palmer could tell for sure which was the right one—Sheffield did not count reading among his accomplishments any more than he counted an affinity for horses—and so Palmer must therefore pose as groom alongside him, shoveling horseshit and touching his cap to the damned frogs as though he'd never faced them across a battlefield, as though he hadn't fought them with every ounce of his strength at Waterloo and again at Dover and then for five years after. It didn't seem to bother Palmer, but Sheffield gritted his teeth when thinking of it.

"Back to work, you lazy bastard!" the head groom snapped behind him. Sheffield had never succeeded in mastering much of the French tongue, but this was a phrase he had learned to recognize after many repetitions, so he sighed and put his back into it. It had been made clear to all the grooms that the entire stable had better be clean enough to sparkle before the Count's guests arrived.

Those guests had been their ticket in, his and Palmer's, for the Count pinched his francs and hardly ever hired extra labor on his estate save for this summer house party, once-a-year. It gave Palmer and Sheffield barely more than a fortnight to get what they'd come for, but at least they'd managed to get themselves hired right off, no time wasted. They'd settled into their position at the bottom of the stablehands' pecking order, Palmer had already started a flirtation with one of the maidservants, and the guests would only begin to arrive today, so they were doing well for time. They had two weeks yet to get the job done. Two weeks in a house full to bursting with rich frogs, which of course made it harder, but a solid two weeks still.

At last the stables gleamed to the head groom's satisfaction, and Sheffield and Palmer leaned against the fence to watch the first carriage come up the drive. It was a lovely light thing, pulled by a team of matched grays, and Sheffield had to set his teeth at the sight. Wicked waste, when life had been so hard for so long back home. It had taken old Boney five years to subdue England even after monsters wearing red and monsters wearing blue had fought to the death at the Battle of Dover—five vicious years of English soldiers employing every guerilla tactic they'd ever learned from their Spanish allies before finally falling to sheer force of Imperial numbers. By that time, southeast Britain was in shreds, cities nothing more than hollow shells and farmland trampled flat. Then the frogs had consolidated their power, and then they'd started the forced migrations. Loyal French generals and landless French second sons got English estates, and the British lords they replaced—those few who hadn't fallen in the war—were either executed or made to go west, joining the refugees who had fled the southeast with nothing but the clothes on their backs.

Fifteen years later, it wasn't much better. Eastern farmland still didn't produce what it was meant to, so hunger ran rampant in the countryside and French garrisons in the cities were fed by supplies brought in by packet ship.

Folk stuffed into the overflowing west mostly worked the coal and tin mines—working for wages paid by French mine owners, and spending their wages on food from shops run by the same Frenchmen. Damned expensive food, when compared to the wages, so the west was hungry too.

And here in sunny France were the frogs, rolling up to the Count's flourishing country estate with bees and eagles worked into the devices of their carriages, indecent low-bosomed dresses on the women making even the highborn ones look like whores. Ordinarily Sheffield didn't let it bother him, seeing as how he and Hull and Palmer got some of their own back with every job, but there was so much waste in one place this time that he found it a hard fight to keep the disgust off his face.

Palmer's eyes flicked to him, quelling. *Don't you dare draw attention to yourself,* those eyes said, as clear as a barked order on a parade ground. *You are not here to offer your opinion, you are here to open the safe.* Sheffield resisted the urge to salute, resolved to stay invisible, and sucked down a calming breath.

And choked on it.

The tall, elegant figure descending from the carriage was a man known to him. An Englishman, in fact, though you'd never have guessed from his clothing—he was dressed like a frog fop, in a rich dark coat cut tight to the waist and padded about the shoulders, a curving shirtfront like a pouter-pigeon, and a ridiculous tall hat. Apparently you wouldn't have been able

to tell from his accent either, or at least so Sheffield had heard French servants saying to one another, in some of the other houses where he'd played at being a groom. He'd heard French servants say a lot of other things about Charles Wilton, come to think of it, and most of them uncomplimentary. Those who licked the boots of their enemies weren't well respected by anyone, even the enemies. *Turncoat,* Sheffield thought. *Bloody traitor.*

Wilton wasn't the only Englishman of rank who had decided to sail with the prevailing wind, but Sheffield hadn't met any of the others, so Wilton received the full dose of his hatred. He'd been a man of wealth and position, a landowner in Kent before the Battle of Dover, and after the battle, managed somehow to maneuver himself into a position of relative power under the new French landlords, collecting taxes or some such. Wilton had gone on to marry a Frenchwoman, eventually moving to Paris with her, and even though she had since died, he was still accepted into the finest circles of French society. With a great deal of laughter behind his back, but Wilton never seemed troubled by that. Whether he was too much of a fool to notice he was being mocked, or whether he otherwise enjoyed his favored position too much to care what anyone said, Sheffield didn't know. Now he watched Wilton preen about with the indecently dressed Frenchwoman on his arm—not his wife, some other woman he'd acquired—and thought about what he'd like to do to all those who'd thrown their lot in with the frogs.

Palmer's hand closed hard over his arm. "Stop it," the Captain said low, in English. "He doesn't matter. You are here for one purpose only."

"I can't stand that traitorous bastard," Sheffield spat.

"You can't stand the frogs either, so you tell me."

"That's—they're different, sir." Sheffield struggled to explain why. "You can't fault 'em for fighting for their side. Maybe some of them were like me, caught thieving and given a Devil's bargain. You fight for your colors. But that Wilton—you're of the same rank, ain't you, sir, you and him? And you didn't go finding a French whore to marry after Dover. You took to the hills and fired your rifle from behind trees at the bastards."

Palmer's face creased in a faint smile, but he said only, "Don't call me 'sir.' You'll give us away."

"Yes, sir—I mean, yes. Palmer." He still couldn't say it without it sounding stiff. "But look here, won't it be dangerous for you? Didn't you say as you knew Wilton back in the day, back before Dover—he knew you as yourself, that is, and you're even using the same name now?"

"Wilton," Palmer said, "is famed for his charm, not his wit. Don't worry, Sheffield. I'm here to do the worrying. You're just here to open the safe."

"Still, sir, a whole fortnight—"

"You're assuming he'll ever once look at my face. He never will, even if I should happen to hold his horse for him." Palmer smiled briefly. "You may trust me on that."

Sheffield did trust him. Palmer would know what the quality did, having been quality himself before Dover—and was damned well quality still, as far as Sheffield was concerned. He'd taken as good care of his men as he could, even when they were all hiding among the Downs and trying to remember what they'd learned in Spain.

Palmer was his Captain, and Palmer had said not to worry, so Sheffield tried not to worry. For a week he kept his mind on his work, shoveling horseshit, cleaning tack, enduring the mockery of his mates for his broken French, and observing Palmer work his magic on one of the tween-stairs maids. Sheffield felt odd, watching that. It seemed all in the way of things when the Sergeant did it, big bluff countryman that he was, but he couldn't help thinking of Palmer in regimentals every time he saw the man hold a door for the overworked lass. He ought to be whispering jokes in her ear instead, Sheffield thought, but he supposed the gentry didn't do that. Palmer didn't rush anything, just coaxed the girl along as he might a mare with a lump of sugar. Sheffield couldn't help wondering if Palmer'd courted his late wife the same way, but wasn't about to ask. Sheffield reflected a few days later that the gentry might know what they were about, as far as women went, for the tween-stairs maid did seem to like Palmer's treatment. Sheffield stored up what he'd seen, thinking maybe he'd like to get a wife of his own once they were home—though it wouldn't be that difficult for him, surely, he a man with a bit of silver in his pockets. Still, though, it was always good to have a backup strategy, and the girl did seem particularly pleased by a courtship that was flowers and smiles instead of bawdy comments. Sheffield supposed she took Palmer for an upper servant come down in the world, superior to the usual sort of man available to her even if he was only an Englishman and nowadays only a groom. She wasn't altogether wrong, if that's what she thought; the only thing she didn't know was how far down the Captain had come.

Seven days into the fortnight, Palmer returned to their loft bunks in the small hours of the morning with a blank face and a terse, "Tonight." The girl had been induced to leave the door open for them, in the expectation that Palmer would come to her. Sheffield wondered if he'd had to promise to marry her, or if he'd maybe offered her silver for her virtue, but thought it would be better not to ask that either.

Palmer snatched an hour's sleep and was up at cock-crow, no sign in his face that any consideration weightier than horseshit troubled his mind. He and Sheffield cleaned tack and hauled water and did not speak much at all. There was no need to speak about the night to come. They had worked it all out well in advance.

The worst part was the waiting about until their mates should fall asleep— the two of them lying there bone-weary and sunk into straw and yet knowing they dared not close an eye themselves. At last Sheffield counted six separate snores from other parts of the loft, and Palmer got softly to his feet. Sheffield joined him. They had mastered the art of getting almost silently down the ladder by that point, and Sheffield had oiled the door days before. There was just enough moonlight to guide their steps through the stable-yard and to the house.

The kitchen door had not been oiled, but then, no one was nearby to hear it squeak. Sheffield stood still in the big, cool, echoing kitchen, waiting for Palmer to lead the way. The back stairs rose up to the servants' bedrooms, but Palmer shook his head, put a finger to his lips, and led Sheffield out of the kitchen and into the main part of the house.

It gave him a dirty little thrill, every time, to be walking through a frog gentleman's home and him unawares. Sheffield smirked a little to himself now. Palmer turned to the right and headed without hesitation up the polished main staircase. His information must have been as precise as usual. Not for the first time, Sheffield wondered where he got it.

A red patterned carpet stretched along the corridor before them. That was fine. Carpet muffled footsteps. Sheffield wondered how much it had cost, and where it had been woven. The doors all looked alike, but Palmer strode along without pausing until he stopped at the sixth one on the left. There he touched his finger to his lips again, indicating the doors all around, and Sheffield nodded impatiently, for they'd been over this. The Count's study was on the same floor as his bedroom and those of some of the guests, so it was even more important than usual to keep quiet. Palmer acknowledged Sheffield's impatience with a smile, and bowed him toward the study door.

Sheffield hunkered down and got to work. He was as comfortable with picklocks as he was uncomfortable around horses—having been bred to the former, you might say, as a countryman was bred to the latter. He'd already had considerable expertise under his belt back when he'd been arrested for thieving and sent to the army at the age of nineteen. He'd found his old profession ready to hand when the frogs finally overwhelmed the guerilla fighters and he had to do something other than fire a musket to make ends meet. He'd found an old friend willing to school him, and he'd graduated to proper safes by the time Sergeant Hull had looked him up and asked if he wouldn't like to put those skills to the service of King, Country, and Captain Palmer.

Forcing the door to the Count's study was dead simple. Anyone could have done it—the Sergeant with his ham hands, even. Certainly Palmer, if he'd been of a mind to learn. Sheffield held the wrench in place and used the pick to lift the little pins inside, one after the other. He was prepared for a long slog of it, given the grandeur of the house, but the lock turned out to be a commonplace little affair after all. It sprang open under his fingers almost before he'd settled into the rhythm of listening for the tumblers. Almost a disappointment. Lucky there was a safe inside, or he'd have said Palmer scarcely needed him at all.

But the safe was a proper salamander, crouching behind the Count's big carved desk like a dog in a kennel. Palmer entered the room first, lighting a stump of candle from his pocket with a matchstick from another pocket and using the makeshift torch to check all the dark corners before he waved Sheffield in. Sheffield went to the safe at once, and as he positioned himself for his work, Palmer drew the door softly to and took up the role of lookout, standing before it with his arms folded. Odd bit of role reversal, that, to have a Captain standing guard for you. It wasn't quite so strange when it was the Sergeant. But then, as Hull and Palmer both said, it wasn't Sheffield's job to worry about such things. It was his job to crack the safe. Palmer blew out the candle, Sheffield having assured him he wouldn't need it, and Sheffield got to work by the faint blue moonlight filtering through the barred casement windows.

Most of his work was done by touch anyway. He twisted the dial with unhurried fingers, listening in the silence of the great still house for the fall of the tumblers, spinning the dial again. It took him about two hours, and for most of that time he was so intent upon his work that they might have fought the Battle of Dover on the other side of those casement windows, and Sheffield would never have noticed it.

Finally the safe door opened, the lock yielding with a snap like a breaking branch that made Palmer spin around. At Sheffield's breathed "Yes," the Captain relit his candle. By its flickering light, Sheffield saw sweat running down the Captain's face, and that surprised him. He'd never seen the Captain nervous before, and wouldn't have thought anything could unnerve him, given he wasn't worried by guerilla fighting or horses or the possibility of being recognized by Charles Wilton. But then, the Captain had never stood guard and waited for someone else to crack a safe. Sheffield could see how that would be nerve-wracking if you weren't accustomed to it.

Palmer left the door at once and came to the safe, and Sheffield crowded out of his way so he could look. Holding the candle aloft, Palmer pulled a litter of papers and books to the floor and started sorting through them one-handed, piling the rejected ones into Sheffield's arms to keep them out of the way.

"Yes," he whispered finally. He looked up, and his eyes were gleaming in the half-light. He set a small note-book bound in reddish-brown leather atop the pile in Sheffield's arms, and reached for the rest to bundle it all back into the safe.

Something moved in the shadows.

Sheffield jerked his head up. A man stood just outside the small spill of candle-light, not quite swallowed by darkness. He wore black—not only a black shirt and trousers, but a black hood and mask as well. He had most definitely not been there the moment before.

He hadn't entered through the door; a glance showed it still pushed to. He hadn't entered through the barred windows; not even someone as slenderly built as he could have managed such a feat. He hadn't been hiding behind any of the furniture or in any of the corners Palmer had inspected. He had simply appeared between one second and the next, nothing heralding his arrival but a flicker of the shadows.

The pistol he held was also black. It caught the candle-flame dully, not glinting as metal would, but the shape was obviously that of a pistol. Without speaking, the man in black pointed the business end at Sheffield and held out his other hand. He wanted the book on the top of the pile, almost certainly.

With only a flash of a second in which to decide what to do, Sheffield jerked his hands over his head and let the papers he was holding cascade to the floor, the brown notebook jumbled amongst them. Maybe the man would bend to get what he wanted, and maybe then Sheffield could overpower him. It was the best plan he could come up with on short notice. He felt there was something to be said for its simplicity.

The man in black apparently thought it had merit as well, for he hesitated an instant.

In that instant, Captain Palmer leaped.

He had been crouched on the floor, half-squatting and half-kneeling. He came upright all at once like an uncoiled spring—a feat more than a bit impressive for a man who had to be knocking on the door of fifty—and his tackle took the man in black at the knees. They crashed to the floor together, and the queer black pistol flew wide.

Sheffield shoved the brown notebook into his breast pocket and caught up the candle-stump. A bit of the fine carpet had caught alight, but he stamped it out. From the floor nearby came thumps and curses—the latter Palmer's alone; the man in black confined himself to grunts—as the two men grappled with each other. Sheffield searched for a weapon to bring to the Captain's aid. He couldn't see where the black pistol had gotten to.

The man in black threw Palmer off, and Palmer fell with a groan. His opponent jumped to his feet, revealing himself to be a young man by the springy way he moved, and whirled on Sheffield, fists already swinging. Sheffield dropped the candle again, and this time it went out. He blocked the first punch by sheer instinct, took the second to the face, and fell over an easy chair, and then Palmer was back up.

From the other side of the wall came voices and footsteps. By the faint moonlight, Sheffield could see Palmer looming up behind the man in black, holding a small table in both hands. The man in black turned from Sheffield just as Palmer brought his weapon down on his enemy's head, and the man in black crumpled. The voices grew louder, and the footsteps were now running. Palmer hauled Sheffield to his feet and they made for the door.

It jerked open just as they reached it, and they skidded to a stop. There, framed by the light of a candelabrum held aloft, a pistol in his other hand, stood the Count. His dark eyes widened with surprise, then narrowed with suspicion.

Beside him, foolish face open-mouthed with curiosity, broad shoulders effectively blocking any escape, stood Charles Wilton.

Palmer spat a curse, and Sheffield muttered a worse one inside his head. He balanced on the balls of his feet, measuring the distance to the Count and his pistol—

An unexpected look of profound irritation crossed Wilton's face. While Sheffield was still trying to decipher it, Wilton pulled back his left hand and slammed it, hard and with all the force of his arm behind it, into the Count's head.

The candelabrum dropped, setting the carpet irrevocably alight. The Count sagged. Wilton caught him with an arm across his throat—the left arm, Sheffield noted, its hand held stiffly as though bones inside had been broken—and with his right hand grabbed the pistol from the man's slackened grip. He pressed the barrel to the Count's lolling head.

Sheffield could only stare.

"Wilton—" Palmer said, in what sounded like anguish.

"Can't be helped," Wilton replied—in English, and crisply, in a tone much unlike his usual easy drawl. "The cover was nearly worn through anyhow. And this night's work pays for all, doesn't it?" Still balancing the Count with his left arm and holding the pistol with his right hand, he looked past Palmer at the stirring man in black. Flames were eating along the carpet, bathing the black-masked face in a golden glow. "Who the bleeding hell is that?"

"Not one of mine," Palmer snapped. Footsteps were thundering overhead and all down the corridor behind Wilton as servants assembled. Guests poked their heads out of their rooms like jacks-in-the-box, bellowing and twittering and exclaiming, some of them almost close enough to see the pistol held to the Count's head. Palmer looked into the darkened hall past Wilton's shoulder, then back at the Count. "Can't you—?"

"No," Wilton said. Sheffield felt heat near his boots and looked down to see a tongue of crawling flame reach the dropped litter of papers and caress it. Farther away, a different tongue slid up the full length of a curtain, headed for the ceiling. The man in black groaned, stirred, and fell back again.

Wilton swung around, holding the Count upright with one hand and pressing the pistol to his head with the other, and the gathering crowd fell back. Wilton snapped an order to them in French, then turned his head to command Palmer in English. "Hurry, go, get behind me!"

Palmer seized Sheffield's wrist again and pulled him into the corridor, behind Wilton's sheltering back and the more useful shelter of the limp Count. Palmer and Sheffield backed down the corridor, and Wilton backed after them, holding the Count as a shield, snapping orders to the gaggle of frog guests and frog servants to keep them still.

The four of them clattered down the servants' stair, through the kitchen, and into the still night outside. The relatively cool air roused the Count—he had not been badly hurt, only stunned—but his interrogative turning of his head froze when he felt the pistol on his temple. Wilton dragged him along, and they covered the distance to the stables at almost a trot.

Behind them, flames rose orange in the windows of the study. Good; that would keep the household busy a while longer. Palmer's eyes gleamed as their awkward cavalcade approached the stable-yard. "Jacques!" he called the head groom's name, in a tone of malicious delight.

Wilton pressed the pistol harder to the Count's temple, and murmured something to him in French. The Count hesitated. Wilton said it again, with an undeniable tone of menace, and this time the Count lifted his voice and repeated the order. A sleepy, bewildered Jacques appeared three words in, and stared in horror for a moment before Wilton snapped at him. Sheffield couldn't make the words out, but *Do as I say or I'll kill your master* didn't need much translation. It was also quite clear that the Count's words confirmed that Jacques should do what Wilton said.

It shortly became clear that Wilton had ordered the two best horses in the stable saddled. Palmer plunged in at once to help Jacques with this arrangement, and Sheffield was glad to help as well. He had, after all, learned how to seem like a groom.

"You have a place to go?" Wilton asked Palmer.

"Yes."

"Right." Wilton raised his voice in French again, and the grooms allowed them to mount and ride away.

Sheffield's role in this partnership was to open safes. Everything else was the responsibility of the men who didn't know how to open safes. It was therefore clearly Sheffield's duty at this moment to keep his mouth shut, spend no energy worrying about what was next, cling tight to Palmer, and not fall off. The last bit was the hardest. Not that he and Hull hadn't made their escape on horseback now and again, but Hull never drove the beasts hell-for-leather as Palmer was doing now. Over on the other horse, Wilton had the Count before him on the saddle, hands bound behind his back. Wilton still held the pistol to the Count's head and appeared to be controlling the horse with his knees alone. Sheffield couldn't fathom how he was doing it.

"I told them we'd let the Count off unharmed an hour's ride away," Wilton said sometime later, "but if we spotted pursuit before that, we'd kill him. There's no sign of anyone following, so I think we'd best be rid of him. Eh?"

"That copse of trees?" Palmer pointed.

They found a stout one to bind the Count to, still with his hands wrenched behind his back. Wilton held the pistol while Sheffield and Palmer worked the knots, and the Count stared at all three of them out of beady dark eyes.

"Traitor," he spat at Wilton's back just as the latter turned away. He said it in French, but Sheffield knew that word.

Wilton whirled back to him. "No," he said in English. "That's the point. I'm not."

He struck the Count across the face with the pistol, and the Count's head snapped back against the tree trunk, then fell forward. Wilton stood looking down at him for a moment before turning back to Palmer and Sheffield. "Perhaps I'd not have done so badly in the army after all, if I'd not been due to inherit," he commented, once more in the light, drawling voice he was known for. "It might have done me better to have an occupation, back when I was a lad. What do you think, Palmer?"

"I think," Palmer said, not giving him the compliment he seemed to be seeking, "I ought to have taken a moment to pull the mask off that other man. I wish we knew where he came from. You're sure you didn't run your mouth off to anyone else?"

"I only *play* the fool, Chris. These days, at least." Wilton gave him a slight, lopsided smile. "Doesn't matter anyway, does it? We've got the prize."

"We have at that," Palmer agreed, and seemed to settle a little. "Let's get home with it and win the war."

Chapter 4

Danby, Yorkshire, August 30, 1885

The overheated little room was absolutely silent for the space of three heart-beats. Then William heard Katarina Rasmirovna whisper, "Bloody hell." Out of the corner of his eye, he saw her grope for the sofa and lower herself into it as though finding her legs inadequate to the task of keeping herself upright. The rest of his attention was captured by the old man who faced him—body bent over a cane, but eyes still alert.

"So you *were* there," Christopher Palmer said in a tone of satisfaction. "After all."

"I was," William said. "I was there when you were wounded at Waterloo." His knees felt as though he was there right now. For a moment, his ears rang with the sound of booming cannon, screaming horses, men crying out as they collapsed halfway to the field hospital. "It was only the day before yesterday, for me. God, *Chris.*" He stretched his left hand toward the old man, an inarticulate and awkward grasp. Palmer took it in a grip of surprising strength. "You did make it back, then. You made it back to England."

"I did." A brief smile added to the wrinkles on Palmer's face. "To meet my son, as you goaded me. I never could be quite satisfied with the idea that I had dreamed that encounter. Why would my dreams clothe you in a uniform of the 52nd? Good afternoon, Katherine," he added, and his lips turned upward in a hint of a smile. "What an interesting visitor you've brought me."

Katarina was shaking her head, eyes fixed in wonder on William. "It never occurred to me..." she whispered, and stopped. She cleared her throat and went on in a voice closer to her own, "It literally never occurred to me they could be telling the truth. But if you know him, Mr. Carter—"

"I know him," Palmer assured her. "This is my wife's brother. He vanished from Hartwich in 1815. And...that's 'Mr. Palmer.'" His chest expanded with the barest puff of pride. "Captain Christopher Palmer, late of His Majesty's Army."

Katarina's breath caught, and she levered herself back off the sofa, pushing back escaping tendrils of hair that clung to her cheeks. "But I know that name. Everyone knows that name. You're the one who—in Provence—that was you?"

"Indeed it was," Palmer said, with more than a hint of pride this time. "Immediately thereafter, I found it prudent to rechristen myself, for reasons I trust are obvious. She's never heard my real name before," the old man added to William. "Nor has Frederick Kent. They couldn't have told you if they had wanted to." Palmer looked past William to the others. "Will you not introduce your friends?"

"Oh—of course. Of course." William turned, donning a veneer of formality that felt as unnatural as new boots. "Miss Barton, may I present Lef—Captain Palmer. Chris, I don't believe you ever met Miss Barton, back in the old days."

"I do not believe I ever had the pleasure, no. Miss Barton." Palmer bowed, correct and old-fashioned, but his eyes glinted as Elizabeth curtseyed in turn. "I have, however, heard a great deal about you. It is an honor to finally make your acquaintance."

Heard about her from whom? William wanted to ask, but pressed on with his duties first. "And this is our friend Mr. Maxwell."

"Emil Schwieger," Katarina introduced the young Prussian. "He has entered Mr. Kent's employ since last we came to see you."

"Captain Palmer," Schwieger said, eyes shining with an almost feverish intensity, "it is an honor to meet you, sir. Your exploits in France are legendary. I knew I was to have the honor of meeting a great freedom fighter, but I never dreamed—" He waved an inarticulate hand.

"You'd have the honor of meeting two?" Palmer finished for him, eluding the compliment as deftly as he might once have evaded a fencing thrust, smiling with open amusement now. He laid a hand on the shoulder of the blinking turtle by the hearth, making it plain this was the second freedom fighter under discussion. "My friend here also bears a name not his by birth," he said. "He has been known as West these many years, but he and Miss Barton met once before that."

"You were a very pretty girl," the second old man informed Elizabeth.

"May I present Mr. Charles Wilton."

Elizabeth's face went pale with shock. "Mr. *Wilton.* Oh…I…What a pleasure, sir."

"He lives more in the past than not," Palmer said, glancing at his friend. "I am sure your remembered face is clearer before his eyes than mine or Janet's. Though he did recognize you as well," he added to Katarina. "So it's a good day, then. Well, now, we cannot entertain in the style I wish we could, but it's a fine day for sitting in the garden, and Janet can put something before us. And then you will solve this mystery for me. At my age, I cannot afford to wait longer than half an hour to have my curiosity satisfied."

"You disappeared," Charles Wilton said to Elizabeth, struggling to overcome the pull of blankets and rise from his chair. Palmer tried to shift around to help him, but Katarina was there first. She drew the old man smoothly to his feet, and Wilton accepted the help, eyes still fixed on Elizabeth. "Everyone said Gretna Green, since you'd climbed out your window on bedsheets and William Carrington was gone too, but Chris always said there was more to it than that."

William's gaze snapped to Elizabeth. *Bedsheets?* Elizabeth gave him a defiant look in response. "It was a cause worth the burning of bridges," she murmured.

"I thought Chris was likely right," the old man went on. "Because you never returned. Or wrote a letter, or anything of the sort."

"It was an odd elopement," Palmer said, recapturing the conversational reins as he led them through the passageway at the shuffling pace that was all he could manage. "Quite a nine-days' wonder, or it would have been, had the war news not overwhelmed it. Many facets of it were puzzling. The two of you could not be traced to Gretna Green—or indeed, out of Hartwich. William had not taken funds sufficient for a journey of any length. And as Charles puts it so succinctly, you never returned. Not though William's father advertised; not at his death; not when the French marched through Kent and we needed every man, able-bodied or not. And so…it never quite satisfied me, that explanation. I kept thinking of Will Carrington in a uniform of the 52nd, and wondering what it was I'd been a part of."

The passage gave way to a blinding bright sky, and then to a scrap of back garden where Janet was laying a blanket upon the grass. She turned back for the kitchen, smiling as she passed them, and Katarina got Charles Wilton settled in one of the two comfortable-looking garden chairs while Christopher Palmer settled himself in the other. The blanket was obviously for the young people and Maxwell. "I'm afraid it's the best we can do," Palmer murmured, and they all hastened to assure him it did not matter.

Wilton looked even more lizard-like out in the bright sun. His blinking bright eyes stayed on Elizabeth, watching as she settled herself. William wondered if it were only his own inappropriate imagination, or if Wilton's eyes had indeed settled upon her shapely ankles as she drew her skirt back from them. "A great shame we never got to dance," Charles Wilton said, leaning down toward Elizabeth in a confiding manner. "I was quite good at it, back then! And everyone said you were the jolliest girl to partner. Not stuck-up like some of the minxes, but game for a good time and with a spring in your step."

"Charles," Palmer said, and gestured apology.

"It's all right," Elizabeth assured him. "I rather imagined they were saying worse things."

"They were saying you eloped." Palmer settled back and regarded her. "Erroneously, so it would seem. What happened instead? What form of magic brings you un-aged to my doorstep—a faerie hill, perhaps? You see, I presume upon my great maturity to insist you tell me your story even before drinking your tea. I ceased being a patient man upon my eighty-first birthday."

William looked at Elizabeth, and then at Maxwell, but there was nothing for it. It was much harder to tell this tale to a comrade in arms than to a stranger. He better understood Maxwell's shaking of the night before. He cleared his throat, but the words still came out hoarsely. "We did this, Chris. We brought Napoleon crashing down upon you."

"It would seem you had a great deal of help," Christopher Palmer said a long time later. The afternoon shadows were growing long across the back garden, and a nearby, a treeful of birds had started a twittering chorus. William kept his eyes on the shadows, and tried to hear the birds and not the cries of dying men.

"Will?" Palmer said. "Look at me."

William lifted his head, stunned at the gentleness in that creaking old voice. Forgiveness was the very last thing he had expected. Palmer regarded him for a moment with eyes that seemed to see a great deal. "I can't remember," he said. "How old are you?"

"Nearly twenty," William said.

Palmer shook his head, smiling a little. "You had a hand in this, yes, but you also had a great deal of help. Unless you have omitted parts of your tale, you did not shoot the Duke of Wellington."

"No. But..."

"No 'but' about it. Waterloo is too great a debacle to be laid at the door of any one man—or any three." Palmer glanced at Elizabeth and Maxwell. "You did not shoot Wellington. You did not appoint Uxbridge to succeed him. You did not retreat across the Channel and invite a siege, and you did not leave a small portion of the monster battalion behind to be captured—"

"Guard our retreat, my arse," Charles Wilton murmured to himself.

"Charles."

"It's what you always say," Wilton protested.

"Yes, but I don't say it in front of ladies." Palmer sighed. "I apologize, Miss Barton. I was about to say— Monsters in small groups can be overwhelmed and taken down, and so what did Uxbridge do? Leave behind a small group. Gave the French the perfect opportunity to figure out how we'd done it and start making their own." Palmer shook his head. "You didn't mishandle the '41 Rising, either."

"All the trouble we went to, getting Frankenstein's journal home," Wilton confided, "and Fitzclarence goes and tips his hand before Bonaparte actually crocks it, and anyone with experience enough to make use of the monster notes is killed."

"Those were terrible years." Palmer's eyes were shadowed. "Charles and I stayed on the Continent for the duration, had to."

"Chris was always going on about living dogs and dead lions," Wilton told them, "but what I said was, better to live to fight another day."

"It might have been," Palmer said grimly, "except we never did. We harried the Imperial rear a bit, perhaps, but we never had another chance to fight them here, not on the ground that mattered. By the time there was an opportunity, we were too old to take a hand in it." He looked up at his guests, and tried for a smile. "Had to hand it over to the young lads. And lasses, of course." He nodded to Katarina.

"Giving us a considerable standard to live up to," Katarina told him, "even before I knew you were the two from the Provence story. You harried the Imperial rear pretty effectively, sir." Palmer snorted, waving that off.

"Wait," William said, caught by the phrasing. "You said—Mr. Wilton, what did you just say? 'Anyone with experience to make use of the monster notes'—is that what happened in Provence? Is Frankenstein the name of the Genevese? Schwieger said something about the Genevese's journal being gotten out of France by a pair of Englishmen—"

"And the penny drops." Palmer's grin took the sting from the words. "Yes, that escapade was executed by the unorthodox partnership of Palmer and Wilton. Our contribution to war effort, as it were."

"Those were the days," Charles Wilton sighed to himself.

"Charles here played a collaborator," Palmer explained, leaning forward a little as he warmed to his tale, "married a Frenchwoman and all, became popular and trusted among the Parisians, and soaked up every useful tidbit of information that came his way. I planned out what to do about it, and hired the skills I needed—mostly from my men, the ones who fought with me the guerilla days. Old Sergeant Hull knew where I could find hands used to burglary, or munitions, or sharp-shooting. Or whatever was needful." Palmer smiled at some memory. "Frankenstein's journal was the *coup* of my career. Second career. Third, I suppose, if you count the guerilla warfare right after 1820 as separate from my army days. In any case, yes, we're the ones who got it out. Wilton, Palmer, Sheffield, and Hull."

Elizabeth looked at Charles Wilton and seemed to only barely stop herself from shaking her head in disbelief.

Palmer caught the abortive movement. "You wouldn't think him capable of it, I suppose," he said. "But you didn't know him very well, did you? Sat with him once in a drawing room for a quarter-hour, if I'm not mistaken? I don't expect the setting showed either of you to your best advantage."

"Nothing to be done, in a drawing room," Wilton said. "Nothing that needed doing—not then, at least. Not until later." He leaned forward with that same confiding air. "First thing my wife ever did was pass along something she'd heard her papa say. She didn't think it meant anything. I didn't act like it did."

"Sometimes you don't know what you can become, until you must become it," Palmer said softly. "I suppose he wouldn't have ever become more than a drawing room fop, had the French not invaded."

"They didn't think I was quality." Wilton smiled like a cat with a mouthful of feathers. "Didn't think I was dangerous. Nor was I, not at first. I didn't learn how to be until later. I was hiding in plain sight by then. Plain sight is a grand place to hide. Those were the days."

"Some philosophers maintain there is nothing on this earth wholly bad," Palmer said, watching Wilton's face. "Wars breed heroes as well as nightmares. The question therefore becomes, would I trade—" He broke off. "To which the answer is, absolutely. You could have roused yourself out of the drawing room at any point, Charles, even without a French invasion. I hope you do—because we are about to stop the French from invading." He turned back to William. "You didn't come to see me, Will, you didn't know I was here. You came to see Kent's old mentor Carter, and there is only one reason I can think of why Kent would send time travelers to his old mentor. Thank God, there's a battle I'm not too old to help fight." Palmer turned to Katarina. "Take young Mr. Schwieger up to my room, and bring down the chest at the foot of the bed. Now—" Palmer turned his attention back to Elizabeth as Katarina hastened off on her errand. "—can you bring the journals and whatnot back with you, or are we restricted to memorized messages?"

"We bring with us the clothing we wear," Elizabeth said, "and the items in William's rucksack. Surely a dossier carried in the rucksack would travel...? Though I don't know if, when this future stops being—if it stops—stops being the future—" She broke off.

"Yes," Maxwell said. His hand drifted toward his throat, then stopped and adjusted his collar in a businesslike manner. "It is possible to carry along items from a timeline that no longer exists."

"As far as I am concerned, you may have it all," Palmer said.

But there was clearly too much for that to be a practical solution. The trunk was so large that Katarina and Schwieger staggered, carrying it between them, and when the lid was thrown back, it was revealed to be crammed to the brim with brittle yellow paper.

"Chris collects old journals and letters," Wilton explained unnecessarily. "Frederick brings them when he visits. Chris says it's easier for us to keep them safe up here, where no one ever bothers to look. And he says someone has to. They're history, and they might be wanted someday."

"Someday," Katarina said, running reverent fingertips over the cracked bindings and yellowing paper, "we'll send the French back where they belong, and Kent will be able to give you a true safe place to store them. A museum to the Resistance."

Palmer smiled at her. "Kat, they're safe enough here until then."

"Plain sight is often safe," Charles Wilton said. "I hid in plain sight in Paris, all those years ago."

Palmer patted his shoulder. "Yes, you did, Charles, and you did it very well."

"*Mein Gott,*" Schwieger breathed. "Is that it?"

Against the side of the trunk, crosswise to the bulk of the documents, nestled a notebook bound in red-brown leather. Embossed on its spine was a coat of arms, an odd shape like an anchor turned on its side. Schwieger reached past Katarina to pull it out, and William was surprised to see his hands shake.

"Frankenstein's journal," Schwieger said, tracing the outlines of the anchor. "I've heard legends of it since my childhood. I never thought I would hold it in my hands." He squeezed it, as though afraid it would vanish.

Palmer eyed him.

"He believes an army of monsters is the best hope for our freedom," Katarina explained.

"I agreed with him, back in '41," Palmer said, "or I wouldn't have risked so much to steal the journal. But that path is closed to us now."

"Why should it be, sir?" Schwieger opened the journal and eagerly rifled through its pages. "Surely there is someone, if not in Britain than elsewhere, who can learn to—" He stopped suddenly and sat frozen, staring down at the book in his hands. William leaned to see what had so distressed him, and saw the jagged gash. The middle third or so of the journal had been cut free of the binding.

"We removed the relevant scientific information," Palmer said. "In 1841. It had to get to England, you see, whether we did or not."

"But—" Schwieger looked up, stricken. "Where is it now?"

"I could not tell you," Palmer said. "Safely hidden, I dearly hope. More likely destroyed, if it has not surfaced in all these years."

Schwieger's face went bleak.

"Hidden," Charles piped up. "We used to hide in plain sight, Chris and I. Those were the days. Plain sight is a grand place to hide."

"More likely destroyed," Palmer said, silencing him with a hand on his arm, "and better so. All Charles and I managed to accomplish in 1841 was to remove it from French hands, and I would shudder to see that small advantage taken from us. It is true Britain cannot again breed an army of monsters—but neither can the Empire. At least there is that."

Schwieger took a long breath.

"Emil, what good could it possibly do us?" Katarina asked him, gently enough. "It was never a practical solution. How could we ever hope to breed a monster army without the Empire discovering it and stopping us? At least we can rejoice that Mr. Carter—Captain Palmer—made it impossible for the French to respond to a British rebellion with monsters wearing blue. Come, we've another strategy in hand now." She rearranged herself on the blanket, sitting at Palmer's feet. "Tell us about Dover, sir?"

Chapter 5

Danby, Yorkshire, August 30, 1885

The night was dark, but full of stars. Elizabeth could see many of them plainly, shining bright through the rustling leaves of the apple tree just outside the kitchen door. They were the same stars that shone down on her father's house in 1815, and she held the thought in her mind a moment, trying to extract comfort from it, before finally concluding that there was no comfort to be had. She leaned against the tree and listened to the rise and fall of voices from the torchlit group a short distance away, grateful she could only make out half the words. Her visit to the convenience had been as much an excuse for a few minutes' respite as anything else.

Behind her, the warm, dark kitchen smelled of bread. Janet had waited until the cool of the evening to do the family baking. Elizabeth found herself thinking of Bronson and Mrs. Bronson and the large shadowy kitchen at Westerfield, and a lump rose in her throat. She wished she had thought to leave them a note. She wondered what had happened to them when the French marched through Hartwich.

If they had even survived long enough to encounter the French infantry. They might well have died before that, perhaps in the Aérostier attack that started the war—though the explosives dropped from those balloons had mostly targeted the protectively clustered Naval fleet, rather than civilian targets on land—or by the monster-on-monster battles that ripped through the countryside once the Empire had control of the Channel and could land its forces. "I do not say he cannot come, but he cannot come by sea," Admiral Lord Jervis had once famously said of Napoleon—and Napoleon had not, in the end, attempted to do so. He had conquered the air instead. His victory at Waterloo had given his military engineers long enough to develop a dirigible that could sail where it would, instead of a balloon that could float only at the mercy of the prevailing wind. Elizabeth had ridden on one of its descendants yesterday, traveling between London and York. She had enjoyed it at the time. Now she wanted a handkerchief to scrub her hands clean of its taint.

"Even if they knew what was coming," Maxwell was saying, "I do not know that Britain would have managed a better defense against it. They underestimated the altitude of which the dirigible fleet was capable, true, but even if we went to Whitehall and informed them, the knowledge would not suddenly enable a ship's cannon to propel a cannonball higher."

"It would tell them where they must concentrate their efforts of improvement," Palmer said. "But no, I do agree with you in the main point. I do not think a group of three could find sufficient leverage to affect the Battle of Dover itself—there are no convenient chokepoints as there were at Waterloo. I think we will need to look farther back. Stop them building the dirigibles between 1815 and 1820, perhaps? Monsieur Coutelle worked out of Charleroi and Madame Blanchard out of Paris, so perhaps—"

"I lived in Paris, for a while," Charles Wilton said. "When we were first married, we lived in London, and there were many Frenchwomen there—wives of second sons and army officials, you know—but the social opportunities in Paris were much greater. I let her think it was her idea. She liked to gossip, and she told me all of what her friends said. We went to dinner parties. No one wanted me there, I wasn't quality, but people invited her."

"And you listened to all they had to say," Emil Schwieger agreed—still in admiring tones, though this was far from the first time Wilton had favored him with such an observation, distracting the group as a whole from its discussion. "It's what made you so successful, sir, I am sure of it."

"Hiding in plain sight," Wilton agreed happily.

"I do not believe three English speakers would gain much traction in post-Waterloo Paris," Maxwell said. "I doubt we would be able to get anywhere close to Napoleon's scientists." He glanced up at Palmer's suddenly lowered brows. "You must trust me, Captain Palmer. I have done this before."

"You will not make me believe you are *helpless*," Palmer snapped, angered for the first time in that long and convoluted conversation. "I spent five years firing my rifle at the bastards from behind trees, without maps of where they would be, let alone a pocket watch or certain knowledge of the future! If Charles and I can burgle a French count's safe, you can damned well use what I tell you to—"

"Do you know, it wasn't lucky eavesdropping that told me about the safe?" Wilton said. "It was cunning. We thought the notebook was in his house, but we didn't know for certain. So I wandered into the study when he had the safe open, so sorry, was looking for the smoking room."

"Brilliant, sir," Schwieger said, more absently this time.

Elizabeth knew she ought to go and help, with the soothing and distracting of Charles Wilton at least, if not with the reading and planning. But the thought of rejoining the conversation seemed to weigh down all her limbs. She leaned back against the tree, obscurely comforted by the bite of the bark on her skin.

Something moved at the edge of the torchlight—a dark movement, blackness against blackness as Katarina rose from the blanket. She made her way across the garden to where Elizabeth stood, walking with the slow aimless strides of someone stretching her back, not the quick pace of one sent on an errand to the house. Glossy black hair rippled over her shoulders. Elizabeth wondered if Katarina's torch-dazzled eyes could see her in the shadow of the tree.

"May I join you, Miss Barton?"

Apparently they could. Elizabeth managed a gesture of something like permission, and Katarina half-sat on the nearby garden wall, one leg hitched up and the other still touching the ground. She rolled her shoulders underneath her man's coat, then took from her pocket a book of matchsticks and a packet of the little cigarillos she called gaspers. She glanced at Elizabeth from underneath her lashes as she shook one into her palm, stopping just short of holding it out. "I don't suppose you…?"

Elizabeth shook her head.

"No, I didn't think you did." Katarina struck a match and touched it to the gasper held between her lips, then waved the little flame out. "Horrible for the throat, these things. But very good for the disguise."

Elizabeth forbore to mention that Katarina was not disguised in any meaningful way now. Katarina drew on the cigarillo. Elizabeth, after watching her a moment, crossed to the other side of the floating smoke and likewise seated herself on the garden wall to await what was coming. Neither of her feet touched the ground, but at least she could maneuver herself onto the stone ledge. She could never have done so in that horrible walking dress.

"I owe you an apology," Katarina said abruptly. She blew out a smoke ring. "I meant what I said before. It literally did not occur to me you could have been telling the truth, until Mr. Carter vouched for your tale."

"I know." Elizabeth ran her fingers along the rough stone of the wall. "I understood that last night. You were trying to protect them. You don't need to apologize. But we can be friends now?"

Katarina turned to face her then. "I should like that, Miss Barton."

"Elizabeth."

"Katarina. Or Katherine, if you prefer."

"Or Kat?"

"No," Katarina said, but she was smiling. "I outgrew that name some years ago. Mr. West and Mr. Carter are the only ones I still permit to use it."

"And Mr. Kent?"

"No," Katarina said, and the smile seemed rather forced now. "Mr. Kent merely forgets at times that I'm no longer fifteen years of age." She took another drag off the cigarillo. "I wonder…would you tell me about the other London?"

"Oh—yes. Yes, of course." Elizabeth hesitated. Where to begin? She did not feel herself equal to the task of explaining Gavin Trevelyan's personal life, and somehow that was all she could think of. It crowded out anything more important. "You sang in a music hall," she said at last, lamely.

Katarina made a little face. "I do that still. Male impersonation acts and bawdy songs for soldiers."

"You served as Frederick Kent's right hand in a massive conspiracy."

"That I do as well. Though it's not so massive, not yet. Give us time."

"You took me all over London," Elizabeth said. "I had never seen anything like it. You had fellow-conspirators everywhere. Friends."

Katarina smiled. "All along city road, in and out the Eagle? Still true."

"It was loud, dangerous, dirty. Horrible, really. I saw a woman shot down in the street by one of the constructs. You said you wanted me to see it, so I would understand why you wanted to bring it down. So I could help. You said..." Elizabeth hesitated. "You said I had the power to change things. No one had ever said anything like that to me before."

Katarina laughed a little, smoke puffing from her mouth. "In that, it would seem I spoke truthfully. Look at all this, and it all follows from what you did at Waterloo. So Gavin got his constructs working earlier, in that other London? Eighteen seventy-six, did Mr. Maxwell say?"

Elizabeth nodded. "You said they seemed angels come to deliver you from the monsters, in 1876. By 1885, you were calling them tigers—that you'd bred tigers to exterminate wolves, and you were still riding the tigers." She hesitated, but she couldn't let this opportunity pass. "I can't think it would be any different this time," she said. "They're too dangerous. You have to help me convince Mr. Trevelyan they're too dangerous."

"You think I can convince Gavin Trevelyan of anything?" Katarina looked deeply amused. She drew in more smoke, blew it out. "In any case, it doesn't matter. You and Mr. Carrington and Mr. Maxwell will make it a moot point, won't you?" The moon was rising, little rivulets of light running over Katarina's loose hair. She watched Elizabeth's face for a moment before continuing. "So he was still a mad inventor and I was still a music-hall girl, but Frederick Kent was a lord. Was Brenda still a miner's daughter? Or were there no humans working the mines?"

"I think it was all Wellington monsters, in—" Elizabeth caught herself. "When her father would have been choosing his profession." *In 1872,* she had almost said.

"I'm just wondering how she left Wales and came up to London, if there wasn't a mine uprising to prompt it..." Katarina trailed off. "Except she wasn't in London. You said you'd never met her. I remember you saying that."

This was shaky ground, though Elizabeth could not quite have said what made her so certain Katarina must not know of the other Brenda's death. Perhaps because she didn't want Brenda herself to know? She could not see how you could ever tell someone *You're not meant to be alive, it was only a mistake.* She didn't want to have to try.

So she did not offer an answer. Katarina looked at her keenly for a moment, then turned luminous dark eyes back toward the group under the torches. Maxwell was reading one of the letters out loud, his voice calm and measured, but something in the set of his face made Elizabeth think of the man who had broken his leg on Mr. Carrington's estate and the way he had howled in pain. William was listening with all his might, eyes fixed on Maxwell's face, left hand idly tracing the chain of the pocket watch looped through his waistcoat. The broken one, as Elizabeth had cause to know, not that you could tell from the outside. William's restless fingers turned it this way and that, and torchlight sparkled from every scratch and engraving.

"You and Mr. Carrington?" Katarina asked, not quite out of nowhere. Elizabeth looked back to find amused dark eyes studying her, and blushed.

"Yes. I mean, perhaps. I mean I...don't know. I think so." Elizabeth, aware that she had given almost every possible answer and that Katarina's eyes had crinkled more with each one, took a moment to compose herself. She looked at her hands. "He kissed me once, but we haven't...talked about it. There hasn't been a quiet moment to do so."

"And you've been rather bowed down, by all this responsibility you've taken on."

That was said seriously, and Elizabeth looked up in something like relief. "Yes, that exactly."

"How old are you, Miss Elizabeth?"

"Just turned seventeen."

"Dear God."

"You told me..." Elizabeth took a deep breath to keep from crying. "You told me I could. You told me I wasn't helpless. So I had to try, don't you see? But now I keep wondering...I keep thinking this could not possibly have been what you had in mind, when you encouraged me to change things."

Katarina looked around. "I can't imagine it was, no," she said at last. "I applaud your initiative, but you'll probably want to aim your cannon more carefully next time."

It hurt, but it would have hurt more if Katarina had contradicted her. Elizabeth would not have been able to bear dishonesty. "I'm sorry," she offered miserably.

"I didn't ask you to apologize." Katarina's tone was matter-of-fact. She lit another gasper. "Just learn from it. Take more care."

"Unmake it."

"That, too."

"Doesn't it...trouble you at all? The idea of all this—I mean, it's the only life you know. The idea of this just not being?"

"Trouble me?" Katarina stared at her. "Do you have any idea—No, of course you don't." She rearranged herself, preparing to answer the question on its merits. "No, Miss Elizabeth, it does not trouble me. I'll take my chances on a different world; it has to be better."

"That has been said before," Elizabeth muttered, still miserable. "You didn't seem to like the 1885 with the constructs, either."

"I'm still prepared to roll the dice on the third alternative. I didn't like the idea before I knew I could trust you, I admit that, but given the premise of your trustworthiness, I agree with Frederick. I'll take the chance. I'd give my own life to take it." Smoke wound into the air from her cigarillo, forgotten in her hand as she frowned over this concept. "I am giving my life, I suppose. I consent, then, if that's what you were asking."

"We can't get everyone's consent," Elizabeth said. "What right do we have to..."

"You have the power and you see the need." Katarina's eyes were intense. "You have no right not to. Consider the consequences, yes, of course. Work out which consequences you want, choose those, work toward them, but don't... don't stand still watching while the opportunity ambles past."

"I would not have chosen these consequences if I could have seen them."

"Yes, well, welcome to the human race, Miss Elizabeth." Katarina tamped out her gasper against the stone of the garden wall. "Anyone walking through time in a straight line has the same problem. You work out the range of probable consequences, you choose the ones you want, and you hope like hell you have correctly gauged what actions you must take to get to those consequences. Then you tie your blindfold on and walk. And correct your course when you can, if the horizon you glimpse through the cloth doesn't seem to be quite the one you want. You think I can see where *I'm* going, working with Frederick Kent to undermine an empire?"

Elizabeth was silent, considering that. After a time, she said, "You wanted to bring it all down, in the last London. You were ready to. Before that, though, you'd been working just to undermine."

Katarina nodded. "Mr. Kent likes the technique. Water wearing away stone, he always says."

There was a pause while Katarina considered the statement. "You make a good point. Not all tactics are right for all situations. There are times when you must seize the chance offered, and times when you'd do better to move slowly and plan well ahead of time. There are times for water on rock and times to throw all your weight behind one strong blow."

"And how," Elizabeth said, "do you know when to do which?"

"Ah, there's the tricky part." Katarina's eyes went to William again. "I suppose you...partner with someone good at different things than you are. Those who seize opportunities ought to partner with those who plan for contingencies. Those who are inclined to still keep planning past the point where action is called for ought to partner with those who will not let them waste the opportunities given. And then...then you and your partner fight it out, case by case." She watched the torchlight on William's fingernails, on the glistening watch, on Palmer's white hair and Wilton's bald head. Maxwell set the letter down and stared at it. Schwieger leaned back into the shadows, where torchlight did not reach. "I think you and Mr. Carrington will do all right," Katarina said. "Like Carter and West. Palmer and Wilton, I should say." But she frowned as she spoke.

Elizabeth wondered if Katarina might be thinking of her own single state. She spoke so warmly of partnership; did she wish it for herself? Might she feel the lack of Gavin Trevelyan's partnership in particular, or was she only wistful in general? Or did something else entirely darken her brow?

"Chris led men on the Downs, in those days," Wilton's voice rose with the smoke from the torches. "They learned how to fight that way in Spain. They raided French camps in the dead of night and attacked supply lines, and the eastern coast was flattened and broken, back then—I don't know what they found to eat, those five years—"

"Yes, yes, sir, we know," William said.

"Don't interrupt me, stop interrupting me, I'm *talking*," Wilton snapped. Schwieger sat up on his knees and reached a soothing hand to Wilton, but the old man shook off the fingers as though they were five separate snakes. "No manners, these youngsters. I'm *talking*."

"I think we've all done enough talking for one day," Palmer said at once, leaning against his cane and rising from the chair as though Wilton's change of mood was a signal. "Come along, Charles, more than time old men like us were in our beds."

"It's not *time* for bed yet." Wilton's voice rose, and Katarina hastily pushed herself off the wall and headed for the little group. Elizabeth slid down as well, but did not follow. Palmer looked up in relief as Katarina approached the edge of the torchlight.

"I let this go too late," he said quietly. "Charles is worst after supper. If we can get him to bed now, he'll be more tractable in the morning."

"Is he always this bad?" Katarina asked.

"Not always," Palmer said, but he looked away.

Katarina went to crouch down beside Wilton. "It's time I said good night," she said cheerfully. "I'm staying until morning—Janet has made up the spare bed for me—so we can visit more tomorrow. Shall I walk you to your room before I retire?"

"No." Wilton jerked his arm away from her. "I'm not tired. Go away."

"It must have been exciting," Schwieger tried. "The work you did in your young days, gathering information and passing it along. How were you never caught?"

Wilton hesitated a moment. "I hid in plain sight," he said at last. "Those were the days."

"Did you, sir? You gathered information from French dining tables?" Schwieger reached to help Wilton to his feet, and Katarina fell back to stand with Palmer. "Will you not tell me about it?"

"They talked in front of me," Wilton said as Schwieger guided him toward the house. "They didn't think I was quality. Didn't think I was dangerous. No one thought I was dangerous; I could walk in when the Count had his safe open."

"My goodness," Schwieger said, urging him gently onward.

"All that, and Fitzclarence made no use of it! Idiot. But we got it away from them, at least." They had nearly reached the apple tree. Elizabeth opened the kitchen door for them, and Wilton included her in his next remarks. "We were the ones who got Frankenstein's journal out of France, you know."

"Yes, sir, I had heard," Elizabeth said, trying to match Schwieger's admiring tone. "Marvelous!" Over his head, she caught a glimpse of Schwieger's face, and the desolation in his eyes startled her. Concerned, she slipped into the kitchen after him.

"Are you quite well, Herr Schwieger?" She kept her voice low, so that Wilton would not hear.

Schwieger turned to look at her in surprise, one hand still firmly under the old man's arm. "Well? Oh, yes, yes, of course." It was not very convincing. He urged the old man to resume his shuffle across the kitchen floor, but Elizabeth kept pace with them. After a moment, Schwieger tried to smile at her. "I have been on the trail of that notebook for many years now. There are stories, you know, and it appears in journals of other men—I have tracked it through journals and tales and history. No one knew what became of it after the Englishmen stole it, but I thought if I could just see Mr. Carter's treasure chest—that was all, just another clue, that was the only reason I wished so strongly to come here. Mr. Kent agreed to allow me my quest as part of his dirigible reconnaissance. I was only hoping for another clue, and then for one instant there it seemed as though Mr. Carter was handing me my—my miracle. And then—nothing. I do not know how I will continue the search now."

Elizabeth nodded. "I'm so sorry." They turned the bend in the corridor and the stairway rose up above them. "Madam Katherine was just saying to me that all you can do is tie the blindfold on and walk," she offered. "And then—and then rechart the course, if the glimpsed horizon doesn't seem to be where you wanted to go."

Schwieger smiled. "In other words," he said, "we live to fight another day. Yes. You are right."

"We used to be able to," Wilton said querulously. "But they won't let me now. I did all kinds of things, back in France. I know how to keep secrets. Palmer ought to let me stay and hear these ones. Carter, I mean. We don't call each other by our real names in front of others."

"It's time for bed," Schwieger soothed. "Look, they're all coming in as well. There will be more to discuss in the morning, and you'll be a part of the council, for we couldn't do it without you, sir. We need the benefit of your experience, all those things you learned from your adventures from the old days. Perhaps, if I escort you upstairs, you will tell me more of them?"

Elizabeth watched, fascinated. Schwieger looked up, caught her gaze, and blushed.

"He reminds me of my old grandfather," he explained gruffly.

Elizabeth nodded, not knowing how to respond. "It's kind of you," she said at last. "I'm…not so patient, myself."

*

She woke suddenly some hours later, from a dream of Wellington monsters looking beseechingly at her through the bars of the Tower of London. For the moment she could not tell where she was. Nothing touched by the silver-blue moonlight seemed familiar—not the braided rug on the floor nor the quilt at the foot of the narrow bed nor the spidery arms of the rocking chair.

She raised herself up onto one elbow, heart pounding, panicking. Then a clipped Prussian accent came to her ears, and she remembered, and went limp with relief.

The Prussian voice paused, and was answered by another—this one quavering, British, and moving slowly through the nouns and verbs of what sounded like an extremely convoluted sentence. Curious and wide awake by now, Elizabeth swung her bare feet to the wood boards of the floor and stood up. The bed creaked and shifted underneath her, and Katarina turned over, muttering something inarticulate before resettling herself. Elizabeth stayed still until it seemed as though Katarina had fallen back to sleep, then she stole across the room and out the door.

Everything was silver and still in the corridor as well. A little fitful light shone from the front parlor, and from there the quavering voice commenced again.

Elizabeth peeped through the half-open door. Charles Wilton sat in his accustomed armchair, well-wrapped, holding forth at some length to Emil Schwieger, who sat at the hassock at his feet. Elizabeth felt herself smile through the pang of heartache, amused and touched at the same time.

"They sent away most of us, you know. Away west. Or worse. Afraid the common folk would rise up and fight if their lord led them."

"But not you?" Schwieger said it in an encouraging tone of voice, prompting for the story.

Wilton grimaced. "How amusing, an English gentleman serving as steward. It was better I do it than leave it to another. I protected...some of them. Saved some from starving, at least. Freedom isn't always what you need first."

"You took good care of your tenants," Emil said.

"Better me than one of the frogs. I was always seated at the foot of the table, you know. I wasn't really quality. Landowner in my own right, when their airships landed, but not quality by their standards."

"You were quality enough that they gave to you a position of responsibility."

"Suited them to have a local man, they said. But they always sat me at the foot of the table."

"Still," Emil said, "they invited you to dinner. And you picked up the secrets you passed on to Palmer, and then Palmer planned the heists, is it not so?"

"Do you know," Wilton said, leaning forward, "the trouble I had to get myself invited to the house party? Palmer said not to bother, but I wanted to be on hand to help. Lucky thing, as it happened."

"My goodness," Schwieger said, admiringly. "You stole it while there was a house party!"

"I hid in plain sight." Wilton let out a sigh. "Those were the days. Everyone talked in front of me, you know."

And so it went on, in and out of the same story, all along the city road and in and out the Eagle. Emil Schwieger, God bless him, sat at Wilton's feet and trod in and out the Eagle with him. Their voices lulled Elizabeth into something close to sleepiness. She listened, standing in the shadows, head resting against the paneled wall, until her eyelids began to droop. Then she stole back to her bed, where she tumbled instantly into dreamless slumber.

Chapter 6

Danby, Yorkshire, August 30, 1885

"Fire!"

The word rent the sleeping air, and William was instantly alert, on his feet, thoughts of tents and trapped horses tumbling through his mind.

"Fire!"

Except he wasn't in a tent. There were no horses trapped; he heard none squealing. He heard frightened human cries instead, female as well as male, and feet scrambling against floorboards. Floorboards? He was in a house. A house in England. Beneath the scent of smoke, the air smelled heavy and rich. Definitely England.

England, yes, right, a cottage in Yorkshire, Christopher Palmer's house, seventy years after the tents of the Peninsula. He remembered now. He was sleeping in an empty downstairs room with Maxwell and Schwieger—camping on the hard floor—while Elizabeth and Katarina shared the cottage's one spare bedchamber and bed, located a little farther down the corridor. And that was Katarina's voice he heard, urgent and commanding. "Fire! Everyone outside!"

William felt as though he had been standing stupidly for hours, but in truth it could have been no more than a count of three. Maxwell was only just disappearing through the doorway in front of him. William caught up his clothing in one awkward handful, and ran. "Elizabeth!"

Smoke choked the corridor, foul-smelling as other-London fog. William's eyes stung just looking at it, but he plunged in anyway, shouting. Maxwell's shirt-tail was just visible in front of him, Maxwell's hoarse voice shouting too. Shouting the same name that was on William's lips. "Elizabeth," he croaked out again, but had to stop and cough, and he knew no one could hear him. Not even Maxwell, just ahead.

It got worse, opaque and smothering. They should have run the other way, William thought. He had assumed without giving the matter any consideration that the fire had broken out in the kitchen, that the correct way to flee was therefore through the front door. But the smoke proved to be thicker at the front of the house. Around the bend in the corridor, an ominous orange light crackled.

There were footsteps on the stair above his head, and he caught the sound of Katarina's voice, speaking with deliberate calm. William turned in time to see her emerge from the billowing smoke as though she were descending from storm clouds, Chris Palmer's arm draped heavily over her shoulders. A sobbing

Janet came after. Katarina's eye fell on Maxwell and William, and she snapped "Outside!" in a much sharper voice than she was using toward Christopher.

They stumbled toward the front door. Out of the corner of his eye and through the shroud of smoke, William caught a glimpse of orange flames devouring the sitting room's curtains and carpet. Before him yawned a doorway, clear black night on its other side. Schwieger and Wilton already stood in the front garden, near the sundial, Wilton excited and voluble and straining to see into the house, Schwieger physically preventing him from going any nearer to the fire.

Two steps into the garden, Maxwell stopped short. "Where's Elizabeth?"

Just ahead of him, Katarina jerked around without losing her grip on Palmer. "She's not here? I sent her out ahead of me—"

"God *damn* it," Maxwell said with feeling, and spun for the house.

But William was already turning, already pitching his bundle of clothing as far into the garden as he could manage one-handed, already swinging back to face the flames. He knew exactly where she was. The trunk. Christopher Palmer's trunk of priceless papers, the entire reason for their Yorkshire journey, the letters and journals that were their only source of information on the years between 1815 and 1885—the trunk had been left in the sitting room when the household retired the night before. William knew exactly what Elizabeth had turned aside to do.

The sitting room looked like the antechamber to hell. Flames replaced the curtains, the elderly wing chairs and sofa, the wooden frame of the curio case. The smoke stung his eyes so that he could hardly see, but he made out the wild-haired figure in the borrowed white night-dress, fumbling with desperate haste at a chest already engulfed by flame. Beside him, Maxwell swore, snatched his own overcoat from the peg by the door, and rushed past William into the room.

"No!" Elizabeth fought him as he flung the coat around her and wrestled her back toward the doorway, but Maxwell had her well outmatched in size and strength. "No, the papers, we have to save the—"

William tried. Crouched down in front of the trunk, it was easier to breathe, though the heat still blistered his skin like a baker's oven. He looked around for something not yet aflame with which he could wrap his hands and save at least one book or two. His desperately searching eyes found nothing, but did note that the hot spitting flames now blocked his retreat. He began to tear off his shirt as fast as he could. One-handed and light-headed as he was, it was not a rapid business.

The splash of cold wetness restored him halfway to his senses, though not enough to immediately realize what had landed on him. "Get the hell out of there!" Katarina snapped from the doorway, and reached to take a second bucket from Schwieger. A second spray of water drenched the nearest curtain, but did not completely douse the fire. "Carrington, now!"

William grabbed his shirt with his left hand, shook the fabric over his arm, and with that meager protection plunged his hand into the center of the chest where the flames had not quite reached. He seized what two or three slender volumes he could grip at once, and then Schwieger's arms closed around him from behind and they were stumbling back toward the hall. Schwieger caught the overcoat from Maxwell and used it to beat out the flame that had begun the journey up William's shirt-sleeve. William staggered, dizzy, glimpsing in a confused way Maxwell's white face and beyond him, Katarina and Schwieger and buckets.

"Carrington, garden," Katarina ordered, and pushed William toward it. "Stay there. See to it the others stay there. Maxwell, help us here!"

William stumbled toward the clean dark air, eyes streaming, throat seared, a tendril of hot pain beginning to bite along his forearm. Elizabeth ran to him out of the darkness, reaching to catch hold of him despite her red and blistered hands. He collapsed to his knees, coughing, and she sank down with him. He let Frankenstein's journal and the other two dossiers spill to the ground so he could pull her closer.

From the sundial, Christopher Palmer watched the flames with a set face. "So then," he said, almost without inflection. "It seems they've found us."

*

They contained the fire before it spread beyond the sitting-room, though the smoke permeated what seemed to be every corner of the house and the furnishings of the room itself were destroyed entirely—sodden where they were not blackened, wallpaper peeling like dead skin. Some of the books behind the glass of the curio case were salvageable, but the contents of the trunk were lost, the brittle old paper disintegrating under the touch of fire and water. All that was left of Palmer's treasure trove were the three volumes Elizabeth's blistered hands and William's burned forearm had purchased: Frankenstein's notebook and two journals of men who had served under Fitzclarence during the 1841 Rising. Nothing on Dover. Nothing on the years between Waterloo and Dover. They had no information on the time period they most wished to affect save what they might have memorized after one reading the night before, or what might be lodged in Christopher Palmer's unreliable memory.

William sat at the kitchen table and rested his head against the wall with his eyes closed as Janet dressed the burn on his arm, but he rose as soon as she was done. The chairs should be left for the older residents of the house, much more shaken than he and much less equipped to handle the shock. He looked about for his clothing bundle, thinking to shrug on the waistcoat. It was not the waistcoat he wanted so much as what was threaded through it; the pocket watch's weight would be comforting. The bundle proved to have been deposited by the cold hearth, where a fourth chair had been placed for Elizabeth. He offered her a smile as he reached past her for his clothing, grateful, as his eye lit on her bandages, that his own burn was on his forearm and he at least had the use of his left hand. He only needed one hand to haul the bundle into the light of the carefully placed candles and sort through it. He pulled the waistcoat free of the rest of it—and his heart seized when he saw no watch dangling from the cloth.

"It's all right," Elizabeth said. "I have it." She held it out to him, cupped between her bandaged hands in a gesture that made him think of a child holding snow between awkward mittens. He took the watch and managed to thread it back where it belonged, feeling more settled once it was in place. Not that the broken watch was terribly useful to them—Maxwell held the whole one—but it was the principle of the thing. He had taken charge of it and would not fail his duty if he could help it. He reached his left forefinger to trace Elizabeth's bandages.

"Does it hurt much?"

"Not very much," she said, and he had to admire both the courage and the ability to tell a lie while looking right into his eyes. He restrained himself from squeezing her hand, but continued to stroke the back of it. She closed her eyes with a sigh and leaned against the wall.

Shuffling steps from down the corridor heralded Palmer's return from his expedition to view the damage. Leaning on Katarina's arm and ominously white about the lips, he appeared in the kitchen doorway. "We're lucky it was only the one room," he murmured, but he sat down heavily, and Katarina demanded of Janet where the spirits were kept.

Charles Wilton looked over from the chair at the far end of the table, where Schwieger was trying to keep him seated and soothed. Wilton had seemed to enjoy talking with him, but now worry turned his face turtle-like again and he tried to rise against the young Prussian's restraining hand. "Chris?"

"All's well, Charles," Palmer said at once. "I'm fine." The second brave lie told in two minutes, William thought. Katarina brought Palmer a glass of brandy, and Chris stared into it before he took a sip.

"Chris?" William spoke up from his corner. This was in many ways not the time, but on the other hand, the question could not wait. "What did you mean, when you spoke outside? Who's found you?"

Palmer did not answer.

Schwieger looked from one of them to the other. "No one, I do not think," he said. "I—it was an accident, the fire."

Katarina looked over at him. "What do you know of the beginning, Emil? I woke and smelled smoke and was two paces down the corridor when I heard you shouting. How did you come to find the fire first?"

"Something woke me," Schwieger said. "Something falling over, I think it was? I listened and heard the sound of someone in the sitting-room. Rattling about, I thought. I went to see who was wakeful, and if he was well. I found the front door open, Mr. West in the garden." He eyed Charles, then Chris, then swallowed. "The candle was on the side table, tipped over, and the carpet and curtains already alight."

"Oh, no, Mr. West!" Janet started to cry again.

Wilton looked at her in bland confusion.

"You didn't leave him in the sitting room, surely?" Elizabeth queried, and Schwieger looked at her. "You and he were sitting and talking there earlier," Elizabeth said. "I woke and heard voices, and I peeped in the sitting room and saw you. Surely you did not leave him there alone with a lit candle?"

"No, of course not!" Schwieger assured her. "That was earlier—hours ago. I saw him safely to his bed, I thought, but he must have later arisen again."

"Wandering the house," Janet said through her tears. "Setting things afire. The whole house might have…"

"I heard the cry go up," Charles explained, "so I went to the garden."

"You went to the garden first, sir," Schwieger said. "I sent up the cry after."

Charles Wilton thought about it, then shook his head. "No. I was worried about the—the papers, Chris, the old ones. Irreplaceable, you know. Important. There was a fire, and I was worried all the papers would burn. So I went out into the garden…"

But he had gone without the papers. If he had taken some of the journals, or been found with any book at all in his hand, William might have believed the tale. As it was, he could not countenance it. The old man must have been pottering around the sitting room with a lit candle, must have been drawn by some fancy to the yard, and must have tipped the candle over as he left. He could see how it had happened, but saw no benefit to anyone of attempting to convince the doddering fool of the truth.

"I've told you, Mr. West," Janet said miserably, "you have to take care…"

"I didn't have a candle," Charles asserted, voice going querulous.

Schwieger spread his hands. "I can only say I saw one tipped over and burning."

"I didn't have one," Charles insisted, and jerked away when Schwieger attempted to pat his shoulder. "How dare you question my word, young sir?"

"There, there, Mr. Wilton." Elizabeth got up from her seat. "You mustn't distress yourself. No one doubts your word, of course not."

Three lies in five minutes, William thought. Katarina watched Wilton and Schwieger for a moment, then suggested she might carefully stir up the fire and make tea.

William drank it gladly, but refused the brandy, suspecting the half-empty bottle to represent the entirety of the household's supply. Maxwell, he noted with some irritation, displayed no such restraint, downing two generous measures with scarcely a word between swallows. Katarina said nothing of this, only sitting down beside Charles Wilton and coaxing the old man into following Maxwell's example. Her unspoken reasoning was plain enough to William's mind: it would be better for all of them if Wilton slept soundly through what was left of the night. Katarina charmed enough of the potent liquid down Wilton's throat that the old man's head began to nod and his eyelids droop, and Janet took one of his arms and escorted him to his bed. Wilton stumbled against her at the doorway and nearly had both of them over, and Schwieger jumped to his feet and hurried to help.

In the end, Wilton left the room with one arm over Janet's shoulders and the other over Schwieger's, the young Prussian clearly supporting most of his weight. Palmer watched the awkward trio depart, rubbing his thumb along the stem of his mostly full brandy glass. Purple shadows stained the crumpled skin beneath his eyes. Katarina came back to the table, drew back the chair beside Palmer's, and sat down.

"Is he often this bad?"

"No," Palmer said, and looked down at the brandy.

Katarina sighed. "Frederick could send you someone. Let us send you someone."

Something like a smile twitched the skin around Palmer's mouth. "Who exactly do you think you could send to look after two ancient anti-Imperialist revolutionaries no longer able to keep from babbling seventy years' worth of secrets?"

"A young anti-Imperialist revolutionary, of course." Katarina looked at the wall over Palmer's head as though names of likely candidates were written there. "Brenda Trevelyan, possibly? If this business of Gavin's takes longer to come to fruition than he thinks it will, she'll need a safe haven in any case."

"I thought she was a member of your company because she had refused to leave her husband's side?"

"Well, but if we could persuade her to leave?" Katarina rubbed her eyes. "I was trying to solve one end of the problem at a time."

Palmer smiled at her, a real smile this time, and patted her arm with one veined hand. "You're a good girl to think of it, but no. I don't want her here. I...can't trust Charles to know what year he is in, from one day to the next. He'd tell her...all our secrets, everything, Frankenstein's journal and all the rest, starting with his real name and mine."

"How can that possibly be worse than her knowing Kent's real name and all the tactics that didn't work in the Welsh mines?" Katarina asked. "Forgive me, but your seventy years' worth of secrets are, many of them, seventy years old. What does it matter any longer?"

"She cannot be made to tell what she does not know. Why do you think I never told you or Frederick who I really was? There's danger."

Katarina hesitated. "Still?"

Palmer blew his breath out. "Yes. Obviously." He gestured to the ruined room down the hall. "I don't want her to know, and I wish you still didn't know. If I'd been thinking faster this afternoon, I might have—have come up with some way to persuade Will to keep my name secret—something. But it all happened too fast." He tilted his brandy glass so that the candlelight burned against the amber liquid, but still did not drink. "I really do not want anyone out there knowing that the celebrated Palmer and Wilton, retrievers of Frankenstein's journal, are helplessly situated here in Yorkshire. And if word does get out, I absolutely do not want a young member of Kent's organization trapped here with us the next time trouble comes tapping at the door in the dead of night."

"I don't think trouble came tapping on the door this night," Katarina said. "I think Mr. West knocked over his candle. I really think you are imagining danger where there is none—"

"I certainly wasn't imaging it back then." Palmer set his snifter on the table with a thump. "God above, Kat, why do you think we changed our names? We weren't wandering about the Continent for our cowardly health, those years after the Rising. Someone knew we had the journal and knew how to find us. Someone was waiting for us in the Count's study that very night, and he or another chased us all over the Continent, hideaway after hideaway and false name after false name. We were waylaid and robbed, our rooms searched, in Rome Charles was kidnapped and questioned by someone whose face he never saw—and the only thing that saved us then was we'd managed to get rid of the part of the journal that mattered, so he honestly could not tell where it was. I assumed our enemies were Imperials, though how the hell they kept finding us I could never tell. I know I didn't betray us, and I'm certain—" Palmer stopped, and swallowed. "I am almost certain that Charles did not either. Nor could it have been Hull —not on purpose—though I suppose perhaps accidentally, he or Sheffield—The persecution didn't stop after the Rising failed; it worsened, in fact; but I could endure that, because we genuinely did not have the notes. We could handle ourselves, Charles and I, and I would have far rather borne the target on my own back than know it painted on someone less capable at home." Palmer sighed and downed the brandy in a swallow. "You protect your own family as long as you can," he said, almost to himself. "Then your responsibility is to the men and women under your command. And then later, under your successor's command."

Katarina rubbed her hands over her eyes again. "God forbid you let your successor or the men and women working for him choose their own risks."

"I do not want any idealistic children taking the axe-blow that's coming for me."

"Mr. Carter—" Katarina stopped, and looked up at him with a half-smile. "I won't be able to stop calling you that, you know."

"It's all right," Palmer said, also smiling a little. "It's been so long—I won't be able to stop thinking of myself that way, either."

"Your service to your country—staying on the Continent to make yourself a target—it humbles me, sir. But that was then. There's no axe-blow coming for you now. Let Kent send you someone to help nurse Mr. West."

Palmer turned the empty snifter between his hands. "Are you unwilling to consider the idea that Charles might have been telling the truth? That he might not have started this fire?"

Katarina sighed. "I don't find it very likely."

"Then you are not considering all the possibilities, young woman. He says it was not his hand. And if it was not his hand, it was someone else's. Trying to smoke us out? Trying to burn my memorabilia? Trying to prevent me telling Will and his friends what they need to know?"

"How could anyone know what you were saying to Will and his friends?" Katarina's voice was the picture of reason.

"The same way they knew to find us in Amsterdam."

"Mr. Carter—"

Palmer slammed the glass down on the table again, so hard it splintered and shattered. Katarina was there at once, pulling the old man's hand away from the glass, grabbing for a cloth to sweep the debris away.

The kitchen was silent for several heartbeats, save for the ticking of the clock.

"All right," Katarina said then, quietly. "You are correct, sir. There is a chance Mr. West's hand did not knock over the candle. Therefore you should let Frederick Kent send you guards. Some of his people do as well looking after themselves now as Captain Palmer and Mr. Wilton did once upon a time on the Continent. If there is some enemy attempting to burn down your house, we would like to catch them." She made it sound nothing but reasonable, but William could see the tactic for what it was—giving Palmer a way to agree to a nurse without sacrificing his pride. "We can discuss that further tomorrow," Katarina continued. "For now, Emil and I could trade watch until morning. It's not so long until dawn. Could you sleep if we were on watch?"

"You're a good girl," Palmer said again. He sighed. "I still think of you as a girl, but you're a woman grown, aren't you? I still think of Frederick as a boy, but he controls a web in London and beyond, a larger force than I ever commanded. He's younger than I was in Provence, but he's no boy, and you're no child either. All right." He levered himself slowly upright, looking every day of his age and more. "I'll leave you the night watch and sleep. We'll talk about setting traps to catch miscreants in the morning."

Katarina rose with him. "As you say, sir. I'll give you an arm up the stairs. There we are, that's right."

"I can help," William said once Katarina and Schwieger had returned to the kitchen. "I could stand one of the watches, if you—"

But Katarina shook her head. "There's no need," she said. She looked herself older by years than she had that evening, but she spoke without hesitation. "We're only indulging our old friend so he can sleep. You and Elizabeth ought to go and sleep as well—you're both hurt, and there's more work to be done tomorrow." She spoke as if Maxwell were not sitting there beside them; but then, William thought, Maxwell was hardly drawing any positive attention to himself. The two glasses of brandy seemed to weigh him down, drowning any words before they got near his lips.

William stretched himself out on his pallet and tried to ignore the sodden, smoke-choked air pressing against his lungs. It did not seem to bother Maxwell—assisted no doubt by the brandy, he had dropped off quickly enough—but William lay wakeful, listening to Schwieger's slow tread make its deliberate circuits around the house. It reminded him vaguely of Trevelyan's loom in the other 1885. Or perhaps the cloth-loom he had seen in Cheshire before this mad adventure had begun. Or a heartbeat. Ka-thunk. Ka-thunk. Rhythmic and measured.

After a time it was replaced by Katarina's lighter step—a smaller loom, William thought drowsily, one spinning quicker. He settled back into sleep then. It was possible to sleep anywhere, even a house reeking of smoke, even a battlefield reeking of death and gunpowder, as long you knew the footsteps you heard belonged to a trusted sentry. And he did trust Katarina—more than he trusted Kent or Schwieger, if it came to it. He trusted Kent only because Katarina did and Maxwell did and Chris Palmer did, only because logic suggested him trustworthy. He trusted Schwieger only because he was one of Kent's company. Only in theory, as it were.

Katarina, he trusted in fact. Because he had shared a battlefield with her before, in the other 1885. Because he had twice seen her plunge into danger without an instant's hesitation, once to save a child and once to grasp a rail-gun. Because she had given him *her* trust, showing him how to affect her 1885 even knowing he might choose to work against her interests. For giving him the opportunity to do *something*, for teaching him a way of moving the world that did not require his ruined arm, he owed her anything she cared to claim of him. Trust was the least he could give her.

He dreamed that they walked home together from Murchinson's, as they had once done in fact. His dreaming mind was vaguely aware that the 1885 around him ought not to feel so real, but he could not remember why. He gave up trying after a moment, and his skin settled into the feel of thick textured fog and watching construct eyes. The damp, smoke-saturated air tickled the back of his throat. Far away in the fog, sentry footsteps walked a beat measured by Trevelyan's loom.

Sometimes the beat faltered, and he knew that was because of the sand Katarina had thrown in the gears. A handful of dust could bring the whole world crashing to a halt eventually, as effectively as a bullet through the shoulder, though not as efficiently. The problem was the need to exist after the destruction. What did one do after?

He asked her diffidently, aware it was no business of his, what plans she might have for after the war. He expected her to say something about Gavin Trevelyan. She told him about her mother the opera singer instead. Her mother had sung at La Scala, and Katarina would like nothing better than to follow in her footsteps. Perhaps it was not too late for her to learn, she said. Perhaps the smoke of London had not irretrievably ruined her throat.

It had been a long day's work, what with dodging artillery in the alleyway and climbing the cliffsides of Orkney, and William felt his jawbones cracking with stifled yawns. It was terribly discourteous, of course, but he simply could not help it. At least Katarina did not seem offended. "There's plenty of time before it rains," she said to him, amusement running through her throaty low voice. "You'd better get some rest. Can't soldiers sleep anywhere?" The cottage smelled like wet wood and burnt cloth, but he stretched out on the pallet anyway.

In his dream, she came back after a time to check that he and the others slept soundly. Like a nursery-maid looking in on her charges, she stood just inside the door, hands on her hips. Her head blotted out the pearly light that came through the windowpane. The light reappeared as she stooped and fumbled with the shadows at William's side, vanishing again when she straightened. She turned for the doorway, and in her hand gleamed a captured star on a chain.

William lay for a confused moment before realizing he was awake. Katarina's dark figure vanished through the doorway. Her quick soft steps retreated down the hall. A moment later, the front door opened and shut.

What had that been in her hand?

William understood it all in a single sickened flash. He rolled out of the bed silently. scattering coat and waistcoat, and sprinted after Katarina on soundless stockinged feet. He ran past the room where Elizabeth slept, past the staircase, past the ruined and blackened sitting room, and out the front door. Katarina was halfway across the front lawn, her bare head gleaming like polished ebony in the gray pre-dawn light.

"Katherine?"

He could not have said at that moment what instinct prompted him to call in a whisper. Later, he realized that it was because the situation was salvageable, because no irrevocable step had yet been taken—just a single moment of poor judgment, and surely she was owed a chance to repent of poor judgment; wouldn't he hope for the same himself? If he raised the alarm, her comrades-in-arms asleep inside the cottage would never trust her again. And that would be too high a price to pay for a moment's impulse, not when he might persuade her to turn and come back to them.

She whirled at her name, and William froze as light glinted off the tiny pistol she held between them.

The pocket watch dangled from her other hand.

"Don't come any closer," she warned, in a low voice that nevertheless carried clear. "Don't shout for them, or I'll shoot."

Deprived of his voice, he had no weapon at all. He had no firearm of his own, couldn't have shot with it left-handed even if he had owned one. If she was as good a shot as her counterpart had been, he could not take her in a rush; she would fell him before he crossed a quarter of the space between them. Even if she missed, she was an athletic young woman nearly as tall as he and had full use of both her hands and no burn on her arm, and he knew where he'd place his wager in that contest. He faced her in the moonlight, not daring to move or shout, as completely unarmed as he had been in Murchinson's, in a contest he must not lose and with no lever long enough to move this world.

For a moment his heart beat in his throat, and it was harder to draw a breath than it had been inside the smoke-choked house. Then William forced the breath into his lungs and set his feet. He didn't have to move the world. He needed only to move one angry woman who held his pocket watch hostage, and surely he could do that. They had shared battlefield danger and a conversation about the future on the way home from the match factory. Surely he knew her well enough to choose words that would move her.

"Katherine," he said. "Katarina. You don't want to do this."

"You do not know one damned thing about what I want or don't," she said.

"That's where you're wrong, as it happens," he said reasonably. "I had the honor of getting you know you quite well, in a different 1885. I imagine there are some differences between you and that other Katarina, but all the important qualities appear to be the same." She looked at him with scorn, but she did not forbid him to speak, so he kept going. "I know you wouldn't leave an injured man on a battlefield. I know you wouldn't abandon a mistreated child. I know you'd turn back to save both, because I saw you do it. I know you fight only the battles you believe must be fought. True, you'll use any weapon that comes to hand and any means you must to ensure your victory—" She clothed herself as a man when that was the shortest path over the ground she wished to cross; she dressed as a woman and dazzled men with her beauty when she needed to distract their eyes from something else; she had primed Elizabeth like a pistol and turned her loose to change history. She had even made a weapon out of a one-armed veteran once, when no other options had been open to her. "—but you're a soldier for your country, no mercenary for hire. You are ruthless in your means, but only in service of a greater cause. So I know you would not steal my only way home if you did not believe it necessary. I therefore believe your tactical assessment, not your motives, to be in error." She was still listening. The length of his speech had settled her feet into the ground, and he did not think she would sprint away from him now, so he took another breath and nodded to the pocket watch in her hand. "Why?" He had been thinking desperately all the time he spoke, and only one theory seemed even vaguely probable. "Because Gavin Trevelyan does not want us to change the past?"

"Yes," Katarina said. "That, exactly."

"And he...convinced you of his position?" William tried to read her expression in the uncertain light. "Or—no, he did not convince you. But you'll take him our watch anyhow—why? Because you love him?"

At that she froze. He might have succeeded in rushing her if he had seized that moment. He did not think to seize it. After a long silence, she parted her lips with an apparent effort and said, "How did you know?"

"You told me," William said. "In that other London."

The pistol wavered for one moment in her hand. Then she firmed her grip. "Do you mean to say...there is a universe in which it is...other than unrequited?"

"No," William said after a moment's pause, and did not feel he told a lie. "It was always unrequited. He was always married. You told me that, too, in the other London. You said—you said that she was dead, but he was still married. That he wore her ring on a chain around his neck, and he might as well wear it on his finger."

"I said that? It sounds as though I was a wise woman."

That was mockery in her voice, not bitterness. William relaxed fractionally. "You were," he said. "You are. Wise and brave both. I know it racks your soul to leave a comrade on the battlefield, but Madam Katherine, do you really wish to prevent us from mending all this, just for the sake of one woman's life?" He knew as he said it that he was taking a terrible risk. She had, after all, been willing to risk as much at Murchinson's for the sake of one child's life—

"Of course I don't want to prevent you!" Katarina snapped. "Did you think I stole this to drop it at Gavin's feet in hopes of his approval?"

William was silent. He *had* thought so. He recalculated as quickly as possible. "If not that, then why? If you want us to change the past—That is exactly what we seek to do. If we are fighting on the same side, why would you take our watch and prevent our changes?"

"Because you won't do it," she said fiercely. "You're already starting to fall in love with these people, already starting to see the threads of their lives as something sacred and not to be broken. Elizabeth is wavering in her certainty already. So you'll get back to London, and Trevelyan will talk you out of it, or trick you out of it, or sneak upon you in the night and destroy this." She brandished the watch. "He won't allow it, don't you understand? Brenda was dead in the other universe. If I can work that out, so can he, and he won't allow anything that will put her in danger. He'd set this whole world on fire—allow the French occupation to stand!—rather than see her come to harm. I don't hate her," she added, in response to what William knew was on his face. "I don't wish her ill. Even if she were gone, he'd never see me for the shadow she cast, so what does it matter? I quite like her, truly. But she's not worth more than this whole world, and he'll never see the larger picture for looking at her. He'll convince you or he'll trick you, but Gavin Trevelyan won't let you do what you came here to do."

"I won't let Gavin Trevelyan stop me." William took a step forward, hand out for the watch, but Katarina got the pistol between them. "You can trust me to do this," he protested. "You did trust me once. We rescued a child from Murchinson's together. You can trust me to do this now." She shook her head. "Katherine, listen to me. You have not made an irrevocable choice yet. Give me back my watch, and I'll never say a word. But if you take it and leave now, you will set fire to your entire life—all your lives, all the possibilities, all the things you might do once this mess is mended. You know that. There is no reason for you to set your life on fire, not when Maxwell and Elizabeth and I can do what must be done." She shook her head again. "This is wanton destruction," he said. "It is not necessary. You need not sacrifice La Scala to this."

Her stillness this time was not frozen. "Freeze" had a connotation of sharp edges. This stillness was deeper, softer, more profound. Something belonging to a small woodland creature. "I told you about La Scala."

"You did. You said your mother sang there."

Katarina breathed a laugh. "Not in this world. No opera would employ an Englishwoman. She was a music hall girl."

"How did she meet a Russian nobleman, then?"

"And I told you that, too. We *must* have been friends." Katarina shook her head. "She said he was Russian; she said they were married, and both halves of that are errant nonsense, though I believed it when I was a child. Mostly people think he must have been a French soldier."

"Your name was Rasmirovna in the other London," William said, "when the French were nowhere near your mother. You looked then as you look now. So I think he must have truly been Russian. And I know she sang at La Scala then, and your voice is like hers, so you could sing there as well if you wanted to."

There was a pause—a tempted one, William thought—but then Katarina said, "It doesn't matter. If the French did not rule this island and an English-woman could sing at La Scala, I might want to sing at La Scala. If the French did not rule this island and Gavin Trevelyan were free, I might want him. But the French rule this island. That's all that matters to me. Gavin will not let you change this timeline. And he knows me too well; he knows what I'll try. I won't have another chance. I can't let this one go. I'm sorry, Mr. Carrington."

Nothing for it, then. William opened his mouth to say the one thing that would definitely change her mind.

A pistol shot cracked through the night behind him, and William's bat-tlefield reflexes hurled him to the ground. He saw Katarina fire one round back, then turn and sprint. William scrambled desperately to his feet as Emil Schwieger pounded past him.

Schwieger held a pistol in an outstretched hand, and was already lining up for another shot. He got off a second round, thankfully missing for a second time, before William barreled into his knees from behind and took him down. "No," William gasped through the tangle of arms and legs and a knee to his abdomen, "no, don't, don't!" He clawed at Schwieger's pistol with his one good hand, hissing at the pressure to his burned forearm.

"You are mad, Carrington!" Schwieger bit out. "You cannot let her depart with your pocket watch!"

"Let her go, it doesn't matter, it's the broken one!" William managed. The windows of the cottage behind him were lighting one after the other, any hope of smoothing this over destroyed with the gunshots. Schwieger stopped strug-gling, looking puzzled. "We have two," William explained around the pain in his gut, "one broken and one whole. She took the broken one!"

Schwieger stared at him in bewilderment. "Then why did you try to coax her back inside?"

"I wanted to give her a chance to change her mind," William said, look-ing into the darkness that had swallowed her. "Everyone should have a second chance. She gave me one, once."

Too late now. If he'd had both his hands, he would have been hard-pressed not to fasten them around the young Prussian's throat. He scrambled to his feet instead and hobbled off at what speed he could manage in the direction Katarina had vanished.

But she had too great a head start, and they did not catch her. For a time her footprints in the smooth mud led them onward, but once the mud turned to meadow it became impossible to track her further. William followed the lonely trail of female boot-prints back to Palmer's house, heart heavier each moment.

The hardest part was going inside to tell the others. Elizabeth pressed one bandaged hand over her mouth, eyes filling with tears, and Maxwell sat down suddenly, as though it was he who had gotten a Prussian kick to the gut. Palmer turned so white William fumbled for the brandy again, and Schwieger hastened to take it from his clumsy left hand.

"And you," William said to him, glad to have someone on whom to turn his fury, "what the devil is wrong with you? Firing shots at your comrade—"

"My comrade appeared to have lost her mind, as far as I could tell," Schwieger snapped back. He sloshed some of the brandy into a glass, and this time Palmer choked down a dose without comment. "I heard some of what she said to you. She was about to hurl herself into the void with the only means we have of changing history—stranding you here—with no considered plan! I meant to injure her, not kill her. I could not know you had two pocket watches and one does not function—"

"You what?" Palmer managed.

"It did not seem important to mention before," William said. "I'm sorry, Chris, I wasn't hiding it, I only...It didn't seem to matter." Since the inadvertent secret-keeping might have just saved them all and any hope of correcting their hideous mistake, he could not find it in his heart to regret it. He tried to force himself to think. "So she'll try it, and it won't work—and then what? Will she come back? Or will she think she's burnt her boats and—"

"Where did she mean to go?" Maxwell interrupted, running his hands through his white hair. His eyes were bloodshot and it looked as though his head pained him after his indulgence a few hours earlier. *Good,* William thought spitefully. "There are only three journals unburnt, and all three of them still here—unless she made her plan before the fire—"

"I—have to check something," Palmer said suddenly, and struggled out of his chair. "Stay here. Wait for me."

He hobbled his way down the corridor. None of them stayed behind and waited—all followed, though they tried to make the distance respectful. Palmer opened the front door to reveal pink sky, and stepped in the garden. He walked over to the sundial and bent down to peer at its brick base. Then he clutched the top with both hands to keep from falling.

Schwieger and Maxwell between them carried him inside, pushing him to sit on the bottommost stair. William knelt in front of him. Christopher had his right hand pressed to his chest, and his breath came in hard gasps. "The journal," he whispered. "She took—"

"Don't try to talk," William soothed him. "Schwieger, we need a physician. An apothecary, something. Do you know the—no, you've never been up here before. Wake up Janet and get her to—"

"No," Palmer gasped. "No, I'm fine, don't send for anyone, no. The journal. Frankenstein's—"

"No, no, sir, it's here," Maxwell reassured him, and seemed about to go and fetch it.

"No," Palmer said again. "The rest of it. Hidden."

William understood with a jolt. "The part you said was no longer in your possession."

"Yes. Lied. No one knew—except Charles. Sundial." Palmer closed his eyes. "Sent it home without us, like I said. Let them chase us—around the Continent. Keep it safe. Came home, and—no one could make use of it—had to be hidden somewhere. Safe enough here. Shaken them off by then. Or so we thought. Behind the third brick."

"Plain sight," Elizabeth murmured.

"So the fire," Maxwell said. "She set the—no, I can't believe that!"

"Think I want to?" Palmer opened anguished eyes. "My granddaughter. Might as well be my...But she knows. Knows the trick. Charles used it. Charles taught her. Set a fire. Then you know—where the treasures are. Funny Charles should fall for it. After all this time." He leaned back against the wall. "Almost funny. For the rest—it's like her. She couldn't trust you to do it. And it had to be done. Very like her."

"Or that foe you mentioned earlier used the same ploy," William said. He wanted it to be that. If it were that, he had not read her wrong, he need not discount as worthless all of his newly won skill in reading people, he was not a fool for trusting her—

"Yes." Palmer looked paler than some corpses William had seen. His eyes slid closed again. "Or that."

"We must know which it was," Schwieger said. He looked, if anything, more shaken than Palmer, but he spoke bravely. "She has a pocket watch that will not work—very well. She may also have instructions for creating monsters, not much use to her without a trained scientist—perhaps she will use them to buy her way back into Kent's good graces?—only dangerous to us if the Imperials lay hands on them. Again, very well, but only if she has them. If she does not have them, your enemy does." Schwieger clenched his hands into fists. "We must know which. We must look for her again, and if we cannot find her, we must return to London today so Kent can be told."

"First we need a physician," William repeated, his fingers on Palmer's uncertain pulse. "Send Janet for one, before you do anything else."

"Quietly," Palmer murmured without opening his eyes. "Don't worry Charles."

"No," William agreed through a thickened throat. "I won't worry him."

Palmer's eyes slitted open at that. "Got too old to fight," he said. "Had to hand it off to the young lads...Will, I can't—can't—see to this. You have to—have to—"

William tightened his grip on the frail hand. "I promise," he said.

Interlude

Vienna, Austria, April 2, 1882

The diagram blurred before his dry and burning eyes, and no amount of blinking would make it come clear. He lifted his eyes from the notebook for the first time in hours, casting an irritated glance in the direction of the window, expecting to see an inconvenient fog rolling in.

To his surprise, he beheld a darkening sky. Evening? How long had he been hunched over the workbench, then? As if in answer, the bells of St. Clement's began to toll, low and melodic. He shifted in impatience as they told the quarter-chime, the half-chime, and the three-quarter chime. Finally they moved into the information he cared about, and he counted the strokes. One. Two. Three. Four. Five. Six.

Six. Six o'clock in the evening. Which meant a few things. One, he had been occupied with models and drawings for something like ten hours. Two, he had not managed to solve the stress fracture problem in time to catch a couple of hours' sleep before his shift at Arceneau-fabrik, despite the ferocious internal resolutions he'd made at dawn. Three, he had not eaten all day either, and if he didn't want to faint while working on the line, he probably ought to correct that omission in the half hour or so remaining before he must begin his walk. He stood up, blinked the black spots away from his eyes, stretched until his neck cracked, and headed over the bare and creaking floor for the kettle.

He grabbed a few biscuits out of the tin while he waited for the water to boil, shoving them into his mouth and holding them with his teeth while he used both hands to gather up the models and bundle them into their hiding place under the floorboards. They took no chances, he and Zimmermann. Should one of their neighbors do something to prompt an Imperial raid of the tenement, there was nothing in a casual glance at the room they shared to suggest that the two of them were anything other than line workers too poor to afford much in the way of furniture. A more detailed Imperial investigation would of course pry up the floorboard, but a more detailed Imperial investigation would sink them for other reasons in any case.

The kettle whistled. Still with the biscuits clamped between his teeth, he poured out a cup of tea. He took up the notebook, intending to put it with the models—then hesitated, eyeing the drawing again. He had a few moments. He sat down on Zimmermann's mattress, setting the teacup on the floor in front of him, dumping the biscuits on a relatively clean portion of blanket and poising the pencil over the paper again.

Sitting down was a mistake. It reminded his body how weary it was. Aching fatigue seemed to rise from his feet and seep up his legs—in a slow inexorable tide, in waves like lapping water. He ignored that data as irrelevant, having no plans to change his behavior to accommodate his body's demands. After all, even when he spent a portion of the daylight hours lying stretched out upon his mattress, he never slept well. His years in Cayenne had left him with nightmares sufficient to occupy all of his sleeping hours for what he suspected would prove to be the rest of his life. And the part before the nightmares started—the part as he began to lose his grasp on the waking world and slip into sleep—was even worse. He knew, for he had once asked Zimmermann straight out, that people other than himself occasionally heard a sound like a low murmur of voices as they fell asleep. He doubted, however, that other people's voices spoke to them. His were mostly smothered by the sound of lapping waves, but sometimes they did cry out his name. His real name, which he had otherwise not heard in nine years. Even when they were alone, he and Zimmermann never called each other by anything but their aliases. He might have even begun to think of himself as the alias, were it not for the voices in his memory crying out "Trevelyan."

Perhaps even they were only his imagination, though. He had to listen hard for them. Sometimes they were almost impossible to hear over the sounds of water and wind, those faint cries growing fainter as the current swept him along, as cold indigo water lapped its way up his legs and numbed them. "Trevelyan—"

He woke with a jump.

The window opposite showed him a sky gone nearly back.

Oh, bloody—

He didn't complete the thought. He didn't have time. He took two precious seconds to hide the notebook, drop the floorboard into place, and drag his mattress over it. Then he grabbed his latchkey and muffler and ran, taking the deathtrap stairs two at a time, hurtling through the front door and onto the darkened street.

Darkened. He was not only late, he was very late. Even if he ran the whole way, he was unlikely to make Arceneau-fabrik before his shift started. But the very last thing his and Zimmermann's combined finances needed was for him to lose this position, so he ran anyway, just on the chance it would make a difference. Mentally he reviewed the maze of streets that lay before him, wondering if there were any shortcut he might take to shave off a minute or two, but nothing suggested itself. He and Zimmermann already took the shortest possible route, avoiding the main streets in favor of less crowded back ways.

The usually uncrowded byways were now nearly deserted, the side effect of being behind his time—most of those who worked night shift in the factory district were most of the way there, and of course those who worked day shift had not yet been released. Usually he and Zimmermann crossed paths at the factory gate, exchanging brief comments on what work the off-shift one had put into their joint illicit operations, but at this rate—yes, curse it, that was the church clock striking seven—they would pass each other on the street. Zimmermann would have plenty to say about Trevelyan losing this job. Trevelyan dropped into a fast walk, rubbing at the stitch in his side.

There was someone pacing him, he realized a turn or so later. There had been all the time he'd been running, though the forefront of his attention had been occupied with other matters then. He slowed his pace a fraction more. The shadow across the street and just visible from his peripheral vision slowed a fraction as well.

A wave of cold like indigo water washed over him, focused all his attention on assessing this new threat. An Imperial? Might his and Zimmermann's Resistance work have drawn attention to itself?

No. An Imperial would hardly blend so successfully into the background of the Viennese *mietshaus* district. Nor would an Imperial bother. Imperials had no need for subterfuge. They had more than enough men and more than enough clout, not to mention the fear of the populace. They favored frontal assault tactics, in the dead of night by preference.

But why would a pickpocket bother working a back street like this? Why would a pickpocket bother targeting *him*? He looked like exactly what he was, a factory worker without two coins to rub together who was shortly to be sacked for being late to his shift. Not exactly a tempting target.

He picked up the pace again. So did the shadow.

Trevelyan weighed his options. At the end of the little byway he currently walked was the gas-lit main road, just visible as a gray patch of light. He might put on a burst of speed until he reached it, and there render his follower powerless by virtue of the larger crowd likely to be walking there. Or there was a true alleyway coming up on his right—he might duck down it, thus enticing his shadow to pursue him into a confined area where Trevelyan could wait for him armed with the heaviest piece of refuse he could find.

Or—there was a third option, just turning left into the byway from the main road. He would know Zimmermann's silhouette anywhere, so tall and thin it gave the impression of being an animated cadaver. Trevelyan might hail him, scaring off his pursuer by the threat of numbers. Or, if he could work out a way to nonverbally communicate the situation in the next few seconds, perhaps they might join forces and make the threat a reality.

He was still weighing his options when a shadow jumped out of the right-hand alleyway, directly into his path, flinging an overcoat over his head as it sprang. Trevelyan wrenched against its grip, but got no purchase before something slammed into his head from behind. The world went bright and then dark.

*

Indigo water twined around his legs, higher with every ice-cold rocking wave, pulling him down into numb stillness. His cramped fingers could no longer feel the planks he clung to. Only his head was warm—a fiery, trickling warmth indistinguishable from pain.

The pain flared into blinding light. He tried to flinch. "Trevelyan," the voice said.

Not in entreaty and not in anger. In satisfaction.

Satisfaction? That was not the way of the memory, nor the way of the dream.

And the water was…distinctly solid, for water. It pressed hard and cold against his knees, slimy and tacky, but not soaking. He was not lying half off a raft, he came to the slow realization, but kneeling on hard ground. Forced to his knees, in fact, by a weight pressing down on his shoulders. The hands he could not feel were not clinging to rough wood, but rather clamped together behind his back, bonds digging into wrists, circulation gone. Trevelyan blinked, and the pinpoint pain before his eyes resolved into the glow of a match. From beyond it, a drawn face surrounded by black hair watched him with interest.

For a moment, Trevelyan could not make sense of it. He was not on a raft. And yet that was Sergei Ivanovich Buryakov's face.

"There," Buryakov said, in a tone almost of affection. "Miss me?"

"I…thought you were dead," Trevelyan managed.

"You hoped," came a second voice—this one emanating from above his head, from the bulk that pinned his nerveless limbs to the ground. It struck his ear like second blow to his skull. *Christ. It's both of them.* He tipped his head back enough to catch a glimpse of Denis Grigorovich Gromyko's humorless expression. Gromyko shook him. "You hoped, is it not so?"

"No," Trevelyan said, though the truth was something more complicated than simple denial. The four of them had been friends once, brothers even, bound by the desperate sorts of ties men form in hell, but if he had thought for a moment there was a possibility of their still being alive…yes, he decided, he would have hoped they were dead.

"No," Buryakov agreed pleasantly. The match spluttered between his blunt fingertips, sparking against his skin, but he did not react. The flickering pinpoint light glinted in his dark eyes and along the silver in his beard. "You did not hope, but you thought. You thought we could not endure the punishments awaiting those who failed to escape Cayenne. An understandable mistake, old friend. Most men could not have so endured." The match winked again, and went out.

Without it, the alleyway was black dark. At a skewed angle, Trevelyan could just make out an inky patch that might have been the mouth of the alley, but he could see nothing else. He fancied he could feel Buryakov move, but could not arrive at certainty before a steely grip closed around his throat and all logical thought was subsumed in the instinctive frantic struggle for air.

"It was anticipating this moment that kept me alive," Buryakov told him in a voice as throaty-warm as a lover's, and squeezed.

The squealing sound of wrenched metal burst through the drumming in Trevelyan's ears. It was not until two or three choking breaths had passed through his swollen throat that he realized Buryakov had loosed his hold. The squeal ended in a sharp clank. *Zimmermann?* Trevelyan thought, in something between hope and dread. Footsteps were sprinting away from him, up the alleyway and toward the inky mouth. His streaming eyes could only just make out the cadaverous form bisecting it, armed with a length of pipe. *Zimmermann. Has he gone mad? Christ Almighty, Nick, run!*

Trevelyan pushed up desperately against the ground he could barely feel, and the bulk behind him rocked for an instant off-balance. It was long enough for Trevelyan to stagger to his feet. Sensation washed back though his legs--shards of pain, waves of ice-cold water. He staggered a step toward Zimmermann and Buryakov just as Zimmermann managed to land a blow that dropped the Russian momentarily to hands and knees. Zimmermann stumbled back, snatching toward his shirt pocket. He looked back at Trevelyan and hesitated one instant.

But only one. Neither of them had quailed on the raft, when the calculation was between two deaths and four, and Zimmermann did not flinch for more than an instant now. Buryakov was down, Gromyko had not yet recovered his balance, but they would both be up long before Trevelyan could get his stunned and stumbling self to safety. Zimmermann struck the match.

Trevelyan approved. He would have done exactly the same thing himself. He didn't even mind the thought of dying in fire. Somehow it seemed preferable to dying in cold water.

A door slammed open just behind him, and a grip closed over his collar as smoothly as if the movement had been rehearsed. Trevelyan rocked backward into darkness as Zimmermann threw the match. The gas-filled alleyway went up in an explosion of orange flame.

*

Cold water lapped over the side of the raft. His legs were numb with cold, his fingers numb with clinging, but his head burned with fever and thirst. Cold water came lapping over the side, and Buryakov and Gromyko dissolved into it, as smoothly as powder from a chemist's envelope dissolving into a glass of water, shouting his name and Zimmermann's. His real name. Zimmermann's real name. Blackened, both those names, for this deed if for no other, for abandoning brothers–in-arms to a place that turned good men mad. And yet could they have done anything else? The world did not run on sentiment; the calculation was a cold one, cold as the lapping water. They could have done nothing to save the two Russians in any case. Hadn't it been better for the world, for their cause, for the Resistance against the Empire, that he and Nick at least had gotten out?

"Have you thought about Wales?" a voice said.

Trevelyan did not know that voice. Moreover, it spoke English—a sound as foreign to his ear after all these years as the syllables of his name. Trevelyan cracked an eye open to investigate.

Once again he did not appear to actually be on a raft. There was no water, and he spied the wooden timbers of a ceiling, and come to think of it, he could feel his legs after all. It was only in contrast to the hot pain in his head that they felt numbly cold. He caught a glimpse of Nick—of Zimmermann—talking with a white-haired man Trevelyan was absolutely sure he had never seen before. They both sat cross-legged on the same floor on which Trevelyan lay. There was no furniture in the little room.

"Is it there you know him from?" Zimmermann demanded, in awkward and guttural English. "The Welsh Rising?"

No. Trevelyan found himself unreasonably irritated that Zimmermann should ask such a stupid question. The accent should have told him the answer—this white-haired stranger was an Englishman. Though there had, to be fair, been plenty of cooperation between the British Rising and its Welsh counterpart, and plenty of similarity. Both had failed with crushing finality. The leaders of both had been transported, to Cayenne or to places like it.

"No," the white-haired man said. "I do...know him, however. In a way. And I know that he will be in Wales in 1883 and London in 1885."

"How?" Zimmermann demanded.

"The same way I knew how to find you today." The white-haired man fumbled at his waistcoat, then held out his hand for Zimmermann's inspection. On his palm lay a—

It looked like a pocket watch. It *was* a pocket watch, surely. Surely only the blow to his head, or possibly the aftereffects of Zimmermann's gas main explosion, made Trevelyan perceive a sea of sparkling images instead of numbers and hands. It was as though the watch were a door to other places, other lands. Other possibilities. He thought, confusedly, of Merlin's cave. Brenda had loved that story.

"This allows me to travel through time," the old man said—or at least Trevelyan would have been prepared to swear an oath to that effect, little sense though the words made. Would Merlin's cave have seemed any more sensible?

"I think he wakes," Zimmermann said.

Who? Merlin? Come to aid Britain in the hour of her greatest need—as though by some reckoning *that* was still to come, not already hard upon them all? Trevelyan could not puzzle it out.

Zimmermann's face bent closer. "Gavin?"

"Don't be calling me that," he muttered, and Zimmermann raised his brows.

"Less damaged than I feared," he said, still in English, presumably for the benefit of the old man who had trapped Merlin's cave in a pocket watch. He helped Trevelyan sit up, and for a moment Trevelyan thought his skull would actually split apart. He swallowed the bile that rose in his throat. Perhaps it was just as well he had nothing in his stomach to vomit.

The white-haired man and the pocket watch were still there. "Am I dreaming this?" he asked Zimmermann.

"No," Zimmermann said. "This man who can travel through time landed in an alleyway in Vienna to save two fabrik workers from their past."

The white-haired man shook his head. "You saved yourselves with the gas-main explosion. I landed in an alleyway in Vienna to make sure you got safely away from the Imperial authorities afterward."

"Why?" Zimmermann demanded.

"Truthfully?" The stranger took a breath as though preparing himself for unfamiliar words. "Because I need your help. I will need your help. I need you to choose to help me."

"Help you do what? You have that." Zimmermann nodded at the watch. "What need can you have of other aid?"

"You would be surprised," the white-haired man said.

"Help you do what?" Trevelyan managed to repeat the question.

The white-haired man took another deep breath, and resettled himself on the floor in the position of one preparing to deliver a lengthy explanation. "I have been trying to save my mother's life for many years now," he began.

Chapter 7

London, September 1, 1885

Kent's face went white. "I'll have her hide for a drum skin."

Schwieger flinched, but did not say anything. His report given, he fixed his eyes on the wall over Kent's shoulder and schooled his face to blankness. William wore a similar expression, Elizabeth noted, and concluded it must be a military trick, a means of fading into the background to escape an angry commander's notice. She glanced at Maxwell to see if he too was employing the technique, but found herself unable to be certain. His face was dull and expressionless, to be sure, but he had not deliberately adopted the self-effacing look in response to Kent's anger. He had looked like that for two days now, for the entirety of their journey back to London.

In any case, Kent scarcely seemed to be seeing any of the four of them. He turned away, shaking his head, taking abbreviated steps as though the ruin of their plans were a physical thing that blocked his path. He put a hand out toward one of the straight-backed chairs, seeking support.

But as soon as the wood brushed his fingers, he pushed away from it, using the chair to launch himself into a stride that made short work of the distance to the far wall. "She's been upset for some time," he muttered, "frustrated at how slowly I move—this has been brewing. But I never thought I had cause to actually worry. How could she think she had to do this herself? *How* could she not trust me?"

"I don't think she mistrusted you," Elizabeth ventured. Kent looked back at her. "I think she mistrusted us. And, ah, and Gavin Trevelyan."

"Yes." Kent had stopped behind the wing chair. He drummed his fingers against the back of it. "Is it true, what she inferred? Concerning Brenda?"

"Mrs. Trevelyan was dead in the other universe," Elizabeth admitted. She had been reluctant to speak these words aloud before, but it seemed a greater risk to keep silent now. "But she was killed by a Wellington monster during a mine uprising. If, in a third universe, the monsters were not present, there's no reason to think she would be in danger. It's—it's—a risk, not a certainty. And another universe holds the same risk for any of you, for everyone everywhere. Would Gavin Trevelyan truly—?"

"Yes," Kent said flatly. "I agree with Katarina's assessment thus far. He loves her...beyond reason. I had the opportunity to observe for myself what he would do to ensure her safety. Leaving comrades on the front line was the least of it." William moved slightly, and Kent turned his full piercing attention to

William's face. "You wish to make a comment about the discipline of my organization, Mr. Carrington?"

"I wasn't planning to comment on it, no," William said mildly.

"This is not the Royal Army as you remember it," Kent told him. "Not even the guerrilla army Carter commanded. It's a patchwork quilt, not a woven braid, and I cannot choose my materials. I make the best use I can of the ones to hand. I forgave Gavin Trevelyan's desertion last year because I needed his talents." He rubbed a hand over his face. "I need them still. Thank whatever God may be he's not here. We have a chance of smoothing this over."

Elizabeth seized on the one statement that seemed tangible. "Where has he gone?"

"He and Brenda were called away on personal business. More precisely, Brenda was, and Trevelyan would not permit her to travel without his protection." The *would not permit* jangled oddly against Elizabeth's ears—oddly, for she knew full well that barely a week ago, such a statement would have seemed nothing but reasonable. Well, no doubt it seemed reasonable to Brenda still. Brenda had never traveled by pocket watch. "They are due to return the day after tomorrow," Kent continued, "not an instant too soon, as certain Russian gentlemen of means are due to call upon us two days after that, and the prototype construct must be in a fit state to present to them when they arrive. We'll never have a real chance of throwing out the French without Russian support, nor a real chance of winning Russian support without something like a construct to catch the Bear's eye. This entire plan is a sequence of tiles, one poised to strike the next as it falls, each balanced as though on the point of a knife, and more than half of them needing Trevelyan's hand to personally push them over. And Katarina knew all that," he added with another flare of anger. "By God, I'll have her hide! A *fire*—" He started pacing again, jerky and unsteady steps. "I would never have believed it of her. Putting that whole household in danger—putting two old men and their housekeeper in danger—men she's known since her childhood—how could she?"

"We don't know for certain that part was hers," William reiterated. He had said that before, was clinging to it stubbornly. Elizabeth knew why. She didn't want to believe it of Katarina either. "Wilton said he did have a candle," William went on. "Palmer said they had enemies."

"You think it was her, though?" Kent looked at Schwieger.

"I—sir, I could not say." Schwieger stammered a little. "We returned here at once because I cannot know for certain."

"And because you knew I could find her." Kent smiled without humor. "I am very good at finding people. Yes." He frowned off into the middle distance, thinking about it. "She has a broken pocket watch, her pistol, and the money in her pockets. Is that all? Did she have anything else, Mr. Carrington?"

"She wore a—a cloak of some sort," William said. "Chris Palmer seemed to think the journal could be hidden inside it."

"I know which cloak," Kent said. "More can be concealed in the lining than you'd think, but still not enough to start a life anew. She didn't take anything else from the house? Not that they have much valuable…"

"She did not," William confirmed. "Palmer and Janet both said nothing was missing, not even loose coins."

"Then she hasn't money enough to get far. Not to Paris—or Petrograd—nowhere by dirigible even if she had the funds, not when she was dressed as Katarina Rasmirovna instead of Colin Ramsey. She could earn her way, of course—" Kent grimaced. "But not so easily in the back of beyond. She did have the railway ticket…I wonder…"

Elizabeth could see the gears moving behind his eyes. He had focused upon the one problem like a hawk's eye fastening upon a songbird's flight, and she thought she knew why. The other problems for which he had assumed responsibility were personal and painful or large and fluid, would sting like nettles or slip like water from one's grasp: the balance between Trevelyan and the time travelers, the need to slip a nurse in under Palmer's guard, the sands of time running out for Wilton. Not to mention the impossibility of aiming time travelers without the directions burnt to a crisp in the Yorkshire trunk. But finding Katarina—that was a small, solid, tangible thing. Not easy, perhaps, but graspable. It must be a relief to focus on it.

Elizabeth wished she had something comparable to which she might give her attention. But there were only three journals left from Captain Palmer's lost treasure horde, none of them having anything to do with Dover, two indeed more memoir than daily account and the last covering only Viktor Frankenstein's unhelpful early life and resuming to record his last days in Orkney. She did not see how she could use them to mend the disaster of Waterloo or anything following shortly from it.

In the place of that problem, what was there to focus upon? Maxwell? His silent defeat was a puzzle of sorts, but not one she knew how to solve. She had banished the exhausted desire to weep for the duration of this interview with Kent, but she felt it creeping back up her throat now.

"Emil," Kent said, "I think we had better start with basic reconnaissance. Do yourself up as a beggar and go for a wander through the music hall district. I'll summon some of the others to do the same."

Schwieger looked startled. "Do you think she's in London, sir?"

"I think it's easier for a woman to earn money in London than in Yorkshire, and I think she had a third-class ticket that would have brought her here." Kent's expression was not really a smile. "I think we ought to search here first before venturing farther afield."

"And you want *me* to go?" Schwieger said. "No disguise of mine will fool Katarina."

"You don't need to fool Katarina," Kent said patiently. "You only need to fool those who might have seen her, and that you can do easily enough. So long as you remember to change your boots for the old patched ones *this time*," he added, voice going rather caustic. "And leave your watch and pocket handkerchief at home. Now, about you three—" He turned from Schwieger to face the time travelers. "I had best find you another place to stay before Trevelyan returns. That will take a day or so to arrange, but I have a day or so to arrange it."

"You'll protect us and our pocket watch from him?" William's tone was studiously neutral. "I thought you just said you needed him."

Kent met his eyes. "I do need him—and his constructs—but I need you and your pocket watch as well. I am attempting to balance on more than one knife's edge. I would understand if you did not trust me," he added, "all things considered. If you wish to take additional precautions, I would not fault your caution or be affronted; but I do most strongly advise you stay here under my protection while you take them." He twitched a rueful smile. "I think we may agree that it is contrary to both your interests and mine to see that timepiece of yours fall into French hands."

William looked to Maxwell—who did not respond, either with words or with a change of expression—and then to Elizabeth. "Our additional precaution might take the form of standing watches," he suggested. "If one of us were always awake with the timepiece upon his or her person, it would be much more difficult for someone like Katarina to make off with it unawares."

"But surely you do not consider that necessary while in the warehouse?" Schwieger protested. It seemed that he was affronted at the insinuation, even if Kent was not.

"I consider it prudent," William said mildly.

"And I consider it understandable," Kent cut off whatever else Schwieger might have said. "Whatever they need do to feel themselves secure, Emil. Now go off about your business, will you?" Still frowning, Schwieger turned for the door.

William touched the back of Elizabeth's bandaged right hand. "I'll take the first watch. Why don't you go and sleep awhile?"

"I—" As soon as she allowed herself to entertain the idea, it was all she could do to keep her eyes open. "Yes—yes, all right. Thank you."

"Sir?" William prompted Maxwell as Elizabeth turned for the stairs. "You ought to rest as well."

The pause that followed was long enough for Elizabeth to make her way up half the stairway. She had nearly come to the conclusion that Maxwell would make no response—he had said so little over the past two days, after all, and nothing at all for hours—when the older man cleared his throat and muttered something about needing a drink first. She almost turned back to dissuade Kent from showing him where the spirits were kept, then decided she was too weary for the argument.

Elizabeth went to bed, Schwieger went off to commence his reconnaissance, and Kent likewise disappeared into the night to conscript other scouts. Maxwell established himself at the dining table with the brandy bottle and a most unwelcoming set to his shoulders. William watched the older man for a moment or so, then helped himself to a candle, and took it and Viktor Frankenstein's journal over to Brenda Trevelyan's wing chair. He sat down, pocket watch nestled securely between his body and the arm of the chair, and began to read.

Frankenstein's French was extravagantly overwrought, and his handwriting extravagantly ornate, but even so they commanded only a portion of William's attention. All the time he was reading, he was intensely aware of Maxwell slumped at the table an arms-length away. One might have fancied the older man turned to stone, were it not for the regular lifting of the glass to his lips. The look of defeat lining his face had first settled there back at Palmer's cottage the previous morning, as the four of them dressed for the masquerade that would take them back to London, and it had not lifted since.

They had taken the train, traveling third class, Schwieger and William and Elizabeth in the guise of poor country folk headed for the city in search of work. In a third class compartment, it was Schwieger's accent and appearance that posed the danger, but he managed by keeping a cap over his tow-blond head and keeping his mouth shut, nudging William whenever something must be done. William might have enjoyed the reversal of roles under other circumstances, but as it was, he was too preoccupied with thoughts of Katarina. And with thoughts of Christopher Palmer, taken to his bed but still bravely claiming the illness that caused the pains in his chest was a slight one, nothing that Charles should be worried over. And with thoughts of Maxwell, who looked like a trapped animal exhausted by struggling, giving itself up for lost. Dressed in marginally better clothing than the rest of them, Maxwell was intended to pose as a servant sent ahead with his master's belongings, thereby explaining the trunk in which their fancy dirigible outfits were packed—but he was so bowed down with misery that he succeeded mostly in giving the impression of a very stupid servant indeed, one who could not keep his mind on anything and spent long hours staring dully out of the window.

Now Maxwell regarded the brandy bottle with the same dull expression. It was an expression William knew; he had felt it often enough upon his own face, back in the days after the Peninsula. It was the look of a man who needed a rope thrown to him.

Unfortunately, William was not at all assured of his ability to use words to craft such a rope. Three days ago, he might have fancied himself becoming rather good at that sort of thing, but now the disastrous failure with Katarina dragged against the back of his mind. Perhaps he was not so skilled at using words to move others as he needed to be. Perhaps the wrong words would be worse than no words at all. But surely sitting in the same room as Maxwell was better than doing nothing; so he sat, reading through Frankenstein's journal with half his attention, considering and discarding one conversational opening after another.

The one he finally chose was nothing he could have predicted. He read the paragraph under his moving finger three times before finally deciding it implied what he thought it did—and then he realized he had a means of beginning a most interesting discussion indeed. He deliberated one moment more, watching Maxwell out of the corner of his eye. Then he exhaled an amused, "Ha!" and waited to see if it would have an effect.

Maxwell's brown eyes lifted incuriously from the bottle.

"I think I've found you," William said.

Maxwell raised his eyebrows, but did not offer any verbal comment.

"In the Genevese's journal," William went doggedly on. He got up and went to join Maxwell at the table, a thumb between the notebook leaves to keep his place. Maxwell's eyes tracked the reddish-brown leather with a little more interest. William set the journal down on the table before drawing back the chair that faced Maxwell's. "You said you had tried to stop him—you tried to redirect his youthful studies—and I have just read of a mysterious stranger doing precisely that. Now where was it—ah, yes, here." He found the paragraph once more and read,

> "On this occasion a man of great research in natural philosophy was with us, and…all that he said threw greatly into the shade Cornelius Agrippa, Albertus Magnus, and Paracelsus, the lords of my imagination…All that had so long engaged my attention suddenly grew despicable. By one of those caprices of the mind, which we are perhaps most subject to in early youth, I at once gave up my former occupations; set down natural history and all its progeny as a deformed and abortive creation; and entertained the greatest disdain for a would-be science, which could never even step within the threshold of real knowledge. In this mood of mind I betook myself to the mathematics, and the branches of study appertaining to that science, as being built upon secure foundations, and so worthy of my consideration. Thus strangely are our souls constructed, and by such slight ligaments are we bound to prosperity or ruin. When I look back, it seems to me as if this almost miraculous change in inclination and will was the immediate suggestion of the guardian angel of my life—the last effort made by the spirit of preservation to avert the storm that was even then hanging in the stars and ready to envelope me…It was a strong effort of the spirit of good, but it was ineffectual."

William looked up from the page to find Maxwell watching with some alertness now. He prodded, "That was you, sir, was it not?"

"That was I," Maxwell agreed, in a voice somewhat gravelly with disuse. He lifted one corner of his mouth in a humorless smile. "Ineffectual. As usual."

It was a response. It was something. It gave him something to argue with. "I wouldn't say that," William protested. "You changed his mind for a time."

"Ineffectually," Maxwell said. "Equally ineffectual were my attempt to remove books from his purview and my attempt to distract him from his Orkney pilgrimage by inviting him to stay with me in Scotland. Not to mention my attempt to lure Brenda Trevelyan from the Wellingtons' path. And my attempt to drive the first monster away from capture by British regulars. And my attempt to change the monster war in 1852." He tipped the brandy bottle vertically over the snifter, and the last thin trickle of amber ran from beveled glass mouth to the chipped glass bowl. "One spectacular disaster after another."

"No," William said sturdily. "One failed attempt after another, perhaps, but none were disasters until Waterloo. You needed our help for that."

Maxwell snorted something between surprise and agreement. There might have been a tinge of amusement to it as well. It was something, William thought again. A crack in the façade. He cast about for an instrument to use in wedging the crack wider open.

"The coincidence of the names is curious, don't you think?"

Maxwell eyed him without comprehension over the rim of the snifter.

"His young brother William," William clarified, "and his betrothed Elizabeth. He goes on at some length about them both. They were paragons of perfection, it would appear, Elizabeth in particular." He flipped back a few pages.

"Her hair was the brightest living gold...a crown of distinction upon her head. Her brow was clear and ample, her blue eyes cloudless, and her lips and the molding of her face so expressive of sensibility and sweetness, that none could behold her without looking on her as of a distinct species, a being heaven-sent, and bearing a celestial stamp to all her features."

William glanced up, trying to invite the older man into a smile. "Not much like our Elizabeth."

"No," Maxwell said with some emphasis, and tossed down a swallow. After a pause, he added, "But his Elizabeth wasn't...exactly like that either. I met her, and she was a sweet girl, but not..." He hesitated, then gave up his search for a word and waved a hand at the crabbed writing. "I suppose," he added, "no one ever is what they seem to be in the pages of a journal. I never thought about it that way before."

William gave it a moment, but Maxwell did not elaborate, so William nudged the conversation forward with another question. "Do you know what became of them? Of Viktor's sweetheart and brother?"

"If you read far enough," Maxwell said, "you'll find out what happened to William. You're not very far in, are you?"

"It's slow going," William defended himself. "The man has the most overwrought style of prose I've ever had to pick through."

Maxwell did not smile. "The child William was the first one to be killed by Viktor's monster. I don't know what happened to Elizabeth. The monster killed Frankenstein once he had what he wanted, but I can't imagine he would have cared about the girl. Perhaps she married someone else."

"I'd have thought you'd say, 'Perhaps she took the veil.' Her 'saintly soul shining like a shrine-dedicated lamp' in the Frankensteins' peaceful home, and all."

"She really wasn't like that." Maxwell peered down into his glass. "Not so—exaggerated, not so perfect, as Viktor's writings would have you believe. Journals...journals lie."

There it was again, that faint note of surprised discovery. William studied the older man. "Do they?"

"Well," Maxwell said, "look at our Elizabeth. They're correct as to facts, I suppose—golden hair, brown curls, that sort of thing—and the instructions for using the pocket watch were all exact." He lifted the glass toward William as if in acknowledgement. "But for the rest, journals lie. No one truly is the way they tell their own story."

William felt as though he had swallowed ice. Maxwell, once more contemplating the empty bottle, seemed unaware of what he had said—or almost said. William cleared his throat very carefully. "You learned to use your pocket watch from instructions in a journal?"

Maxwell nodded as though it were obvious. "There was no one nearby to teach me."

William let the breath out, drew another one. "I thought you'd said your parents were time travelers?"

"They were. I received a trunkful of their effects after my aunt's death—when my cousin inherited her house. His wife came across it while cleaning out the garret. Just after my thirtieth birthday, that was. Among other items of less interest, the trunk held a stack of journals no one had ever bothered to open and a pocket watch—" He waved at William's waistcoat. "—that obviously no one had ever popped open either. And suddenly...quite a lot made sense that never had before. It was like watching a door swing open. I read through the journals they had kept of their adventures—my father was a methodical man, and it was he who wrote enough about the watch that I could infer how it worked—but my mother wrote only of adventures. Fables, one might have thought, or adventure stories such as boys read, except there was the watch to prove it true. Doors opening in dazzling profusion all around me. I wanted to...do the sort of things they had done."

William was rationing his breaths so carefully each one hurt. "You knew them only from the journals?"

"They died when I was small."

"Died?"

"Vanished," Maxwell said, "actually. My aunt told me they died abroad, but I discovered later there had been more of mystery to it than that."

"And—and did you solve the mystery, once you had the journals?"

Maxwell shrugged. "I did not arrive at a certain solution, but I was able to make an educated guess. In her last entry, my mother wrote of wanting to see the court of Henry VIII, and, well, it's easy enough to see what happened in consequence. Or some of what happened in consequence, at least. I'm missing a portion of the story, obviously, for the watch somehow made it back when they did not, but...the court of Henry VIII was one of the first places I tried to go." He downed the last of the brandy in his glass, and added, "I tried over and over and over again. I can't make the watch take me there. There is nothing I can do to save her."

So you've spent the rest of your life trying to save everything else, William thought bleakly.

"She was brave," Maxwell said. "Outspoken. She never shied from meeting head-on what needed to be met—and he was brave too, in a different way; he never gave up until a solution was found. I learned that from their journals, the way they spoke of each other. All I could think, all these years, is that they would have known what to do. No one would ever apply the word 'ineffectual' to either of them. Except—" He turned bleary eyes to the leather-bound volume sitting closed in front of William. "—journals lie. No one's really so perfect, seen close."

No, William thought, *no one is. The Lord Seward of Katarina's description flawlessly executed every plan, and the Kent I've come to know is only just holding it together with a hundred tradeoffs. The man who saved us so spectacularly in an alleyway our first night in London drew Elizabeth's anger later for, after all, only improvising as he went along. Disillusionment is the order of the day. Journals lie. And you didn't want Elizabeth to see whose picture was in your locket. Dear God.*

He could ask. He could ask right now, and Maxwell, well past too drunk to have control of his tongue, would answer. If he asked, Maxwell would answer.

William moistened dry lips. "How old were you, when they vanished?"

"Just over a year, so I am told."

God. "This was—what, 1820 or 1821?"

"Autumn 1819."

So he had truly been born in 1818. Somewhere in the north of England—one might as well assume that was true as well. To a mother who was brave and outspoken and whose child had no memory of her, God have mercy. What was the next question? *Whose face is in your locket? How did you know at once we were time travelers? What is your full name?* Anything he asked, Maxwell would answer.

At the end of the corridor, at the edge of William's awareness, a key scraped in the lock of the warehouse's door. Maxwell looked up, tensing suddenly at the possibility of danger, shaking off the outermost layer of the drunkenness that weighed him down. "It's all right," William soothed him, but the moment had broken like a pricked soap bubble. The sound of footsteps followed the sound of the key, and then Kent's weary, unshaven face poked around the doorway, Schwieger's equally pale and bristled one hovering at his elbow.

"Any of that left?" Kent asked, nodding toward the bottle.

Maxwell tipped it experimentally, then looked surprised at its lightness. "There doesn't seem to be."

Kent did raise his eyebrows at that, but did not pursue the subject of his guest's ill manners. "I suppose it is not as though I need it to sleep in any case," he said instead.

"No news?" William ventured.

"None. Except of the negative sort, I suppose. I can tell you a great many places Katarina is not." Kent sighed. "All well here?"

"All's—quiet, at least," William said. He could not bring himself to call it "well," not even for courtesy's sake. Not when Katarina might be stirring up Wellington monsters against them even now. Not when the first of Trevelyan's construct army hunkered malevolently in the laboratory down the corridor. Not with Maxwell's unintentional confession ringing in his ears. The pocket watch ought to provide a means of making it right, William thought in a rush of despair, but without Palmer's dossiers to point the way, the past presented itself as a tightly woven tapestry, not a collection of threads that might be tugged free or detangled.

When Maxwell drunkenly insisted it was his turn to look after the pocket watch, William let him take it. Maxwell wasn't fit to have charge of it, of course, but there was nothing to be gained in pointing that out, and William knew he wouldn't sleep in any case. He didn't sleep through Elizabeth's guard shift either, and then it was his turn again. By the time it was once again Maxwell's responsibility to guard the watch, the older man was sober (and recovered from his headache), and William could scarcely keep his eyes open. He collapsed into sleep without a second thought.

Chapter 8

London, September 2, 1885

A hand on his shoulder woke him. His dry eyes blinked open, flinched closed again at the glare from the candle. Kent shifted without speaking, interposing his cool shadow between William's eyelids and the attack of the light, and William was sufficiently grateful to attempt opening his eyes again. The light was mostly behind Kent now, lighting his tawny hair with a halo of gold and shrouding his face like a veil. He waited a moment or two, fingers still warm on William's shoulder, watching William's face. Then, apparently satisfied the younger man would stay awake, Kent removed his hand. William brought the words from what seemed an immense distance: "What—time's it?"

Kent did not move to consult a pocket watch. "About an hour after sunset."

Just over halfway into William's selected sleep period, which went a long way to explaining the difficulty he was experiencing in rousing himself. So why was Kent rousing him? He looked at the older man more sharply, but Kent was not nearly agitated enough for there to be an emergency. So why—?

"My people have brought me a list of three likely theaters featuring newly hired dark-haired singers," Kent said in a whisper calculated not to disturb the sleeping Elizabeth next door. "I want you to come with me tonight."

"You want me to come?" William repeated. "Why?"

"It's asking for trouble to go walking alone in that part of the city," Kent answered. "I need a companion—a stirrup-man, if you will—and Schwieger is out scouting again."

"I can't do anything to help you in a fight," William pointed out, struggling upright. "I thought you had an organization full of bodyguards?"

Kent sighed. "Not any I particularly want to witness the conversation I must have with Katarina if we catch her. You already know the worst of what lies between us; you saw it yourself. Indeed—" The intense blue eyes narrowed, shrewd and considering. "—by your own account, you came closer to changing her mind than I would have imagined possible. It might be better that you approach her tonight, since you seem to know how to reach her."

"I did a poor job of it last time—" William said in automatic self-deprecation, but he was already levering himself up off the mattress. By chance or by design—probably the latter—Kent had offered bait he found irresistible. Yes, William wanted to talk to her again. He had to talk to her again. He had to know how badly he had misunderstood her, how badly he had overestimated his new skill at persuasion, how badly he had failed in that first attempt to reach her.

"Elizabeth is asleep," Kent continued, still softly. "Maxwell is on watch and, for a wonder, sober, perhaps because we're out of brandy. He can look after her."

William paused in the act of reaching for his boots. "They are not to come along?"

Kent leveled a look at him. "There will be enough quick tempers in this confrontation already—enough hotheadedness in Katarina's skin. I don't need to double or triple my chances of disaster, and I could hardly bring a girl like Elizabeth to theaters like this in any case. No. They stay here." He turned for the stairway. "Step lightly. That fourth step creaks, remember."

William did remember. He managed to avoid creaking the fourth step by skipping it entirely, and he otherwise moved as silently as he could manage.

Which was apparently not quite silent enough. Halfway down the stairs, he heard movement behind him.

"William?"

Damn.

He turned enough to look back up the stairs. Elizabeth stood just at the top, blanket wrapped around herself, curls in wild disarray, feet bare. Her voice was smeary with sleep, and he wasn't sure her eyes were all the way open. "Where are you going?" she asked, sounding very uncertain. "What's happening? Is there something wrong?"

William hesitated. Kent, a step below him and likely invisible to Elizabeth's limited range of vision, reached out in the darkness to give William's forearm a silent warning squeeze. William looked back at him, and saw Maxwell watching the entire scene from the lamplit corridor below. The white-haired man shook his head once.

He didn't like lying to her, but they were right, both of them. William turned back. "Nothing's wrong," he soothed. "All's well. Go back to sleep."

She frowned at him, rather vaguely. He was becoming more convinced every instant that she wasn't in any meaningful way awake. "Yes," she said after a moment, and turned back. He didn't breathe again until he heard her lie down.

And then he almost called her back. It hardly felt right, after all they had done together so far, to tell her an untruth now, even one so passive. He stood irresolute on the stair for a full count of five before Kent's quiet voice recalled him to himself. William hesitated one breath longer, then followed Kent to the door. Very likely they would return before Elizabeth had awakened in any case.

*

A second thunderstorm had passed through the previous afternoon, leaving pools of stagnant water to warm on the streets and yet still doing nothing to break the heat of the air. William walked straight through a rain-puddle before Kent could stop him, and bit back a curse at the water splashing his trousers.

Kent unsheathed the dark lantern—a little late, from William's perspective, but at least the rest of the journey would not be hazardous. The streets were as dark as London in some other century. The lantern-light pricked out a pattern in the water on the cobblestones. William followed where Kent led.

Once out of the warehouse district, the streets proved livelier than they had been in the deathly still early morning. Curfew had not yet chimed, and the few patrolling soldiers William saw did not seem disposed to prevent those men with coin to spend from spending it in any manner they chose. Not that there was much to buy—the shops Kent led him past had largely bare front windows, largely empty shelves. Only here and there did unappetizing foodstuffs stare back at him—limp-looking fish, pale pigs' feet, skinned sheep's-heads. Perhaps because of this scarcity, the tavern at the end of the street appeared to be doing a thriving business. By the smell, it was offering some greasy meal to go with the gin. Outside, girls dressed in nothing to speak of called to passers-by. William found himself profoundly grateful not to hear Katarina's throaty tones issuing from any of their painted mouths. At least they weren't searching for her among that company.

Kent led him under the torch that blazed out front and through a cloud of cheap tobacco smoke generated by the loafers bantering with the painted girls. A faded sign proclaimed the tavern to be the something "and Bottle"; William didn't have light to see the top word. The window facing the street was papered with bills he also had no light to read properly, but they seemed to have something to do with promising a performance. So this was the music hall. No, they could certainly not have taken Elizabeth here. Not dressed as a boy, not dressed as herself, not in any guise.

Immediately within the door, a steep and narrow staircase loomed. Kent mounted it without hesitation, and William followed. At the turn halfway up, a man in clean, if cheap, finery presided over a box half full of coins. "'Evening, gents, fifty centimes for the dress circle," he greeted them. "Or pay a franc and enjoy the pleasures of the box seats."

Kent rummaged in his pocket, clicking coins suggestively. "I heard you have a new singer," he said. "Dark-haired girl?"

"Indeed we do. Pretty lass, well worth hearing. Fifty centimes for the dress circle, franc for the box seats."

Kent handed him two silver coins, and the man lifted the barrier. "Right this way," he said, bowing them through and gesturing up the staircase. "First show's just about to start."

Rowdy voices drifted down the stairs, and at the top they found their way blocked by a chattering crowd of men in laborer's clothing. Kent shouldered briskly through, and none of them appeared to take offense to being jostled. William followed in his wake. Kent turned abruptly right and ducked into a partitioned recess, where two benches sat on either side of a rather battered-looking table. The benches boasted neither cushions nor backs, but Kent gestured him to sit. These were apparently the box seats. William gingerly lowered himself onto a bench, half expecting it to give way beneath his weight, relieved when it responded with nothing more disastrous than a creak. He looked around and identified the stage, presently draped with a dingy blue curtain. Behind him, the standing crowd—occupying what apparently passed for a dress circle—pushed and called greetings to each other and took occasional, furtive puffs of pipes. The smoke twined up into the still air and hung there. William had been to fine theaters and—er—less fine ones, among genteel crowds and unruly brother soldiers, in England and abroad, but he had never been to one so depressing.

It was better once the show began. Accompanied by a jangling pianoforte and rather better-played fiddle, singers dressed in something approximating cheap finery offered a series of comic songs no more offensive than any William had heard at music halls in his own time. A pair of good-looking redheaded girls performed a step dance; the fiddle player gave a solo; and then, with some fanfare, announced their "new talent, the lovely Miss Alice Yates."

It wasn't Katarina. This girl was younger, pretty rather than possessing anything like Katarina's elegant beauty, singing in a sweet and tuneful and utterly unremarkable voice. Kent stayed until the show was over anyway—out of politeness to Miss Yates, William assumed, although it might also have been due to a reluctance to push back through the dress circle or a fear that there might have been two new dark-haired singers debuting this night. He was on his feet almost as soon as the curtain touched the dusty boards of the stage, however, and William followed his long strides down the stairs and out of the theater.

"One down, two to go," Kent said. "We'll try The Eagle and Crown next. Quick march, and we'll be able to reach it before the second show starts."

The name ought to have told him what to expect, but William did not make the connection until they topped the stairs of the second establishment and beheld their way blocked by a crowd of men in blue coats. He felt himself stiffen all over, and Kent, beside him, closed a hand over his arm.

They didn't shoulder through the crowd this time, William noted distantly, mostly preoccupied with the effort of keeping any reaction from reaching his face. Instead, Kent ducked through gaps and offered apologies in French whenever his shoulder happened to brush that of a man in uniform. He had not reserved a box seat this time either; William, looking around, observed all of those to be taken by soldiers. Right—so they must take care not to draw undue attention. William therefore set his feet, set his teeth, and turned his eyes toward the stage. Blue uniforms pressed against him on every side. French conversations rose around him, smothering.

The girls who tripped out onto the stage were attired as one might expect would appeal to a houseful of soldiers, and gave a performance that raised raucous calls from their audience. William had not previously observed any young lady raise her foot to the level of her eye—certainly not a row of them, in time with music—and other under circumstances might have found the sight diverting, but he disliked exceedingly playing a member of a French audience watching English girls disport themselves so. The next act seemed at first to be better—a duet of girls, one fair and one dark, singing some fairly innocuous song that had the audience joining in for the chorus—until something in the quality of their faces made William start to wonder. Were they—could they possibly be—

"Yes," Kent murmured in his ear. "They're boys. Don't react."

They were followed by a girl who was indisputably a girl—she removed enough of her clothing over the course of her song for William to be absolutely certain of that fact. Also dark-haired, but not, thank God, Katarina either. Then came a comedic sketch, mostly in French, which William followed well enough to wish he did not.

When the program moved on to the singing of patriotic songs—involving all of the singers so far presented, boys and girls, and prompting the audience to roar back during the chorus—Kent squeezed William's arm, and they escaped.

"Well," Kent said, sucking in air as though his throat pained him or perhaps his gorge was rising, "that's degraded some since last I attended a performance."

"Did you really expect Katarina to take employment here?" William demanded.

"Who do you think has the money to hire new performers?" Kent said. "I expected her to take employment at The Bridge and Bottle, frankly. I was clinging to the hope we would not have to go to the Ten Bells. She's too good for that place. But if she needed work and they were hiring—" He sighed, and started down the street. "It's worth a few minutes, if we can get in while the show is still on."

The third tavern proved to be a fair walk from the second, and down streets it became clear Kent did not know well. He had handled himself with easy confidence as they approached the other two music halls, but in this part of town his confidence was more of a deliberate projection. His eyes flicked incessantly to alleyways, storefronts, street signs, and he let out a mostly stifled breath of relief when the tavern rose up before them at last.

It had not been painted any time this century, as far as William could tell. The sign had nearly rotted away, displaying only "ell" to his questing eyes. "Hell," perhaps. Even the torch stuck outside smoldered in a sullen way.

Inside was even worse. The fine decorative tile that had once graced the entryway was now stained and cracked. Guttering candlelight hindered rather than aided attempts to see further than a hand span before one's face. At least the disgruntled mutter of voices enjoining Kent to close the door were all speaking English.

Though the second show of the night was halfway through, the tables were nothing like fully occupied. Kent's coin bought them one in a discreet corner with a reasonable view of the raised platform that served as a sort of stage. Upon it, a blonde woman well past her first youth was singing some maudlin love song in a cracked soprano. She was followed by a mouse-haired girl who didn't look more than fourteen and didn't sing any better than her older counterpart. Kent ordered two glasses of gin, perhaps because he needed the fortification for what lay ahead, and they settled down to wait.

William knew it was her the moment she stepped onto the stage, despite the unhelpfully guttering candles. He was somewhat surprised to find he could recognize her silhouette when she had bound and padded it to make it male, but apparently he could, for he was sure of her before she opened her mouth. The husky rich voice was an unnecessary confirmation.

She was dressed in clothing that appeared to be intended to represent a wealthy gentleman's evening dress, and she performed a sketch, parts sung and parts spoken in an exaggerated French accent, about the lazy and luxurious life it was her—his?—privilege to lead. The meager audience chuckled in parts, but overall seemed too resentful of the truth behind the comedy to remember to find the exaggeration amusing.

They liked it better when she got to the end of the description of her persona's daily life, and began to mime undressing for bed. Some of the men dispersed about the tables might well have not recognized her for a woman in disguise until that moment. They laughed and applauded as she stripped off the bulky coat, undid the tie, unbuttoned the shirt almost to its midpoint, and as a final touch, pulled off the topper and shook down her cascade of dark hair.

Kent's fingers drummed the table before them. "She's too good for this," he muttered.

With her hair down, her coat off, and her shirt half-unbuttoned, Katarina embarked upon the second song in her repertoire. In this, she portrayed herself as a woman—a daring woman, holding up an invisible skirt to go wading in the sea, inviting the audience to imagine her trousered legs bare. The skirt went up—and up—and up—and the men in the tables leaned forward as though she were indeed about to reveal something indecent. She did not, even in mime, dropping the invisible hem chastely back to her ankles just as the song ended. The audience grumbled and laughed in equal parts, leaning back in their chairs and exchanging remarks with each other.

So it went on. Her next two songs were recognizable as versions of the ones that had been sung in the "Bridge and Battle," but with hand motions and inflections that rendered them tawdry instead of sweet. As a finale, she offered something that sounded for all the world like a children's song, resuming with startling ease the posture of a young man, though she left her coat off and her hair unbound.

"Half a pound of tupenny rice," she sang, picking up an imaginary bag with her right hand and setting it in the crook of her left arm. "Half a pound of treacle." Another bag added to the first. "That's the way the money goes—" Her left hand pulled her pocket inside-out, proving it empty. She shrugged, and picked up her abandoned coat from the chair she had flung it over. She held it out as though to the audience. "Pop goes the weasel!"

"Weasel and stoat," Kent murmured inexplicably. "'Popping the weasel' is slang for pawning one's overcoat. Usually to buy food."

Katarina had set down her imaginary bags of provisions, and now sauntered down the stage with her coat over her shoulder. "All along the City Road," she said, and William recognized the words of the rhyme she had made brief reference to in Yorkshire. "In and out the Eagle." She tipped the contents of an imaginary glass down her throat. "That's the way the money goes—" The proof of empty pockets again, and once more she held out her coat. "Pop goes the weasel!"

The audience chuckled its understanding and approval. Katarina flashed them all a suddenly very feminine smile, and set the coat down. She minced back across the stage, clearly as a woman, hips swaying, finger teasing the unbuttoned edges of her shirt. When she opened her mouth again, even her voice had changed—still throaty, but now with a velvet edge. "Up and down the City Road…"

William was reminded of the women on the street corners outside the Bridge and Bottle and the Eagle and Crown. The rest of the audience was apparently reminded of the same thing, judging from the comments they called.

Katarina grinned, picked up the chair on which she had draped her coat, swung it around so that its back was toward the audience, and straddled it. "Up and down the Eagle." The audience roared. "That's the way the…money comes." She grinned as they laughed. "Pop goes the weasel!" It was very obvious that she was no longer speaking of pawnbroking.

Kent drummed his fingers harder.

Katarina jumped up again, recaptured her masculine posture, and propped one foot on the chair. "All along the eastern coast, the lion blows the bugle. That's the way the Eagle falls—"

William froze.

"Pop goes the weasel!" Katarina's smile was steely edged now. Her hands mimed settling a rifle against her shoulder and firing it, and William thought of Palmer, fighting for five years all along the eastern coast.

"Half a pound of tupenny rice," she finished. "Half a pound of treacle. Cockerel for Sunday tea—"

"Is the cockerel still the symbol of France?" William asked in a whisper.

Kent's teeth flashed white in the dimness. "Not of the Empire, but of France herself—indeed it is."

"Pop goes the weasel!"

Most of the audience seemed to appreciate the sentiment, applauding and muttering, but a few shifted uneasily. Katarina's eyes swept over them, and she laughed, feminine once again. "I've no time to plead and pine. I've no time to wheedle. Kiss me quick and then I'm gone—" She blew an exaggerated kiss to the audience, and caught up her coat. "Pop goes the weasel!" She was off the stage almost before the last syllable left her throat.

"Get up," Kent said, just loud enough to be heard over the wave of applause. "We'll wait for her by the stage door out back."

*

Elizabeth stared at Maxwell over the globe of the lamp. "Gone to find Madam Katherine? But—but I asked him and he said—William lied to me?"

"He said what was needful to keep you safely here," Maxwell told her. The lamp light glinted on the chain of the pocket watch at his waist, his to care for. His folded hands rested atop Viktor Frankenstein's journal. A teacup—not a brandy glass—was just visible in the outermost ring of light. Maxwell was washed and brushed and neat today, and his calm brown eyes regarded her with the air of a schoolmaster—the air of the man in command. He had looked that way in the alley the first night, and she had taken the act for truth then, but much had happened since.

"He lied," Elizabeth repeated. "So did you. So did Frederick Kent. How dare you?"

"I believe Kent phrased it as not wishing to have a loose cannon aboard his ship," Maxwell replied. "Clever turn of phrase, that. If you had known, you would have wanted to come. If he had denied you permission, you would have taken matters into your own hands. And we really can't afford to hand any more victories to the French."

"I've done nothing you have not done," Elizabeth shot back, "except to succeed where you failed. You don't know better than I what is best to be done. Your judgment is not more valuable than mine—"

"I am three times your age at least," Maxwell snapped. "I have been traveling for longer than you have been alive."

"—fine, then perhaps it is now, but it certainly wasn't when you first began traveling. You think you know better than everyone. You thought you did even at the beginning. I'm not a pawn in your chess game, Mr. Maxwell, or don't you understand that? You can't move me into position, assume I'll stay there, and declare your aim achieved! I've as much soul and mind and heart as you, as much right to move myself about the board!"

"Because that worked so well at Waterloo?"

"You were the one who insisted on handling Waterloo in a twenty-four-hour scramble! William and I both wanted to arrive earlier, find a way to talk with the Duke, and explain to him what actions of his would lead to the future we had seen! But you assumed—implied—you said we could not trust him to act as he ought. And by that you meant, we could not trust him to act as you wanted him to. As though the Duke of Wellington were a pawn on a chessboard too, to be coaxed into position with a carrot or bludgeoned from behind with a whip. Have you ever dealt straightly with anyone? You sent me a pocket watch but chose not to share your knowledge of its power. You chloroformed John Freemantle rather than sharing knowledge with the man who commanded him. You tried to kidnap Brenda Trevelyan instead of delivering a plain warning—"

Maxwell slammed closed Frankenstein's journal and stood up with a suddenness that knocked his chair to the floor.

"—you blindfold all of us and tie our hands and push us into place, and then you're surprised when we react by fighting for freedom! You're angry when our struggles unbalance your idea of—"

He was already through the doorway. His boots struck the stairs with furious emphasis. If there had been a door upstairs, he would surely have slammed it.

"—of what should be," Elizabeth finished, addressing the empty room. "I am so *tired* of *everyone* treating me this way! Petting and tricking and deceiving me into doing what they think I should." She jerked Maxwell's abandoned chair upright, plumped herself down in it, and flipped open the cover of Frankenstein's journal.

When Emil Schwieger returned some three-quarters of an hour later, Elizabeth was still sitting furiously upright in Maxwell's chair, turning each leaf of the notebook after an angrily precise interval.

Schwieger paused in the doorway, a greeting on his lips, then stopped short. "Has something happened, Miss Elizabeth? Where is everyone?"

"'Everyone' is pursuing plans from which I have been excluded," Elizabeth said. "That's what has happened," she explained, and Schwieger winced in sympathy.

His bright blue eyes moved about the room. "Where is the pocket watch? Is it not your turn to guard it?"

"Maxwell has it with him." Elizabeth gestured to the loft above, and Schwieger followed the wave of her hand with his eyes. For a moment, she thought he would excuse himself and mount the stairs, but instead, after a slight hesitation, he entered the sitting room. He paused at the table, hand hovering as though to draw back the chair to her right.

"May I?"

"Oh, of course." How nice that someone asked her permission for *something*. Schwieger drew the chair back, seated himself, and glanced at her reading material.

"Unfair of Herr Maxwell to carry off the pocket watch," he offered. "Since it was first your possession, if I correctly understand?"

"No," she admitted grudgingly. "That one is in fact his possession. I destroyed mine."

Schwieger looked startled. "You did? How could you possibly?"

"It's…rather a long story."

Schwieger smiled a little. "I have an hour at least before I have to go back out on patrol." He paused in an inviting sort of way.

Elizabeth hesitated, trying to decide if she wanted to begin the recital.

"I intended to make some tea, to have with my supper," Schwieger added. "Would you like a cup?"

It sounded homey and comforting and very nice indeed. Some of the anger drained from her skin. "Well—thank you, yes." She stood as he did, and began her story as they made their way to the scullery.

It was complicated enough to fill all the time it took Schwieger to measure tea and then all the time they waited for the kettle to boil. Elizabeth reached her conclusion just as the first whistle pierced the air, and Schwieger shook his head in wonder, pouring. He handed her one of the cups, and they returned to the table in the sitting room.

"These pocket watches," Schwieger said, "they defy understanding. Where did you acquire such a magical device, if not through Mr. Maxwell?"

She started to say, *In fact, it was through Mr. Maxwell,* then decided she would rather not tread that story all the way through again. "It was sent to me at my father's house in Hartwich. No letter of explanation, nothing to identify the sender."

"Extraordinary. And where did Herr Maxwell acquire his?"

"He found it in a garret, he says."

"Is that all the explanation he gave? He did not say where the garret was, or the year?"

Elizabeth shook her head, surprised at his intensity. "Why does it matter?"

"A device may be unique," Schwieger said, "but if there are two, there are usually more than two. I cannot help wondering if there are objects of magic and power scattered throughout Britain—or Europe. In garrets, perhaps. If there are more to be found, I should rather like to know where. I should also like to know where they came from in the first place. Is it not a cause for your curiosity as well?"

"I suppose it will be eventually," Elizabeth said. "My attention has been… consumed by more immediate problems."

He smiles. "Fighting monsters and disarming constructs. A heavy burden for one so young."

It would have annoyed her from Maxwell, and from Katarina it had made her throat tighten, but something in Schwieger's voice made Elizabeth smile. "You're no older than I am," she pointed out, mock-offended. "Are you?"

"Ah!" He grinned a little. "I cannot tell. A great secret madame."

For some reason that made her want to smile again, though she could not have said why it was amusing.

"It was really that bad, under the constructs?" Schwieger went on.

"Really truly," Elizabeth said. She did not feel like smiling now. "And before that, it was really truly that bad under the monsters you wish returned to life."

Schwieger's smile took on a grim edge. "The monsters I once wished returned to life," he corrected. "That option is no longer open to me, thanks to Katarina."

"Or to some unknown enemy," Elizabeth reminded him.

Schwieger nodded. "I am not sure which option I like less," he said after a time, looking down into his teacup. "Is it worse to think our comrade could act so? Or is it worse to think some enemy of Palmer's took the notes and the Imperials will soon be crafting monsters against us?" He tilted the cup so that the lamp-light gleamed against the tea, then rotated it slowly, watching the gleam trail along the surface of the liquid. "If the latter—perhaps it is just as well Trevelyan has started to walk his present course. You said, in the other

London, his constructs were all that allowed Englishmen to defend themselves against the monsters?"

"No," Elizabeth said, "no, no—that is, yes, you recall correctly, but that was how it all started in the other London as well. You must not return to that path."

"But the path is malleable, surely? We might use Trevelyan's tool differently. And it is just a tool, is it not? It matters for what purpose it is used. The evil is in the brain that directs the hand, not the tool in the hand's grip."

"Not this tool." Elizabeth shook her head, refusing to yield an inch. "A tool that confers such tremendous power—it—it—summons men who will misuse it. The men of that other London, those who built constructs to fight monsters—Trevelyan himself—did not intend constructs to ever be used against Englishmen, but the 'wheel turned itself,' Lord Seward said."

Schwieger studied her. "So you truly believe the only solution is to prevent the initial construction of the self-turning wheel. You truly believe that."

Elizabeth nodded. "Yes."

"I suppose I must trust your judgment," he said, "since you observed the other London and I did not." Had anyone ever placed trust in her judgment? Elizabeth felt a little dizzy, thinking about it. "You thought to do so by indirect methods," Schwieger went on, "by recreating the sequence of events so no one would ever think to build the first construct. Kent is a great proponent of indirect methods—as is Maxwell, apparently. But you—" He smiled at her, blue eyes brilliant in the lamp-light. "I think you are more like me. I prefer direct action. I think you do as well." He hesitated a moment. "The wheel does not turn itself yet," he said. "It has not yet made its first revolution. Therefore, a direct act can still prevent that first revolution from ever taking place." He set the teacup down. "I believe I can offer you a better alternative than Maxwell's indirection."

*

"Go around the corner and meet her at the back door," Kent said as they reached the mouth of the alleyway that stretched behind the Ten Bells. "I'll wait here."

William stopped still. "You'll what?"

Kent prodded him back into motion. "She might well run if she sees me, but she's not afraid of you."

No, William thought with an inward grimace, of course she wasn't afraid of him. She had proven that outside Palmer's house. *Am I bait?*

"You'll be able to coax her into a reasonable state of mind," Kent continued with another nudge.

Right, because he had done so brilliant a job of that back in Yorkshire. *Yes, I'm bait.* He considered telling Kent what he thought about that, but it was more important they talk with Katarina than that he stand upon his dignity. William gritted his teeth and stepped into the alleyway.

The torchlight of the street was dim enough, but he was night-blind without it. Anything at all could have been lurking in the darkness before him. He picked his way step by step over slimy cobblestone and piles of muck, eyes fixed on the small spill of light from the lamp in the Ten Bells' back window.

The door beside it swung open while William had still half of the distance yet to traverse. *Katarina,* he thought, and made to quicken his step, but the figure was too short and slight. She turned her head, and the lamplight shone for an instant on her face. The little mouse-haired singer.

"'Evening, love," a voice from the shadows greeted her.

Of course there would be other men besides William waiting outside the stage door. He should have expected that. Young men assembled outside stage doors everywhere, to meet the girls who had lately been performing and invite them out to supper. Of course it would be so here as well as everywhere else.

Not that this man seemed so very young, though. Something in the voice, and in the bulk, suggested middle age. Nor was he issuing anything so mealy-mouthed as a supper invitation. The girl shrank back from him, uttering what certainly sounded to William like a mew of dismay, and the man stepped to close the gap between them, pressing her up against the wall. The lamplight shone on his greasy black hair.

This is really no business of mine, William thought. Moreover, if he got into a fight with this man, he would surely lose, and might well cost them their only chance to speak with Katarina. It was not his business, and there were much larger problems to hand that needed his attention.

There had been much larger problems needing his attention when he escorted Christopher Palmer to the infirmary, too. And when he had fetched the child Meg out of Murchinson's. William sighed, and lengthened his stride.

"All right there, miss?" he called.

The black-haired man jerked around, but without loosening his grip on the girl.

From the other side of the lamplight, a second man—just as large, this one with iron-gray hair—stepped into William's range of vision. "Keep walking," he advised.

William stood still. "If the young lady asks me to leave, of course I will." He pitched his voice a little louder than was natural. They would probably take it for nervousness—and they wouldn't be wrong, as far as it went, but he was also hoping to attract some attention. Kent's, by preference, but someone from inside might do as well.

"I said keep walking," the gray-haired man growled.

"I'm waiting for someone who sings here," William said, still too loudly. He glanced from side to side as surreptitiously as he could. There was a small crate visible atop the refuse to his left side, empty, half broken, wooden slats splintered. Not much of a weapon, but it might do. "She's a handsome woman, tall, dark hair." Was there, he wondered with rising irritation, some reason Kent was not coming to offer his services? "Perhaps you'd like to wait with me, miss?" he added to the girl.

The little singer gave a gasp, and then all at once started to struggle. The black-haired man shoved her back up against the wall, holding her without effort, and his companion took a step toward William. His big hands balled into fists, and a smile showed more teeth missing than present. William tried not to break eye contact as he lunged to catch up the crate.

A crack like breaking ice split the stillness, and the iron-haired man jumped and swore, shaking his right hand as though something had passed close enough to sting it. William turned the lunge into a duck, folding himself against the wall, out of range. His eye just caught the glint of lamplight off the barrel of the pistol aimed through the window. The black-haired man saw it too and backed away, letting go of the girl so suddenly she almost fell.

The whip-crack split the air again, once, twice, and one of the men yelped with pain. Both of them took off running after that, and the mouse-haired girl scuttled off in the opposite direction. William scrambled upright just as Kent came pounding up behind him—finally—and the stage door opened to reveal Katarina's furious set face and dead-steady pistol.

There was no sound except for three people's quickened breathing, as Kent and his former lieutenant faced each other. The dark eyes did not flicker, and nor did the blue.

"Who were you aiming at?" Kent bit off at last.

For a moment, Katarina did not seem to understand the question, but then her eyes went wide. "I was aiming at precisely what I hit!" She added, "And you're both welcome, I'm sure," before deliberately lowering her arm.

"I think my confusion is understandable," Kent said. He folded his arms for all the world as though there was not an angry armed woman just before him, for all the world as though there had not been a nearly deadly conflict in this alleyway a moment ago. "You seem to have declared yourself an enemy to me and mine."

"Kent," William said, "I thought we came here to talk reasonably—"

"Ask William Carrington here how he left Christopher Carter," Kent barreled over him. "Ask him what effect your fire had on the old man's health."

"*My* fire?" Katarina stared at him. "Who's been telling you lies? I never set it. Charles West knocked over his candle—"

Kent shook his head. "I might have believed that if your theft had not been discovered."

"That—my—That was a different matter altogether." The look on Katarina's face was something between impatience and shame. "The fire was no help to me. It almost destroyed my chances of getting away clean. Why would I choose to give myself fewer hours of quiet in which to run? Yes—" Her eyes went to William. "—I picked the time traveler's pocket. I confess that. I took the watch." She did not look down to her belt, but the hand that did not hold the pistol dropped to caress something that hung there. "Quite a Celtic tale," she added, almost conversationally. "I sold my honor for a worthless trinket. My entire life up in smoke and nothing to show for it but a broken thing I can't even pawn. We walk forward blindfolded, always, trusting the path we walk to take us to the destination we've chosen, and sometimes we choose very badly indeed." She sighed. "I certainly would not have chosen this consequence if I had been able to see it. Did you know the watch was worthless, Mr. Carrington, when you faced me in the garden?"

"I did," William said.

"Was there some reason you did not say so at once?"

"I did not..." William hesitated. "I didn't want that to be the reason you came inside."

Katarina breathed half a laugh. The lamplight glinted on her loose hair, on the pistol in her hand. "Well, yes. I suppose I see that. You would hardly have been able to sleep easily any night following."

"I don't mean it that way," William said. "Or at least, not only that way. I wanted you to come in because you—because I—Because you give people second chances. Children taken to match factories, Peninsula veterans with missing arms—And you deserved one of your own. I owed you at least that."

Katarina watched him. He could not read her expression. "Then I think," she said, "I must thank you for offering me the chance to choose differently."

"Madam," William said, swallowing, "it was the very least I could do."

"Does that mean you trust my word, William Carrington?"

He met her dark eyes. "Yes."

"For some unknown reason," Kent cut in acidly. "He may, but I do not."

"You don't believe Wilton could have knocked over his own candle?" William protested. "Or that Palmer's enemies could have—?"

"Not the latter, certainly. Think, Carrington. You went looking for Katarina after you tangled with Schwieger. You and Schwieger both went looking, outward from the house, trying to find her footprints by the rising sun."

"We followed them for a short way," William agreed, "but then she cut across a field."

"But that short way was dirt, was it not? You saw her footprints leading away from the house. Did you find any others leading toward it?"

William closed his eyes, trying to remember. "No," he said, surprised as the realization occurred to him. "I hardly thought about it at the time—I was thinking of following her—"

"No footprints," Kent said. "No outside enemy to set the fire. It was set by someone in the house."

"By Charles Wilton, then," William argued. "As we thought at first. Wilton knocking over his candle."

"That is possible," Kent admitted. "I can see it. He knocked over his candle, he feared for the precious papers, he fetched them from their hiding place. Katarina might have taken them from his hands when she guided him out of the burning building—might not have even realized what she held until later. If that is the truth—" His eyes returned to Katarina's face. "—if my former lieutenant is guilty of only opportunism, all she need do to settle her debt with me is hand me the Frankenstein papers."

"The what?" Katarina's eyes went from one of them to the other. "What," she said then, very carefully, "are we talking about?"

"Chris Palmer hid something priceless in the sundial," William said. "In the morning it was gone. We think Charles Wilton rushed to it when he saw the house in—"

"—house in flames," Katarina finished. "How—odd that the trick should work on him of all people. I suppose he is not who he once was— Frederick." She interrupted herself all at once, as though understanding had abruptly and forcibly descended. Her eyes were suddenly fixed upon Kent's face. "Frederick, it was not I who played that trick upon him. Listen to me. I woke and smelled smoke. At the end of the corridor, I saw flame, and Schwieger getting Mr. West into the garden. I ran upstairs for Mr. Carter and Janet. I went nowhere near the sundial until we all assembled there. I didn't have time." Her words were coming faster now. "Frederick, I don't have your papers. On my honor—what honor I have left, at least—it wasn't I who took them." Her eyes bored into to Kent's. "Do you understand me? If I did not take them, and no enemy's footsteps approached the house, you have a different problem."

*

"We couldn't go in there!" Elizabeth protested, aware even as she said it that her tone lacked something of the necessary conviction. Schwieger apparently heard the lack as well, for his eyes crinkled.

"But we could. We could slip in and away again, and leave behind a solution for this problem you have taken it upon yourself to correct."

"I thought the laboratory was kept locked," Elizabeth faltered.

"It is, but there are locks and there are locks. The proper locks are all on the front door. The one sealing the laboratory is a formality, and I could get it open. And then...only think." Schwieger's voice went low, persuasive. He leaned forward, and his hand went out, almost as if he would lay it over hers, but he stopped just short of that intimacy. "That great hulking enemy of yours has no power yet. It sits there waiting, quiescent. Helpless. We could do...something. Something simple, so that it will fail before the eyes of Trevelyan's investors, so he'll have no backing to build more."

Elizabeth shook her head. "He will certainly repair it."

"Materials are scarce," Schwieger said. "And these emissaries from Russia are due in only a few days. Trevelyan himself does not return until tomorrow midday. In time, perhaps, other emissaries will come, but between now and then, no construct army will be built. Sometimes victory is achieved by holding the line against assault after assault, until reinforcements can arrive—no? Prevent him and prevent him and prevent him, and the terrible future you have witnessed will not come to pass. Come—we can do this now."

"I—" The temptation was momentarily dizzying. So overwhelming was its pull that Elizabeth found herself on her feet without realizing she had made the decision to rise. "I—No. No, wait." Schwieger waited patiently, as she had bidden him, while she struggled to form her thoughts into words.

"That would be as bad as what Mr. Kent did to me tonight," she said. "It would be as bad as what Maxwell does. And what Maxwell does never works as he wishes it to. Of course it does not. Ruin his prototype, and Mr. Trevelyan will make another. Frighten Brenda and she will flee from rescue, thinking it abduction. The only way to change Trevelyan's actions is to change his mind, surely. He must choose not to create the future I saw."

"We all start so," Schwieger said, not unkindly. "Everyone holds fast to ideals in the beginning. Later one realizes that it is sometimes necessary to force the change required, by fair means or foul."

She shook her head, unable to summon an argument, knowing only she did not agree.

"You need not take any action you do not wish to," Schwieger said, and turned away. But something in the briskness of the movement told her he was headed to the laboratory, to force change by foul means. She took a quick step into his path, throwing proper manners to the wind where they belonged and catching hold of his arm.

"Don't," she said. "Wait."

He hesitated.

"Let us discuss it, at least?" she said.

He turned to face her, standing very close indeed. She knew enough of men and women now to read the look on his face. She dropped her gaze from his, trying to decide what to say next, and her eyes fell on the glint of gold at his waist, almost completely hidden by his ragged clothing. In her memory rang Kent's impatient voice, telling Schwieger to leave his pocket watch behind if he was going on patrol dressed as beggar. Why would he take such an obvious risk in defiance of orders?

All at once she felt cold.

"What's this?" she said, before she had time to be afraid of what would happen next. She reached for the glint of gold—trying to remember despite her racing pulse how Katarina might essay this touch, trying to make her questing fingers coquettish as well as curious.

His hand shot out and grabbed her wrist. And then she was sure.

Elizabeth's fingers closed over the watch as Schwieger pushed her away from him, and the timepiece came free with a ripping of cloth. Schwieger swore and grabbed for it, and Elizabeth twisted desperately to get free. Beneath her bandages, the blisters on her palms burned all over again, but she did not let go of the watch.

She got one good look at the golden orb between her bandaged palms— larger than was customary, too heavy for its size, carved with leaves and vines and a bird and the rising sun. Then Schwieger's hand closed over her arm again. Elizabeth kicked at him—and missed—but did knock over one of the chairs, which was almost as good from one point of view, since the noise would surely attract the attention of her comrade upstairs. She would never defeat Schwieger in a physical contest, not without help.

She added her voice to the clatter of the falling chair. "Maxwell!"

Schwieger had her arms now, but she had both hands wrapped around the pocket watch. She bent over it, squirming and straining against the grip bruising her skin, drawing up her knees and folding almost to the floor to shield the watch from his grasp. *No, no, I won't give it back, I won't let you use it here—I don't know what you mean to do—who are you?* "Maxwell!" she shrieked again.

"Elizabeth?" His boots thundered down the stairs. Schwieger got an arm around her chest and forced her upright, using his other hand to pry apart her fingers. She caught a confused glimpse of Maxwell appearing in the doorway, coat off and collar undone, white hair wild.

Elizabeth jerked and wrenched and managed one instant's freedom of movement for her hands. She launched the watch into the air—not well and not far, but it skittered across the floorboards in Maxwell's direction, and he lunged forward and caught it up.

Schwieger released his hold upon her wrists, and Elizabeth tried to follow the watch in a lurching, inelegant bid for freedom. But before she managed to get her stumbling feet underneath her, there was something cold and sharp against her throat.

"I don't want to hurt you." Schwieger's voice grated against her hair. Maxwell had said those very words, that first night in the alleyway, but it hadn't sounded like this. "Don't make me hurt her," he repeated, looking over her head at Maxwell. "Put it down."

Maxwell hesitated what seemed to be an endless moment. He looked down at the pocket watch, open in his hand. The blade pricked against Elizabeth's skin. Maxwell's face tightened, and he tossed the pocket watch onto the dining table.

"Step back," Schwieger ordered.

Maxwell took a step back toward the doorway, arms slightly open, hands held away from his body. "You have what you want," he said. "Now let her go."

Schwieger leaned forward, quick as a striking bird, and caught the timepiece by its chain. Elizabeth fought him for one instant before his grip closed hard again.

"Stop it," Schwieger said to her. "I don't want to hurt you. I didn't come here to hurt anyone." He held her against him with one arm, knife in the other, watch dangling from its chain in his knife hand. "I came for the monster notes. I never wanted anything more, and you locals were never meant to be involved." Elizabeth could only just see how the light danced in little sparks off the watch chain looped over his hand. She could not see the knife at all, of course. "You have no idea what horrific a future this world is hurtling toward! It hasn't happened yet, I can still stop it, you have no idea what we'll start doing to each other twenty-nine years from right now unless someone stops it!"

"Then you have what you came for," Maxwell said, almost calmly. "So let her go."

Schwieger shook his head. "One thing more," he said. "Your watch too."

"That's not yours to take," Maxwell informed him.

The knife whispered against Elizabeth's skin. "It very much is," Schwieger said. "You must be mad if you think I'll leave it in your hands and you free to do more damage. Put it on the table, or she comes home with me as hostage for your good behavior." Maxwell hesitated. "Now!"

Maxwell sagged, dropping his eyes as though in defeat, his hand moving to unfasten the pocket watch from its fob.

But the rest of his body didn't look defeated. Even as his hand moved toward his waistcoat, his shoulders were squaring and his knees bending just slightly, and Elizabeth knew exactly what he meant to do. Maxwell wasn't William, not one to offer a stream of reasonable words until they weakened the resolve of the enemy holding the weapon—not even when the weapon threatened someone dear. Maxwell would act at once, would act boldly, would act before fear could make him hesitate and hesitation could strengthen his enemy's position. It was not always the right approach—Katarina had been right; sometimes you needed to act fast, but other times you needed to take pains—but it was an approach Elizabeth understood without needing a pause for thought. She was exactly the same way herself.

Her boot heel connected with Schwieger's knee at the same moment Maxwell launched himself through the space that separated them. Schwieger staggered, the blade scratched across Elizabeth's skin, and Maxwell crashed into them. The three of them fell in a tangle of limbs. Elizabeth tried to kick free, but someone's elbow drove into her middle, and she fell back, breath gone from her lungs, only dimly realizing it when Maxwell shoved her clear of Schwieger's reaching hands. She heard a fist connect with flesh, and the knife clatter to the floor.

Elizabeth blinked tearing eyes. She saw Schwieger on his back, Maxwell atop him. The older man was trying to pin the young Prussian with his greater weight, but Schwieger had both his hands plunged into Maxwell's collar, fastened around Maxwell's throat. Maxwell's breath came in little coughing gasps, and his face flushed red. He let go Schwieger's shoulders with one hand, then the other, reaching to pry at the choking fingers. Schwieger snatched one of his hands away from Maxwell's collar—and grabbed not for the knife, but for the pocket watch that had fallen beside it.

Elizabeth made a desperate effort to roll upright, retched, and sagged back. Somewhere behind her, a door slammed. She heard running footsteps, Kent's voice shouting something.

Schwieger's hand closed into a fist over his watch, his thumb pushing the side button twice in rapid succession. Maxwell scrabbled to free his own watch from his waistcoat, or his collar from Schwieger's grip, but the young Prussian jammed the top button home. He and Maxwell vanished in a flash—not of light, but a momentary brightening of color, and then a movement as though the air around them had folded itself in half.

Maxwell's locket fell through the space they had been, trailing its broken chain like a shooting star until it clinked to rest on the floorboards.

Interlude

Carmonton, Wales, November 18, 1882

Brenda Evans knew better than to be out by herself after dark on the road between Cardiff and the mines, but one unlucky chance after another had befallen her, and so here she was, a good hour from home yet and the shadows slanting hard toward evening. She thought about turning back, deferring her journey until morning—but she did not personally know anyone who ran a boarding house in Cardiff, and badly choosing her night's accommodation could be as hazardous to her safety as being waylaid on the road. Then there was the expense, and her father would worry. She looked at the sky. Surely she could make it home before full dark. Surely the road could not be so dangerous. She tightened her grip on the reins.

If only her father's chest cold had not laid him low for a solid month, she might have made this journey in October, when the days stretched longer. If only the prices in the miners' store were anything like reasonable, or the selection anything like practical, she might have deferred the journey altogether. But though she could make do with the Bureau store for everyday, she relied upon the annual Cardiff trip for winter necessities, and with her father out three weeks' wages and doctor's bills to pay besides, it was even more needful she pinch francs where she could. Not that Dr. Cadwallader cheated them— quite the contrary; he was neighborly enough; it was his trap she was driving— but he had to live as well as anyone else.

If only she had gotten an earlier start this morning. If only the doctor had not been called out on a case, so that he might have accompanied her as he had first suggested. If only she had managed to find all she needed more quickly— Brenda sighed. "If onlies" did no one any good. Here she was. At least if she was waylaid, there was plenty in the cart other than herself to tempt a man—which was a comfort as cold as the nipping fall air, but better than no comfort at all.

It could easily be so much worse, she knew that. She and her father were, in fact, among the more comfortable residents of Carmonton. There was his pay from the mines, and her pittance from teaching, and only the two of them to feed, so they could put by a bit now and then. Without that savings, and without her teacher's salary, his long illness might have been a disaster rather than merely a trial. A decade ago, it would have been impossible for her to contribute to the household income unless she went to work in the mines herself, but the recent reforms—prompted in part by that horridly condescending young Frenchman—meant that it was no longer lawful to employ small children in the mines. The government Mining Bureau must arrange schooling for the miners' children instead, and must therefore employ an instructor, and so here she was, Miss Evans, the old maid schoolteacher who also kept house for her father.

It wasn't the sort of life she had dreamt of as a child, but it wasn't so bad. Sometimes well-meaning Carmonton women asked if she wouldn't rather be married with a home of her own, and she had even been courted briefly, now and again. By the self-important French reformer, in fact, as well by a young doctor who had briefly worked with Cadwallador, and in an occasional and desultory fashion by Cadwallador himself. She had encouraged none of them, however. It wasn't that she lay awake nights crying for Gavin Trevelyan—not any longer, at least; not for years—but no one else had any savor beside her memory of his sharp gray eyes and deft, clever fingers. She would probably have to marry once her father died, but she had no desire to rush the event.

Cardiff had receded into the distance behind her, and the lights of Carmonton had yet to come into view. The road bent around in a lazy curve, wood to one side and sloping farmland to the other. The low sun cast red light over the barren fields. If she squinted, she would be able to see the church tower of old Pendoylan, where her father's father had farmed before the French came. Pendoylan was there still, as was the surrounding farmland. But now between the main road and the old village lay the shanty-town, where the landless folk lived.

There were too many people in Wales now, as the French in the east drove the English west and west. With so many wanting to till Welsh soil, the Farmland Bureau could set the rents as high as it chose, with predictable results. Those who could not pay were forced off their land. Some, like Brenda's father, went to work in the mines. Others went to scrounge work at the city ports. The rest, not yet desperate enough to leave, scratched what living they could as laborers, and in the evening came home to shacks whose walls leaned drunkenly to one side and whose roofs were hardly enough to keep out the damp. The shanty-town was the last refuge of widowed women, men too ill to work, and men who had been discharged from the mines.

That last group was the most dangerous. Many of them knew her and how she earned her living, and considered her the Bureau's creature. That morning, two had shouted some abuse that Brenda had driven away from as quickly as she dared. That had been in the daylight, and she must now drive past them in the dark—what had she been *thinking*, not turning back to Cardiff while she had the chance?

Sometimes, if she chanced to be out of doors at night in Carmonton, Brenda might have to walk past men from the mines easing their woes in the tavern. She always straightened her back and moved unhurriedly, lest she catch their eyes by scurrying. She straightened her back now and tried to drive the pony-trap the way she walked, and the curve of the road brought her to the edge of the shanty-town.

There was no one lingering in the November chill to see her. They'd gone inside to what meager meals the day's earnings could buy them—she could smell the smoke of their cooking-fires—and she wanted to shake herself for a goose. There was no one here to harm her, and soon she would be home.

A shadow moved from the side of one shanty and Brenda's heart leaped into her throat. In the summer she would have thought nothing of it, but surely there were not leaves enough to cast such a shadow now? She looked more sharply at it, but it was gone. Just a nervous fancy, or someone skulking there and watching her? She hit the pony, but it quickened only briefly before settling back into its usual sullen walk. She glanced back twice as the pony labored up the hill away from the shanty-town, and the second time she thought she saw movement again.

*

But no one sprang from the brush to waylay her. The sky was blue-black when she reined the pony to a stop before her father's gate, and she fumbled to unload her parcels as quickly as she could. Da would be home from the mine before long and wanting tea.

The kitchen was dark and cold, but Brenda did not bother to light a candle. She hurried to and fro down the short garden path, carrying her parcels in awkward armfuls and dropping everything helter-skelter on the table. She snatched a warmer shawl from the peg before running back into the dark, nipping night. She must hurry and return the pony to Cadwallador, then get back home, tidy up, and start the evening meal.

There was a light burning in Cadwallador's parlor when Brenda drove the pony into the yard, and Brenda felt herself release a breath she had not known she was holding. She need not walk home alone, then. She could ask him to escort her. She hadn't realized how much the shadow had unnerved her, how little she wanted to walk even the short distance unaccompanied, until an alternative presented itself.

But Cadwallador did not come out to help her unhitch the pony. Brenda guided the sullen little beast into its stall, rubbed it down, got its supper, and Cadwallador still did not appear.

She hesitated in the dark between the barn and the house, looking through the window into Cadwallador's brightly lit parlor. She could see the man himself seated in his armchair, slumping a little, staring at the fire. He must surely have heard her drive in, so why on earth did he not come out to meet her? Was he asleep? Perhaps he was. His tousled dark head rested heavily on his hand.

Then his other hand came up, and Brenda could see the glass of amber liquid it held. Cadwallador tipped the entirety of its contents down his throat in one gulp and straightened enough to pull the decanter closer.

So that was it. She would rather not have his company, in that case. Brenda wrapped her shawl more tightly about herself, bent her head into the quickening wind, and started the walk home. Fast, with her head down, plowing through the shadows, refusing to think about the shadow that had watched her from the shanty-town. Likely it had been nothing. Nothing had happened to her on the road; nothing would happen in Carmonton. Not even here, not even in this lonely moonlit stretch between Cadwallador's house and the main road.

A branch snapped somewhere in the dark behind her.

Brenda's stride hitched only for an instant before she forced herself onward. If she ran, whatever it was would chase her. If she screamed, would anyone hear? Cadwallador, maybe, but he might be too far gone to take notice—

A shadow rushed at her all at once, from the side, a flurry of light and dark in her peripheral vision. She tried to dodge, but her feet tangled in her skirt and she stumbled. A hand seized her arm, jerking her upright, and another hand clapped over her mouth like a blow, with enough force to rattle her teeth. "Don't scream!" a voice rasped in her ear, low but urgent. "Brenda, don't, please! I only want to talk with you!"

She knew that voice. It went straight to her spine, with the sort of jolt his fingers on her skin had once given her, and she stopped struggling at once. He took his hand from her mouth in response, and she twisted away from his grip on her arm to see his face. It was older, thinner, bearded, but she would have known it anywhere.

"Mother of God," she breathed. "Gavin."

*

"Owen Jones," he told her once she had stirred up the fire and set the kettle to boil. "You oughtn't throw my name about, not even within these walls. I haven't used Trevelyan in…quite some time."

"You were not," Brenda said slowly, "properly released." She had known that from the moment she recognized his voice in the wood—either he was escaped or he was a ghost—but saying it aloud in her firelit kitchen seemed to somehow make it real. She took two plates from the cupboard as she did every night. Then she reached for a third.

Gavin moved aside so she could arrange them on the kitchen table. "I was transported for ten years," he reminded her. "Anything over seven, you can't come back at all. When your time is served, you have to stay as a settler."

"Word never came to us you'd escaped," Brenda said. *I thought you were dead.*

He smiled just a little at that, the quick sidelong half-twist of the mouth she remembered, and the sight set her blood jangling in her veins again. "They'd not be eager to have it widely known. Half of what makes Cayenne so fearsome is the convicts believing no man can break free. It's hard—took me three years of catching at every possible chance—but it's not impossible. You need to know something of currents, and…and it helps to have good men aiding you."

"It was a great many of you escaped, then?" Brenda began cutting bread and cheese, marveling with one corner of her mind at the oddness of this. Gavin Trevelyan stood warming himself at the fire in her kitchen, chatting over details of his escape from the French prison colony for all the world as though he described his day at the mines. She had not seen the man in twelve years. How could it feel so natural to prepare his supper?

"Four," Gavin said, and a shadow quenched the smile on his face. "In the beginning. Only two of us made it out in the end."

The oddness rose up in a wave, and Brenda let the knife fall, clattering. "What are you *doing* here?"

Gavin looked up. "I had to see you."

"No. I don't mean that." She clenched folds of her apron in her fists. "Where have you been these nine years?"

"The West Indies first," he said. "America later. Vienna, most recently. I have been...learning things. Working with...clever people."

Working with the Continental Resistance, then. Continuing the struggle against the French that had gotten him transported in the first place. He had been free on the Continent, working against the French, for *nine years* with never a word to her. "You could not have sent me a letter?"

"It didn't seem a wise plan," he said, and she had to acknowledge there was truth in that. "Brenda, I didn't think I'd ever be coming back here. It was better you forget me. I said I wanted to see you, and I meant just that—I expected to find you married, and if you had been I wouldn't have revealed myself, I'd have contented myself with a glimpse and left you in peace—"

"So what brings you to Wales, then?" Brenda studied him. "It wasn't only to see me. You wouldn't risk your life for a glimpse of me this autumn when you hadn't for nine autumns past, not unless something had changed. What's about to happen?"

There was a silence while she met his slate-gray eyes, still sharp and fierce, despite the lines around them. She did not drop her gaze, and at last one corner of his bearded mouth turned upward in a reluctant smile.

"You're too clever by half," he said. "I should have remembered that."

"Well, then? Something's about to happen, isn't it?"

Gavin studied her another long moment. He nodded, but as he shaped his lips into "yes," Brenda's father opened the kitchen door.

*

"Sir, it will be different this time. It will." Gavin spoke so fast the words stumbled over each other. "We know what we did wrong twelve years ago, and we won't make those mistakes again. The man who leads us—he's an Englishman whose family once was noble—he's organized us into small companies, all over the countryside. No one knows anything bar what goes on in his own company. Many don't even know who they work for, not higher than their own local commander. If any of us except Kent himself were arrested, we could tell the French almost nothing. The collapse of one company does not mean the collapse of the Rising."

"Lad," John Evans said, not unkindly.

"We've invented a way to coordinate over distance," Gavin went on, heedless. "We can pull all the little companies together at the last moment, strike in many places at once—many cities, many mines. And once we prove we can take the mines, we can expect help from the Russian Empire. The Bear wants to bloody the Eagle any way he—"

"Lad." Brenda's father did not raise his voice, yet something in it made Gavin Trevelyan fall silent. John Evans looked at him for a time without speaking, then reached to pour himself more tea. "It's written in the papers," he said conversationally, "there are French reformers pushing to give Britain seats in their Parliament. The new young Emperor does not have his father's or his grandfather's antipathy, and—"

"Sir, that proposal is an insult." Gavin was out of his chair at the thought of it, pacing the small kitchen. "First, that Parliament is a toothless joke; Napoleon III has all the power there is securely in his fat little hands. Second, the land is ours by right, stolen from our grandfathers, and we're to be grateful for a Parliamentary sop? Condescending French schoolboys—"

"Those condescending French schoolboys do well with their power, now and then." John Evans' voice was still mild. "It's because of them the Bureau now teaches the children of the mines."

Gavin made a gesture as though he were throwing aside that small concession, or possibly throwing it against the wall. "Do you not want to see the Eagle driven off our soil?"

"I do," Evans said, "but I do not believe you and your bright-eyed compatriots can do it, any more now than you could in '71. You did not see what the countryside was like, after."

"No. I saw the inside of Cayenne, instead."

"Where you paid for the choices you had made. While here in Wales, women and children who knew nothing of your cause also paid for the choices you made. Ask Brenda what it was like, if you will not hear it from me."

Gavin's eyes met hers briefly, then fell. She wondered what he had seen reflected there.

"I will not take part in your madness," Evans said. "I believe we better serve Wales by keeping the peace. It is already better for children now than it was for me in my youth, and if we do not tug the Eagle's tail, perhaps it will grow better still. In any case, it could be much worse, and I will not help you bring about those days again." He fixed Gavin with suddenly stern hazel eyes. "For the sake of what was between my daughter and you, I'll not tell anyone I saw you here. But you'll leave here at once. Take the rest of the bread if you're needing it, and the cheese as well, but don't darken my door again. If you do, I'll have no choice but to tell the gendarme—to protect my daughter and myself. Understand?"

Gavin did not take the bread. He swallowed hard and looked at Brenda.

Her father looked at her, too. "You're not to have a thing to do with him again, you hear me, girl?"

She heard him. She nodded, and Gavin's face went blank, and then he was through the kitchen door before she could say a word. That night, she cried for Gavin Trevelyan for the first time in twelve years.

*

She woke in the cold November dawn half-wondering if she had dreamed it. When she hurried downstairs to stir up the fire and start the porridge, the kitchen looked the same as it ever did—shutters tightly bolted to keep out the cold, long splintery cracks in the floorboards letting the cold seep in anyhow, the dishes washed and put away, and the kettle waiting to be filled. The table's three straight-backed chairs were pushed tidily into place, as they were every morning. It seemed impossible that Gavin Trevelyan could ever have sat in one of them.

Her father took his usual place at the table in his usual placid silence and consumed his usual porridge and tea. He was not abnormally curt with her, nor abnormally gentle. He did not mention Gavin's name. She tried to, but choked on it.

After Mass, she cooked as lavish a dinner as their meager pantry would allow, and the third chair at the table stared at the back of her head all the while. Cadwallador came to smoke a pipe with her father and while away the long Sunday afternoon, and Brenda might have gone to visit a friend, but she went to her tiny bedchamber instead. She could not have said what she did there.

Eventually the afternoon drew to a close and it was time for her to prepare the evening meal. And then tea was done and she could go to bed. She felt as though the world had retreated from her, as though she moved ghost-like through it, as though she'd been faerie-cursed to silence.

Well, and the last was close enough to true. It was true enough to say she'd been swept up by the Wild Hunt for an evening, for an hour, alive to possibilities and sparkling futures and the dazzling riptide of life, then plunked back down at home with her tongue sealed to prevent her speaking of the fair folk. Plunked back down in the real world because she had not seized the chance of riding with the Hunt while she could.

The next morning, she made porridge and washed the breakfast dishes and walked off to the schoolhouse, as she did every Monday. She walked back that evening, head down against the wind, wondering if she had spent the past twelve years only half-alive. And how long it would take to become re-accustomed to the feeling.

*

She came home to find the door ajar.

It was like being doused in ice water. Brenda blinked once at the forced lock, then straightened, noticing for the first time that day that a patch of intense blue sky peeped through the usual coal smog, that one of her new shoes had rubbed a sore place on her instep, that part of the lintel had rotted through and really ought to be repaired— She should have been afraid, she realized later, finding the lock picked and someone in her home, but in the instant it did not even give her pause. She ran inside. Gavin was sitting in her father's chair.

He jumped to his feet as she entered. "Forgive me intruding—" he started.

Brenda dropped her schoolbooks and rushed across the room and straight into his arms. "I thought you'd gone," she said into his chest.

He shook his head, chin pressed against the top of her head. "I had to see you." His hand came up, hesitantly, and smoothed down her hair. After a moment's pause in which he appeared to assess whether she liked it, he did it again. "I don't want to cause trouble for you," he said then, but he did not stop stroking. "Tell me to go, and I will."

"No," she said. The Wild Hunt came careening headlong through the boundaries sensible folk built, offering madness and hope and the chance to gather up what you'd let slip through your fingers. She leaned back just far enough to look up into his face. "No, I do not want you to go."

He closed his eyes for a moment, in disbelief or gratitude or some other excess of emotion. But when he opened them, they were as intent as they had ever been, and he held her off at an arms-length. "Can you come walking with me? I want to show you what we are doing. Or will your Da be home too soon for you to risk it?"

"No," Brenda said, "not for hours yet." She swept the scattered books up and onto the table. "Where shall we go? Oh, but wait—" She looked up from the arithmetic book, struck. "Won't it be dangerous for you? How can you be going abroad in the day?"

"Where we're going, there's no danger of anyone recognizing me as Trevelyan," Gavin said, sidestepping the second question. "There's more of a danger that you'll be recognized as Brenda Evans. But I thought of that. I brought you something to wear."

*

The cloak was ragged and threadbare and itched something awful, and the dirty kerchief that hid her hair smelled so terribly of onions her eyes watered. But Gavin was right: not one person they passed had looked at her face. The two or three Carmonton housewives they encountered at a distance all took her—and Gavin, for that matter—for shanty-town folk who'd come to ask about a mine job and been turned away, and in the shanty-town itself, most of the eyes were too dulled with misery to spare much attention for unfamiliar features.

The slant-walled hovel Gavin brought her to was so full of men Brenda could not see how they all fit. Some of them were rough-looking enough to frighten her, but others wore their shanty-town garb as uneasily as she did and did a poor job indeed at aping the local slang.

"Miss Evans?" asked the most egregious offender in this regard, a man with tawny hair surrounding a handsome, fine-boned face. No one could have looked less like a Welsh miner. Well, he might pass himself as a merchant driven out of business, Brenda thought, and took his offered hand.

"Frederick Kent, at your service," the man said.

"'Kent himself,'" she quoted, remembering Gavin's earnest argument with her father the night before last.

Kent chuckled. "Is that how your young man describes me behind my back? What a delightful counterpoint to all the time he spends arguing with me to my face." But he laid a hand on Gavin's arm as he spoke. "Useful arguments they are, too. I couldn't do without him, Miss Evans. He's the second most valuable man I have. He and Mr. Carpenter here—" He gestured to a man in the shadows Brenda had not even noticed until that moment. "—magic up whatever we need."

"Not so," Carpenter declared, stepping forward. Perhaps it was only Mr. Kent's jesting use of the word "magic," or perhaps it was due to her reflections on the Wild Hunt earlier that day, but Brenda was reminded for a fanciful moment of the tales in which wizards formed men from shadows or wisps of smoke. Carpenter was even taller and even thinner than Gavin, and everything about him was the color of ash or coal—dark suit, curling black hair, black beard, gypsy-brown skin. Against the backdrop of all this darkness, his eyes shone a startlingly blue-gray. "The magic is Mr. Kent's, in providing the materials," he corrected. "Young Jones and I build from them using principles of chemistry and engineering. There is nothing mystical to our work."

She had already suspected the name "Carpenter" to be an alias, for he did not look at all like an Englishman, and his voice confirmed her suspicion beyond doubt. His accent was guttural and languorous at the same time, thick and rich and chalky. She had never heard anything like it before. "What do you build?" she asked.

The men all glanced at each other. "Well," Kent said, "for instance." He drew her over to what should have been the dining table, motioning Gavin and Mr. Carpenter to follow. "All right, you lot, find something else to do," he added to the others, and the kitchen emptied of men. Brenda blinked. "Show her your wares, Carpenter."

"These," Carpenter said, running his hand down a pile of long poles laid on the tabletop, "are signal rockets. They rise up into the air, hundreds of feet up, and there explode." He caressed the pole. "Lovely fireworks, all different colors, prearranged signals to resistance cells all over Britain. Far less dangerous than a messenger—to both the mission and the messenger. Those I invented myself, though your Mr. Jones refined them some. These—" He laid a hand on a second set of poles. "—are Mr. Jones' own invention. A pike, that folds so a man may hide it beneath his great-coat. Truly! No chemistry there. All you need to make it is a blacksmith." Carpenter favored Gavin with an approving look. "And then there is the house in Cardiff—most of that work was that of your Mr. Jones."

Brenda turned to Gavin, who seemed both embarrassed and pleased. "It's a safe house," he explained. "In the very center of town, overlooking the green, the best possible place, but no one knows it's anything but an old abandoned merchant's house. I made some false panels and trapdoors, nothing so very difficult. The signal rockets are the true genius here, and that's all Carpenter."

Brenda fingered the cold rods. "A way to send messages all over Wales at once. Pikes hidden under coats. A way to take back the mines, all at once. I think I see."

"But will you help?" Kent asked her. She looked up to find his intense blue eyes focused on her alone.

"Oh, yes," she said, surprised he thought there was a need to ask, and his smile was like summer sun chasing all the chill from the little room. She found herself smiling back without consciously deciding to do so.

But Kent's eyes were still serious. "Your father will not."

Brenda hesitated. "My father says you can't win. That it'll make it worse for all of us, another Rising."

"What do you think?"

"I think—" She didn't know how to say it. *I think I was asleep for twelve years and didn't know it and then the Wild Hunt came to my doorstep and offered—* She looked at Gavin. *I think I didn't know how much I grieved for his death until he came back. There's never been anyone like him, and I can't know he's this close and doing something this dangerous and stay safe at home as though it's nothing to do with me—* "I think it would be worse not to try," she said at last. "Even if it didn't work, at least you would feel alive while you were trying."

That smile could have brought daylight to the Pit. "You were right," Kent said to Gavin. "And then some. Welcome, Miss Evans. We are very glad to have you here."

*

Brenda made it back to her house a scant quarter hour before her father was due, but managed to have the tea mostly prepared before he walked in the door, and if he noticed the blazing fire had done less than usual to warm the kitchen, he said nothing of it. She escaped to her room soon after the meal was done, lest the glee singing through her veins betray itself on her face.

Gavin snuck back to see her twice more that week, and late on the Saturday night, appeared under her window. "You were right," he told her. "Tommy Davies was the man to speak to. We've got some sympathizers among the miners now, and one of our own men hired on. Kent's headed back to Cardiff, and that's where I should be too."

Brenda nodded. *Ask me to come with you,* she thought. *I'm part of this now. I chose to be. Ask me.*

He licked his lips. "When this is over, I'll come back if I may."

It wasn't what she wanted, but it was something. "I'll wait," she promised, and his crooked sidelong smile lit up his whole face before he slipped away into the dark.

*

Winter came, and drove its icy winds through the cracks in the floorboards. Brenda shivered through her walk to and from the schoolhouse, taught her students spelling and sums, cooked breakfast and tea for her father, and dodged Cadwallador's occasional diffident advances. Bone-chilling winter gave way to sweltering summer. Now and then whispers reached her ear of possible unrest in Cardiff—maybe the beginnings of another Rising—but the word "maybe" was always attached to the rumor. The French thought there might be treasonous activity afoot, but could not pinpoint where. Kent was a careful man.

Gavin came to see her now and again. It was like being betrothed to a faerie, she thought—he would appear out of nowhere, turn the world upside down for a day, and leave her seeing it all differently. "Sometime this autumn," he said. "As soon as we've weapons enough. The men in Carmonton Pit are ready." Brenda thought she knew which ones they were—the youths who had taken to nodding to her when they passed. They'd been told to look out for her and her father when the Rising started.

"How will you get weapons into Carmonton?" she asked Gavin.

He shook his head. "It's better you don't know."

"I could see you, when I come to Cardiff to do the autumn shopping," she suggested.

He hesitated. "I would like that, but—no, you'd best not. I want you safe from it all. When Cardiff's ours, there will be time enough for us to enjoy it."

"I chose to be a part of your Rising," she said. "I'd like to do more than—"

But he was already shaking his head. "You've done more than enough, you told us who to approach in the Pit and who to avoid, you helped us get our message through without attracting the gendarme's attention. You've done your part. I need to know you safe, love." Nothing she could say would persuade him to give her a more active role in what was to come.

*

Little Risings were to happen in pits all over South Wales, all at once, coordinated by Mr. Carpenter's rockets. Gavin was to be in Cardiff with Kent, at the center of the web. He had warned her that he might not be able to get away to see her before it happened, and so she was not overly surprised when Tommy Davies stopped her as she came home from a Friday evening spent sewing at a friend's house.

"Owen Jones sends his best, Miss Evans," he told her, and slipped a phial into her basket with a movement that was meant to be casual. "Tomorrow afternoon, he says. You give this to your Da tomorrow morning, it'll keep him home. Nothing dangerous, just—" Tommy rubbed his belly, and Brenda nodded. She wasn't sure if it was excitement or fear that burned through her. A little of both, perhaps.

It will be all right, she told herself. *Da won't be hurt, and it will be over soon, and then the mine will be ours and then—*

She was almost calm by the time she reached her own front gate. There she saw Cadwallador's trap parked beside the long white Bureau-granted fence, his tied pony nosing the ground for nonexistent grass. Beside the pony's bent head, the gate swung open, loose on its hinges. Brenda caught herself thinking, *I'll have to get that mended,* and then almost laughed. How absurd of everyday life to go on when the world was about to change.

She slipped through the half-open gate without creaking it and moved up the garden path unhesitatingly, despite the dark. She knew every step of the path as well as she knew the lines on the palm of her hand. As she reached for the latch, she heard Cadwallador's voice inside.

"Tomorrow," he said, and Brenda froze. "Second shift in the Pit. There's a group in Cardiff plans to take the armory at the same time, and then the city watchtower, and then they'll send a detachment to reinforce the rebels here. It's all right—the Imperials will be ready for them, they're moving into Cardiff tonight, and we've a surprise or two in the Pit itself. Now, John, the safest place you can be is my house. Pretend you're taken ill about noontime, get Brenda and go, and I'll be there to let you in. It'll be over by sundown."

Brenda stood frozen in the dark.

"How do you know?" her father asked.

"One of the boys they suborned in the mine had a change of heart. He got scared and told the gendarme, and the gendarme's used me as a go-between to the Cardiff Imperials, so the boys in the Pit wouldn't know they'd been betrayed."

A boy in the Carmonton Pit wouldn't know anything about Kent's larger plan, Brenda thought. Only one small corner of it. "If any of us except Kent himself were arrested, we could tell the French almost nothing," Gavin had said, and Cadwallador hadn't mentioned anything except the Pit and Cardiff. The other spokes of the wheel, isolated as Kent's plan dictated, were likely still unbetrayed.

But Gavin was in Cardiff.

"Which boys in the Pit?" her father asked. "Who do we need to fear?"

"They've told me to hold that secret, John. You can't accidentally betray what you don't know, after all. Some of our boys, a larger lot from Cardiff, that's all you need to know."

"Is a lad named Owen Jones one of them?"

"Why?" Cadwallador asked, voice gone sharp. "You know him?"

Brenda's heart hammered. Her father seemed to take an age before replying.

"One by that name came by here last fall to look for work in the Pit," John Evans said at last, "and I didn't like the look of him. Shifty-eyed fellow. I only wondered."

"Apparently he's their weapons-wright," Cadwallador said. "My informant has heard the name."

And he's in Cardiff, Brenda thought. *He's in Cardiff, and he doesn't know he's in danger.* How could she possibly get a warning to him? She wished, foolishly, for a rocket of her own.

She could wait until Cadwallador left, then try to persuade her father to take her to Cardiff with a warning— But even as she thought the words, she knew them for the coward's way out. She could do that. She could pretend it counted as doing something to help Gavin. But she knew how that story ended. Her father would refuse, would lock her up safe somewhere for her own good, and she would weep there, helpless, as the Rising failed and her true love perished. That was how the ballads went. And then sometimes the girl died of a broken heart at the end of them, and sometimes she lived on past the ballad's end, and Brenda wasn't sure which was worse. She had wept for Gavin's supposed death when she was sixteen, and so now she knew what happened when the girl lived past the end of that sort of ballad, what happened in the wake of Risings.

Nothing. That was the hell of it; nothing happened. There was suffering at first, yes, as you endured Imperial punishment, but eventually even that reminder faded, and the heartbeat of everyday life resumed its rhythm. You got used to it all again, numbed by the necessity of living. You drove past the shanty-town thinking, "Well, it's not so bad."

If she once walked into that house, she would never have the chance to leave it again. She'd be trapped inside until a hedge of briars grew up over it.

Brenda turned. She walked very quietly back down to the trap, and unhitched the pony from the trap. She led it at a walk until she was a short ways down the lane, then found a stone to use as a mounting block. The pony didn't like having her astride its bare back, and Brenda didn't much care for it either, but they'd be faster without the trap. She kicked the pony's sides hard, and it trotted.

*

It was one by the bells of St. David's by the time she reached the sleeping city. She sat on the horse's warm back, hidden by the shadow of the bell tower, needing a moment just to tremble. The moonlight had been scanty, and the road from Carmonton a potential disaster of branches and rocks and rabbit holes. She had spent every jarring step of that ride expecting to be thrown the next instant. She wanted to sob. She couldn't yet.

Gavin's cursed care for her safety meant she had never been to the house in Cardiff. It overlooked the green and seemed to be only an abandoned merchant's house, that was all she knew. Well, she would knock on every door of she had to. At least she knew where the green was. She walked the horse down the darkened streets, flinching from every alleyway shadow.

None of the houses seemed to be in good repair. She picked the one that looked least as though anyone inhabited it and hesitated for a long, shivering moment. Then she swung down from the pony's back, found a fence post to which to tie the lead rope, and limped on cramped leg muscles to knock on the door.

No one answered.

Brenda hesitated a long moment before rapping again.

"'ere!" a querulous voice snapped nearly at her feet, and her heart jumped into her throat. "Stop making that row!"

"Oh—I—" She backed up, but not quickly enough. A shadow rose from the pavement, catching hold of her arm before she could flee. A metallic scrape heralded a dark lantern opening, and red-rimmed eyes peered at her out of clothing that seemed to be no more than a bundle of rags. The scent of gin rose all around her.

"Who're you?" the drunk demanded.

"I—I—I'm looking for Owen Jones," Brenda managed. "I—do you—he boards here, I think?"

"Who are you?"

Was it only her imagination, or did he sound less drunk that time? Less Welsh? Was it possible he was one of Kent's guards? Why else would he want to know who she was?

"I'm Owen's betrothed," she said. "I come from Carmonton. Do you know where he is?"

"Never heard of 'im." The voice sounded like dismissal, but he did not loose her arm.

Brenda resisted the urge to struggle. "Well, to the best of my knowledge, he boards here. With a, a Mr. Carpenter and a Mr. Kent."

"No one lives 'ere, girl."

If he were a guard, he would be determined not to give them away. And rightly so—Brenda might have led her father here, or the gendarme. There might be men waiting to rush upon the house once she induced those within to open their doors. She knew herself to be trustworthy, but could not blame the guard for fearing a trap.

"Then I am sorry to have disturbed you," she said. "Let me go, and I'll be on my way." She leaned closer, into the miasma of gin, and whispered. "Tell Frederick Kent that one of the Carmonton miners betrayed him to the Imperials. They know about the Cardiff and Carmonton plans for tomorrow. Nothing else as far as I know." The hand did not tighten on her arm, nor did the eyes flicker. Was she wrong? But she was committed to the course now. "I'll walk away. You can wait as long as you like to be sure I'm here alone. Just give him the message by sunrise." Now she twisted her arm against his hand. "Let me go."

Go where, though? What if he spoke the truth, what if he was what he seemed, what if Gavin did not live here? Ought she to knock on other doors? But if he was a guard, that might make her seem untrustworthy. Perhaps she should ride away, but she knew of nowhere else to go in Cardiff—

The fingers dug into her arm. "Oh, no," the man chuckled. "You oughtn't rush off. Too cold a night for a little thing like you to be out."

Brenda's heart started to pound. Could she have been wrong? Oh God above, if she had misjudged—

The hand squeezed her arm twice. She didn't know what that meant. "I've got some nice warmin' stuff in a little bottle just over here," the man said. He propelled her toward the shadow from which he had arisen.

Brenda tried to plant her feet into the ground, but it did no good. "No," she whispered, then tried to speak more firmly. "No, let me go."

"Oh, come, lass, 'ave a 'eart. Give us a kiss and I'll give you a sip."

"No—no." She turned her head aside from the gin-soaked breath.

"No call to be so 'igh and mighty." There was an ugliness to the voice now. "Out by yourself this time of night, you're no innocent maid."

She pushed against his chest, but his grip on her arm drew her closer and closer. He pulled her, step by stumbling step, toward the shadow of the house. All at once he shifted his weight and pushed her up against it and a helpless little cry burst from her lips.

And nothing happened.

The man eased away from her. "Ah, you're no fun," he said in disgust. And more softly, "Forgive me. I had to know you really were here alone. If you were bait, your defenders would have rushed in." Brenda gaped at him. "Go on!" he said loudly. "Get off with you!" And in the whisper again, "Go around to the back and knock in sets of three on the kitchen door. You can deliver your message yourself." He pushed her away from him.

She fell. She was scrambling up almost before her palms touched the dirt, stumbling at a half run out of his reach and into the yawning dark shadow that ran along the house.

There was a light in the kitchen window. She almost fell against the door. She remembered to rap three times. "Let me in!" she pleaded, not knowing whether she was playing a part or not. She rapped three more times. "Please, let me in, he wants to hurt me—"

The door jerked open under her shaking fist, and Frederick Kent caught hold of her as she barreled inside. "Brenda! What on earth—" He was in his shirtsleeves, tawny hair backlit by a single candle, and his arms closed fast around her, solid and sure. "Are you hurt? Is someone after you?"

"No," she said. "No. Your—your guard, he frightened me, but he was—he had to—I understand. There's trouble in Carmonton. I came to warn you."

Over her head, Kent spoke without raising his voice: "Get Jones. Now." The kitchen was full of people, she realized dimly. She could barely make them out through the tears in her eyes. Kent bent back toward her. "You came yourself?" he said. "You came alone?"

"I took the doctor's pony," she said, and he laughed a little, hugging her to him so she could feel the rumbling vibration through his chest. It was not at all like Gavin's embraces—no lightning-quick, questing fingers, nothing to stir the blood, nothing she need squirm away from. She relaxed into it instead, taking a deep breath of warmth and strength and safety. She wondered fleetingly if this was what it was like to have an elder brother.

"Brave girl," Frederick Kent said, and held her off. Her eyes were still blurred, but she could see the approving smile. He kept his hands on her shoulders. "Tell me."

*

"Imperials are moving into Cardiff tonight," Kent's ringing tones cut through the chatter of voices, "to be in place to stop us at the armory tomorrow night. They're not in place to stop us now." He looked around the room, at the stacked weapons and eager men who looked back.

"But our men aren't all in place either," someone from the crowd objected—a balding older man who put Brenda in mind for a brief wrenching moment of her father. "That was the whole idea of doing it the night after market day, get them all to come into Cardiff as they would anyhow."

"We do this now or not at all," Kent said. "Either way, we send up no red rocket tomorrow. Carmonton will know not to rise. They're compromised; we can't risk it. We'll have to leave it to the other mines." He looked around the room again. "I'd like to put an armory behind them. I'd like to be holding the armory when the Imperials get here. Wouldn't you?"

An approving murmur rose from the others. In the corner where they stood watching, Gavin's fingers tightened over Brenda's hand.

"Once we have it," Kent said, "we can take Cardiff. Once we take Cardiff, we can hold it long enough for the Bear to come and aid us!" He paced through the circle of candlelight, then turned and paced back, looking at every face in turn. "It's a risk," he said. "We don't have all the men we planned for. But it's still possible until the Imperials get here, and impossible once they take possession. What do you say? Shall we? Will you follow me?"

There was no question that everyone in the kitchen would follow him anywhere he chose to lead.

"Then arm yourselves and form your companies in the yard!" Kent said. "Carpenter, a moment of your time—"

"I'll show you where you can hide," Gavin said, squeezing her hand again to get her attention.

"Hide?" Brenda looked at him in dismay. "No, I want to be with you! Surely there's something I can—"

"I don't want you anywhere near the fighting," Gavin said. "It'll be over before dawn. Once we hold the armory, I'll come and escort you to it in safety. For the moment, the safest place in the city is right here. I'll show you the secret panels, the places to hide, in case someone unfriendly should come looking."

*

It was two by the bells of St. David's when they left. She waited all night alone in the house—trapped atop a tower, trapped behind a thicket of briars, frozen in amber. In limbo, which she decided somewhere around four that morning was unquestionably the worst part of hell. She fancied she could hear shouting from the direction of the armory. She was certain she could hear rifle shots. She imagined Gavin bleeding his life out in a Cardiff street while she paced this floor here.

The sky was lightening when a click from the ground floor roused her out of a doze. She scrambled upright, and had her hand on the latch of the false paneling before she heard Gavin's voice call her name.

She met him on the stairway, and even in the adequate light she could see the exhaustion on his face, the blood on his clothes. "None of it's mine," he reassured her. But he leaned against the wall as though he could hardly keep himself upright.

"It's over?" she asked, not quite daring to hope. "The armory is ours?"

"It's over," he said. "We failed to take the armory, and now the Imperials are here. Kent and his men are holding out against them for now, but they won't last long. We've got to leave the city."

*

The caves in the mountains north of Cardiff had been well-provisioned by Kent's people, and though dank and cold, were not comfortless. Survivors of the abortive Cardiff rising trickled in over the next few days, many hurt, all with the eyes of those who had looked into hell. Later they were joined by others from further off, who brought news of other arms of Kent's organization. Some of the Pit uprisings had succeeded, but most of the other cities had faltered in their resolve to rise once they heard of the Imperial cruelty in Cardiff—and without urban support, it was unlikely the mines could be held by their workers against the Empire's troops. The Welsh Rising had died at birth.

Kent himself was among the last to join the refugees. Brenda watched as he made his way through the knots of huddled figures, stopping to speak to each one, to offer praise for courage in combat or concern for an injury, to quietly give the news of a comrade's death or ask for news of one still missing. He reached their corner last of all, and crouched down. "Brenda," he said. "I have you to thank that anything at all was salvaged from this disaster. You saved everyone in Carmonton who meant to rise and would have died trying. I wish I had made as good use of your warning in Cardiff—but even there you saved everyone who hadn't yet joined us, who still lives to fight another day."

She smiled a little, not knowing what to say.

"Jones," Kent said then, in an entirely different tone of voice. Brenda looked up, alarmed. Gavin did not rise, but his back stiffened a little where it leaned against the rock wall. Kent was regarding him without a smile. "Is there something you wish to say to me?"

Gavin looked straight into his eyes. "I'd do it again," he said. "One man more or less at the armory could not have affected the outcome, and no one else in this city would have made her safety his first concern."

"Wait," Brenda said. "You didn't have— I thought you'd had permission to go and fetch me. You left them there?"

"It was bad enough losing you when I thought you safe and happily wed," he snapped. "I'm damned if I get you killed."

"Nick Carpenter was shot just after you left your post," Kent said. "He died almost instantly."

A shadow passed over Gavin's face—but he banished it the next instant, replacing it with defiance. "I'll still act exactly so next time. If that means you want me gone, say the word."

Kent studied him for several moments. "Those are your terms?"

Gavin gathered himself as though to push off from the wall and stand. "Yes."

"Done," Kent said.

Gavin stopped.

"I do not," Kent said, "want you to leave. I want you to stay—and the understanding that you will put her life before any of ours is an acceptable price for your services. I intend to return to London to retake control of my operations there. We'll need to refrain from direct action in Wales in the near future, but there are plenty of other ways to sour the Eagle's satisfaction with his British prize. Plenty of other ways to disrupt the Empire, plenty of other ways to court the Bear. Most of these men are country operatives—I'll arrange for them to join other companies in Wales or the south of England—but I want you to come to London with me. Carpenter's boots need filling. I want you to fill them. You have ideas, I know you do. Different ones than his, even."

"Impractical ones," Gavin managed after a moment. "We haven't funds or materials enough—"

"Let's say I had ways to acquire funds," Kent said. "And let's say it would be easier to acquire materials in London, where there are at least a few factories to scavenge from. Let's say you didn't need to worry about that part of it, because I would. I'd get you what you need to build those weapons you sketch whenever there's a pencil in your hand." Gavin stared at him. "I mean what I say," Kent assured him. "Tell me what you need."

Gavin continued to stare for a moment, then his eyes seemed to focus. "To begin with," he said, "a priest."

Kent raised his eyebrows. "Are you thinking of Carpenter? I had thought to find someone to say a Mass for the souls of all we lost—"

"No," Gavin said. "He— It wasn't so very important to him, you know that. I can't imagine it mattering to him whether we observed the proprieties or not."

"Then if not for Carpenter—?" Kent paused interrogatively.

Gavin took a breath. "For me." He turned to face Brenda, somehow shifting one leg beneath himself so his seated position turned into something more like kneeling. "I'll have to leave Wales," he told her. "For good this time, most likely. I don't know what fortune I'll find in London, or if I might not journey on from there. I've got two francs in my pocket and all I can offer you is a life looking over our shoulders for the Imperials, but—" His gray eyes bored into hers. "Will you marry me?"

Brenda looked right back at him. "Yes," she said, "if I have your word you'll never again leave me behind. Where you go, I go."

Gavin's jaw tightened. She waited. His jaw tightened further.

"If I can't have your word, we don't need a priest," she said. Over Gavin's shoulder, she thought she saw Kent's mouth twitch.

"Those are your terms," Gavin said at last.

Brenda nodded.

"It's an...acceptable price." He looked as though the concession tasted terrible in his mouth, but he forced himself to say it anyway. "I give you my word."

"Then yes," Brenda said, "I'll marry you. I'll—I'll go to London with you first and marry you when a priest can be found, if we must do it in that order."

"Excuse me." The deferential throat clearing came from one of Kent's men, sitting a few feet away with his back up against a cave wall and his knees drawn up to his chest. "I don't believe we were introduced earlier, Miss Evans. George Spencer. As it happens, I am an ordained minister of the Presbyterian Church."

Brenda blinked.

"I assure you," Mr. Spencer added, "we are not all the monsters Imperial propaganda makes us out to be."

"I—never thought you were," Brenda managed. That was not quite true; she had never thought about the matter at all. "I only— I don't think I've ever met a minister before."

"You may have and not known it," Mr. Spencer said. "We tend to keep quiet, for obvious reasons. I could not help but overhear your conversation, and I wondered if I might be of service?"

Gavin nudged her. "If it's important to you to have a priest," he murmured, "we can wait until we get to London."

"No." It was the same feeling as turning from her father's door. Surely if she did not seize this chance, it would vanish and she would wake up in Carmonton—not even in hell—in limbo, which was worse. She chose to ride with the Hunt. "It's not important. I'd rather be married now."

"You'll excuse me," Kent said, getting to his feet with something like a smile briefly easing the tension on his face. "I have a great deal to oversee if we're to move on in the next day or so."

George Spencer recited the Presbyterian wedding service from memory. "We can't very well have printed prayer books, after all," he pointed out in answer to Brenda's raised eyebrows. "Owen Jones, will you—"

"No," Gavin said.

Everyone within hearing turned startled eyes in his direction, but Brenda understood.

"That's not my name," he explained to the minister. "And I've burnt and blackened this one so badly it's no protection for either of us. I'll do this…as myself."

Names have power, Brenda thought. *Isn't that what they always say of faeries? Once a faerie gives you his true name, he is bound to you forever after. And cannot flit off and leave you behind.*

"I, Gavin Trevelyan, take you, Brenda Evans, to be my wife."

Chapter 9

London, September 3, 1885

William sat at the dining table, swirling the last dregs of cold tea in a handleless cup, not really listening to the conversation going on upstairs between Kent and Katarina. He could catch no more than one word in three, and he gave his attention to no more than half of those; most of his mind was elsewhere. He fancied he could feel the weight of the little silver locket in his breast pocket as well as the weight of history resting on his shoulders, factually impossible though both those notions were.

In the far corner of the room, Elizabeth was curled up in the wing chair they had all insisted she rest in. At least she had not been badly hurt in the scuffle with Schwieger, the blow to her middle having caused only bruises, not broken ribs. The blisters on her palms had burst and bled during the struggle for the Prussian's pocket watch, but Katarina had known how to tend them and bind them up again. Now Elizabeth cradled the broken timepiece between her bandaged hands, looking down on it as though it might spontaneously return to life and thereby provide a solution to all their problems.

If William closed his eyes, he could see the gold glint of the second pocket watch—the useful pocket watch, the *working* pocket watch—at Maxwell's waist as Maxwell and Schwieger fell together into nothingness. Each time the memory presented itself before his inner vision, William thought of something else he wanted to say to Maxwell on the subject of recklessness and planning ahead. In those moments, William wanted Maxwell safely returned to them for no other reason than to be absolutely certain he would have the opportunity to deliver the lecture.

And then he would look over at Elizabeth, and know she had only been saved from the fate of falling through time with Schwieger because Maxwell had not hesitated, and want to praise Maxwell's quick thinking. While still, simultaneously, wanting to berate him for not planning more than an instant ahead. *There is something comforting in the statistical inevitability,* Maxwell had said when Elizabeth and William turned up to rescue him in Orkney. There was, William supposed, something similarly comforting in Maxwell's antics provoking this dual reaction of pride and exasperation from William in particular. In some other context, it might have been amusing.

But there was nothing comical in the current circumstances. Nothing at all. Without a working pocket watch, they could never set right their terrible Waterloo mistake. More to the point, without a working pocket watch they could never get home. Worst of all, without a working pocket watch in Elizabeth's possession, there would never be one for Maxwell to find in a garret—and then all of this came crashing down like a construct felled by a rail-gun, peppering the alleyway with destruction even as it collapsed to its knees. William brushed a hand over his shirt-front, for what comfort was to be found in touching Maxwell's locket.

He had seized it almost before it hit had the ground, while Kent and Katarina were still rushing to Elizabeth's aid and before he could know for certain what secret it contained. He knew now. He had tucked it away in his pocket to keep it hidden from the warehouse inhabitants, the secret being no business of theirs. He had not exactly meant to hide it from Elizabeth as well, but she had, oddly enough, yet to ask him about it. Perhaps she did not even know he had it. Perhaps her eyes had been too blurred from the pain of her injury—a blow to the solar plexus was a most unnerving pain the first time one experienced it—to have noticed it fall or noticed him catch it up.

It was heavier than any talisman had any right to be. Elizabeth and Maxwell, now both his responsibility. *You protect your own family as long as you can,* Christopher Palmer had murmured to himself, thinking no doubt of the wife and son who had died during the harsh years after Dover. And, *Was it unclear what I meant, when I said 'keep her safe'?* Maxwell had snapped at him in a barn outside Waterloo.

Perfectly clear, William had told him then. *Have you advice as to how?*

He hadn't known how to protect her then. He didn't know how to protect either of them now. How in the world was he to save them both?

At the corner of his vision, light glinted off the gold casing of the broken watch as Elizabeth turned it over in her hands. William looked over at her, and she must have caught the movement out of the corner of her own eye, for she spoke without lifting her head. "Where do you suppose he is?"

"Twenty nine years in the future, or a little more?" William said. "At least, I imagine that's where Schwieger came from and meant to return to." He knew she was not speaking of Schwieger, but it was Schwieger's watch that had dictated Maxwell's fate.

Elizabeth shook her head. "Schwieger's timepiece could have been set to some other time and place."

"Unfortunately true," William was forced to respond.

"He could be anywhere."

Also unfortunately true. William did not reply.

"I wish—I wish there were some means that would allow me to know he was well." Elizabeth's curly head came up from the watch, blue eyes bright in the lamplight. "This is twice, you know—three times if you count the fire in Yorkshire—that he's taken a mad risk trying to keep me safe. And in between the night in the alleyway and last night, we quarreled so—I wish I hadn't said some of the things I did. I wish I could make it right by going and helping him now."

William said, in a voice he tried to make gentle, "But we can't. This isn't like Orkney. We don't know where he is, we don't know when he is, and even we did, we'd have no means of traveling there."

"There must be *something*," Elizabeth argued. "I can't sit here and do nothing—" As though in illustration, she wriggled off the wing chair, careful not to rest any weight on her hands. William started to reflexively scrape back his chair, but Elizabeth waved him back down. She came to take the seat across from him, setting the broken watch on the table between them. The cracked faces stared at them for one instant in silent reproach before Elizabeth snapped the casing closed and turned the watch over. "Do you know how to pry off the backing here?"

William looked up, startled. "And do what?"

"I don't know yet. I only want to see inside. I want to do something."

And it was, he reflected, better she have something to do. Looking inside a broken pocket watch was a safer task than many she could have selected, so William picked it up to look at the backing. Neither his left hand nor her bandaged fingers were capable of prying it loose, so he got up, telling Elizabeth he intended to look for a tool to aid them.

He almost collided with Katarina, just coming through the doorway. "A tool for what?" she asked. And then, "Forgive me, I couldn't help overhearing."

Katarina looked tired, William thought. Well, and small wonder. She had come rushing back to the warehouse with them to rescue Elizabeth and Maxwell from Schwieger; she had stayed the night, making tea and looking after Elizabeth's injuries and subsequently making breakfast; but something in her movements seemed to suggest she was visiting the home of a friend rather than returned to a home of her own. Before William could decide whether he wanted her to know why they needed tools, Elizabeth explained, and Katarina gamely applied her own fingernails to the casing. William tried not to twitch at the sight of their watch in her hands. She had returned it to him with some ceremony the night before, after all. He had said he trusted her.

The backing popped away, and the three of them stared down into a mass of broken gears and levers—some snapped, others whole but knocked out of place and no longer meeting the teeth of their neighbors. The gears and levers surrounded a gleaming black cube perhaps the size of a blueberry, which flashed lights of many colors as the fourth face had once flashed images.

Katarina stared at it. "What is that?"

"I've no idea." William fished out his own pocket watch, and motioned for Katarina to open its back as well.

Elizabeth leaned closer to the magical timepiece. "That part doesn't seem to be broken."

"How would you know?" William could not help asking.

"Well, I don't. But it's—it looks like it's—it appears to be engaging in some activity. Your watch has nothing like it, so perhaps that's the time-travelling part?"

"Perhaps so," William acknowledged, looking from the inner workings of his perfectly functional timepiece—gears turning around each other, ticking in a comforting manner—to the sad collection of quiescent metal bits that made up Elizabeth's. They reminded him somehow of a battalion routed and scattered by an enemy advance. On the other side of the lamp sat Frankenstein's journal, its odd embossed seal also seeming slumped and defeated. "And if it *is* the time travelling part, what then?"

"Then," Elizabeth said slowly, "perhaps all we need to mend my watch is a watchmaker."

William looked again from the simple turning gears of his timepiece to the far more complicated jumble that made up the other, and then, eloquently, back to Elizabeth.

"Well, yes," Elizabeth said in response to his look, "perhaps a genius watchmaker, then." But she did not seem at all perturbed by the idea. A familiar spark kindled in her eye. "I believe Mr. Kent has just such a man in his employ."

Katarina looked up at her in alarm. "Did none of what I did or said make any impact? You cannot possibly be considering putting this into the hands of someone who has every reason to destroy it. He won't allow anything that risks her life."

"May I infer," Frederick Kent said from behind them, "you are discussing employing my weapons-wright as a watchmaker?"

Katarina made an exasperated noise.

Elizabeth turned on her. "Can you recommend someone else of like skill and similar trustworthiness?"

"Trustworthiness is the issue," Katarina said. "The only way I can see you securing his cooperation is if you somehow keep him from realizing the risk to his wife."

"You're as bad as Maxwell!" Elizabeth said with sudden fire. "Tricking people like that doesn't work, it's never worked. That's the one common thread in all Maxwell's misadventures. Don't you realize—" She tapped the fingers of her bandaged right hand on the embossed seal of Frankenstein's journal. "—that no one has ever tried to persuade the Genevese student to alter his behavior by showing him proof of what would result? Maxwell tried to subtly redirect his youthful studies, tried to dislodge him from his path at University, tried to tempt him into visiting the Scottish mainland instead of going on to the Orkneys—Maxwell's usual style, trickery and misdirection and chess—and none of it worked. Of course it didn't. Of course that sort of thing never works. For one thing, those manipulated might well later stray off their path, since they've no way of knowing where it is. That's what happened with Frankenstein. Young Viktor was lured away from his dangerous studies for a time, but reverted back to them later.

"And if those manipulated do awaken to the deception—" She paused to level a look at William, and he understood this to signify that the "awakening" was not a metaphorical turn of phrase. Elizabeth had expressed her opinion on last night's untruthfulness quite clearly; they had argued; they had mostly reconciled, but it seemed she still harbored some feelings of anger. "—they become determined to leave the path they have been tricked into walking. That's what happened with the Duke. Had we persuaded him to change his battle plan, he might have done; but once he realized someone had been attempting to trick him into a course of action, he became determined to return to his original course." She added, "Convince me to curtail my behavior, and I might. Lock me in, and I'll climb from the window."

Or seize Maxwell's sleeve and make him take her to Waterloo. William contemplated it. Might Maxwell have well gotten further with her if he had explained why he wished to keep her safe, instead of acting in a way that made her feel like a child locked in her bedchamber? It was an interesting notion.

"Is that what you intend to do?" Katarina asked. "Go and persuade the Genevese?"

"If I had a working pocket watch," Elizabeth said, "yes."

"Hm." Katarina looked at the watch, but in an unfocused sort of way, as though different visions presented themselves to her. "If I could have seen this consequence," she said after a time, slowly, "I would not have chosen it. Well. You may be right. Perhaps someone ought to allow Viktor Frankenstein the chance to choose the future with the blindfold off his eyes. But if you want to have any chance of actually getting there to speak with him," she added, once more in her customary manner, "you had better see to it Gavin Trevelyan never learns what he is risking."

"You say that like she's a piece on a chessboard," Elizabeth said. "*You* say that, and yet—" She shook her head. "If I'm right, I won't be able to get what I need through trickery."

"Emil Schwieger seemed to find success tricking Charles West," Katarina retorted.

"We don't know that! Yes, he got away with the papers, but for all we know he carried the seeds of his own destruction with him. We don't know how his adventure will end. We do know how Maxwell's adventures have ended, and none of his deceptions have ever worked."

"More practically," Kent said, "I cannot imagine you successfully deceiving Gavin Trevelyan in any case. He'd discern it, and the backlash would shake the earth." He paced a few steps, thinking. "You'll lose nothing by waiting a day or two. If Maxwell can return for you, he surely will in that time. I'd prefer Trevelyan spend all his attention focused on our imminent Russian investors, in any case."

"If I had a working pocket watch," Elizabeth muttered, "you wouldn't need them or Trevelyan's constructs."

"I still might," Kent told her. "Even if Trevelyan were willing to try to mend your watch, he might fail. Even if he succeeded, you might fail. Even if you succeed, Emil Schwieger might undo what you do, and in any of those cases,

I will need a secondary position to fall back to. I will need a weapon to use to fight this war, here and now."

"That's fair," William said, but Elizabeth shook her head.

"That will retort upon you as they did on their former masters," she said. "You'll throw off the French the way your counterparts exterminated the Wellingtons, but then you will be left with the constructs and no use for them, riding the tiger, caught in the gears that turn themselves. I told you what the British government did when they had constructs ready to their hands to be used as weapons; surely it will all happen again unless we—"

"Convince those in power to act differently?" Kent said.

Elizabeth stopped.

"I'll be the one to lead the Rising," Kent said. "So I'll be the one who holds the power at the other side. It will be mine to say what use we make of our weapons afterwards. You have warned me of the consequences, and I give you my word that I will not take that path now I know where it leads. You've delivered your warning, Elizabeth. You've ridden your courier's mount through the battlefield and the forest without losing courage or sight of your goal; you've put your message safe into the general's hands; you've done well. Now stand down." He held Elizabeth with his eyes. "I'm not a pawn either. The future stretches before me, mine to write. You have told me what I need to know, and now you need to step back and trust me to act."

"Oddly enough," Katarina murmured, a small smile on her lips, "you are speaking with one of the few men in history who may be trusted to keep that promise."

Kent turned to look at her, pain in his eyes. "You think that, but you won't come home?"

She hesitated—then shook her head. "We're still fighting on the same side. If you need me, a message to the theater will find me, and I'll let you know when I find something better. But no, I won't come back here. I think...I know...I need some space around me, room enough to move freely, try out some of my own ideas."

"Kat—"

"You saved me," Katarina said. "Back then. I needed an elder brother then—or even a father, I suppose. I'd be dying in a gutter by now, if you hadn't taken me into Carter's organization—I know that, and I'm grateful. And I've done well enough for you since, haven't I? Working within the lines you've drawn? It's only...after all this time, I can't tell whether they are my lines too. I won't be able to tell until I see how I walk when there's no path laid out for me."

William looked at Frederick Kent's face and decided the older man did not understand. He wasn't sure he did himself, for that matter. But Elizabeth nodded as though it made perfect sense to her. Katarina pushed herself away from the table, brushed Kent's cheek with a kiss, and walked over to the scullery door. She reached around inside the room, then straightened, holding a single packed carpet bag. She must have packed it sometime the night before. William had been right; she had never meant to stay.

Kent roused himself. "But your things. Don't you want your trunk? I bought it for you as a gift, remember—"

"I'll be needing to travel light," she said. "You'll find a use for it here. I'm not going far, Frederick, truly. We're still on the same side."

Kent shook his head, but tried to smile. "I'll see you out, then."

William listened to their steps echoing down the corridor to the front door. He heard the door open and close, but Kent did not immediately return. William could picture him standing quietly in the entryway for long enough to compose himself. He had, after all, lost so much in the past week.

"It's disappointing to find Madam Katherine taking the position she does, this time," Elizabeth said, turning the pages of Frankenstein's journal. "She was so different in the other London. She took me out and let me see everything—I asked her if she wasn't afraid I'd betray her to the authorities, and she said, 'I didn't think you would,' but I could have, you know. She'd given me enough freedom that I could have. She let me learn everything and then let me choose. No one had ever given me a gift like that." She looked up then, her expression almost pleading. "Surely, surely, Viktor Frankenstein is owed no less?"

Viktor Frankenstein was the farthest thing from William's mind right at that instant. He was considering the words in another, more personal light. Was a choice only freely made when everything possible was known about it? Or where there times when revealing the future amounted to changing it? His fingers moved to touch the locket. Knowing what he now knew did not change his intended path, but if it changed hers, surely it was dishonorable to purchase his own desires with that coin. Or was it more dishonorable not to share with her all the knowledge he himself possessed?

A click and the scrape of metal down the corridor proclaimed a latchkey opening the front door. William turned toward the sound in surprise, not altogether unhappy to be distracted from his thoughts. Not Katarina returning, surely? Wouldn't she have given Kent back his latchkey?

It was not Katarina returning. The voices greeting Kent spoke in a Welsh lilt, male and female, and Kent answered them with pleased surprise at their early arrival. Three sets of footsteps returned along the corridor. Gavin Trevelyan's broke off halfway, his voice saying something about stopping in the laboratory, but Brenda continued up the passage with Kent.

"I have much to tell you," Kent was saying to her. "It has been an eventful few days."

"Let me just go upstairs long enough to lay aside my things," Brenda answered, "and then yes, of course, I wish to hear it all."

Elizabeth jumped to her feet, light burning in her eyes.

"Elizabeth?" William started to ask, but she was already making for the door.

She paused just long enough to whisper, "I must go and speak with Mrs. Trevelyan. Before anyone else does—" and was gone before he could manage a reply.

Chapter 10

London, September 3, 1885

Elizabeth stood on the topmost stair, red curtain hanging inches from her nose, becoming aware that she had not drawn a breath since running from the sitting room. She drew one now, trying to steady her fluttering heart, then tapped with the knuckles of her bandaged hand on the bannister—what she could manage in place of knocking on a door. "Mrs. Trevelyan?"

The rustling sounds on the other side of the curtain paused. "Miss Barton?" Brenda's surprised voice came back.

"Yes. If you are not too tired from your journey, may I speak with you?"

"Now?" Brenda queried. "Oh—well, of course, dear. Come in."

Elizabeth drew aside the curtain. It was rude, of course, the very definition of inconsiderate, to chase up the stairway someone only just returned home from traveling. But she could not wait. She had to talk to Brenda now, before Kent could share the situation with her or with Trevelyan, before Trevelyan's mind could calcify into a position on the matter. She had to speak with Brenda while there was still a chance of Brenda persuading her husband.

Brenda greeted her with arms full of dark cloth, and an expression than seemed tired though still perfectly amiable. Her eyes widened as they fell upon Elizabeth's bandages. "My goodness, Miss Barton, what's happened to your hands?"

"That's…one of things I wished to speak to you about." With a start, Elizabeth identified the cloth as the pieces of Brenda's dark blue walking dress. Loaned to Elizabeth some—what was it, seven days ago now? Packed by Elizabeth into Kent's trunk before they left Yorkshire by train. And left by Elizabeth in the trunk, in the Trevelyans' bedchamber, for the two days since. She had not even thought to unpack it, brush it, and arrange it where it belonged. A small thing in the grand scheme, perhaps, but no fit return for hospitality and kindness. She came to help with it now, offering what apologies she could.

"Your gown," she began, inanely. "I'm so sorry, Mrs. Trevelyan. I entirely forgot—"

"No matter," Brenda assured her. "And no, no I can do this, you've hurt yourself. Sit and tell me what's happened."

Elizabeth took the indicated seat on the edge of the closed trunk, and found that she had forgotten all of the speeches that had flashed through her mind, seeming so brilliant, on the run up the stairs. "I…hardly know how to begin. I—so much has happened since you departed." She watched Brenda lay out the basque and commence buttoning all the tiny buttons from chin to waist. She had to find some more natural way to lead into what she wanted to say. Still lamely, she tried, "Mr. Kent never mentioned what took you away?"

Too late, she remembered that Kent had called it a private affair, but Brenda did not seem to mind the question. "Gavin and I went to see to...a new arrival to the city," the older woman said. "Someone I knew before my marriage. Though I would have gone to help him settle into London life even if I had not known him personally," she added. "When Frederick hears of a Welshman come looking for work, he usually sends me to deliver greetings and see if the newcomer can't be recruited into the Resistance. If he can, all well and good, and even if he can't, he's usually willing to give me information enough for a pamphlet."

"A pamphlet?"

Brenda looked up from the armful of skirt she was shaking out. "About conditions in the mines, or Cardiff, or among various folk in London or the countryside. You saw some of them the night you arrived."

"I did—but give you information? I thought, from what Mr. Trevelyan said, that he wrote them..."

Brenda smiled. "They're published under his name, yes, because his is a name to conjure with after the two Welsh Risings—and no one would take seriously anything written by 'Missus' anyone—but I'm the one who actually writes them. Gavin's very good at keeping the printing press running, but he's rubbish at putting words to paper, and after all, I once taught the writing of compositions."

"I had no idea."

Brenda pinned the skirt of the walking dress in place and smoothed down its flounces. "Well, but we've scarcely had the opportunity to talk, have we? It's what I can do. I want people to know what life is like, in the mines and in places like them."

"Other Resistance fighters?" Elizabeth guessed. "To fire their souls with resolve?"

Brenda shook her head. "Well, to be sure, but they're already with us. I want the folk who aren't Resistance fighters to know of it. The English who marry French, the ones who muddle along thinking, 'This isn't so bad.' I'd be pleased to catch the attention of French reformers, too. Gavin hates them on principle and Katherine doesn't care for them much either—she imbibed her opinions from Mr. Carter, and he'll never see the French as anything but villains to aim a musket at. But I knew a French student when I was a girl—he courted me, as it happens—and he worked to make it law that the Imperial Mining Bureau educate the children of the miners. Because he heard how bad it was, and then came to see it with his own eyes. The one law's not enough, of course, not by half, but it's something. Perhaps I can provoke another something, do you see?"

"Water wearing away rock," Elizabeth said.

"What Frederick always says, yes."

"Do you...does that mean you do not support Mr. Trevelyan's plan, then? You do not wish to see a Rising, with constructs and all?"

"I should very much like to see us rise against the Empire. But until that time comes—am I to do nothing? I haven't the luxury of doing nothing." One of Brenda's hands brushed the front of her gown, a gesture that might have been nothing but smoothing away a wrinkle in the cloth.

"A time to wear away stone with water and a time to strike one hard blow," Elizabeth said. "How do you know which is which?"

"I don't think anyone does," Brenda Trevelyan told her. "We all—what is it Katherine says? Tie on the blindfold and walk."

Elizabeth would never get a better opening than that. "I think I see a way I can strike one hard blow," she said. "I think I can make it better for you, and for the children you and Mr. Trevelyan will have. For the children I myself... may have, someday. I think I know what I can do." She took a deep breath. "I had better start from the beginning."

She told it all—the journey north, the surprises that had awaited them in the Yorkshire cottage, the fire. Katarina's theft. Schwieger's treachery. Last night's confrontation and Maxwell's disappearance. Brenda sat down with a thump on the other end of the trunk partway through, and listened to the rest open-mouthed.

"I think I know what to do, now," Elizabeth finished in a rush. "I think I know who I must speak with and what I must say. If I could only get there." She opened her bandaged hands to show Brenda the pocket watch, its backing pried off to reveal the gleaming cube flashing its bursts of light.

Brenda drew back. "What is that?"

"I don't know," Elizabeth said. "Nor does William, nor Mr. Kent, nor Madam Katherine. But it doesn't seem to be hurt. I mean, it could be—I don't know what it's meant to look like—but all those lights, it doesn't look broken, does it? Only the gears around it have snapped. Mr. Trevelyan has the skill to mend something like this, surely, but...but they all tell me he won't help."

Brenda watched her. "Why do they think so?"

"Because of you." Elizabeth had to stop to breathe. "In the other London—I was afraid to tell you this, but in the other London, he was a widower. You'd been killed in an uprising of Wellington monsters the year after your marriage. And they all say—Madam Katherine and Mr. Kent and all of them—say he won't help us change this, because it might put you at risk again."

"Oh," Brenda said. "Oh, I see." She reached out and took the watch, with its sparkling secret, out of Elizabeth's hands.

It was a much calmer reaction than Elizabeth had expected or wished for. Her heart sank.

After a moment, Brenda looked up with lips quirked in a small smile. "Were you hoping I would fight at the touch of restraints?"

"Er," Elizabeth said. "What makes you think—?"

"Because Katherine would. Nothing makes her angrier than the idea of someone else deciding what risks she might and might not take, and you're very like her."

"But you're not," Elizabeth said, heart sinking further. "I suppose I should have realized that. You don't mind wearing that horrible corset and you don't mind your husband and Mr. Kent telling you what to do. I don't suppose you ever did anything like climb out of your window and run away from home."

Brenda's eyes crinkled. "I'd no need to climb from the window, that's true."

For a moment Elizabeth did not understand. Then she felt her eyes widen.

"I eloped with Gavin," Brenda explained. "Or I ran away from home and joined the Rising. Depending on how one chooses to tell the story."

"But I—I thought you said you weren't like Madam Katherine—"

"I said," Brenda repeated, "that I do not react as violently as she does to the idea of a constraint. But I do understand why she left today. I am sorry for it, but not altogether surprised, for she has been struggling against Frederick for some time now. I left home myself when I was a little older than she is now, because the briar hedge around my life was smothering me. I don't blame her for doing the same."

"But now you regret it?"

"By no means. I only...I have come to see that...it's not quite so simple a thing as I thought it was, leaving. I'd thought of it as a thing requiring courage, and so it is...but nowadays I think so is staying. Leaving is often the easier of the choices, one burst of courage to slice through the briar hedge and done. Staying—wherever one chooses to stay—means you need courage enough to keep pricking your hands on the thorns as you clear away their stranglehold on the roses. Choosing roses to care for isn't quite the same thing as allowing the briar hedge to trap you."

"I don't understand."

"I know you don't." Brenda smiled a little. "I don't regret throwing my lot in with the Resistance, I don't regret stealing a pony to warn Gavin, and I don't regret choosing his way over my father's. But...when I think about having my own children, I begin to see my father's point. The name Trevelyan is one to conjure with, as I said, but it conjures dark faeries as well as light. I think about the danger that might come to my son because of his father's choices, and I begin to understand my Da." Brenda sighed. "At least I got to tell him that."

Elizabeth quirked puzzled eyebrows at her.

"It was he we were settling, in a boarding house on the city outskirts," Brenda said. "He's too old and feeble now to work in the mines, and he's got no daughter's teacher's salary to help him keep body and soul together back home—" She broke off. "But we'll find some work for him, somehow."

Elizabeth did not know what to say in response.

Brenda ran the watch chain through her fingers. "If Gavin mends this for you and you go back..."

"Yes?" Elizabeth tried not to pounce.

She must not have quite succeeded; Brenda looked up with a brief smile. "If you change it all, she might die, this other Brenda. She might be in danger."

"Yes."

"But what happens to me? Do I—stop? Or does this all go on, do I stay here and some other Brenda grows up in another world?"

"I don't know," Elizabeth said.

The silence should have been broken by ticking, but of course the pocket watch was silent.

"But we could take you somewhere," Elizabeth rushed on. "You and Mr. Trevelyan could leave with us, and we could find some safe place before this all starts, so that even if we fail, you and your family could be..."

Brenda was shaking her head. "If there's any chance this world will continue after your changes, then no. I won't walk away from it. What I do here helps, even if only a little." She looked down at the pocket watch. "But I think I hope it vanishes and I'm left with no memory of it."

Elizabeth blinked. "Then...does that mean you'll help me?"

Brenda smiled at her, but her eyes had gone a little distant. "Frederick asked you if you were an angel or a genie. Jinn are a sort of faerie, aren't they?"

"I think so," Elizabeth said, bewildered.

"The Wild Hunt comes offering chaos. Chances, changes. Not certainties. Those who want certainties stay where they are. Where it's maybe not safe, but the dangers are known, so it's safer." Brenda met her eyes. "It could be worse, whatever third world you create."

"It could be," Elizabeth said, because to say anything else would be a lie.

"But it could be better, and I owe my child something better if I can manage it. If I'd wanted to be safe, I'd have stayed in my father's house—so the Wild Hunt it is, then. Once more." She stood up, pocket watch in hand. "I'll go and speak with Gavin."

*

Kent cornered Elizabeth while the argument between the Trevelyans was still raging in the laboratory. Elizabeth had sat upon the stairway to wait it out, miserably unable to draw her attention away. Both Kent and Katarina had been quite right, she was forced to concede in the privacy of her own thoughts. Gavin Trevelyan was as resistant to the idea as they had predicted he would be. It was his voice she could hear, dully, through the closed door. Brenda's tones were still soft and reasonable, even after all this time.

Kent's tones were soft also, but dangerous. His eyes glittered. "I thought I made it clear," he said, "that I desired you to wait until the Russians had departed before distracting Trevelyan's mind with this matter. If I did not believe you to be sincere in your professed principles, I would think you guilty of an attempt to change history by sabotaging construct creation."

It was exactly what Emil Schwieger had tried to entice her into doing. She still wasn't certain why. Only to remove her from the situation, lock her in the laboratory perhaps, so that he might more easily steal Maxwell's pocket watch? Or because he genuinely had desired the prototype destroyed, so no constructs would menace his future monster army?

Not that it mattered now. Elizabeth brushed away the intrusive thought and met Kent's angry eyes. "I am not attempting to sabotage anything. It was only that the matter couldn't wait. Either we would tell him about Katarina and Schwieger and the broken watch, and he would understand what we wanted and speculate as to why we were not asking for his aid. Or we would tell him not one word, and that in itself would arouse his suspicions. Either way, by the time you granted leave to broach the subject, he would already have made his decision, and not even Mrs. Trevelyan would be able to change his mind."

"She may well not be able to change his mind now," Kent muttered.

But she did in the end. Elizabeth was still sitting on the stairway when Brenda emerged to tell her that her husband had agreed to attempt a repair of the timepiece, despite the risks to his wife, for the chance it might offer his child.

"Of course," William said when Elizabeth went to tell him. "He has a family to protect. In any way he can."

*

Trevelyan spent about half his time over the next two days scrounging materials, making sketches, and creating molds. He claimed these activities to be necessary for the repair of the watch, and snarled at any requests for further detail. The other half of his time, he spent cleaning, arranging, and polishing the laboratory and its prototype inhabitant—and then re-cleaning, re-arranging, and re-polishing, despite already-gleaming veneers.

Brenda engaged in similarly frenzied activity in the sitting room and scullery, and Kent spent hours out conversing with those among his contacts who were assisting the discreet Russian arrival onto English soil. When he was within the warehouse walls, he either paced the sitting room or pretended cheerful calm, the latter so obviously a manifestation of iron will that it was painful to watch. Faced with this choice of company, William and Elizabeth spent as much time as was practical assisting Brenda.

The morning of September 5th started very early. Kent dressed himself to glittering perfection, added top hat and gloves and walking stick, and left to meet his Russian envoys. "Someday," he murmured, "I'll have secretaries to bring foreign dignitaries to me. For now, I expect they will understand..." He did not go alone; but the two large and burly men who called for him at the warehouse door were obviously bodyguards rather than members of his future parliament.

As the hour drew close to noon, Elizabeth laid the table under Brenda's fretful direction. William watched, praising everything, as subtly and yet consistently as possible, until the worried line between Brenda's brows eased. At last she took off her apron and went to smooth her hair, and Elizabeth smiled at William. "That was kind of you."

He lifted his good shoulder. "It was no great effort. The sandwiches do look very fine indeed."

A knock came at the door—three sets of three. Kent and his Russians had arrived.

Brenda came tripping hurriedly down the stairs, holding up the skirt of the dark blue cage-dress. "I'll answer it," she said. "Miss Barton, go and fetch Gavin out of the laboratory, won't you? Make him put on his coat if he hasn't already!" she added over her shoulder, and disappeared around the curve of the corridor.

Elizabeth would have greatly preferred some other task, but there had been no time to argue. She heard Brenda begin to undo the latches as she herself headed reluctantly for Trevelyan's laboratory.

The heavy iron-bound door was pushed to, but not locked. Elizabeth tapped on it and pushed it open in the same movement.

She had never seen the place so clean. The papers that had been scattered over the worktables were now stacked in one shadowed corner; the tools that had littered the floor were hung from hooks that she had not even realized were nailed into the wall. The now-revealed bare boards of the floor had been neatly swept. It was pleasant in here, Elizabeth thought, dim and cool like a cellar, offering a little relief from the sticky heat of the rest of the warehouse. Was that due to the cavernous ceiling? Or only to her imagination telling her that shadows ought to be cool?

In the middle of the room, illuminated by the orbs of three lamps, stood the eight-foot-tall construct prototype, gleaming silver and copper patchwork. Trevelyan, likewise dressed in the crispest shirt she had ever seen upon his back, was engaged in rubbing some imaginary spot from its hide with a rag. He glanced up as she entered, but did not say anything.

Elizabeth took a step inside, then another. The loom was silent now, the blacksmith's bellows at rest, the hearth below them cold—nothing to distract the eye from the construct. She remembered how, when she was a small child, spiders had frightened her, despite Bronson's often-repeated reassurances that there was nothing to fear from them and Mrs. Bronson's telling her how they ate nastier bugs. She remembered a large spider building a web in the corner of the kitchen step, and how scared she had been to walk past it. She remembered the day that, after hearing some tale of a valiant knight braving fearsome things to rescue a lady, she had decided she must not be a coward either, and approached the disgusting thing, step by terrified step, to see how close she could get before her skin ran cold. Entering the laboratory was like that. The construct repelled her more than the spider ever had.

Trevelyan finished his polishing with a flourish, and stepped back to survey his creation. "Beautiful, isn't it?" he said. Deliberately, she thought, and it made her jaw tighten.

"I hate these things," she said clearly. "I loathe the sight of them."

Trevelyan folded up his rag. "They're necessary," he said.

"They will not be once my watch is mended."

"Come to speak of it," Trevelyan said unexpectedly, and walked over to the nearest work bench. He closed his hand over something that gleamed momentarily dull gold in the lamplight. When he turned, Elizabeth saw it was her timepiece, and her heart seized in hope. Trevelyan handed it to her without ceremony.

Elizabeth stood speechless for a moment. The watch was warm from where his hand had covered it, and it ticked with reassuring regularity. "You've mended it?" She fumbled to undo the clasp.

"Partway," Trevelyan said. "I don't think there's anything to be done about the pictures." Indeed, the fourth face was cold and lifeless still. "But you can use the dials to set it now." Elizabeth eagerly ran a fingernail over them, and they responded to her touch. "I don't know if it works, of course," Trevelyan added. "Can't very well test it, can I?"

"Mr. Trevelyan, you've—you've—I can't thank you—"

"Ah, that'll do." He turned away with a look, not of embarrassment, but something more like genuine disgust. It stopped the words in her throat.

"We've no more time for this in any case," he went on. "They're here, aren't they?" Not waiting for her reply, he headed for the door.

"Mrs. Trevelyan says I am to remind you to wear your coat," Elizabeth said to his back.

Trevelyan muttered a sigh, took the waiting coat from a peg, and wrestled his shoulders into it without breaking stride. Elizabeth hastened after him, out of the laboratory and down the corridor. Kent's voice came from the sitting room, warm, expansive, welcoming.

Elizabeth rounded the corner behind Trevelyan to see the small room crammed full of people. Kent's two burly bodyguards stood against the far wall, along with their obviously opposite numbers from Russia—though the Russians did look more like secretaries than bodyguards, in neat drab clothing that might have been appropriate for a clerk, with top hats and walking sticks in hand. Kent, Brenda, and a short, dark-haired gentleman with a black beard and a glossy black coat occupied what space there was in the center, and Brenda was following Kent's words of welcome with some of her own. The short, black-bearded Russian seemed to have been bowing over her hand, for he held it still loosely in one of his own, carrying both top hat and cane in the other.

William effaced himself toward the doorway as Trevelyan entered, making room for him, trading places. He joined Elizabeth under the lintel.

"Ah, and here is the man of the hour," Kent said. "Mr. Luzhkov, may I present Gavin Trevelyan."

Trevelyan strode one step into the room, hand outstretched—and froze. Elizabeth could not see his face, but she could see the way his shoulder muscles suddenly bunched with tension, and panic sang through her veins. She tightened her fingers on William's sleeve.

The dark-haired Russian standing at Kent's side turned from Brenda to face Trevelyan fully. Elizabeth's nerves were keyed up to such a pitch that she had to bite back a squeak at the sight of his face. The entire left side of his face was a mass of scar tissue, white and shining, eye covered with a patch. With the right side of his mouth, he smiled, and Elizabeth thought of the way an injured dog bared its teeth. "Trevelyan," he said.

"Buryakov," Trevelyan managed, bringing up the word as though it came from a long distance. His hands clenched and unclenched and made little searching motions from side to side, as though attempting a conjuring. "I thought you were—"

"Dead," Buryakov said. He slid his right hand along the length of the cane he held in his left. "No. Not by water and not by fire."

"Trevelyan?" Kent said. "What is this?" His voice sounded like a master rebuking a subordinate, but his eyes were on the Russian and not on Trevelyan. Brenda backed a few steps away. The four men against the wall had likewise tensed, watching.

Trevelyan ignored them all. "You've a score to settle with me, true enough," he said to the Russian, both hands outstretched now to show he carried no treacherous weapon, "but for the moment we have a common enemy, and it's my laboratory has the means to defeat them. Let's call a truce for now. You won't be able to develop an army of constructs without me, after all."

"Constructs may prove useful to Russian interests," Buryakov agreed. He paused a moment, as though thinking about it, eyes resting on Trevelyan's face. Still watching Trevelyan, he tucked the cane under his left arm, and a pop of sound pierced the air.

Kent's tackle took him down a second too late. Smoke from the end of the walking stick clouded the air, but Elizabeth could still see Brenda collapse, folding like a ragdoll against the table of teacups and napkins. Trevelyan cried out something inarticulate and surged forward, and the four men at the far side of the room plunged into the fray as well. William jerked Elizabeth around the corner.

"It is not death I owe you," Buryakov/'s voice rose above the clamor. "It is hell."

"Laboratory," William said, pulling Elizabeth along with him. "Weapons—"

The little construct watched them impassively as they tumbled through the doorway. Another two sharp pops reached Elizabeth's ears from the direction of the sitting room, followed by a smashing sound that had to be the rickety table and its plates and cups crashing to the floor. Mostly the sounds were shouts and thuds, less frightening than artillery, but there was no doubt the Russians would kill if they could. Elizabeth's heart hammered even faster at the thought. Was Brenda already dead?

William grabbed a heavy pointed tool from over one of the workbenches, handed it to Elizabeth, and caught up a second for himself. They ran back toward the corridor.

But they arrived back in the sitting room to find the worst of the conflict over. Buryakov lay still in the middle of the floor, a neat red wound in the center of his forehead, eyes open and fixed on the ceiling. Kent's two bodyguards were in the process of binding the wrists of one of the Russian bodyguards, while Kent himself kept the other pinned against the wall, a pistol to his head.

The second Russian was talking. "Madness! Not orders! Orders were to inspect weapon! Boris and me, we do not know Luzhkov means this!" He twisted a little, and Kent pressed the pistol more firmly to his head. The Russian stilled, but kept talking. "You think we want trouble with Imperial Police? Orders were to come in quietly and go out quietly and make no trouble for Russia!" Kent's bodyguards finished with his companion and advanced toward him. His eyes rolled back toward Kent again. "I help you with Luzhkov!"

"Which is why you're not dead now," Kent said evenly. "Bind him and gag him," he ordered his men. "Let's hope the Imperials give us time enough to sort this out."

Elizabeth had seen no sight of Trevelyan or his wife until this moment, but when Kent's bodyguards took charge of the second captive, they moved enough to allow her line of sight to the corner behind the overturned table. Trevelyan was kneeling there. Blood soaked and stiffened his left sleeve and more ran from a cut on his forehead, but he seemed unaware of his injuries. Brenda lay in his arms.

Kent turned, taking in the tableau the instant after Elizabeth did. "Oh… God," he said.

William ducked around the various obstacles and dropped down beside Trevelyan, muttering something that sounded like reassurances, but his face changed when his fingers touched Brenda's throat. Elizabeth, hastening to join them, did not need to be told.

"For some reason," Trevelyan said quite calmly, "one never envisions one's sins being visited on others."

"We were not ordered—" the second Russian captive began, in what sounded like a tone of distress, but got no farther before a gag was shoved into his mouth.

There was a pause.

Trevelyan eased Brenda's body very gently to the floor, carefully cradling her head. His eyes went from her face to William's, then to Elizabeth's. Then he pushed himself to his feet, reaching over his wife's body at the same moment to snatch the watch from Elizabeth's hand. She almost pulled it back, but Trevelyan batted her away with a snarl. "Kent's right, that might have been enough noise to draw down Imperials," he said. "You'll want to be well away before they get here. That doesn't leave me much time to work."

He had pushed past her and was most of the way out the door before Elizabeth found her voice. "I thought you already fixed—"

"I lied," Trevelyan snapped. "But there's only a few more gears to put right." He vanished in the direction of the laboratory.

"Right," Kent said quietly. "Mason, Stuart, I can't thank you enough. Now get the hell out of here. Katarina's singing at the Ten Bells these days," he added as the men scrambled to comply. "Wait until tomorrow to tell her what happened. I don't want her coming here today or tonight." He turned to William. "Pack up whatever looks useful. Food, weapons. Bullets. If Trevelyan can't fix the watch after all, you'll have to come with us. Elizabeth, we'll need—" He rubbed his forehead. "Take the blanket off Kat's bed."

She stumbled to obey him. She knew what he wanted it for. She took the one off his bed too, in case he wanted it for the dead Russian.

Trevelyan emerged from the laboratory just as she was handing Kent his blankets. Without saying a word, he opened the watch and showed it to her. This time the fourth face was working. This time she did not feel particularly moved to thank him.

William ran down the stairway, rucksack in hand.

"Never mind the packing," Kent said. "Just go. I don't know how much longer we'll be safe here. You're my best chance of victory now."

"You could come with us," Elizabeth said, looking from him to Trevelyan, knowing even as she spoke how stupid the words must sound—and indeed, Kent was already shaking his head, something almost like a smile on his exhausted face. "You two could help us mend it," she persisted anyway. "And then be safe, afterwards—"

"For what imaginable reason," Trevelyan said tightly, "would I want to do that?" He shoved the watch into her hand and closed her fingers around it. "You tell Viktor Frankenstein—from me—that foreknowledge is a gift. One I'm sure he has done nothing to deserve, and one he has no right to squander. Knowing the consequences with time enough to turn back? I'd sell my soul for his second chance." The edges of the watch cut into her palm with the force of his bloodstained grip over hers. "Fix it. You're the only one who can fix it."

Elizabeth's eyes blurred, and William took the watch gently from her hand.

"The journal—" she said.

"I already have it," he said. His head was bent toward the timepiece, watching intently. She started to ask what he was looking for, but the universe went bright and dark around her before she could speak.

Chapter 11

Danby, Yorkshire, June 5, 1764

The brook proved to be as peaceful as it had looked on the fourth face of the pocket watch. Quiet green meadow stretched around it in every direction—free from the constant grinding undertone that had plagued construct-governed London, but saved by birdsong from the heavy dead silence of French-occupied London. Best of all, a weeping willow arched over the brook itself, dipping its leafy tendrils in the water, perfectly positioned to conceal anyone who sat under it from the eyes of chance passers-by. The brook was a good place to regroup, to cry, to shake. Even to sleep a little. Elizabeth found herself profoundly grateful for the safety it offered. As she surfaced toward wakefulness, she found herself almost ready to begin again.

"Are you feeling better?" William asked as she turned toward him. From his cross-legged sitting position, he could only just reach to brush her curls away from her forehead with his good hand. She wasn't sure if he had slept beside her, or if he had been sitting up and keeping watch the entire time she rested.

She had to admit he asked a reasonable question, considering her hysterical sobs of some hours before. "Yes," she said after a moment's consideration. She did indeed feel better, if still rather strained around the edges. The remembered image of Brenda Trevelyan's body made her throat tighten all over again, but she supposed that was natural. She supposed she had been long overdue for weeping.

"Good," William said. "That's good. Do you think you could you manage a bit of a walk? I want to show you something." What might have been a smile touched his lips. "I think I know where we are."

He led her through the tickling knee-high grasses to a small copse of trees. On the other side of the wood, the ground fell away in a smoothly curving hill. Below, lush green farmland shone emerald under the summer sun. Beyond the farmland clustered the red roofs of a village, and prominent among them rose the spire of a stone church.

"I am almost certain," William said, "that we are looking down upon Danby. See the church tower? The coach brought us by the road that curves around it. There on the far side—" He gestured, and Elizabeth squinted to see the little cottage nestled among the green. "—is the house where Christopher Palmer and Charles West will retire to live out their old age."

"Oh," Elizabeth said, surprised and then pleased. After a moment, she added, "Why should it feel so much like coming home?"

"We found old friends the last time we were here?" William suggested. "Or we've so often looked upon the brook it seems like an old friend itself? I couldn't say with certainty. I only thought it might…lift your heart."

"It does," Elizabeth said. She went closer to the edge of the treeline, leaning against a fallen pine and looking down. "What do you suppose the year is?"

"Before 1820," William said, voice pinched with distaste. "There's no tricolor flag flying anywhere in the village I can see, and the church has not yet begun to crumble."

"It's lovely," Elizabeth said. "So peaceful, without the Eagle overshadowing it. I almost wish we could stay."

William turned to her. "Do you?"

"Well," Elizabeth said, "no. Not truly. There's so much we must go and do." She could see Katarina falling in an alleyway, Maxwell falling into nothingness, Trevelyan's burning eyes and bloodstained hands. All of them were depending on her to somehow put this right, and she wanted to do it for them, of course she did. "Only I think…I wish…I wish we could go and do things, and then come back here between times."

William smiled a little. "A pleasant green haven," he said, "for the times in between the adventures."

She knew whose words he was quoting. "I have a greater appreciation for pleasant green havens than I did a week ago. Was it only a week ago we had that conversation in Orkney? It feels like a year."

"Some weeks are longer than others," William said. "A pleasant green haven, to rest from adventures. Does that mean…have you given any thought to… what you want to do next?"

She looked at him in amazement, and he hastened to clarify, "Go to Orkney and convince Viktor Frankenstein of his error, yes, of course. In—" He paused to hook his own pocket watch from his belt and check the time. "—another eight hours, as soon as the timepiece permits. I meant…after that. After the war. I mean when it's over, when we've done what we must and this is mended, I mean when the days stretch out before you and you can fill them however you like, what do you want to do?"

"Oh," Elizabeth said. Had he somehow known the careful thought she had been giving to this very topic? "I want to do things," she said, and for a moment it was his turn to look amazed, but she went on, "Real things, not stitch samplers. And *do* things, not—" She gestured inarticulately with her bandaged hands. "Not just see them. I used to want to see things. Now I want to do things."

William nodded understanding. "With the pocket watch?"

Elizabeth hesitated. "Perhaps? But it's so…so big in some ways, I'm a little afraid to…" She trailed off, then started over. "I suppose I was thinking something different. I was thinking if only we could set Waterloo right, if only we could make it so there were no monsters and no constructs plaguing our future—after that, we'd be like Frederick Kent, you know. We could know what was coming and work to divert the stream."

"Yes," William said at once, and she had to smile.

"And you?"

"That," he said. "The same. I'm not my father's heir, but I do have enough of a position to have a responsibility. I keep thinking of the child Meg, and there are so many others who need—knights, I suppose. I think there might be ways to play the knight even with—" He gestured to his right shoulder with his left hand. "If I could learn to write left-handed, or hire a secretary—I thought—I thought I could run for Parliament, perhaps. Become a philanthropist or a reformer. Write pamphlets. I could change what must be changed. I could try, at least."

"Walk through time in a straight line," Elizabeth said. For some reason, a swelling in her throat made it hard to swallow. Free roses from briars. "Write the future."

"Yes," William said, "that exactly. I want to go back home and write the future. And there's something else I want. Something I need to ask you." He took a breath. "I'd never forgive myself if I didn't ask. But you do understand that you need not do anything except what you choose? You have a pocket watch, Elizabeth. You can do anything, go anywhere, live however you like. You needn't stay in Hartwich once we set things right. You could go somewhere where your life could be more like Katherine's, if that's what you wish. You needn't marry just to escape your father's house. You needn't marry anyone if you do not wish to."

The swelling had spread to her heart now, which seemed to have grown too large for her chest. Her ribcage ached under its beating. "I needn't," she agreed, not steadily. "I suppose, given no practical necessity driving me toward the married state, I would only consent to marry for love. Were you going to ask me something?"

He must not have understood what she meant, for he said it like the words were a glove flung down. "Will you marry me?"

"Yes," Elizabeth told him.

"Yes?"

"Yes. Don't look so surprised! I thought you knew I—"

He caught hold of her then, slid his good hand up her arm to her face and then around the back of her head, and most effectively stopped her from talking. Sometime later, he said, "I did know. I thought you…I thought you might not be ready quite yet. I thought perhaps you'd say you wanted to travel more first."

"I thought we could travel more afterwards. Together?" She nestled against his chest. "By ship?"

He laughed a little. She could feel the vibration shiver through them both. "How conventional of you."

"Brenda Trevelyan—" This time Elizabeth managed to say her name without breaking down in tears. "Brenda Trevelyan said she wouldn't leave her 1885. She said it needed her. She wrote those pamphlets her husband printed, did you know that? We could just run off, you and I; we could set up housekeeping in a time and place easier than the one we were born to, but...but I think our 1815 needs us."

"Yes," William said, and tightened his left arm around her.

"Everyone will think we did run off, and then came back, but my parents will want it smoothed over." She had been thinking about this for days. "They won't want a scandal, so they will most likely give their consent and let us have my dowry. But then we—we needn't stay in Hartwich itself. We could take a house somewhere else—"

"Somewhere in the north," William said. "Somewhere near here, perhaps. A green haven to rest in between adventures."

"Perhaps we could use the timepiece now and then after all," Elizabeth said. "Go to other times and places just to see them. Very carefully. We'd need to be sure to take care, of course—we'd need to be sure to come back. If we—when we—if we had a child, we wouldn't want to disappear and never have him know what became of us..."

William stiffened. Elizabeth tilted her head and looked up at him. "You know," he said at last.

"I—there is something I suspect," she said. "Is it something you know?"

He sighed. He took a step back from her, drew Maxwell's locket from his shirt pocket, and put it into her hand.

It was warm from the heat of his body. Elizabeth slid her fingernail along the join until she found the clasp, and the two halves sprang apart. It was not exactly a surprise to see her own face looking back at her.

The woman in the miniature seemed only a little older than the face she beheld every day in the glass, and much of that effect was probably due to the dressing of the hair under a cap as befit a married woman. Elizabeth enjoyed one instant of satisfaction in having her expectation proved correct before a sense of frustrated disappointment settled on her shoulders. "I see," she said. "I was hoping it was both of us."

William breathed a laugh. "And here I thought I was going to surprise you."

"You knew for certain," Elizabeth said, looking up at him. "I was only guessing."

"I didn't know for certain until the night he and Schwieger disappeared," William corrected her. "Until then, I was only guessing too."

"What made you think so?"

"A hundred little things. Some things he said when he was drunk. Some things he didn't say. In the Alps they have avalanches, a hundred snowflakes combining until half a mountain collapses—it felt like that. I sat there talking to him that night, and it felt like something I had known for a long time. I couldn't say exactly when I started knowing."

Elizabeth nodded slowly. "I know when," she said. "It burst upon me like a thunderstorm. It was the night of the fire, he pulled me out of danger—and I thought after all he's done for us—not just my life, but my *life*, the watch—all of this, the chance to do something—I ought to name my eldest son for him. I hadn't realized until that moment that he never gave us but the one name."

"Yes," William said. "I noticed that as well, sometime during that drunken conversation."

"Once I saw that, a hundred little things fell into place. His mother had a dress like mine,. Madam Katherine knew I'd come from Kent. Madam Katherine acted as though she knew a great deal about me, in fact. Maxwell used my first name when he presented me to her, but you'd introduced me to him only as 'Miss Barton.' It felt like—like an avalanche, as you say. I sat there wondering what had been inside that locket he was so glad I hadn't opened."

"Yet you didn't ask?"

"I—was afraid." That sounded even more absurd said aloud than it had in her head. "Or no, not afraid exactly. But if I asked, he would answer, and I was afraid it—" She bit her lip, then blurted it out. "I was afraid it wouldn't be you. And then—and then I wouldn't know what to do."

A flush spread over his cheeks. "I was afraid of the same thing," he admitted. "That it wouldn't be me. And then I was afraid it would be, and I worried you'd feel obliged. I didn't want you to wed me only because you thought you owed it to Max. I finally decided I would ask the question first, so I'd know in my own mind you really wanted to. He knew your Christian name. He sent you the watch. I knew you were part of his story. But his father could have been anyone."

"His father the *time traveler*," she pointed out.

"His mother the time traveler owns the timepiece. She could share it with another if she chose. And so there I was—we were speaking of choices freely made and all knowledge freely shared, and I couldn't share the whole truth because I didn't have it myself."

"Most of the time we cannot see the consequences we choose," she said. "Foreknowledge is a rare gift. The rest of the time you tie on the blindfold and walk. I want to marry you because I wish it, and because you wish it, and—and that's as much and more than most people have."

"So it is." His left arm wrapped around her waist, drawing her close. "Maxwell Carrington," he murmured after a moment. "A firstborn son not named for his father. How tongues will wag."

"It won't be the queerest thing we do," Elizabeth retorted. "At least, not the queerest thing I plan to do. And it could be 'William Maxwell Carrington,' did you ever think of that?"

He laughed, and she laughed, and then she shuddered and clung to him. "We have to fix this. We have to fix this, too. Living forward. He can't grow up without parents, he can't know nothing of us but journal entries, we can't abandon him to a life that ends with him hurtling through some unknown time with Emil Schwieger—"

William hugged her. "He won't. We won't. We know what the consequences are, now. We can choose to avoid them. We'll make it better for him."

"He's still out there somewhere right now," Elizabeth whispered. "Even if we succeed with Frankenstein, Schwieger will still have the papers, and Maxwell is still there with him, wherever 'there' is. Or maybe not even—Schwieger could have pulled a knife on him the instant they were alone, do you realize that?"

"No," William said definitely. "He could not have." Elizabeth stared at him in astonishment, and he elaborated, "Trevelyan knew Maxwell in Vienna. The Maxwell he met in Vienna knew the three of us would arrive in occupied London, in 1885, in need of shelter. He hadn't done it yet, so he must therefore survive whatever danger he is in now—at least long enough to do it."

"Oh." Elizabeth rested her forehead against William's chest. Her knees felt suddenly wobbly. "So we may see him again. I so hope we see him again." William moved his hand up her back, running his fingers through the tangle of her curls. She relaxed against him, letting the motion soothe her jangled nerves. After a time she thought of something. "But the Frankenstein papers. Schwieger will still have them. Even if we convince Viktor in Orkney, Maxwell will have to stop Schwieger—"

"He will." William spoke without hesitation. "We can trust him to do his part while we do ours. And we can trust him to come back to us if there is any way on earth to accomplish it. We can trust him."

"Yes." Elizabeth found herself suddenly just as certain. William's conviction was contagious. She straightened, and his brown eyes were there to meet hers, warm and steady and unafraid. She was even able to smile at him. "Very well, then." She took a deep breath. "We had better give our attention to our part. How shall we accomplish our task in Orkney?"

Interlude

Orkney Isles, September 1, 1790

The red-gold sun hovered in the western sky, readying itself to begin its slow liquid descent into the sea. Viktor Frankenstein watched it from the window above his sleeping pallet, and reflected that there was no point in recommencing his labors now, as he would shortly be deprived of light sufficient for his employment. True, he had, on previous occasions, worked day and night with a pause only long enough to light candles—but his store of candles was at the present moment sadly depleted, and he had been warned often enough of the deleterious effects of incessant labor upon his health. If he spent himself too freely now, he would have no reserves to draw upon when the next fever of inspiration seized him.

Admittedly, working fits were not so common with him now as they had once been. Indeed, he had for some days been possessed by that mood wherein he found it impossible to prevail upon himself to enter the laboratory; he knew he ought, but a kind of dragging lassitude seized hold of him and rendered him still. Today, his limbs actually ached with fatigue, as though he had been climbing the cliffside—which he had not; it had been many days since he had even walked upon the stony beach of the sea. *Perhaps I have taken ill already,* he reasoned with himself, *some sickness brought on by the unhealthfulness of this barren and lonely life.*

In that case, it was surely better he rest himself, lest he bring on a complete collapse of the sort that had occurred three years before. He would therefore swallow a draught to aid in slumber, sleep long and soundly and awake refreshed, and then upon the morrow plunge himself into his work. He had not much further to go. One final effort, and the task would be complete, the race won, his life once more his own. *With my promise fulfilled, the monster will depart forever. He and his loathsome mate will find a remote and desolate corner of the earth to dwell in and will never again trouble me.*

The words echoed in his mind a moment, but he had resolved to put thoughts of work aside for the night, so he therefore pushed them off. He reached instead for his sleeping-draught. When not exhausted from a day's and night's incessant labor, Viktor found it difficult to sleep—his limbs and fingers twitched, and his thoughts seemed to twitch as well, jerking observation and conclusion together into a structure he found himself reluctant to contemplate with any great attention. Not that he had ever taken deliberate council with himself and chosen to look away from the tower of conclusions his mind constructed; he had merely never as yet chanced to examine it closely, though the portion of his brain responsible for edifice-building persisted nightly at its task. To address this complaint, he had evolved the custom of dosing himself at bedtime with a small quantity of laudanum. The tincture slowed the work of his inner edifice-builder and scattered the internal building materials to the four winds, and thereby enabled Viktor to gain the rest necessary for the preservation of life.

By the time the sun touched the sea, Viktor had swallowed enough of the potent brew to achieve the stillness of thought he desired. Indeed, perhaps he had been overgenerous with his mouthfuls, for the vista of sea and sky seemed to tilt as he turned his head. He rested his chin upon the window ledge, and watched with dreamy satisfaction the breaking of the waves upon the rocks. A good stretch of stony beach was visible, the tide being nearly at its ebb. Viktor fixed his eyes upon this. He observed the monotonous yet ever-changing pattern of the waves dashing upon the stones, and thought of Switzerland.

No vista in his home country had the smallest trait in common with this desolate and appalling landscape. Here the hills rose barren above the salt spray, and no more than five hardy families scratched a living upon the rocks; at home the vine-covered hills were thickly scattered with cottages, and the placid lakes reflected a blue and gentle sky. This was a place of torment and struggle; his long-forsaken home, a land of serenity.

Thoughts of home led him inevitably to thoughts of Elizabeth. His cousin had eyes the color of those lakes and that sky. Her hair was the brightest living gold, her lips and the molding of her face perfectly expressive of sensitivity and sweetness. Her saintly soul shone like a shrine-dedicated lamp in his father's house, every sweet glance from her celestial eyes a blessing to its inhabitants. She cared for Viktor's father, in the last year grown feeble with age and loss; she played the part of elder sister to Viktor's brother Ernest; she tended the graves of Viktor's mother, dead these several years of scarlet fever, and of Viktor's young brother William, killed some months before in circumstances that still made Viktor's soul shudder within him.

He was surely the man on earth least deserving of Elizabeth Lavenza's angelic regard, and yet she had bestowed it upon him—upon *him*, Viktor Frankenstein—and waited now for him to complete his travels abroad and return to take her hands in marriage. Would that he could leave this place at once and fly to her—but he dared not engage in his loathsome occupation in his father's house, dared not poison the lives of those whom he loved, and so dared not return home until his work was done. For as long as the term of his imprisonment upon this sterile island lasted, he might behold his Elizabeth only in his thoughts.

At least he found those vivid enough, particularly in that time between sunset and moonrise, particularly with a body relaxed by laudanum in preparation for sleep. He could almost see her standing before him now, pure-skinned and golden-haired and ethereal, and the landscape he glimpsed behind her was made up of placid lakes rather than frothing gray sea.

For one heavenly instant, she might have been solid enough to touch. Then he blinked, and she and the serene lake vanished, and there were only the angry Orkney waves.

A young man and young woman stood together upon the barren shore, gazing out at the water. In a dim way, Viktor found this occurrence odd. He could not have been asleep, for the sun had sunk no more than halfway into the sea; and yet he had not seen the young people arrive, neither walking from one end of the beach, nor from the other, nor disembarking from a fishing-boat. He watched them idly, wondering from whence they might have come.

The boy and the girl looked about themselves, at the stony beach and then at the sea and then up at Viktor's cottage perched on the cliffside. The girl was bareheaded, and the salt breeze whipped her hair into her eyes, tangling the curls into snarls. She clawed her tresses back with an impatient hand, and made shift to tie them, but they escaped again. The boy pointed out to her the path that at low tide led from the shore to the cliff; the girl nodded; and the two of them started up it, side by side. The young man had a deformed arm, which dangled as he walked.

They were wearing the most extraordinary clothing. Not only was the girl without hat or kerchief, but she also appeared to be without a gown, to be clad what certainly looked to Viktor's eyes to be nothing more than a shift. The boy wore a coat of plain material, more like a laborer's than a gentleman's—and a battered rucksack was strapped to his back, confirming the impression—yet for all that, he was plainly no Orkney fisherman. Neither he nor his companion bore any resemblance to the starved and bent creatures with whom Viktor shared his island. They were straight-backed, and apparently healthy, save for the boy's arm—and bandages on the girl's hands. Where had they come from?

Viktor contemplated the notion that they might not be there at all. It would not be the first time he had seen what was not there after taking his sleeping-draught, though usually he fancied he beheld his distant family, or shrank in fear from a vision of his loathsome nemesis. He had imagined before now that the monster had burst upon him, seized him from his sleeping-pallet, and dashed him to the floor.

The boy and the girl gained the top of the cliff and continued along the path that led to Viktor's front door. He watched from the window, still uncertain if he beheld a vision but incurious of the answer. The vision stopped in front of his window, the girl and the boy looking at each other before the latter stepped forward and spoke. "Monsieur Frankenstein?"

He did not answer for a moment, trying to decide whether any of his previous visions had addressed him by name. The young man cleared his throat and tried again.

"Viktor?"

"Yes," he said, distracted from his musing, and looked up. "Who calls me?"

"My name is William," the boy said.

It was not the first time he had seen the shade of his murdered little brother, though this was the first time the vision had taken the form of the man his brother might have grown to become. He searched the youth's face for any sign of the child he remembered—not that a man nearly grown should be expected to possess rosy cheeks, but perhaps something in the smile—or perhaps the eyes—

William hesitated, then turned to draw forward the wild-haired girl dressed in a shift. "May I present," he began, then stopped and fell back upon informal manners. "This is Elizabeth."

Viktor looked over at her in sharp interest and sharper alarm. "No," he said after a moment's scrutiny, in great relief, "no, you're not." He had feared for a moment that his betrothed had come herself to bid him come home—and he would not have her within a hundred miles of this place—but though the eyes of the girl before him were blue, they snapped and sparkled and had nothing of serenity in them. Nor was the hair golden, nor the countenance characterized by ethereal sweetness. This was not his Elizabeth. His Elizabeth was safe at home.

"No," the girl agreed, pushing back her tangled curls again. "Not your Elizabeth."

He did not think he had spoken aloud, but of course if she was his vision, she would know his thoughts. "You're his Elizabeth," Viktor concluded, looking at William. "If my innocent brother had lived, he would have grown into a man who had a love of his own. Are you then a vision of what might have been, come to reproach me for my crimes?"

"The shadow of what may be, only," the girl murmured. "No, sir. My surname is Barton. This is Mr. Carrington. We're spirits of what is yet to come, but we are not your ghosts."

"I am a man of rational principles and scientific education," Viktor declared. "I do not remember to have ever trembled at a tale of superstition in my childhood, or to have feared the apparition of a spirit. Darkness had no effect upon my fancy, and a churchyard was to me merely the receptacle of bodies deprived of life, which, from being the seat of beauty and strength, had become food for the worm. I had not then, and I have not now, a weakness of understanding such that finds comfort in the belief of ghosts. Though it is true," he added after a thought, "I have since seen things in which most people would not believe, and it is no superstition to believe in what you have seen, or extrapolate other facts from what you observe. If there is a way to bring dead flesh to life, could not the departed mind be preserved in some way as well? That which we think of as personality, as memory, as principles? The soul, in other words?" He peered at his brother William. "Might you not be indeed true representations of my beloved dead?"

William turned to Elizabeth and switched from French to English, rather an odd thing for a vision of Viktor's to do. "I do not believe we may call this a choice made with free will and all the consequences known."

The girl's face registered dismay. "Is it madness?"

"No," William said, "it is opium. At least, I cannot tell if the other may be true as well, but certainly to begin with— You may trust me," he added. "I had rather a lot of the stuff when I was wounded, and the dreams it gave me still make me shudder. We cannot call this a choice freely offered and freely made until M'sieur Frankenstein understands who we are."

Elizabeth nodded, and looked Viktor over in a way that made him wonder if he were a vision of hers, rather than she being a vision of his. "How shall this be accomplished?"

"Time," William said. "Fresh air. And tea, if there is any in there. You seem unwell, sir," he added to Viktor, in French. "Allow us to come in and tend to you."

"I have feared," Viktor agreed, "that I have fallen ill from my unhealthful life of solitude…" By then the boy had left the window for the door, and before Viktor could remember how he had intended to end the sentence, the two young people were standing before his pallet.

The girl was not so gentle and tender a nurse as his Elizabeth, but she made distressed sounds over his pale and emaciated condition, and brought him a handkerchief dipped in water to soothe his brow. William spoke again of tea, and turned toward the kitchen.

"No!" Viktor tried to rise, but the room swam and he fell back. "You must not—must not—trespass—into my laboratory. There is a—a scientific project—of great importance—"

"Yes," William said, "we know, sir. If you keep tea in this outer room, I assure you I have no desire to enter your laboratory. It smells unpleasantly of rotting meat in there. To be sure, it smells rather like a battlefield infirmary in here," he added, turning away and surveying the littered and untidy chamber. "Ah—I see a kettle. And a canister…" He picked his way over the debris on the floor and lifted it from the mantelpiece. "Is this tea?" Viktor did not answer. The young man uncorked the canister to verify the matter for himself, then managed to fill the kettle and stir up the fire, working one-handed all the while. Viktor wondered why his imagination should have crippled his brother.

"Your illness will be eased by fresh air, sir," William told him, and gave Viktor his left arm to lean upon as he made the few steps from pallet to door. William settled him on a broad flat stone, and soon after Elizabeth joined them and pressed Viktor's own mug into his hands, steaming with strong tea. The sun had set, but the moon had not yet risen, and the night was full of the rumble and hiss of the waves below. Viktor swallowed the tea and let himself float along on the sound.

*

"I must beg your pardon, sir," Viktor said, a very long while and some three or four mugs of tea later. He studied the young man by the light of the rising moon, wondering how he ever could have mistaken him for his brother. Other than the fair hair, they shared not one feature in common. The young man's eyes were brown, not blue; his lashes fair, not dark. "I must have seemed a madman," Viktor continued, "with my wild speech. I have been ill, as I told you, and sometimes my dreams take such possession of me I cannot tell them from the waking world, and…my young brother, a beautiful child whom all adored, was killed last year, murdered in a most horrible way. They said our maidservant Justine killed him for the miniature he wore, but…" He trailed off, as he had so often before. Of what use was it to attempt this story? Who would believe that a being whom he himself had formed and endued with life had confessed to Viktor its authorship of the crime? There was no point in making the attempt. "But…"

"But they were wrong," the girl Elizabeth said. "The fault was your monster's."

For a moment, Viktor could not perceive the sense of her words. Then his mug slipped through his fingers and broke into slivers upon the rocks before.

"How did you know that?" he demanded, leaning toward her.

She met his eyes without flinching. "I have read the record you made of it," she said, and pulled from William's rucksack a notebook bound in reddish-brown leather.

Viktor at once sought the book's accustomed resting-place in his pocket, expecting to find she had purloined it while tending him earlier. To his astonishment, the book was there. He drew it forth and stared at it, looking from it to its fellow in Elizabeth's hands.

She opened her copy and turned it so he could see. The pages were covered with a hand he recognized as his own, though the light was too dim to allow him to discern words. With frantic haste he flipped through the book that had been in his pocket. The same hand covered the same pages, in the same pattern.

"This is the journal you kept from the day you left Geneva for England," the girl said, "until the day of your death." Some of the pages that should have belonged to the middle of her copy were missing, excised by a knife-blade, only jagged nubs of paper remaining. After the gap, however, his writing once more appeared upon the pages. The girl who was not his Elizabeth turned to a leaf perhaps three-quarters of the way to the end. "Do you see this final entry? It was made the fourteenth of September, seventeen hundred and ninety. On the fifteenth of September, you will finish the female monster, and that is the day upon which the male monster will have no further use for you and will end your life."

Viktor stared at the page, and then up at her face, straining to perceive her expression in the darkness.

"We should return to the cottage," William said quietly behind them. "As little as I fancy the company of what inhabits the kitchen, we must have candles for the rest of it."

It took some rustling about before William discovered a cache of candles, the existence of which Viktor had quite forgotten. There were, it transpired, more than enough to bring almost an illusion of daylight to the cramped front room. He might after all have pursued his researches in the laboratory tonight… though perhaps it was just as well he had not. He let William guide him to the rickety table he used as a writing desk, and the young man set before him both the reddish-brown journals.

It is a trick, Viktor thought, staring from the one to the other. *It is a copy to which they have added, in order to compel some action from me...*But how could that be? His notebook had resided in his breast pocket for most of a year. Their copy of it was exact in every detail save for the missing pages—including even the musings he had thought of this morning, but had not yet set down. How could this be known to anyone save himself?

"How do you know this?" he managed from a dry throat. "How do you come by this?"

"I was born in 1798," Elizabeth said. "My friend Mr. Carrington and I lived to see the world that your creature and his wife and their offspring wrought. This device—" She nodded to William, and he unthreaded a pocket watch from his waistcoat, popped it open, and laid it on the table where the candlelight shone most strongly. "—allowed us to travel backward in time, so that we could warn you of what we saw. I am here to ask you not to create this world."

"Offspring," Viktor whispered. "No. No, he promised me, that if I created for him a female creature to follow him into exile, they would quit Europe forever—and every other place in the neighborhood of man—"

"He lied," William said, looking Viktor directly in the eye. "He betrayed you. You have suspected his treachery before now, have you not?"

It was that thought, that conclusion, that structure he had shied from in the dark watches of the night. Those were the words he had sought to drown with laudanum. Now the words burst upon him, loud as a carillon of bells, impossible to ignore. They deafened him.

"At least," Elizabeth amended, "he may have made the pledge in good faith. That I do not know; I have no power to see into his heart. But I can tell you with absolute certainty that he will break his word. He will leave you dead in your laboratory a fortnight from now—I *know*, I saw your body lying just there, inside the kitchen door, and I saw your creature take his newly freed wife to the mainland. Their offspring will run free through the Highlands, prey upon the unfortunates who dwell there, and cause the capture of one of their number with their misdeeds. Once a creature has been captured, it will become possible for others to duplicate your experiments, and monsters will be created to serve in the British army."

"And in the French." William took up the tale. "If you look closely at this watch, you will see it displays images of things that have happened or will happen—see, here, this battle being fought upon English soil? Monsters wearing red and monsters wearing blue, and helpless men falling to their ferocity. That is the Battle of Dover, fought between French monsters and British. Here—" He reached again into the rucksack, and drew out a notebook bound in black leather, and a second bound in green cloth. "—I have the accounts kept by men who lived in the devastated world that was all that remained after the battle. Finally, I have seen with my own eyes the massive weapons that humankind creates decades later to rid themselves of the plague of monsters, and the damage these weapons do to their wielders as well as to their targets."

Viktor looked from one of them to the other, feeling faintness swirl in his head and nausea swirl in his gut. The sense of peaceful floating that had encompassed him when they sat on the cliff top had vanished. In its place, a creeping dark exhaustion settled over him. Every shadowed corner of the room seemed to be hiding a dreadful thing, or perhaps an angelic being that gazed at him with accusing eyes.

"Please," the girl said, and looked at him with an expression that might, for that moment of softened entreaty, have been mistaken for one belonging to his Elizabeth. "Don't do this."

"Take your time, sir, and read what we have brought you." William moved out of the light, setting his feet firmly as though to dissuade himself from impatience. "I have no wish to hasten you to a conclusion; I rather wish to convince you as one rational man to another."

Viktor swallowed the sickness in his throat and drew the green cloth notebook toward him. "When I was ten years old, the monsters came," it began. "When I was a man, I joined Fitzclarence's Rising." It went on to tell of nights spent in caves, of farmland trampled flat and women and children starving. As Viktor forced his way through the words, the pocket watch sat open upon the table, occasionally sparking to life with colored images so bright they hurt his eyes. It seemed to return with particular delight to the picture of monsters ripping each other apart, and at last Viktor buried his head in his arms with a moan.

"It is true," he cried. "I have feared deceit on the part of the demon, but I have refused to consider it carefully. Perhaps he has lied to me and does not mean to keep his promise to avoid the habitations of man. Or perhaps the fault will lie with her—" He had to raise his head to wave a hand toward the kitchen door, and once he beheld the steady gazes of William and Elizabeth, found himself compelled to address them with his thoughts. "Three years ago I created a fiend whose unparalleled barbarity desolates my heart and fills it forever with the bitterest remorse. I am now about to form another being, of whose dispositions I am alike ignorant; she might become ten thousand times more malignant than her mate, and delight, for its own sake, in murder and wretchedness. He has sworn to quit the neighborhood of man, and hide himself in deserts, but she has not. Perhaps they will stay in the Highlands because she—who will in all probability be a thinking and reasoning animal—will refuse to comply with a compact made before her creation." His thoughts carried him on, floodwaters racing to the sea. "A race of devils will be propagated upon the earth, and will make the very existence of the species of man a condition precarious and full of terror. The wickedness of my promise bursts upon me—and yet—it is a promise; I have given my word—and I fear the fiend's threats if his craving is not satisfied. Can you not—" His eye fell upon the gleaming pocket watch. "Can you not take this device and go to my student apartment in Ingolstadt, to that lonely cell wherein I conceived the first loathsome demon—can you not show the man I was three years ago what will result from his folly, and save my young brother and the good Justine and—"

He stopped, because Elizabeth was shaking her head. "No," she said. Her blue eyes were bright with tears. "I would if I could, but another has already used this device to attempt just such a change. He went about his work too subtly, we think."

Viktor looked at her, puzzled and distracted from his tirade.

"A man of broad shoulders and brown eyes," William said, "an Englishman by his speech, who would have attempted to dissuade you from your course of study at Ingolstadt."

Viktor could not recall him. "There were many such, my course of study being the very opposite of orthodox."

"Or perhaps you remember a man of that description staying with your family in Geneva?"

Viktor tried to cast his mind back. "Stay, I do remember such a visitor to my father. He was a great researcher into natural philosophy, and upon the occasion of a lightning strike that destroyed an ancient oak tree standing upon my father's property, he explained to me the theory of electricity and galvanism. All that he said threw greatly into the shade Cornelius Agrippa, Albertus Magnus, and Paracelsus, the lords of my imagination, and for a time I gave up my dangerous researches. When I look back, it seems to me as if this almost miraculous change of inclination and will was the immediate suggestion of the guardian angel of my life—the last effort made by the spirit of preservation to avert the storm that was even then hanging in the stars and ready to envelop me. It was a strong effort of the spirit of good, but it was ineffectual. Destiny was too potent, and her immutable laws had decreed my utter and terrible destruction. When I went to university, I drifted back to my dangerous occupation."

"So you see, it has already been tried," Elizabeth said, "and therefore it cannot be tried again. The consequence of the choices you made then are set in stone, Monsieur Frankenstein. But—" She took a breath. "—the consequences of the choice you make tonight are yet to be written. You have not made it yet. You are making it now. You need not choose to create—" She gestured to the litter of papers on his writing desk. "—this world."

"Usually," William said, his voice low and intense, "we must make decisions in the darkness or the twilight, with the path ahead obscured. We choose consequences not knowing what they are. God knows, I have myself." He looked at Elizabeth. "We have, the both of us." She nodded, face somber. "But you, Monsieur Frankenstein, have the opportunity to freely choose your destiny— seeing clearly all that lies down one of the two paths open to you." He tapped the book of wartime memoirs. "Do you choose to bring this world into being?"

"No," Viktor whispered, bile rising in his throat at the thought. "I have no right, for my own benefit, to inflict this curse upon everlasting generations. I have been struck senseless by the creature's fiendish threats, but now I see clearly. If I do not turn from this path of destruction, future ages will curse me as their pest, whose selfishness had not hesitated to buy its own peace at the price

of the existence of the whole human race. No, I will not serve you, monster!"
This he howled at the ceiling, a defiance flung in the teeth of the demon he fancied always to be watching him at a remove. Then he dashed into his laboratory
before his resolution could fail.

There he seized a kitchen knife, and fell upon the thing manacled to what
had once been a kitchen table. He ripped free the stitches in the flesh—upon
which he had so painstakingly toiled only a few days before—and the body that
might have become a female creature fell apart into a lifeless pile of limbs and
organs. The room did, as William had observed, stink of rotting meat, and Viktor feared he only contributed to the stench when he kicked the various body
parts into separate corners—as though they might spontaneously gain life and
movement and crawl to reattach themselves once his attention lay elsewhere—a
ridiculous thought, but one that momentarily possessed his mind with terror.
Trembling with passion, he then attacked the apparatus itself, smashing glass,
casting half-brewed potions and serums to the floor, twisting delicate utensils
into mockeries of their former shapes. "The notebook," he gasped then. "From
my writings this madness might be replicated by another—will be, you said—"
He addressed those last words to Elizabeth and William, who stood in the
doorway watching him. Then he seized a candelabrum and his journal, and
rushed into the yard.

The moon was a slender crescent that barely competed with the stars, and
both of them were overwhelmed by the flare of his torch. He kicked wood into
the shape of a bonfire, ripped pages from the notebook to use as kindling, and
set it alight. When the fire caught, he tore the book to pieces in a kind of frenzy,
feeding page after page to the greedy flame and watching it leap ever higher.

At last it was done—his life's work reduced to nothing but ash and the
heaps of rotting flesh inside the house—and he turned to the two who had
saved him from himself. To his horror, Elizabeth still held the second notebook,
the one from the future that foretold his death. Firelight glowed against the
calfskin bindings.

"No," he whimpered, looking at it. "I destroyed—"

"You did," Elizabeth said. "Those who travel in time and that which travels
with them are protected from the ravages that befall those living forward." She
smiled a little, and added, "The physical ravages, at least."

"But—" Viktor said.

Elizabeth met Viktor's eyes. "We did not come all this way and risk so
much to leave this intact for another time traveler to find. I choose to destroy it,
as well." She walked past him and dropped the notebook into the bonfire. The
three of them stood quiet and watched it burn.

"It's done," Viktor whispered as the last piece of charred ash fell to the
ground. "I never shall and no one else ever can complete this work."

William closed his eyes and let his breath out in a long sigh, and Elizabeth
seemed to suddenly find her knees weak; she stumbled a little, and William
slipped his left arm about her waist to steady her.

"Hist!" Viktor cried, seized with terror. "He's there! He watches!"

Both the youngsters snapped alert, and William pushed Elizabeth toward the cottage as he ran past the dying fire to look into the darkness. All three of them were silent, listening. The sea roared in Viktor's ears.

"There is nothing there, sir," William said, returning. "The moon and stars give light enough when you are beyond the fire, and I saw nothing move."

"No, no. He is there. He is sly!" Viktor strained his eyes, but saw nothing moving either. He was not even sure he had seen movement the first time, but he knew with every fiber of his being that his dread creation had followed him in his travels, had hid itself in caves or taken refuge in wide and desert heaths, and now observed the destruction of all it required for future happiness. Was that wind he heard, or a howl of devilish despair and revenge?

"You must go," he said to the boy who was like his brother and the girl who stood beside him. "Gather your things and leave this place the way you came. You must not be here when he comes! He will revenge himself upon me for the breaking of my promise, and I accept that it must be so—I choose that consequence of my miserable folly—but I will not watch while he harms others in my stead. Go from here!"

They gathered together their papers and the watch, Viktor pressing them to greater haste with every breath. When they had collected their belongings, he almost pushed them to the door.

"Come away with us," William urged. "Leave this place at once, take a boat and go to your friend Clerval."

"I would not have Henry near me when I face my nemesis," Viktor told him. "You must not be here either. Go!"

Elizabeth paused one moment longer, however. "Thank you," she said, and reached to take his hands. "You have saved us."

"You're not much like my Elizabeth," he told her, "but I think you might be an angel after all. One of a different complexion."

She blinked at that, and then William was taking her hand and urging her onward. Viktor watched, heart hammering, as they ran across in the direction of the fallen-in barn. Nothing lunged from the darkness to menace him, and they finally vanished from his sight.

Viktor returned to his pallet, took up his post at the window that faced the sea, and waited.

Chapter 12

Orkney Isles, September 1, 1790

They ran into the night, heading for the ruined barn, and nothing lunged from the darkness to menace them. "There was nothing there," William whispered as they gained the shelter of the building. "I saw nothing; I heard nothing; he is afraid of something only he can see."

"Perhaps it was not just laudanum, then," Elizabeth whispered back.

They waited, holding still, for long enough that she started to shiver from the wind and the reaction to the interview they had just concluded. Hearing absolutely nothing that might indicate the presence of a monster, they dared to light the dark lantern ("I shall miss the matchsticks when we go home," Elizabeth murmured) and found a more comfortable place to sit. Half of the building's roof had fallen in during past winter snows, but the other half seemed sound enough, and under this, they made a nest of somewhat moldy straw and sat back to take stock.

William opened the pocket watch and set it down where they both could see it. The fourth face was asleep. Elizabeth thought of discretion—just in case there was something lurking about outside after all—and covered it with a fold of her skirt.

"We can't leave until it shows us we've changed something," she said.

"We couldn't leave before tomorrow in any case, unless we stole a fishing boat," William pointed out. "In all honesty, Elizabeth, I do not think there is anything out there. Viktor Frankenstein carries his phantasms with him."

"I think that makes it more urgent that we stay until we are sure he will not change his mind back," Elizabeth said. "Otherwise, he might see some phantasm that threatens him as effectively as we convinced him."

A flash of colored light through the white fabric of her skirt proclaimed the fourth face to have awakened, and she snatched it up eagerly.

And beheld monsters tearing each other to pieces at the Battle of Dover, while dirigibles loomed over their heads.

Tears sprang into her eyes, but she tried to keep them out of her voice. "It's not a failure yet," she said, as though saying it could make it true. "The images did not change immediately after Waterloo. It only means we must stay until we are sure."

"Which we shall." William too spoke with deliberate cheer. "We'll be right here, should it prove necessary to waylay Viktor Frankenstein and change his mind again." She might have been fooled by his voice, if there had not been light sufficient for her to see the clenching and unclenching of his left hand. "Come here," he added. "You must be cold."

She nestled against him, and they watched the slice of sea and sky visible through the space where a door should have been. The winds died down as the high tide came in, until at last the water seemed quite gentle, almost motionless under the eye of the quiet moon. A few fishing vessels specked the water, and now and then the breeze wafted the sound of voices, as two night fishermen called to each other. Eventually even those voices ceased, and Elizabeth almost drowsed in the silence. The pocket watch cycled through the brook, the ship, the knights on the mountainside, the desolate street of 1885, the Battle of Dover, and a drowsy darkness of its own.

Suddenly a splash reached Elizabeth's ear. Startled, she lifted her head from William's chest. Another splash, and she felt all William's lean muscles tense beside her. Elizabeth reached out careful fingers, took up the pocket watch, and quietly shut it, lest its light betray them. Then she held as still as she could and listened.

She identified the sound after a moment—the rhythmic swoosh and splash of oars in water. Another fisherman, come long after his fellows had gone to their beds? Somehow she did not think so. She craned to see more of the ocean through the broken door, and was rewarded by the sight of a boat coming into the bay from the mainland. It had only one passenger, but as he leaped into the shallow water to bring the craft to shore, she could see the enormous height and the overlong gorilla-like arms. At this distance, she of course could not see the scars that creased his dead face.

She shrank back against William, and he held her. There was nowhere for them to go, and indeed they dared not go far. They must hear what happened between Frankenstein and his monster.

The monster climbed the cliffside with some dislodging of stones, but no grunts of effort. Elizabeth had a perfect view of it as it crested the cliff, pulling itself up with its huge muscled arms, its scarred face betraying no effort at the motion. It set its feet on the cliff top and straightened with an ease that hinted at the greatness of its strength. The moonlight shone full upon it, and she recognized the lines and scars and stitches of the face that had loomed over her a week ago and two weeks from now, in this very cottage. A casual swipe of its hand had flung her hard to the floor. She had not quite had time to be afraid of the hulking, hard-eyed beast then, but she did now. How would Viktor possibly hold out against its threats, if its very appearance was so daunting?

The monster stomped past the barn, displaying no apparent interest in it, and circled around to the back of the house. Elizabeth knew exactly when it reached the kitchen window; the creature's howl of anguish and fury split the night. For an instant she was back in the alleyway, that first night of this mad adventure, held by Maxwell's urgent hands against a cold brick wall. Watching over his shoulder as a monster fell, shrieking, to a construct's Gatling-gun fire.

She blinked, and she was in the barn, pressed close to William's side, feeling the patter of his heartbeat and the quick rise and fall of his chest. The monster stomped past the barn again, reached the front door of Viktor Frankenstein's cottage, and yanked it open.

Elizabeth tried to remember to breathe.

"You have destroyed the work which you began," the monster's hoarse voice came from the direction of the cottage, strangled guttural voice mangling the French words. With the door and windows both open, the words carried clearly over calm water and through the calm air. "Do you dare break your promise?" the creature went on. "I have endured toil and misery: I left Switzerland with you; I crept along the shores of the Rhine, among its willow islands, and over the summits of its hills. I have dwelt many months in the heaths of England, and among the deserts of Scotland. I have endured incalculable fatigue, and cold, and hunger; do you dare destroy my hopes?"

"Begone!" Viktor Frankenstein responded, but in a voice that quavered. "I do—I do break my promise. Never will I create another like yourself, equal in deformity and wickedness."

"Wicked!" The monster let the word echo for a moment. "If I am wicked," it continued, "who made me so? Did I not tell you, upon the occasion of our former parley, that my vices are the children of this forced solitude which I abhor? My virtues will necessarily arise when I live in communion with an equal. I am as you made me; if you had not created me a form so hideous that all recoil from it, if you had not cast me forth to dwell in a world that despised me, I might have become a being of love and benevolence." The monster's voice caressed the next words—slowly, lovingly. "If I were not so horrible that your brother William called me an ogre, he and the maiden Justine would be living still. Any crimes I have committed must be laid at your door."

Elizabeth had felt some pity for the creature at the beginning of this speech, but rage boiled inside her at its conclusion. *At Viktor's door? His alone? The first evil was his, certainly, but the second was yours. Did someone take your hands and place them about William Frankenstein's throat?*

"Murderer of my brother!" Viktor Frankenstein replied. "You swear to be harmless, but you have already shown a degree of malice that should reasonably make me distrust you, and with every breath you remind me of your past villainy. I believe vengeance is all you live for now, and this request a feint that will increase your triumph by affording a wider scope for your revenge. I will not aid you."

"Slave, I before reasoned with you, but you have proved yourself unworthy of my condescension. Remember that I have power; you believe yourself miserable, but I can make you so wretched that the light of day will be hateful to you. You are my creator, but I am your master—obey!"

This command was followed by a crash and a cry, and then a longer, higher-pitched scream. Elizabeth tensed to jump up and run, but William's hand closed over her wrist.

"We have to do something!" Elizabeth whispered, struggling. "Protect him somehow—"

"What are you going to do?" William hissed in her ear. "Build a weapon sufficient to take the monster down?"

"Shall each man find a wife for his bosom," the creature wailed from the cottage, "and each beast have his mate, and I be alone? I had feelings of affection, and they were requited by detestation and scorn. Are you to be happy, while I grovel in the intensity of my wretchedness? Yes, I live for vengeance now! I may die, but first you, my tyrant and tormentor, shall curse the sun that gazes on your misery—unless you here and now commence the creation of a second companion for me."

"I refuse," Frankenstein gasped, "and no torture shall ever extort consent from me. Shall I create another like yourself, whose joint wickedness will desolate the world? You may torture me, but I will never consent."

There was a long, long silence. "Man," the creature said then, "you will repent of the injuries you inflict."

"Devil," the man replied, "cease, and do not poison the air with these sounds of malice. I have declared my resolution to you, and I am no coward. Leave me; I am inexorable."

"I go," the monster said. "But you shall reap what you have sown. I shall be with you on your wedding-night."

"If that is to be the fulfillment of my destiny," Viktor Frankenstein replied in a tone of great weariness, "if that is the hour I shall die, then let it be so. That consequence I cannot undo, but I will not sacrifice the whole human race to ensure my safety. It would be an act of the basest and most atrocious selfishness."

There came then the sound of a blow, and a heavy fall, and cry. Then silence. Then the monster stomped from the cottage, scrambled down the cliffside, and cast its boat upon the water. Propelled by the monster's strong arms at the oars, the little craft shot toward the mainland with the swiftness of an arrow, and was soon lost amidst the waves.

Elizabeth released her held breath in a long and shaky sigh. To her intense relief, new sounds came from the cottage: a man's groan, a scrape of a chair over a wooden floor, uneven footsteps and water splashing from a jug into a bowl. Viktor could not be badly hurt, then.

Elizabeth's hands shook as she located the pocket watch and opened it. The fourth face was alight, and showed the image of the meadow. Wind rippled through the grass and dimpled the surface of the water.

The water turned gray and menacing and rose into a looming ocean wave. It crashed down upon the little ship, and for a moment seemed to have overwhelmed it, but the ship struggled back upright.

Its flying pennants turned into the banners of the mountainside knights, whipped out straight and proud in what appeared to be a strong wind. The dazzle of sunlight on armor almost blinded her. William shifted impatiently, then resettled himself, holding still but with his left hand clenched.

The images disappeared and reappeared. The ship fought with the waves and the knights rode out to battle and the meadow lay drenched in peace, but no image of monsters tearing each other apart at Dover materialized.

"Are they off the chessboard, then?" William asked the air—in a whisper, as though he feared angering whatever force supplied the images.

As if in answer, the embattled ship dissolved into the London street.

William and Elizabeth bent their heads over the watch. The street was shrouded by mist, through which a gaslight burned. In the background, factories rose aggressively against the horizon, pumping from their chimneys smoke that thickened and yellowed the fog. The place did not, thank God, have the dead and desolate feel of the London Napoleon's Empire had crushed beneath its heel. But no constructs marched through it, either—the yellow fog was split by no blue lightning.

"They're not there," Elizabeth said. "Neither of them are there—" And then she burst into tears.

It was a brief shower, quickly spent, and William assured her, entirely understandable given the strain they had both been laboring under. She scrubbed her face dry with his handkerchief and settled back to study the image of the London street when it reappeared.

"It's—better," she said, belatedly cautious. "It's different, at least."

"Then it has to be at least a little better." William raised his head to give her a shaky smile. "We'll go and see tomorrow."

The thumps and scraping sounds from the cottage had not ceased. "What is he doing in there?" Elizabeth wondered.

"I cannot imagine." William eased away from her, stretching. "Shall we go and see?"

They were quiet and careful, and Viktor was too occupied with his employment to spare any attention for the window. He had lit all the candles again, and by their light was walking to and fro, folding garments and placing them into trunks, adding the remnants of his mostly destroyed chemical apparatus. A great red mark stood out lividly on his cheek, and he walked as though he had sustained an injury to his leg—after a moment, Elizabeth identified with a jolt of sickness the odor in the air as that of burned flesh, and guessed what kind of injury—but for all that, an odd aura of peace hovered about him.

"He is packing," William whispered. "Perhaps he is going home."

Viktor Frankenstein left the cottage in the small hours of the morning, carrying a large basket. He hesitated for a moment before descending the cliffside path, looking about him. "Little brother?" he called. "Elizabeth? Are you still near me?" Hidden once more in the barn, Elizabeth and William looked at each other. Before they could decide whether to answer, Viktor kept talking as though they had. "I will keep my promise. I go now to commit to the ocean what remains of my horrible experiment. I shall not have the tools I need to attempt it again, and I will not leave the remains of the female creature to terrify the innocent inhabitants of this island. In the morning, I go to Clerval in Perth."

He descended the path, put his basket aboard a little skiff, and sailed away from the shore. Elizabeth watched him until he vanished from her view.

"He was brave," she said to William. "Mad, perhaps, and selfish all his life until now, too arrogant and self-absorbed to see what affect his actions had on others, but brave in the end. If he cared for his own life more than a future he would never see, he might have yielded to the monster's threats."

Viktor Frankenstein did not return. The sun rose, and the wind picked up, and the waves crashed below, but there was no sign of the returning skiff. The watch in Elizabeth's hands, however, continued to show the third 1885 and continued not to show the Battle of Dover, so—

"The change seems to be holding," William said. "I think we have done what we came here to do."

They slept in shifts, and the sun made its long summer path across the sky, and Viktor did not return. But nor did the fourth face change its cycle of images. At last the hour grew late enough that they might use the watch for travel again, and Elizabeth tried combination after combination of dial settings, trying to convince it to take them to Waterloo, that she might see what transpired in the absence of monsters. The watch proved immune to this desire, and likewise refused to take them to 1820 in Hartwich. But when the image of the third 1885 appeared, and Elizabeth tentatively brushed her thumb over the knobs, the Orkney sea and sky wavered momentarily out of existence.

She let go at once and sat, breathing. "Did you feel that?" she asked William. Foolishly; she could tell by his expression that he had.

"I would like to go and see what the future looks like now," William said. "Then we can decide if any other adjustments seem worth the risk."

"Forward, then," Elizabeth said, more bravely than she felt. "To see what we have wrought."

Interlude

Waterloo, Belgium, June 18, 1815

John Freemantle felt every burst from the cannon as a jolt through his breastbone. At least the blasts no longer tore through his eardrums; his ears had been ringing for hours now, muting the roar into something almost manageable. His horse, a big bay possessed of considerably more battlefield experience than its rider, bore the noise stolidly, with no more sign of discomfort than the occasional twitching of an ear.

The British and their Belgian allies had been under heavy fire for most of the afternoon. In Freemantle's opinion, "heavy fire" made it sound more civilized than it really was. The term did not adequately convey the experience of facing down cannonade while enormous iron balls ripped through the ranks, leaving bloody pieces of men wherever they struck. The senior officers seemed unfazed by the carnage, but John Freemantle was only twenty-five and had not long served as aide-de-camp to the Duke of Wellington, and it was all he could do to feign calm.

The pounding crashed to a halt, and Freemantle would have stumbled if he had not been mounted. The battlefield was not quiet, not by any means, but the relative silence was as abrupt as being doused by cold water.

"Prepare to receive cavalry!" came the shout, and Freemantle, wrenching his nerves back under control, looked about for the Duke. His Grace was for once near at hand, and moreover actually headed toward the position of relative safety his rank demanded he assume. Freemantle spurred to his side, and the square slammed closed around them, infantrymen three ranks thick. The outermost rank knelt with bayonets at the ready, and that was the real reason for the superb effectiveness of the infantry square formation against a cavalry charge. Horses could not be made to leap into bayonets.

A bugle call pierced Freemantle's ringing ears, and then the square was surrounded by the thunderous rush of men on horseback. Freemantle experienced it only as a movement of air and a shuddering of the ground. He could see nothing but the scarlet-coated backs of the men guarding him.

The wave crashed against the infantry squares. The ground shook under Freemantle's feet.

And the charge broke, as it had broken eleven times before. The men within the square, Wellington and his aides-de-camp, were as safe as it was possible to be on the battlefield of Waterloo. For a long time afterward, the only sounds outside the square were of swords clashing and men screaming. Then the French cavalry retreated for the twelfth time, and the artillery resumed.

Wellington swatted aside the broad red infantry backs at once, ignoring the entreaties of the aides who wished he would not so expose his person to danger. No one could possibly replace him, as his subordinates pointed out again and again, but the Duke paid no more attention on this occasion than he had on any other. He was invariably to be found riding along the lines, demonstrating to the men his calmness and composure, giving terse orders and the rare word of encouragement. Wellington was not a demonstrative man and had not the gift of inspiring his troops with words—but he was right there with them, in the thick of the fight, and his men respected his courage as they did his skill. Sometimes, Freemantle reflected, that respect went farther toward encouraging battle-weary soldiers than warm words would have done. He did appreciate why Wellington so publically scorned attempts to keep him safe.

He judged the men to be in need of Wellington's encouragement at the present moment. The British force had never been strong to begin with—"my infamous army," Wellington had once said bitterly in Freemantle's hearing—and after the day's pounding by Napoleon's troops, they were in a sorry state indeed. Between injuries, deaths, and desertion, the line along the ridge was stretched nearly to breaking. An entire Belgian brigade had fled in panic, the British cavalry had destroyed itself in a useless charge on the French line, and General Blücher's Prussian reinforcements, promised the night before and sorely needed, were still nowhere to be seen.

Freemantle followed the Duke back onto the open field as other aides emerged from their own infantry squares. Wellington's staff re-gathered itself around him, eyeing the battlefield and shaking their heads.

"If the Prussians do not come, there is no way we can hold until nightfall," Canning muttered, and Freemantle gave his fellow aide-de-camp a startled glance. No one had dared say it quite so bluntly before now.

"They will come soon." General Muffling spoke unhappily. He somehow managed to appear at Wellington's side, like a drooping-mustached Greek chorus, whenever anyone raised the question of the missing reinforcements. Muffling was Blücher's liaison to Wellington, and he had been predicting the imminent appearance of said reinforcements since first light, over and over in almost exactly the same phrasing, while the sun rose high and men died under fire and the hopes of their comrades dwindled. "General Blücher attacks the Emperor's flank down in the village, but once that skirmish is won, then...then, surely..."

He trailed off. No one nearby gave him any aid in completing his sentence.

"Well, gentlemen," the Duke said, as though offering commentary upon an inconvenient rain shower, "they are hammering us hard, but we will see—"

He got no further. Something caught his attention—his aides turned to follow his gaze—and a British officer on a black horse came tearing down the ridgeline, mud spraying from each striking hoof. He waved as he rode, screaming something over the sound of cannonade, words no one could possibly hear. The Duke raised a hand in acknowledgment.

The black charger skidded to a halt, and the rider nearly fell from the saddle as he saluted. Freemantle recognized him, though his face was drawn and splattered with mud: a staff officer named Kennedy.

"My lord," he gasped. "La Haye Sainte—the farm—fallen. Overrun. The French pursued our men—engaged Von Ompteda's battalion—destroyed it. The whole battalion, my lord. Gap in the center of the line."

Wellington did not hesitate. "I shall order the Brunswick troops to the spot. Go and get all the German troops you can, and all the guns you can find." Kennedy saluted and wheeled his horse, and the Duke swung to his aides. "Canning, my compliments to Colonel von Butlar, and the Brunswick Corps is to advance to the center immediately. I shall join them there. Gordon, my compliments to Major Norcott, and I wish a small detachment of the 95th to go into the forest and retrieve those Belgians who retreated so precipitously a short time ago, as their presence is desired to reinforce the center. Freemantle!" Freemantle barely had the chance to touch his heels to his horse's side before Wellington was galloping away from him.

*

Gunsmoke hung thick over the crossroads that had once been defended by Van Ompteda's battalion, and Freemantle winced to see the pitiful stratagems being employed to fill the gap in the line. As Wellington rode up, officers from all over the ridge made for him, and their reports were identical to a man. The center had suffered the heaviest of Napoleon's heavy fire since early that day, and so many of their men were now dead or injured that—even with the Brunswick troops supporting them—they would be unable to hold their positions in the event of another French attack. And the French would attack; it was only a matter of time.

"The Prussians *must* come," someone muttered. "If they do not—"

"I am not saying *I* mean to retreat," another officer said, speaking the word aloud for the first time, "but the line may break, and we must decide what to do if it does..."

Wellington ignored that, turning to greet yet another officer stumbling toward him. "How do you get on, Halket?"

"My lord, we are dreadfully cut up," the man said simply. "Can you not relieve us for a little while?"

Wellington paused one beat. "I fear I have no one to send."

"Surely," Muffling said weakly, "surely it cannot be much longer before General Blücher..."

"But until that time," Wellington said, "it is impossible."

There was silence among his officers. Even the noise of the artillery seemed to be faltering. Freemantle strained his ears—everyone was straining their ears—trying to discern if there were drumbeats mixed in with the musket fire. Was the French infantry preparing to march?

"Very well, my lord," General Halket said. "Then we will stand until the last man falls." He turned to gaze where everyone was gazing, at the crossroads hidden from sight by swirling dust and smoke, from which a column of French troops would doubtless shortly appear.

Wellington turned abruptly to Freemantle. "Lieutenant Colonel," he said. "I desire you ride along the ridgeline until you encounter a Prussian commander—it does not matter which one. You will give him my compliments, and tell him that I am in desperate want of troops not yet battle-weary, who can join the fight upon the left so that I may move some of my men to plug the gaps in the center. We understand his commander is delayed, but we require his assistance at once, immediately, at this very moment. Do I make myself clear?"

"Yes, sir!" Freemantle snapped a salute, clapped his heels to his horse's side, and clung tight as the animal shot off along the ridge.

He could not maintain the speed for more than a few minutes. The ground was littered with the dead and the dying, with abandoned muskets and bits of smashed wagons, and where it was not so littered, the soil had turned to slimy churned mud that sucked at his horse's hooves. Over this morass, gunsmoke hung as heavily as a fog upon a northern moor. Freemantle, hardly able see five paces ahead, was forced to slow his horse to a walk. Maddening, but if the animal broke a leg, the rider would be lost, and thus also the message, the battle, the war, the kingdom—

Artillery still thundered behind him. Freemantle could not hear the pop of musket-fire over that all-consuming roar, but an occasional spark of light did pierce the gunsmoke cloud he road in, and by that he was able to place the French skirmishers who still harassed the British artillerymen. His only consolation was they could not possibly see him either, and thus could not aim at him. A musket-ball would be as disastrous to his message-bringing as would an injury to his mount.

Farther down the ridgeline, the musket-flashes came with less regularity and the pauses in between them grew longer. In the lulls, there was no light— only swirling gray smoke before his eyes and the deafening ringing in his ears, and he might have been traveling through a wasteland where nothing lived or breathed. Now and then he came to a patch where the smoke hung less heavily and the ground came abruptly into view, and then he started back from the staring eyes of the mangled corpses there. He wondered if it were possible for a battle to end with everyone on both sides killed.

The smoke thinned at the same time the worst of the roar faded behind him, and then Freemantle could dismiss that ridiculous fantasy for what it was. He was not, by any means, riding through a wasteland. Indeed, he was closing upon the left of the British line, so far along the ridge that he could just discern the tip of the Placenoit church spire through the last gray wisps of smoke hovering in the air.

Now he could hear the shouts of men overtaking the deafening thunder of the cannon. He felt as though he had returned to the real world from the realm of the faeries, not that he would ever admit nonsense of that kind to anyone. He drove his heels into the horse's sides.

The bay burst past the end of the line and onto the Ohain road, running full tilt now that nothing restrained it. Freemantle scanned the valley below, able to see now that he was out of the haze of gunsmoke, and his eye lit upon a group of blue uniforms. They were not marching north from Placenoit, but rather west from the woodland that lay toward Wavre, so they were not the troops Wellington had been trying to hasten all afternoon, but must instead be some newly arrived portion of Blücher's army. Not that it mattered. They were Prussian; therefore they were allies; and they were close and not currently under attack.

Cold with sudden, sweaty relief, Freemantle turned the bay's head and plunged down the slimy hill. Several times he felt the horse slip, but the animal managed to regain its footing each time, and Freemantle reached the valley without either being thrown or going down under the flailing beast. The Prussians were arriving from the wood in a long, straggling line. Those already arrived had assembled in a loose formation, resting after their long march over rough ground. They looked up at him, most with the incurious manner common to tired foot soldiers.

Freemantle rode among them, asking for their commander in English, in painfully simple French, and in the two or three words of German he could command. Those two or three words were, fortunately, sufficient—indeed, he hardly needed to speak at all, for his scarlet coat told them what he was, and incurious or no, they pointed him up the line almost before he opened his mouth. Freemantle kept following their directions, hoping this quixotic quest would in fact lead to the commander. At last a thin, unhealthy-looking fellow identified himself in broken English as a staff officer and motioned Freemantle to follow his equally thin and unhealthy-looking horse—and then Freemantle came face to face with Lieutenant General Hans von Zieten.

The General looked him once up and down. He was a solidly built man in his middle-forties, balding and somewhat red of nose and cheek, but shrewd of eye and decisive of manner. "Ach, Colonel," he said, in heavily accented English. "What news have you?"

English, thank God. Freemantle abandoned the French he had been rehearsing without an instant's regret. It would be much easier to give a complete explanation in his mother tongue, and even persuasion might not be impossible. "It goes badly, sir," he said, and rapped out the rest of Wellington's message.

Von Zieten nodded. His jowly face remained imperturbable and his hands loose on the reins, but his eyes darted everywhere, watching his straggling mass of men struggle through the mud and come into formation. Occupied with monitoring their progress, he did not quite look at Freemantle as he made his reply. "Tell the Duke himself not to distress. I shall come as soon as I my corps have assembled, and see, that will be soon enough."

Freemantle shook his head. "Sir," he said, with enough urgency that von Zieten's eyes came back to him, "I fear His Grace cannot wait. He was most clear upon that point. I am to say he needs aid now. He must have reinforcements sufficient to fill the gaps in his lines."

"His Grace will know it is the strategy of a fool to piecemeal send a corps into battle," von Zieten said. "When they form a force that can some good do the English, then I will bring them."

"Sir—no, sir. I cannot return to the Duke with such a message." Freemantle wondered if that flash in the shrewd eyes was surprise, or anger, or both, but he could not pause to worry over it. He plunged on. "His need cannot brook an instant's postponement. The outcome of this day teeters on the balance now, at this very moment. If reinforcements come immediately, victory is ours; but if they are delayed even by minutes, I cannot say what will happen."

Von Zieten did not answer at once. He studied the corps still assembling itself, then looked past Freemantle up the hill. Then he turned away and snapped something in German. The officer who had escorted Freemantle at once kneed his horse to his General's side. Von Zieten gave him curt, harshly chopped-off orders that Freemantle could not follow, and the man galloped away.

"I may tell the Duke you will come?" Freemantle gathered his reins, but von Zieten shook his head.

"First I send my lieutenant to reconnoiter."

"Sir—" Freemantle began, unable to keep the impatience from his voice, but von Zieten held up a hand to cut off his half-formed protest.

"I your duty understand, Colonel," he said. "But duty I have also."

There was nothing Freemantle could say to that. Sweat slid down his back in cold droplets as the minutes ticked past. The bay, picking up on his unease, shifted to the left, then to the right, then to the left again. Freemantle tried to relax the muscles of his legs and stop his right hand from fidgeting on the rein. He achieved only minimal success, but von Zieten did not comment. The Prussian corps continued to arrive from the direction of Wavre and assemble itself into ranks.

The thin staff officer mounted on the thin horse shot back toward them. He reined up with a flourish and gave his report in a bark; von Zieten answered him as abruptly. Then the General turned to Freemantle, and there was something so like gentleness on his square red face that Freemantle stiffened in alarm.

"I am sorry," von Zieten said. "My lieutenant reports to me the sight of men in red coats running. From the ridge and to the forest they run. Wellington's line has broken, and he retreats; my corps no good can do him now."

"No," Freemantle said stupidly. "No, sir. It is not possible."

But of course it was. Freemantle remembered the men staring at the crossroads, the swirling gunsmoke that could have hidden anything at all, the French column that was sure to emerge from it sooner or later. If it had been sooner, if the attack had come while Freemantle picked his slow and careful way over the ridge, then it was indeed possible for Wellington's ragged force to have broken. The British could well be in full retreat, running for the Forest of Soignes. Freemantle could picture it, and it felt exactly as though the earth was crumbling under his feet. As though the churned mud of the battlefield was pulling him under its slimy surface.

"We to where good can be done go," the Prussian said. "We those at Placenoit reinforce. You come, Colonel, if you wish." The thin staff officer was now riding up and down von Zieten's columns, shouting, and even as Freemantle watched, the corps turned, and began their march away from the ridgeline. Away from Wellington, away from the fleeing British, away from the lost battle.

"No, sir," Freemantle said, forcing the words out of the hollow place in his chest. "My place is with His Grace. By your leave—"

He turned the bay's head without waiting for permission, and numbly pointed the horse back toward the ridge. Behind him, von Zieten's corps filed away toward Placenoit. The thump of their boots sounded like a funeral march. *It's over,* Freemantle thought dully. *We've lost.*

Something moved at the edge of his vision, and he looked up. Galloping down from the ridge as though all the hounds of hell pursued him was a solitary man in a Prussian uniform. He had lost his hat somewhere, and his gray hair and mustache blew in all directions. So wild did he look that Freemantle took a moment to recognize him as General Muffling, Blücher's liaison officer and Wellington's Greek chorus. The man was riding without a care for the treacherous mud—indeed, the horse stumbled and skidded with every other step, and Muffling seemed to haul it back to its feet by main force each time—and he shouted as he rode, desperate words that Freemantle was too far away to hear. *Does he come to warn of the British rout? Warn his countrymen to save themselves?*

Muffing saw him and reined his horse so hard the beast reared straight up. "Mein Herr General?" he demanded of Freemantle once his mount was back on the ground. "Where? Do you know?"

"Yes," Freemantle managed, pointing. "I have just—"

"Bring me!" So commanding was his tone that Freemantle's intended words—an inquiry regarding Wellington's health and safety—stopped in his throat. He turned to ride back the distance he had just covered, Muffling at his side. Blue- and green-uniformed Prussian columns flashed by as they pounded along the valley.

Von Zieten had not moved far from where Freemantle had left him, and Muffling rode straight up to him, earning a raised eyebrow from the square-faced General. The wild-haired liaison officer began a tirade in German, then looked over his shoulder at Freemantle and switched to English. "What is it you do, sir?" he demanded of von Zieten. "This man brings you a message from the Duke—"

"The Duke the field flees," von Zieten interrupted.

"This is not true. You are mistaken, sir." Muffling paused for one gasping breath. "What you saw were wounded, sir, wounded and prisoners. The British are not in retreat, they are standing fast. But by Gott, sir, if you do not come to join them at once, the battle will be lost in truth."

Von Zieten hesitated, looking into Muffling's face. "This is true?"

Muffling switched back to rapid German. Two incomprehensible sentences into his explanation, von Zieten swung away from him, bellowing a command. The command was taken up by his officers, and the southward-marching columns of men stopped in their tracks. At another bellowed order, the columns turned. They marched away from Placenoit; they marched to reinforce the British.

"You have saved us, sir," Freemantle said. Von Zieten seemed to think the compliment for him, as indeed it could have been, and waved it off with one hand as he cantered away to lead his men. But Freemantle had meant it for Muffling, and it seemed Muffling knew.

"I could have saved nothing had you not been here," said the man with the drooping mustaches, beaming at him and reaching out to squeeze his arm. "How could I have found mein Herr General in all of this disorder? Had you not brought me straight to him, I could not have presented him a true report. It is you who won the battle this day."

Freemantle pulled away, embarrassed. "I must return to the Duke."

"Indeed." Muffling released him, still beaming. "Bring him this good news."

Freemantle kicked the bay, and it leaped forward.

He did not dare to hope. Despair had come so close to enveloping him that he could not shake off the last lingering touch of her fingers. For the entire ride back—through the sloppy churned mud, up the hill, through the smoke cloud, and around the detritus of massacred men and ruined weaponry—he found himself plagued by secret nightmare visions. The British had not been retreating when Muffling left—very well—but for all anyone knew, the line had since broken and they were retreating now. He imagined cresting the ridge to find his countrymen slaughtered, a line of French infantry bayoneting the last few who could no longer offer any defense. The scene etched itself so plainly before his eyes that he was almost surprised to find it not true when he reached Wellington's position.

But the French infantry had not yet advanced. The British were still holding. The Duke was where Freemantle had left him.

"They're coming," Freemantle said.

Wellington nodded once, as though the conversation concerned a dinner invitation.

Within a quarter hour, von Zieten's advance guard was in place at the end of the British line, neat in their blue coats and oilskin caps, somewhat disheveled from the long march over rough terrain, but seeming fresh from the parade ground when compared to Wellington's battered troops. Wellington ordered the cavalry to leave the left and reinforce the crumbling center, and his lips turned upward slightly as he followed their progress through his spyglass. He slapped the instrument into Freemantle's hand and moved to give another order, and Freemantle lifted it to his own eye, curious to see what Wellington had seen.

It was astonishing how much the set of a man's shoulders and the tilt of his head could tell you. Even with the spyglass, Freemantle could not read anything as specific as expressions, but he saw the shift in posture move from man to man, all along the center of the ridge, as the cavalry came to reinforce the position. The men in the center had considered themselves under an inevitable sentence of death a moment ago. Now they glanced over their shoulders at the horses and straightened as though they still had a fight left in them after all.

The reaction of the men on the left was even more dramatic. Positioned as they were, they could not see what manner of reinforcements approached from their rear, but they heard the drums and the marching feet, and some caught a glimpse of the flag. The words ran through the ranks of exhausted men like wind through a ryefield: "The Prussians have come."

The artillery did slacken now, and the skirmishers finally withdrew, and from down in the valley came the drumbeat that heralded the French infantry advance. But the men who would have despaired at the sound half an hour before grinned a little instead. Freemantle was at Wellington's side as the Duke rode along his lines, redeploying artillery and infantry now that he had the reinforcements to permit him to do so. He was not grinning; but then, His Grace never grinned.

With the infantry redeployed to his satisfaction—more than a thousand of them lying down beneath the crest of the ridge, where they were both safe from the guns and hidden from the advancing French—Wellington took a position high above them. On horseback, he was a distinctive figure in his blue civilian dress and cocked hat, and Freemantle had a sick qualm at the thought of skirmishers and lucky shots. He was not the only one so concerned, apparently, for the rest of Wellington's aides were likewise drifting closer to him, metal filings drawn to a magnet. Not that there was much they could do in the defense of the hypothetical lucky shot, and Wellington rolled his eyes when he lowered his spyglass and saw them all. "Gentlemen, we are somewhat thick on the ground," he told them, with an accompanying flicking motion of his fingers, and Freemantle and the others sheepishly moved a few paces away. "Better," the Duke said, and returned to his spyglass. "And—ah, yes. Here they come."

Even without a spyglass, Freemantle could see precisely which French troops were advancing over the sloppy churned mud of the valley. The Emperor, expecting victory near at hand, had sent in the Garde.

The Imperial Garde was the elite of the elite of Napoleon's troops, distinctive by their height and the bearskins that were part of their campaigning uniforms, usually held in reserve until the moment of victory and partially for that reason never defeated. The day was traditionally as good as won when the Garde took the field, and certainly the rest of the French troops assumed this would be the case at Waterloo as it had been so often before. They cheered as the tight columns passed, a wave of sound that started faint but grew into a crescendo from every part of the valley. The British peppered them with grapeshot, but they kept coming, and French infantry from elsewhere in the field joined them in support. The main column headed straight for the crest of the ridge, where the Duke waited atop his horse with his aides clustered around him.

No British infantry opposed them.

The Garde came faster.

Wellington waited until they were no more than fifty paces away, then drew in his breath. "Now is your time! Up! Make ready! Fire!"

From the perspective of the Imperial Garde, Freemantle thought, it must have seemed as though British soldiers exploded out of the earth at their feet. The men hidden behind the crest of the ridge jumped up and pumped volley after volley into the approaching column, and the French soldiers paused for a moment in sheer disbelief. Three hundred of them fell in the first sixty seconds, and then the British drew bayonets and charged, shouting.

The Garde, said to know how to die but not how to surrender, broke at the sight.

"The Garde is retreating!" It was shouted all over the battlefield, in triumph by the British and in horror by the French. The rest of the French infantry joined the Garde in flight. Some isolated fire resumed from the French side, but Wellington acted as though he did not care. He snatched off his hat and waved it over his head, sending what remained of the British cavalry and infantry charging after their fleeing foe. "Forward and complete your victory!" His voice pierced the chaos. "Look, they fly before us! See them off our land!"

"For God's sake!" Freemantle heard someone else shout in exasperation. "Don't expose yourself so!" He turned his head in time to see a horseman come pounding past. The man reined up beside Wellington, and Freemantle saw that it was Lord Uxbridge, the Duke's second in command. Uxbridge's words were lost in the surrounding noise, but his gestures suggested he was attempting to persuade the Duke of the need for some caution. Wellington shrugged him off, as he had shrugged off all other similar arguments that day. Uxbridge persisted, and Wellington seemed to answer tersely, then made an obvious gesture of impatience and drew his mount an exaggerated step backward. He turned from Uxbridge to continue the coordination of the pursuit.

A sound like the snapping of a tree branch hit Freemantle's ears, and he looked over just in time to see the red stain blossom and spread fast on the white cloth of Uxbridge's trousers. Wellington swung around in the saddle, catching his second before he could slide to the ground, holding him with one arm as Freemantle struggled through the press toward them. Uxbridge's face had gone the color of whey. "By God—" he said in hoarse surprise as Freemantle reached them. "I've lost my leg."

White fragments of bone poked from the mangled hole that had been his knee, stark against the dark blood. "By God," Wellington said, "so you have." Uxbridge's eyes fluttered closed. "Freemantle—" the Duke commanded, and Freemantle reached to take his limp burden. "See to him," Wellington said, already turning to the job still to be finished. "Get him behind the lines."

Freemantle summoned a couple of soldiers with a snap of his fingers, and with their aid managed to ease Uxbridge off his mount. As they turned for the relatively safe ground where the wounded were being tended, he paused to take one last look at the battlefield. The road that led out of the valley, the route back to France, was choked with blue-coated soldiers.

*

It was well into the evening and the light was fading before the sound of trumpets and hoofbeats pierced the cooling air, and the rest of the Prussian reinforcements came thundering from the direction of Wavre. By then the tide of the battle had definitively turned and their aid was not so desperately required, but it was still warmly welcomed by Wellington's decimated men. The Prussians, not exhausted by ten hours of fighting, took over the pursuit of the fleeing French.

General Blücher himself led the Prussian cavalry. Of course he did; no one had expected him to do anything else. Blücher had always led his men from the front, and at seventy-two said he was too old to learn new habits. The handsome, white-haired, fierce-eyed Prussian rode up to La Belle Alliance as though the inn belonged to him, rather than holding the dubious distinction of having housed Bonaparte and his officers the night before. In a scene no courtier could have more perfectly choreographed, Wellington came up the road from the opposite direction at the same moment, and so the two commanders met for the first time outside Napoleon's abandoned headquarters.

"Quelle affaire!" Blücher commented in greeting, lifting his hat and gesturing with his other hand in the direction of the churned mud and rye that was the battlefield.

"That's all the French he knows," Wellington muttered to Freemantle, and Freemantle almost choked with the unexpectedness of the jest. But then Wellington recovered his usual courtesy, lifted his own hat, and, asking Muffling to serve as translator, replied to Blücher's pleasantry with one of his own. "Indeed, sir, it was a damned nice thing. The nearest-run thing you ever saw in your life."

"Une belle alliance," Blücher noted with a wave toward the signpost that proclaimed name of the inn, and chuckled. He leaned forward in the saddle, holding out his hand, and Wellington shook it. The battle was won.

Epilogue

London, September 7, 1885

Lord Seward's second best carriage was a gorgeous thing, light and fast in the brougham style, with huge high wheels polished to gleaming and his lordship's arms etched in exquisite detail on the door. Brenda thought she was probably supposed to be awed by it, but awe could not quite penetrate the giddy glee that bubbled in her throat as the expressionless coachman handed her in.

The inside was even more beautiful than the exterior. Brenda ran her gloved fingers over the satin-smooth wood, then pressed her palm against the red velvet seat cushion. It pressed firmly back; this carriage was sprung to within an inch of its life. Brenda could hardly restrain the impulse to bounce on the seat, and a sidelong glance at Gavin's faintly twitching fingers led her to suspect he could hardly restrain the impulse to crawl underneath the thing and take it apart. The coachman climbed into his box above them, and the matched snow-white horses whisked them through London's gaslit streets and to Cinderella's ball—or at least to the Royal Opera House, which was nearly the same thing.

Brenda glanced at Gavin again, handsome but very stiff indeed in unaccustomed evening dress. His eyes slid sideways to meet hers, and she bit her lip to keep from laughing aloud. "All our neighbors will have been staring," she murmured, mock-distressed, reciting the lines of a modest little housewife come from the country. "We could have so easily taken a cab."

"A man in my position," Gavin replied, "must not insult his lordship by refusing a kindness such as this." The words might have sounded reproving to someone who didn't know, but Gavin said them in his own voice, the soft sing-song of Wales instead of the clipped correctness of London, and Brenda grinned to herself. He was reciting lines as much as she was. This was a game they played together.

It was all a game, the life they lived in London. They had a fine house in Kensington—not a gentleman's house, but the sort that might be occupied by a professional man worthy of respect—a physician, say, or a barrister. Their rank did not require them to keep a carriage of their own, thankfully, nor did it require them to entertain in the glittering style of Lord and Lady Seward— merely to accept an invitation from Gavin's patron now and again, with suitable murmurs of gratitude for his kindness. Brenda wore correctly fashionable gowns to those dinner parties, and Gavin spoke like an Englishman when in conversation with Seward's other guests, as he did with his colleagues at the University.

Within the walls of their own home, it was different. They had taken care that it should be, ever since that evening during their first London winter when she had chanced to read aloud "The Lord of Burleigh" from a collection of Tennyson. When she had reached the line, "the burden of an honor unto which she was not born," Gavin had gone still as stone in his chair on the other side of the hearth. Brenda had looked up to find his eyes fixed on her, taking apart her expression as his fingers might one of the delicate contraptions he built. He was no better with words now than he had been as a boy, but the worry in his eyebrows spoke volumes. She laughed aloud, and then so did he, surprised, relaxing.

"It must never be like that," he said, giving the words the inflection of Wales. He got up and crossed to her, dropping to one knee beside her chair and taking the book from her hand. "If you are unhappy, say the word, and we'll go straight back to Pendoylan. I'll be the eccentric who insists his genius can only thrive in country privacy; I can play that part as easily as this. I'd have to be here sometimes, of course, but—"

Brenda shook her head. "There's no need. It's better for you to be here, and I'd rather be with you than anywhere. And I'm not certain," she added after a moment, "we'd now fit into Pendoylan any better."

Gavin sighed agreement, but his eyes were still anxious. "You don't mind? Much?"

"I don't mind at all." It was true. She was playing a part every time she stepped out her front door in the role of London matron, and she might have preferred it not be so—but within these four walls she was herself, and so was he, and she needed nothing else for happiness.

"I do worry about the baby, though," she added after a little while, rubbing at her middle. "He'll grow up thinking this is all there is. He won't know who he is, or who we were before we came here."

Gavin thought about that, turning it over in his head like an engineering problem to be solved. "That will never do," he declared, and from then on, they played the game more deliberately. Gavin continued to speak like a Londoner nine-tenths of the time—but he spoke like a Welshman inside his home, and Brenda herself made no attempt to shed her accent. They hired an English nursemaid, and later English governesses and tutors, but they took the children to Pendoylan for each summer holiday. They accepted Lord Seward's kind gifts of theater tickets and rides in his carriage, but when no such were offered, they went to Covent Garden in a cab and enjoyed the music as much from the stalls or the gallery as they did from Lord Seward's box. One behaved as one must to advance one's husband's career—but as long as you knew who you really were, Brenda thought, that was all right.

Now Lord Seward's second-best carriage joined the tangle of heavy four-wheeled cabs and light two-wheeled hansoms and other elegant private coaches pulling up outside the Royal Opera House. The coachman sprang down to open the door for them, then stood aside while Gavin swung out and reached to hand his wife safely to the pavement. There was a brief pause while Gavin's hand strayed to the clasp of his evening-cloak as though he wanted to pull it off and toss it into the carriage; but he surrendered to decorum, left it where it was, and waved the coachman off. Brenda could not blame him for the impulse. She could almost feel the curl wilting out of her hair in the stagnant heat of the evening. A truly horrid odor rose from the horse-pies in the roadway, and off to one side a flower girl hawked wares that looked more than two-thirds dead.

Gavin set his top hat on his head with one gloved hand and offered her his arm. They joined the crowd milling toward the great white columns of the entranceway.

"Mr. Trevelyan?" a voice said almost in Brenda's ear, and she jumped back.

Gavin turned in a swirl of cloak, stepping between her and the speaker so smoothly it might have been unconscious.

"I apologize for disturbing you, madam," the young man added with a bow in Brenda's direction. He was nice-looking enough, and pleasantly spoken, and he did truly sound contrite for startling her. But he was dressed in the most extraordinary costume—beneath a battered traveling cloak, Brenda glimpsed a brass-buttoned cutaway like something out of a painting—and he eyed Gavin with an unnerving eagerness. "But it is Mr. Trevelyan, is it not?"

Gavin regarded him, one eyebrow raised almost at the level of his top-hat brim. His eyes swept the young up and down. "It is," he said, and now he was using his cool public voice, antiseptic in the correctness of its accent. "But I do not believe I have the pleasure of your acquaintance."

"My name is Carrington, sir," the boy said; "we met some little time ago, at—"

Gavin raised the eyebrow again. "I would remember your face," he said. "I admit it is not particularly distinctive, but I have an exceptional eye for such things; I would remember." He turned his back on the boy, and Brenda winced a little. She had never enjoyed this part of the game they played.

"It was at a dinner-party." Mr. Carrington padded after them like an eager puppy. "A Mr. Maxwell introduced us—"

"And that is quite impossible." Gavin turned to face him. "Young man. I can only assume that you desire me to take you on as a student. And that, knowing of my oft-repeated determination to work alone and unencumbered with the business of teaching, you decided your best chance of securing a position within my laboratory was to pretend a previous acquaintance. If you thought this tactic either was original or had any probability of being effective, you were in error. Nor do I find it endearing that you considered me naïve enough to fall for so crude a ploy." They were drawing attention, Brenda realized, her toes curling inside her boots. On one side of the pillars, elegant men and women turned their heads in well-bred not-quite-curiosity. From the other side, coachmen and loungers likewise watched the show. The flower girl with the wilted blooms stared with particular anxiety, and there was something odd about that, Brenda thought. But she could not get a good look at the girl past Gavin, and Gavin's cold eyes stayed on the stammering young man. "Moreover," Gavin concluded, "unless you have tickets to Madame Rasmirovna's performance, a circumstance I consider most unlikely given your attire, it is inappropriate for you to impede the progress of those who do. Good day to you, sir." He turned in a swirl of cloak, keeping himself between the young stranger and Brenda as he escorted her inside.

*

"So the Trevelyans are well," Elizabeth said, pulling her cloak more tightly around herself. The evening air was as still and hot, but surely the gown under the cloak would attract more attention. She let the limp flowers slide out of her hands to the cobblestones. They were swallowed by fog and shadows before she heard them hit.

"The Trevelyans are well," William agreed. He had made a show out of buying all her flowers and sweeping her away with him; let the music lovers outside Convent Garden think what they would. Now he turned both their steps to an alleyway where they might talk a moment undisturbed. "As is Madam Katherine. 'Madame Rasmirovna.' Good for her."

Elizabeth leaned against the alley's brick wall and looked about her. She could see little, between evening shadows and thickening fog, but her mind's eye ran through the day's images. There was no Murchinson's, but there were many places like it, where bedraggled underfed workers straggled out of the gates at nightfall. There were no constructs and no monsters, but men in soldiers' uniforms begged for alms on street corners. Gavin and Brenda Trevelyan took Lord Seward's carriage to the theater—and Elizabeth was happy for them—but children sold flowers for pennies a stone's throw from the glistening carriage wheels. "It's...better," she said cautiously.

"It's still bad," William agreed with the tone rather than the words. "Better, but still bad." He offered her his arm. "So now we go and fix the rest of it, living forward."

"Water wearing away stone," Elizabeth agreed. "And...and we trust Maxwell to find his own way home."

"Because we must. And because he can." William squeezed her hand between his elbow and his ribs. "Right, then. One final question. What sort of wedding shall we have?"

Elizabeth stared at him.

"We must decide before we set the watch," he explained. "The nineteenth of June, eighteen hundred and fifteen—but where? Back to Hartwich? Or to Gretna Green?"

"Oh, I see." Elizabeth thought about it.

"I gave the matter some consideration," William said, "and I think we can avoid a scandal if we are careful about it. You slipped out of your window to meet me at the orchard, true, but I came straightaway to your parents like a good lad and asked for your hand. We could have a proper wedding, guests and gifts and bridesmaids and wine at the wedding breakfast, everything done as it should be, and no one could say a word against us."

Elizabeth made a valiant effort to restrain the shudder, but failed. William laughed at her. "Right, then. Gretna Green?"

"Gretna Green," Elizabeth said, and William handed her the watch so she could set the dials.

Timebound

Coming Summer 2017!

Waterloo, Belgium, June 18, 1815

John Freemantle felt every jolt of the cart like an explosion within his skull.

At least, he thought it was a cart. He had reason to think so; he had been carried semi-conscious in a cart once before, and it was not an experience one forgot. The sickening arrhythmic lurches, each one as bone-rattling as it was nauseating, had nothing in common with the plunging deck of a ship or the joggle of a properly sprung carriage. Moreover, each jolt seemed to give rise to a fresh bout of moaning in a variety of registers, from sources surrounding him at close range. Then there was the smell—sweat and blood, vomit and urine. He was becoming more certain every instant that his initial impression had been correct. He was in a cart.

What he could not determine was why. Freemantle cast his mind back, trying to recall some sequence of events that would logically end with his person residing in such a conveyance. The battle had been going badly, he remembered that. The British and their Belgian allies had been under heavy fire from the more numerous French. Between injuries, deaths, and desertion, Wellington's line was stretched almost to breaking, and when the news came that the farm La Haye Sainte had fallen, Wellington had no fresh troops he might move to plug the gap. The promised Prussian reinforcements had still not arrived, and so there was nothing for the Duke to do but—

Freemantle remembered with a jolt worse than anything the cart could throw at him, and jerked upright. Or tried to; he only got halfway before pain spiked through his temples and he sagged back down. The Duke had summoned the special battalion. The Duke had sent him, John Freemantle, to summon the special battalion. But something had ambushed him in the woods. And he could dimly remember, as though recalling a dream, a girl with a minx's face and an impossible pocket watch—

"Battalion," he croaked.

"Easy, John."

Freemantle turned his head toward the voice. The movement seemed to take a long time, and a green blur swooped across his field of vision as he did so. He wasn't sure if he had opened his eyes, or if the sickening haze was present only behind his lids.

He squeezed his eyes hard shut, then forced them open. This time they focused enough to recognize James Warren. Warren was propped upright against the side of the cart, chest and right shoulder bound with blood-soaked bandages, face paper-white except for the dark shadows under his eyes.

"Battalion," Freemantle said again. "Burnley. I was—" The cart jerked underneath him, drowning the faint flicker of memory in a flood of queasiness. Freemantle drew a deep breath, holding it until the worst of the sickness past. "What—happened?"

"You were thrown from your horse," Warren said. He spoke almost without inflection. The gray eyes that regarded Freemantle seemed unnaturally wide, unnaturally steady.

Freemantle made one more effort to sit up, and this time managed it despite the spike of pain through his skull. "The message—"

"Hit your head," Warren added, as though that were the question he had asked. "They took you to the village to recover."

"The message, James. The battalion—"

"Didn't come," Warren said.

"Oh, God." The blur of green crashed over his head like an ocean wave. There had been a girl and a pocket watch and an impossible story, and he had—chosen not to bring the message? But no, that was impossible, that was a fever dream. Surely he could never have chosen to betray Wellington. Surely he was guilty of nothing but failure. "Oh, dear God."

"I wasn't there," Warren said, as though he were talking in his sleep. "Leeches wouldn't let me leave. But I heard. Heard the others talking. They said His Grace was waiting on the battalion. They said it looked like the Prussians might reach us—they were even in sight. But then the infantry broke under the last French charge. The Prussians thought the day lost, and made tracks. It didn't take long after that…"

"But the Duke," Freemantle said, struggling to comprehend it. The girl had said they could win without the special battalion. And because of that, Freemantle had chosen to— He shied away from the memory. "Never beaten—all those times on the Peninsula—conjuring possibilities from thin air—how could the Duke—" He stopped at the look on Warren's face. "Dear God. No."

"He was trying to rally them," Warren said hoarsely. "He was—being conspicuous, the way he always—Lord Uxbridge rode at him, shouting, 'For God's sake, don't expose yourself so!'—and then—A lucky shot, they said. Uxbridge was so close that the Duke's blood—the Duke's blood splattered—" Warren choked. He coughed, and the crimson stain on his bandages darkened and spread.

"Under Uxbridge," Freemantle said. It was the only part of the paragraph he could absorb. The other intelligence was too momentous, as though the universe had been pulled up by the roots, or broken and reformed into something entirely new. He could not comprehend it. He pushed it instead to the back of his throbbing brain. The girl had said that, to save the future, he must not bring the message. And he had believed her, as mad as that seemed now, he had chosen— "We're under Uxbridge. What are we about?" He looked around himself. Bleeding and hastily bandaged comrades-in-arms lay wedged and piled around him, groaning with each fresh lurch of the wheels. Past them, the green haze would not come into focus.

"Retreating," Warren said, still expressionless, eyes still staring. "Bonaparte sent in the Garde. Immortals. Undefeated."

"Retreating," Freemantle repeated. She had said they would win. "Where to? Brussels?"

"In Brussels," Warren said, "they are preparing feasts to welcome home their Emperor."

Of course they were. The Belgians had always been more French than Dutch, had never been likely to stand with Napoleon's enemies in the event of the Emperor's victory. Some had fled the battlefield, and some— Freemantle had an instant's memory of Belgians in the Forest of Soignes, but it fled when he tried to grasp it. The effort struck through his head, a blinding spear of pain. The girl had a handkerchief, and a pocket watch, and a glib tongue, and he had believed her, and he was worse than a traitor, worse than a fool. She must have been a French spy. If she were real at all. Perhaps she wasn't real. He wanted her to not be real.

If she were not real, this was not his fault.

"Bonaparte's done it," Warren said. "Separated us from the Prussians. They retreat across the Rhine, we back to the North Sea while the route home is still open to us. The French pursue, but Uxbridge left a small band of monsters to cover our retreat. He thinks they will be enough. He takes the rest home to garrison our shores. It's too late to use them any other way."

"Too late," Freemantle repeated. The words tasted awful on his tongue, slimy and nauseous.

"Not your fault," Warren said suddenly. But it was. "Even Wotten said so, when he came to fetch me from Mont St. Jean. You hit your head. The Duke oughtn't to have waited. He delayed too long in sending a second courier. He delayed too long in sending for the monsters in the first place."

Freemantle's guts twisted inside him. "No," he said, as the sky throbbed in time with the throbbing in his temples. "It wasn't his fault. Never his fault. It was mine—mine—I failed—I caused—" She had said, The message must not get through, and he had said, I have a plan. His hand had thrown the lamp, struck the guard, misdirected the message, lost the war. "I caused this. Oh, God."

He was no longer wearing his pistols. But a polished-smooth handle still rode on the belt at Warren's hip. Freemantle reached out, and Warren was too drunk on his own injuries and grief to stop him seizing hold of it.

Read the continuation of Elizabeth, William, and Maxwell's adventure
as they try to set time right...again

in

Book 2 in the Keeping Time trilogy

Coming Summer, 2017

stillpointdigital.com/timekeeper

Keeping Time

It's 1815, and Wellington's badly-outnumbered army stares across the field of Waterloo at Napoleon's forces. Desperate to hold until reinforcements arrive, Wellington calls upon a race of monsters created by a mad scientist 25 years before.

It's 1815, and a discontented young lady sitting in a rose garden receives a mysterious gift: a pocket watch that, when opened, displays scenes from all eras of history. Past...and future.

It's 1885, and a small band of resistance fighters are resorting to increasingly extreme methods in their efforts to overthrow a steampunk Empire whose clockwork gears are slick with its subjects' blood.

Are these events connected?

Oh, come now. That would be telling.

Timepiece
Timekeeper (Summer, 2017)
Timebound (Winter, 2018)

stillpointdigital.com/keeping-time

Stillpoint/Prometheus

Interested in fiction that will bend your mind and heart?
Sign up for news, giveaways, and more at
stillpointdigital.com/prometheus/news

HEATHER ALBANO is a storyteller, history geek, and lover of both time-travel tropes and re-imaginings of older stories. In addition to novels, she writes interactive fiction. She finds the line between the two getting fuzzier all the time.

Heather lives in Massachusetts with her husband, two cats, a tankful of fish, and an excessive amount of tea. Learn more about her various projects at heatheralbano.com.

Read more from
Stillpoint Digital Press!

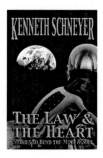

Exploring the seams where humanity and technology, society and individuality intersect, Nebula- and Sturgeon-nominated author Kenneth Schneyer presents thirteen mind-bending, thought-provoking tales of near and far futures that will amuse, amaze, and unsettle. The law will change, and the heart will change, and the heart will change the law. These stories confront the question of just what makes and keeps us human.

Samurai, assassins, warlords…and a girl who likes to climb.

Though Japan has been devastated by a century of civil war, Risuko just wants to climb trees. Growing up far from the battlefields and court intrigues, the fatherless girl finds herself pulled into a plot that may reunite Japan -- or may destroy it. She is torn from her home and what is left of her family, but finds new friends at a school that may not be what it seems.

Magical but historical, Risuko follows her along the first dangerous steps to discovering who she truly is.

StillpointDigitalPress.com